MIDNIGHT FALLS

(SKY BROOKS BOOK 3)

MCKENZIE HUNTER

McKenzie Hunter

Midnight Falls (3rd Edition)

MckenzieHunter@McKenzieHunter.com

ISBN: 978-1-946457-91-2

ACKNOWLEDGMENTS

Each time I write an acknowledgment, I can't help but be humbled by those who have given so generously of their time to help me. Mom, Tiffany Dix, Sheryl Cox, and Gregory Caughman, thank you so much for encouraging me to take this journey and being there every step of the way. Marcia Snyder, I don't have the words to express how grateful I am that, even while battling breast cancer, you were there offering whatever assistance you could. Your character and strength is something I will always admire and I am glad to have someone like you in my corner.

Stacy McCright, I have said it before: every author should have a "Stacy" in their life. Thank you for your honest, constructive, straight-no-chaser feedback. I will always have a love-hate relationship with your critique e-mails and I am very grateful for them and for you.

Thanks to my cover artist Hampton Lamoureux. A special thanks to John Harten and Luann Reed, my editors, who went above and beyond with helping me create a book that I hope my readers will love.

Last, but definitely not least, I want to thank you, the reader, for giving me a chance to entertain you with my work.

CHAPTER 1

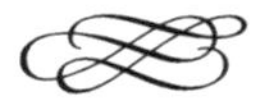

Josh stood in the middle of the diaphanous shell. I pressed against parts of it, trying to find a weakness in the barrier, but it held firm. His mocking grin remained as I whispered several words and pressed against the protective field that remained even after three failed attempts. It was the strongest he had ever made. I could feel the strength of the magic he used. Even if I couldn't feel it, I could see it in the strain on his face. His cerulean eyes turned a shade darker as he called forth stronger magic.

It wavered; his eyes eclipsed even darker trying to hold it. The words fell freely from my lips and specks of orange and blue flailed in the air, and the wall dropped; the light crystals of its existence dissipated into the air.

"Very good," he said softly as he walked to the sofa and dropped onto it.

Just as I was about to take a seat in the chair across from him, a glass tumbler flew in my direction. My hands quickly flicked in the air and it changed direction, crashing into the door across the room, sending shattered pieces everywhere.

The exasperated breath made small waves over his lips. "You didn't have to break it."

"You didn't have to attack me with glassware," I shot back with a grin.

The remarkable control Josh had over magic, even when he was fatigued, was impressive Effortlessly, from his seat on the sofa, he gathered the broken glass and cleaned it away without as much as lifting his head from its resting position against the back of the sofa.

"You've improved so much in the last three months," he said.

With practice, my ability to control defensive magic now rivaled Josh's.

"I think we should try spells again," I said.

It was only when he lifted his head and those intense perceptive eyes held mine that I saw the guilt about our shared secret. We were living in this perpetual state of denial and never discussing the source of my magic, which was something we danced around. It was the dirty little secret that we would probably take to our graves. I never admitted that I held on to some of the dark magic that Ethos forced into me as an effort to kill me, and Josh didn't mention that he knew that when he saved me from it. We had mastered the beautiful art of denial. We never discussed it even after I'd performed a spell and things went terribly wrong.

I was gifted with the ability to change dark magic to natural and we speculated that I could learn to do the reverse with dark magic. Most days I had convinced myself that I could master it completely, but sometimes I doubted it. It didn't feel like Josh's magic, natural, but it wasn't quite dark and draconian. But it was stolen dark magic. The more I thought I was controlling it, the more the reins of my control seemed to loosen. I often wondered if we were being foolish and naïve to believe that diablerie wasn't inherently evil and was at the mercy of the one who wielded it.

"I think we should wait," he finally responded after giving it a long consideration. His tone held a level of guilt rather than apprehension. Protective fields and defensive magic were easy; they just used a minor amount of magic, leaving the core of it untouched. Performing spells was where you delved into the essence of it, forcing it to react to your command. Casting a spell wasn't like the other things—they seemed harmless in comparison. Spells changed the dynamics of the world, altering and manipulating things. If done correctly, they were majestic, obliterating any feelings of powerlessness while draining their source, which is why they were hard to do with borrowed magic. But my magic wasn't borrowed. The source was dead and I had taken it from him.

He sat up, concentrating on his hands for a long time before he looked around his new place, which he had moved into just a little over a month ago. He brought many of the things from his high-rise condo in the city to his new home; a three-bedroom Art Moderne ranch. I was curious to know what eclectic person decided something so unique, with its odd curves and peculiar design, would not look conspicuous in the Midwest. It did, which was why it was hidden away nearly half an hour from the city. The stainless-steel appliances, expensive hardwood floors, vibrant modern colors, and empire blinds didn't seem to improve his post-dorm/fraternity house decor, which probably irritated his brother each time he visited. The scarred coffee table fit the oversized microsuede dark blue sofa that was slept on more than sat on. The odd accent chairs must have been a gift because they seemed out of place, and far too traditional for his style. The worn geometric area rug wasn't worth keeping in his first place, let alone packing and moving somewhere else.

It was different from his condo that I had loved, but it gave him what he desperately needed—privacy. After we had a few accidents with magic, staying in his condo wasn't really an option, especially after the homeowners' association asked via a nicely worded form letter from their attorney that he leave.

"Do you think we were wrong for keeping some of Ethos's magic?" he asked softly.

Oh, I guess we are talking about it now.

"I don't know," I admitted. "But look how far I've come in just a few months. Imagine how much control I will have in a few more." My denegation seemed far more convincing than I felt about it.

He took his time responding. "Maybe we should go back to the way we were. Just get rid of the dark magic and I go back to loaning you mine."

I shook my head. "Loaning it makes you weaker. Why do that when I can just improve my skills with magic I already have? I can do this, Josh. *We* can do this. Right now it's hard, which I am sure it was for you when your strength increased."

"Hmm, where did this confidence come from?" he asked with his trademark half-grin, but fragments of tension still remained as he studied me with cautious eyes.

It was false bravado, and although I wasn't sure about the magic, I just wasn't ready to give up so easily.

"But we need to be careful. You already know how most witches feel about were-animals and magic. I just want you to be safe. The lower-level witches have a more difficult time detecting the variations of magic, but the stronger ones are more sensitive and skilled. With circumstances as they are, it's better not to raise concerns. And you've caused enough," he said.

"Variations?"

"If magic has been performed and I have ever been around that witch, I can tell who performed it." Josh had once described it as a fingerprint. Each witch had their special imprint that marked their magic. Problem was that if the witch were unknown, then the owner couldn't be matched. "Were-animals are the same way. If one walks into a room, other were-animals know it's there, and the same is true with vampires."

"Well, I am sure the deadly fangs are a big sign as well," I joked.

He laughed. "That, too."

Were the *circumstances* he spoke of in regards to his brother Ethan, the pack's Beta? I suspected that there was more to him than just being a werewolf, although he continued to deny that there was. Did Josh know?

"Tell me about Marcia," I said. The Creed was the governing body of the witches. At one time, it was led by the five members, equal partners in dealing with the witches. But over the years, Marcia, the strongest of them, had emerged as the leader and the others had been reduced to just council. Technically, they were supposed to lead as one, but if they were to name someone as a leader, then it would be her.

Last year I had found out I was a Moura Encantada, responsible for protecting the Aufero, a mystical object, and Marcia had it in her possession. It wasn't supposed to be that way. It had been my mother's responsibility to protect it, but upon her death, I inherited the obligation, and I'd already failed. Marcia somehow had it, and I was sure she wasn't going to give up such power anytime soon. I had no idea how I was going to get it. And I had to have it. It was a life or death matter. The last Moura Encantada that allowed her protected object to be taken had been found dead.

"What do you want to know?" he asked casually, wondering, I was sure, about my new interest in her. His smile was missing its usual wayward lilt; it was stiff and forced. The relationship between him and the witches had always been strained by his dual loyalties. He managed it, but it wasn't without difficulty.

"Before she acquired the Aufero, how did they punish the witches?"

Josh came to his feet and started to slowly walk the area, my attention following his every movement. Josh wasn't a hard person to keep your eyes on. The deep, alluring blue eyes and defined angles of his features were captivating. "The same as she does now, she takes their magic. I guess the worst thing one could do to an angel is clip their wings," he said, and the smile vanished quickly as his eyes became heavy with concern.

"But the Aufero can pull the magic from them by sheer will. How did they do it before?"

"They used a spell."

"Just like that, 'bam' and you're magicless?"

"It's not that simple. There is usually a hearing and then they decide what level you will be demoted to. Most penalties are short-term. But most witches don't fare well when such limitations are forced upon them, especially if they've lived the majority of their life with the ability. There isn't anything that can be done about it. Some are punished for just a year, usually for small infractions: practicing in forbidden magic, usually dark arts or necromancy. For some reason, there are many of us that feel the need to practice such a dangerous craft. The Creed punishes a witch if a human is hurt as a result or for practicing what they consider forbidden magic. Recently, the punishments have been stricter for minor infractions that, in the past, only warranted general counseling. Things like spells that were poorly executed and put the witch at risk of being discovered. Just like you all, we want to maintain the same level of anonymity about our existence."

"And the harshest punishments?"

He made an attempt at a scowl but seemed to lose interest. "Removal of magic completely or punishments to a level five are reserved for witches that perform a *rever tempore*. Most of the time, the punishment is even more severe."

He didn't need to say it; we both knew what that punishment was—death.

He considered my look of confusion and explained, "It's a spell to reverse time"." "You have to be very strong and very gifted to do it, and still most of the time it fails. But if successful, the witch can go back to a specific time within twenty-four hours. Someone desperate enough to do the spell is usually trying to correct something really bad; consequences usually do not mean much to them at the time, and the risk of losing their magic or death is inconsequential."

I stared at him with a newfound fascination, my head a whirlwind of thoughts as I imagined the ability to go back in time. Of all the magic we'd done and all the things I had seen and heard, this had to be the most intriguing.

Josh's gaze stayed on me for a long time, sensing my interest. "You don't just change *your* twenty-four hours, Sky—you change *everyone's*. That is why it is forbidden. Losing your magic may be your best punishment." His watched me with concern for a long time. "It is a spell that under no circumstance should be performed. It's dangerous."

I got his message loud and clear: *Don't try to learn how to do it and don't even think about asking me to teach it.*

"These are strong witches. I can't believe they stand idly by while their magic is stripped from them and don't try to stop them."

"Some do, but you have one witch going against the five powerful witches that make up the Creed. I am strong, but not stronger than the five of them," he said.

He took up a spot in front of me. "If you don't give in willingly, it is stripped from you by force, and it is quite painful, I hear. Of course, there is a penalty for your resistance." "But it's not like this is done casually. For such a severe punishment, it must be a unanimous decision."

I was sure the trial was just a formality and that the witch's guilt and level of punishment had been established before the so-called trial occurred. His voice hinted at it, although his words didn't. I'm sure those found guilty rivaled the Creed's strength. Was there truly a hearing, or was it just a show, a display of false democracy that truly did not exist? Where were the bylaws, a written account of what was deemed punishable by the demotion of your magical skill? But I climbed off my high horse quickly, because the were-animals weren't any better. Of course, there were laws that we lived by, but some were vague, giving the Alpha far too much power of interpretation.

The uncomfortable silence between us was odd. We dwelled in a place of unrestrained comfort—we understood each other. Josh had always been very intuitive and I suspected he knew I had more inquiries but for some reason resisted pressing the issue.

"I need to get the Aufero," I admitted.

He simply nodded. "I know. I'll help you."

"No. I may have to take it, and you assisting will only make things worse." It was such a delicate line that he walked by having to split his loyalties between the pack and the witches. I wanted to find the Aufero and take it. The further he was from this situation, the more plausible his deniability.

People in the otherworld didn't have a problem with segregation. They dealt with each other as little as possible and when they were forced to interact, it was usually in a state of contention, which made Josh's relationship with the Midwest Pack an atypical and very fragile situation. The pack needed Josh and would never do anything to damage the frail tapestry of the situation. If things went badly with Marcia and me, they would want Josh as far from the situation as possible, and my act would be viewed as that of a rogue were-animal, unsanctioned and unauthorized.

Josh's situation wasn't any better. As a blood ally to the Midwest Pack and younger brother of their Beta, it would be difficult for him to keep my secret if he deemed it pertinent information for them to know. Our friendship teetered on a fine balance, complicated by our personal obligations to the pack. He was more fettered due to the intrinsic bond he had with his brother.

Josh was strong, although not as skilled as someone of his level should be. His alliance with the were-animals made him a target. I was sure they were just waiting for him to mess up so badly that he would be the next witch in front of them being divested of his power as a penalty for some minor infraction.

I didn't want anyone involved. "But I do need a favor from you," I confessed, my eyes dropping to the floor, avoiding his heightened interest.

When I finally glanced up, he flashed a smile and leaned against the sofa, crossing his arms and exposing a new addition to the multitude of art that covered his body. It was a textured tribal tattoo that wrapped around his forearm, covering the scar left when he had been slashed by a claw a few months ago. Even when he was doing the most innocuous of acts, there was always a hint of mischief to him that made you feel like he had an intimate relationship with trouble. "Okay? What do you need?"

"I need us to go back to the dark realm. Do you remember that spell?" I mumbled, briefly lifting my eyes to meet his.

The smile vanished, retreating into a worrisome grimace. He found his composure but not before he started to bite at his nail bed. It was his nervous tic—his tell. But he had every right to be apprehensive. It was a caustic reminder of the time he was nearly killed when a witch connected to dark magic tried to kill him in order to steal his magic.

"Yes, I remember the spell and that time quite well," he said.

"Can we do that again?"

"Why?"

"I think I know where the Aufero is. When we went there the first time, for the Gem of Levage, I saw an orb that fit its description." I grabbed my purse, pulled out a folded piece of paper, and handed it to him.

"I didn't know it was important until Chris told you about the Aufero."

He looked at the horrible scribbling on the paper. "And what is this?"

"I don't have an eidetic memory, but it is pretty good. I tried to draw everything around it so that I could find where it is being kept," I said. "But it was over two years ago, everything is fuzzy. I just need another look. "

"Okay, I'll do it for you," he said, although I knew he would rather be raked over hot coals.

We stood in the middle of the living room. In anticipation of something bad, a scowl overtook his features. Strong magic drifted off him and spiraled around us. His usually cerulean eyes, now a deep indigo, held mine, and he took my hand in his. He clasped my hand firmly, stepping closer and invading my space. I wondered if he could feel my magic the way I felt his. Did it feel odd—wrong somehow? Did he relive that day that Pala had tried to kill him and steal his magic instead of helping him get into the dark realm?

I shivered at the nearly faded images of us straddling this realm and a magical one, where so many elusive objects were hidden with the use of strong magic. He waited a long time before he took out the knife. His eyes were vacant as they wavered, barely able to meet mine. No matter how many times we did it, a knife sliding over my hand was always painful. I winced. The blade slicing into his skin didn't seem to bother him. But I guess a person who had as much body art as he had was accustomed to a certain level of pain, probably even welcomed it. As he placed his hand in mine, our bond came quickly. As soon as he whispered the final words of the spell, I was yanked into a sea of darkness. I called for Josh but he didn't answer. This was different than before. No objects revealed themselves as I walked through the caliginous abyss. Breathing was difficult, and I was bathed in the heavy mist that surrounded me. Something was wrong. The dark feel that occupied every inch of the room and the dank coolness that enveloped me were definite signs that I wasn't welcome.

But the farther I walked, the warmer the air became, and the brighter my path. A new world slowly revealed itself to me. I heard Josh call, but I couldn't see him. It didn't look like it did the first time we had visited. Before it was full of things, hidden by the cloak of dark magic, but now there were fewer items. I searched for the Aufero, an orange luminous globe. A shadowy figure moved in the distance, and I lost focus on the reason I was there as I followed it. The slim figure darted in and out of the mist, just a glimpse of him appeared, and then I heard a loud shriek. Like a siren warning me of danger. I quickly changed directions and looked for the Aufero. As though it had waited for me to discover it, the glowing sienna ball pulsing at spastic beats was a beacon that I followed until I was in front of it. Everything revealed itself as if I were looking at a portrait. The dark wood curio that housed it, the odd painting of a woman with her arm outstretched to the sky, her dark dress angled out by the wind, all worked as markers that would ensure I could find it again. The room brightened, giving me every opportunity to identify it if I needed to. A sparrow hung on the wall, and odd cylinder-shaped candles were mounted to the wall, a garnet triple goddess symbol hung over a marble counter. On the tiles of the floor were symbols intricate and different in each space; they would be easy to identify.

I started back, trying to follow Josh's voice, which had become louder with each step. A figure moved so quickly to my distant right it was just a blur. As my eyes adjusted to the quick movements, I recognized it. Ethan, or someone that looked so like him he could pass as his double. The moment I was close enough to identify him he disappeared. When I turned to find Josh, Ethan's double stood in front of me. He had all his features except his skin, which here was bronze, his eyes vacant and gold. Our skin nearly touched. He was just about to touch me when I remembered Josh's instructions two years ago when we were in the dark realm and encountered a bronze man similar to the one standing in front of me. "Don't touch him, and if you ever see someone like him outside this realm: run."

And that is exactly what I did. Before he could touch me, I ran through the space, draped in darkness, calling Josh. I screamed, but my words were captured in the darkness, as we remained in unyielding silence. The fog increased, making it hard to see anything. The smell of sulfur and fire bloomed in the air. Breathing was difficult and my vision was compromised as my eyes started to tear up. I heard a strange gurgle and ran toward the sound. Josh's hand was wrapped around his own throat, trying hard to pry an invisible strangler off him. Just as I whispered the words to release us, something sharp sliced into my side.

Lying on the floor next to Josh, I panted softly as the remnants of strong magic lingered. My side ached.

"I hope you got what you needed, because we are never doing that again," he finally said, sitting up.

I continued to lie on the floor thinking about everything I'd seen in there and trying to make sense of it. Josh hovered over me. "Are you okay?

I nodded, but I wasn't. My side was throbbing.

"You're bleeding," he said, rearing back on his heels to get a better look.

I followed his gaze and found my shirt was sodden with blood. He jumped up and went to the bathroom and came back with a towel and bandages. Before I could object, he lifted my shirt and starting cleaning away the blood. My skin gaped open from an incision that was just deep enough to need bandaging. "It will be okay by tomorrow," I said, but he lingered just a little too close.

Personal space was a concept that Josh often ignored. He glanced down and smiled. "All better," he said.

But it wasn't all better. The longer I was away from the dark realm the more distant it seemed. I winced when I sat up to grab a piece of paper and pen off the coffee table and started scribbling down the patterns and shapes I had seen and everything I could remember about the dark realm and the Aufero, while Josh just looked over my shoulder. I wished we could have grabbed it then, but the dark realm just allowed you to see things, never touch. Which made the bronze man and whoever stabbed me even scarier. How did they survive in such a place? Why did they stab me? They weren't trying to kill me, maybe not even hurt me. Was it their way of pushing me out? If that was their plan, they succeeded, because I was glad to be out of that place and didn't have any intentions of going back.

I wasn't an artist, but a person could look at my picture and definitely find what was drawn on it. But I couldn't seem to get the image of the man that looked like Ethan out of my head.

"What's wrong?" he asked.

I wanted to tell him I had seen Ethan. I should have but it sounded crazy when I said it, and in my head I could only imagine what it would sound like out loud.

"Nothing."

"Did you get what you needed?"

And so much more. I simply nodded my head.

He brushed the damp hair from my face. "You're burning up. Are you really okay?"

No, I wasn't okay, but I wasn't hurt. I felt different, but I couldn't pinpoint what it was. "What *is* Ethan?" I blurted.

His face scrunched, giving me the look I suspected you would give one descending into madness. "What do you mean?"

I was positive Josh knew that there was more to Ethan than met the eye. Josh was more inquisitive in the past, but now he seemed to be in a place of acceptance. "He's a werewolf, like you, Skylar."

That was the problem. Ethan was more like me than he would admit. I wasn't just a wolf. I was death masquerading as a werewolf. I didn't survive my birth as a result of a vampire trying to turn my mother and me in utero. The conflicting changes were too hard for my body to handle, and like any other person would, I died. In an effort to save my life, my mother transferred a spirit shade from her to me and gave up her life in the process. I'm alive because I host a spirit shade named Maya. Because of my unusual birth and death, I could and would never be *just* a werewolf.

Ethan could break protective fields, something were-animals couldn't do. Dark creatures had an unusual aversion to him. There was something very odd about him, yet each time I questioned him, he was quick to tell me he was *just* a were-animal.

Josh handed me a glass of water. I emptied it quickly. I sipped on my second glass slowly, as he stared at me from across the room. He was too perceptive to not know something was wrong, but I wasn't sure if he really wanted to know.

Josh tried to convince me to stay longer, and usually I would have. We always ended our practice sessions the same way: sitting on the couch, snacking on the various junk foods that dominated his diet as we drank an unwise amount of alcohol while watching a movie with better special effects than storyline. But today I just couldn't stay because keeping what I saw to myself was going to be difficult anyway, and there wasn't any way I could maintain discretion doing typical post-magic activities. Today I needed to get as much distance as I could from Ethan's brother.

CHAPTER 2

I always glanced at the small sign written in gold script: PLEASE DO NOT TOUCH THE ART, before I stepped closer, keeping my hands at my sides and struggling to obey what should be an unspoken rule. The most avant-garde work in the city was displayed in this gallery. Most up-and-coming artists and sculptors held their shows here and it was the home of many modern pieces by local artists.

This was a good ending to a very disappointing day of searching for the Aufero. I knew what the place looked like. The problem came with actually finding the building. The dark realm didn't give you an address. It only revealed objects that were ordinarily hidden by dark magic in the real world. The last time when we looked for an object there, we knew it had been somewhere Josh was familiar with—the vampires' home. Now I was blindly going into various places. I had narrowed it down, based on the surroundings, to either a boutique, a candle shop, or a magic shop masked as a metaphysical store. Three metaphysical stores and the candle shop were a bust.

The art gallery was a welcome escape. No one asked me if I needed help anymore because I usually scanned the new paintings and sculptures, then made my way to my favorite portrait. But I made it a point to pause for a moment, to study the pieces, the way Claudia, the owner and Ethan's and Josh's godmother, had taught me. It seemed to be her goal to encourage me to appreciate work on a different level other than just considering it "pretty," "provocative," or "nice."

Although each piece fascinated me, it was a simple portrait at the far end of the gallery that always garnered my attention. It calmed me and always made life seem a little less complicated. When I joined the pack, I knew it would be more than signing my name on a dotted line and showing up for the next members' meeting as I waited for them to tell me what dish I needed to bring to the next pitch-in. They had taken complexity to a new level. Why did I need to know the history? Wasn't American history enough? And finances? American Express, my mortgage company, and the utility company were the only things I felt obligated to give money to monthly. So when I was told I had to give 10 percent of my income to the pack, I was ready to give them my two weeks' notice, the finger, or whatever was needed to separate myself from them. Questioning them on what the money was used for and what I got out of giving it to them quickly became a moot point when I received a quarterly statement, and a 60 percent return on my investment. I didn't ask any questions, I just took the money and hoped the mistake wouldn't be soon discovered. But I was realistic. They didn't make mistakes like that, nor were they likely to let me walk away without consequences. It was something I accepted as being part of the Midwest Pack. The advantages of joining them outweighed the disadvantages. I needed them.

"Why this one?" Ethan asked. He stood close. The warmth of his body brushed against my back, his breath bristled against the nape of my neck. I inhaled a deep breath because now I felt like I was suffocating. Ethan had an overwhelming presence. After two years, I thought I would have gotten used to it. But I hadn't.

I didn't know how to answer that. What drew me to this picture was still a mystery to me. I continued to stare at the portrait of two boys lying on a bed, the younger of the two in peaceful slumber; his blushed cheeks and ruffled hair made him seem angelic. The older one was propped on his elbow, watching over him. His face was intense and far too troubled for someone of his age. The pale blue walls offered a tranquil backdrop for the portrait. Each week I came into this gallery to look at this portrait, finding something new and intriguing about it. Today I noticed a shadow just to the right of the slightly ajar doorway as flecks of light filtered into the room. There was a story to this picture that I was missing and it pulled at me each time I saw it. What was it trying to tell me? This wasn't art. It was a puzzle. Tightening my hand into a fist calmed my urge to touch the painting.

I shrugged an answer as he took up a place next to me, focusing his attention on it, too.

Once I asked Claudia if she knew the boys. She took in the picture as though she hadn't seen it a million times. Her smile, which was usually pleasant, was weak and forced. Her response was "I do believe we all know boys like that. Sweet and docile when they are asleep, but when awake, mischievous like rascals."

"Let's have dinner tonight?" Ethan requested.

Ignoring Ethan had become a talent I had perfected to a delightful skill. This time I just couldn't. Instead, I scoffed at the request, glanced over to look at him, and said, "No."

"No?" he asked. A smug grin reached his eyes, gunmetal with a hint of blue. Then it crept over his lips; obviously he wasn't used to being denied. "Why not?"

"I don't like being lied to or threatened and every time we're together you do one or both. So, no, I don't want to have dinner with you," I said firmly.

He moved closer. "You're the one who wanted to talk. I am

giving you an opportunity to do that and I will answer any questions you may have."

That piqued my interest. I turned and scrutinized him for a long time; his features held the same sincerity as his voice. His chestnut hair was short again, accentuating his defined features, which were usually stringent and tight as though he was physically carrying the weight of the world. I had a hard time believing any of it. "You will answer them truthfully and promise not to give me any of those silly lies of omission that you are so fond of?" I challenged.

He nodded.

I considered the invitation. I didn't want to have dinner with him, but my curiosity overshadowed my apprehension. Worst-case scenario, he reneged and refused to answer my questions, and I would have the pleasure of walking out on him.

As I pondered the invitation for a few moments longer, unable to fully commit, he crossed his arms. "I will see you at eight," he said.

"I will meet you at Gigio's at six." That was early enough for it not to be considered a date. I didn't want to date Ethan, and based on his behavior toward me most of the time, he didn't want to date me, either. Six o'clock was a perfect non-date time.

"I will be at your house at eight with dinner," he said as Claudia approached. He turned toward her, and before I could object, he looked over his shoulder. "If I am going to be subjected to your inquisition, I do believe privacy is necessary."

His smirk deepened as he turned his attention to his godmother.

"Ethan, I'm so glad to see you," she said with a thick South African accent. Always impeccably dressed, today she wore a peach pantsuit, a pearl necklace and bracelet set, and beige gloves. She was never without gloves. Not only was she an empath, she was also an auteur. She could predict your future simply by touch. The gloves helped make life easier for her. If they were on anyone else, they would have looked silly, perhaps even pretentious. But with her refined, elegant looks, they fit. Most of the time her deep brown waves were pulled back into a bun. Today she wore them down; loose waves flowed around her face just shy of her shoulders, flattering her parchment skin.

Ethan smiled and greeted her with an air kiss on each side of her cheeks, avoiding touching her skin.

"You have to promise to visit more. Brunch Sunday, okay?" she suggested.

When it came to Claudia, Ethan and Josh were reduced to amicable and compliant children. "Sunday will be great," he smiled, agreeing without hesitation.

Then Claudia turned her attention to me. "You should join us," she offered.

No thank you, I think dinner tonight is more than enough. I kept my snide remarks to myself, gave her a genteel and fake cloying smile. "Of course." There would be enough time to come up with an acceptable excuse to cancel.

"Wonderful." She beamed. Then she did something odd: her cheek pressed lightly against mine, where she held it for a few seconds. I wasn't sure if it was intentional, but I knew in that brief moment she could see my life. I attempted to read her expression, but there wasn't anything there, just the same cordial stock smile that she used on her many patrons. It was her inviting smile that coerced you into trusting her and ignoring her complex skills that would otherwise cause apprehension.

She took my hand in hers and held in casually at her side. "Your lovely friend is becoming one of my favorite patrons. Her curiosity is inspiring. I see why you're so fond of her, she is quite charming," she said with a broad smile.

"I am quite fond of her. And her curiosity, if nothing else, is quite *charming*," he said. His broad, mocking, and deceptive grin annoyed the hell out of me, but instead of calling him on it, we stood there smiling at each other like two idiots.

Fond? Charming? I had to shift my attention from Claudia to Ethan. Ethan often had a questionable relationship with the truth, especially when it came to giving me answers to what he considered sensitive information. Now he was just lying for sport. Most of the time he was mocking me for what he perceived as incompetent behavior, or threatening me. At what point had that fondness developed? Most people didn't do that when they were fond of you. But with Ethan you never knew. That might be his twisted version of a mating ritual.

When Claudia beckoned him to follow her, the cynical smirk on his face was the true declaration of his feelings as he turned to follow her. What was the jackass award he seemed to be constantly vying for? A car? Caribbean trip? International vacation? Soon Ethan was the furthest thing from my mind as I directed my attention to a new painting that had a price tag on it that ensured I would never be its owner.

As a passive act of aggression, I refused to clean my house for Ethan. He was an uninvited guest. But I closed the door to the room claimed by Steven, the pack's fifth, and my pseudo-housemate who continued to deny he lived here. Yet, my guest room was now occupied by his clothes, furnished with his urban cottage-style beechwood furniture and an absurdly large flat-screen television that covered the greater part of the wall opposite the bed. And his monthly contribution that he claimed was for the food he ate coincidentally covered half the mortgage every month. I didn't want a housemate, and he claimed he wasn't one. Now I just considered him to be the guest that had stayed too long.

Whatever he was, he had made his presence apparent. Textbooks were laid haphazardly on my coffee table, men's workout magazines crowded my magazine rack, research articles always fanned out around the sofa, and I don't think he ever hung up a jacket. Initially I attempted to straighten up after him, but often it seemed like I added to the disarray, maybe even made it worse. Amidst what he called "organized chaos" was a system and he was the only one who could figure it out.

Despite my aversion to the idea of a housemate, I liked having him around. He'd gone to Georgia after his mother took over as Alpha of the Southern Pack, after the former Alpha was killed. He had been gone for nearly four months and I had missed him the whole time.

Five minutes before eight and I scanned the thirty-two questions on my iPad again. There were really just twelve actual questions. The others were just variations of the same question. Experiences with Ethan left me cynical. The master of half-truths and lies of omission forced me to be creative with my questions; maybe he would trip up and I would actually get the real answer.

Eight on the dot, Ethan knocked at the door. He handed me a large rectangular gift box before ducking back out of the door to bring in two large carryout bags from a favorite steakhouse in the area. I wasn't aware that they did carryout—they didn't last week. Ethan was an arrogant narcissist and—or perhaps because—the world around him bent to his will.

He headed to the kitchen and placed the bag on the table, removed the food before searching through the cabinets for plates, utensils, and silverware. "Open it," he urged.

Sliding my fingers along the seams of the box, I separated it with ease. I nearly dropped it when I finally got a glimpse of the contents. It was the painting that I had admired over the past year and a half at Claudia's gallery and that she had always refused to sell me. "How did you get this? She said it wasn't for sale," I said. Countless times I had asked her to sell it to me, offering her amounts of money that often made me feel foolish for my willingness to depart with such an exorbitant sum for a painting. Each time, she had pleasantly let me know it was for display only.

"It wasn't," he said.

"But she sold it to you?" I asked.

He shook his head. "No. I asked her if I could have it so that I could give it to you." He studied me for a long time. "You seem to really like it." He smiled. "I wanted you to have it."

From just inches away, the colors were more vibrant and the details more intricate. I touched it, something forbidden when in the gallery. "Thank you." I couldn't decide what was more astonishing: that I finally had it in my possession, or the fact that I did was because of Ethan.

Distracted by the painting as I placed it against the wall, I was inattentive as Ethan finished setting out the meal. It wasn't until he handed me a piece of red velvet cake that I acknowledged his presence. "You seem like a dessert-first type of woman," he said as I followed him back into the kitchen.

I am sure there was an insult in that comment, but I didn't care, because I *was* a dessert-first type of woman. I grabbed a fork and my iPad off the counter and took a seat at the table and starting eating the cake. Scrolling through the questions, I read off the first one, starting with something easy. "You are able to break wards, how?"

He placed two plates on the table. "Can I at least take a bite before you start questioning me?" He set the plate in front of me and placed a glass of wine next to it.

I slid the wine aside; dealing with Ethan, I didn't want to be compromised in any way. He moved it back in front of me. "It's a gift from Claudia. Just take a couple of sips. I can assure you the next time you see her she will ask for your thoughts about it. She will consider it an insult if you haven't tried it."

I took a sip. It was really good. Its deep coloring was a direct contrast to its light berry taste, which lingered. I would expect nothing less from a gift from Claudia. I continued taking small sips from the glass as I waited for him to take a seat. As soon as he did, I repeated the question. I was on edge, fully aware that I might never have another opportunity like this.

Taking a long draw from his glass, he said, "My mother was a witch, I inherited it. In skills that Josh falls short in, I seem to excel. I shouldn't have been able to do anything because I was a werewolf, but things never happen as they should. When my mother noticed that I was able to do magic, she suppressed it." He answered me between bites. He looked so bored and indifferent, I halfway expected him to lay his head on the table and take a nap. All this time I had waited for the truth and he presented it like he was giving me a recount of his trip to the BMV.

"Suppressed it?"

"With iridium. I spent most of my childhood with either an iridium cuff or iridium injected into me," he admitted.

"Injected into you? Couldn't that have killed you?"

"It wouldn't be any worse than if Marcia or the others found out. She is a purist. Since she has taken over the Creed, she's done an exceptional job at eliminating any anomalies that she is aware of. A wolf with the ability to use magic would have been a target for her."

My mouth opened in a disgusted gasp. Purist or not, the idea that she would kill a child based on her beliefs made me sick.

"Agendas do not discriminate based on age. Anomalies grow into adults that become problems. Delaying it because of a soft spot for children doesn't make the problem go away or be any less dangerous," he said. The fact that this didn't bother Ethan was more disturbing than the witches doing such things. Beliefs had to have boundaries, which definitely should start with not killing children.

"What is the fifth protected mystical object?" I asked.

"I don't want to answer that."

"You said you would give me the truth."

"That is the truth. I don't want to answer it. Next question," he said firmly.

I glared at him as my lips lingered at the rim of the glass before I took a long drink. *How should I proceed? Should I kick him out?* For several long moments I had that debate in my head. Ethan relaxed back in his chair, a hint of a smile on his lips as though he sensed my conundrum.

"Did you really love Chris?" I am not sure why that was so important to me. I didn't understand him, their relationship, and how a couple of months ago, he was willing to let her die rather than let her be changed into a vampire.

His pewter eyes turned cold. "That is neither relevant nor your concern."

He was right. It wasn't, but I just couldn't understand how he could let his ex, someone that everyone considered his weakness, die. Was he incapable of accepting that we all had weaknesses, and she was his? Or was the idea she was his a factor in why he allowed her to die rather than live as a vampire?

"I want to know, and you promised you would answer my questions. You already avoided one. If you aren't going to answer my questions, then you need to leave."

Why was I trying to figure out what went on in his mind? He was a puzzle to me and foolishly I was hell-bent on figuring it out. This was one of the pieces of the complex thousand-piece puzzle that was Ethan. I didn't know why I needed to do it. I likened it to people climbing Mount Everest. You climbed it, now what? The same was true with Ethan. What happened once I figured him out? Would I consider him less of a jackass? Highly unlikely. Would his acts be less cruel? His bad temperament more tolerable? Yet I couldn't stop myself from trying to figure him out.

"Yes. I did."

He crossed his arms over his chest, a stone cold look that would never relax.

"You let her die," I said.

"So?"

So. For a few minutes, I was speechless. Their relationship was the definition of narcissism and dysfunction and could only exist between people like them. Her commitment to her job and his to the pack trumped whatever existed between them and they were resigned to continuing to live that way.

"I couldn't let someone I love die without doing everything possible to save them, even if it meant letting her be changed to a vampire," I said. Ethan had made the decision not to allow her to be changed after she was badly injured in battle. If it weren't for the intervention of Kelly, the pack's nurse, who went against Sebastian's and Ethan's decision to let her die and helped Demetrius, the Northern Seethe's Master, change her, Chris would have died that night.

The stern features didn't relax as I attempted to hold his platinum-ice gaze as long as I could. Eventually I looked away. There was something about the higher-ranking were-animals that made it impossible to hold their gaze for any extended period. Long periods of eye contact were considered a challenge and they had a way of relaying that you didn't really want to do that. Their connection to their inner beast was so intrinsic that there didn't seem to be any part of them that could be considered human.

"Well, that is one of the many differences we have. I wasn't going to be responsible for making a vampire, especially one created by Demetrius with the ability to be as dangerous as Chris. Next question."

"But—"

"Next. Question."

I took a sip of wine and then skimmed the questions. "How long have you known about me and what I am?"

This question took him too long to answer, so I settled in for a creative lie. The amused smile coursed over his lips. "I said we would have an honest conversation and I plan to honor that. You might as well have a neon sign on your face flashing everything you are thinking because it is that easy to read. When we took you to Claudia, it wasn't the first time you had met her. You may not remember. You may have been eleven or twelve when she met you in a store. Do you remember her?"

I shook my head. Claudia wasn't the type of person you forgot, and I racked my brain trying to think of when I had met her. Did I ask her why she wore gloves? Did it not strike me as odd because it was winter? Her accent should have stuck with me, because my mother was fascinated with language and often I waited at her side while she asked a person questions about their culture while expressing her love for their language. She hadn't found one that she didn't think was a thing of beauty. She spoke four languages fluently. I was content with English and my barely passable Portuguese. I spent most of my childhood trying to cancel my lessons. But since I was half Portuguese, it wasn't an option to my mother. In hindsight, I was glad she made me stick with it.

"And what did she think of me?"

"You were still young, but she found you to be peculiar. She could tell you were a were-animal that hadn't emerged and suggested that we keep an eye on you. So we did. You didn't really prove to be a danger, so we checked in periodically. It was quite a boring job for whomever was tasked with it. It wasn't until Josh came to us with the request that you needed to be protected that you proved to be remotely interesting."

Of all the anomalous and creepy things I knew about the pack, this topped it. They had been watching me off and on for over a decade.

"Then why didn't you want me to join the pack?"

"Sebastian sees you as an asset. I still disagree and you haven't shown me anything since we've met that has changed my opinion. You're impertinent and irresponsible. Before, the only person who had to deal with your screwups was your mother, and given what she had to work with, she did an exceptional job. Now your carelessness is our problem. We are now tasked with the immense responsibility of protecting your life. I don't think it is worth the risks," he admitted in a low, thin voice.

He leaned into the table, and his deep gaze held mine. "As a Moura, you have your benefits, but I am not sure if the cost-benefit is really worth it. Those responsible for guarding things of such power must possess some of their own. At all times it should be controlled, never the other way around. I have not seen anything in you that would prove that you have the ability to possess or control anything of power, even your wolf half. At best, you're an endearing mess; at worst, you become an obligation that could hurt this pack. You're witty; it's good fun for a laugh or two. You're kindhearted, which means you will be trampled by those in this world. You blush when you're upset, you make unwise decisions when you are scared, and you are incapable of getting people to see a reality you wish them to believe. These are not the qualities of one fit to survive in this world. I figure far too many pack resources will be wasted trying to keep you alive," he said, and then he rested back in his chair and watched me.

I lingered over his words. "'Incapable of getting people to see a reality you wish them to believe'? You mean lie? I am sorry I do not possess the qualities of a deranged psychopath and haven't perfected the fiendish art of lying. Please, let me apologize for being sane and not an unconscionable degenerate. You of all people should know that you can never mistake kindness for weakness; they are not mutually inclusive."

Defending who I was to Ethan would not change anything. His mind was made up about me, and mine about him.

"Of course they are, but in your case they aren't. Your ability to manipulate magic can be an asset; however, of the many people I have encountered, I do believe it is a gift wasted on you," he said freely. "I still think taking on the responsibility of being your babysitter, and honestly that is what we will be for you, was one of the few unwise choices Sebastian has ever made."

I wanted to ask more questions, but honestly, I couldn't take any more of his *truths*. Instead, I smiled, plaintive and easy, as I scrolled through the questions on the screen and then asked the one that jumped out at me. "Why are you such an ass? I am sure you've already won some type of award for it. Why keep at it?"

His eyes narrowed. "Is that really on there?" He leaned in to look at the illuminated screen.

I nodded and tapped my finger right next to the question and turned it to face him. A condescending smirk lit his face. "Do you really want to waste time on silly questions?"

"Okay, here's another: what happened in your life that caused you to be such a jerk? Are there any mood-altering medications that you aren't taking enough of or too much of that make you act like this?"

He chuckled. "You said you wanted the truth and I gave it. I'm not one to coddle people or to temper my words because of sensitivity. I advise you to toughen up, because that is more likely to happen than me changing. If you don't want the answers, then don't ask the questions."

He was right. I wanted the truth and couldn't get angry that it was delivered by an acerbic narcissist who derived a level of pleasure from being tactless and candid. I took a deep breath and scrolled through my questions again. "The Tre'ases were afraid of you, and your presence sent Ethos into a violent rage. What is it about you that causes them to respond like that?"

He relaxed back in his chair. "I don't know."

I could feel the heat of my irritation brandishing my skin. The master of illusion and lies was back to his old ways.

He continued, "I've often wondered the same thing, but I don't know that answer. I am an anomaly; there are many that simply hate me because of it." He watched me with acute intensity. "I guess we are alike in some ways," he teased, pointing out the same thing I had acknowledged just a few months ago. Before he vehemently denied we were anything alike. What had changed?

His silence always put me in a bad place, and I waited, feeling as though each thing he did had an ulterior motive. It was as though we were playing chess and he was the reigning champion and I was just a novice.

"You know what I wonder?" he asked, his perceptive gaze fixed on me with full intensity. "Why Ethos was so lenient on you. He could have forced you to do whatever he wished—but he *asked*. When you stabbed him, he could have just as easily killed you—but he didn't. Do you ever wonder why, Sky?"

Of course I wondered, but sometimes ignorance was the most blissful thing imaginable. I was sure Ethan was about to snatch me from that place. He grabbed our glasses, went to the counter, and refilled them. Then he went to the living room and waited for me to join him. Obstinacy had me planted in my seat trying to gain back the control that Ethan had taken. After a few minutes, curiosity—my worst burden and flaw—had me taking a seat next to him. He handed me the glass. I placed the wine on the table next to me.

"You are aware of Maya's story?" he asked.

I was aware of the diluted version his brother had told me. She was born to a witch named Emma, but was killed before she reached the age of two. Legend told a different tale of a child who died in her sleep, but two years ago when I was stuck in the *in-between*, we spoke and she told me about her murder. Like any mother faced with the death of a child, she did what she could to save her life. Emma went to a Tre'ase to help restore her life, which she did. But like the tricksters that they were, the Tre'ase didn't give her a body to store her returned life in. Maya was cursed to go through her existence using others to host her in order to allow her to live.

"I am not sure how accurate the information is. Perhaps it is a tall tale or some twisted variation of the truth, but it is my understanding that Emma had another child, a son. She kept him hidden to keep him from Maya's fate, and he grew up to be who we now know as Ethos."

He waited for me to react, but I wouldn't give him the satisfaction of it. *Breathe.* It was such a simple task just minutes ago, and now it had become an extreme undertaking. I took another sip from the glass as I processed the information.

Ethan continued, "Wouldn't it make sense? After all, when he was reunited with his sister, he asked for her help in controlling the vampires and the were-animals. Even after her betrayal, when she stabbed him in the middle of battle, he never retaliated. Instead, he relinquished his power to her. Unfortunately, the fragile body that hosted his sister wasn't able to contain it."

Ethan, as always, watched to see what grew from the seeds that he planted. I took another long draw from my glass, an inept attempt to soften the information, slowly savoring the robust flavors of currant and blackberry. I wasn't sure if it was the wine or the information, but it was bitter against my palate.

"What are you able to do?" he asked after a stint of silence.

"What do you mean?"

With the look of amused arrogance he said, "The magic that you kept—or should we keep pretending you didn't?"

I could have denied it, but I was just getting tired of all the silly games Ethan and I played, so I decided to share. It was my show of good faith. If I showed him my hand, maybe he would do the same. I shrugged. "Not much." I waved my hand and the napkin danced across the table; then it soared toward us.

I held his curiosity as objects moved around the room in a simple choreographed production.

"Impressive. Besides making napkins bounce around, and I assume all your clothes in the morning as you make them dance around the room, what else can you do?"

Did he have a camera in my room? My mornings were always filled with a pre-dress performance as I made my clothes flounce in a mawkish production: flying pants, prancing shirts, and my underwear twirled around in an overzealous show. I concentrated; a thin golden silhouette surrounded me. Ethan sat up and took notice, examining it closely. He pushed into it, but it held. He pushed harder and it pressed him back into the sofa.

"Drop it," he requested softly.

After a long moment, I released it. It shattered like glass hitting the ground with a thud; fragments of its existence illuminated the room for minutes after it fell. It was too strong and I didn't have the same control of it as I did with Josh.

"What else can you do?"

"Nothing."

He didn't seem convinced. "Josh hasn't allowed you to do any spells?"

I shook my head.

He took out his phone and pulled up a document, then gave it to me. "Read this," he said, then he leaned over the sofa and poured a few water beads out of the vase next to us, then placed them in my hand. "Change them," he instructed.

"Sure, what do you want? A bunny? Bird? Lizard? Kitty?" I teased.

The straight line of his lips barely curled into a meager response. "You can't produce something organic from an inorganic. No one can. But you should be able to change the form."

He waited patiently as I stared down at the unevenly formed pebbles that filled my hand. I didn't have any idea what I wanted to make. Instead, I focused on combining them, leveling them until they melted into each other. Slowly, they warmed in my hand, solidifying into each other as a formable slate, which I eventually shaped into a small basin. Sparks of orange, blue, and crimson formed a small fire in it, which started to spread uncontrollably. Before it overwhelmed the small space, Ethan smothered the flames with a wet towel. But the bowl was too hot, singeing my hands. I dropped it, and he caught it just inches before it hit the floor. I hurried to the sink, ran cold water over my hands. Ethan took out a cube of ice from the freezer, and cradled my hand in his as he massaged it with the ice cube.

Three ice cubes later, my hand felt better and I was sitting next to Ethan on the sofa. He handed me my glass of wine. "I do believe I've underestimated you," he stated with a renewed interest. "You are becoming very powerful. Impressive." He gave a faint smile.

For a brief moment, his thoughts commanded his attention. "To untapped power," he said in a low voice as he lifted his wineglass to me. I tapped my glass lightly to his and hesitated before I took a drink, still thinking about what I had done. Power: I was becoming it. It still hummed around me, coursing lightly over me. Even when I borrowed magic from Josh, it never felt like this. Something had changed, and for some reason it seemed greatly enhanced by Ethan's presence.

I put the glass on the table as I started to feel the effects of it. My eyelids twitched and became too heavy. I had to work at keeping them open.

"Are you okay?" Ethan asked.

I made another futile attempt to open them. "Too much wine. It always makes me sleepy," I said.

"Lie down," he said, sliding off the sofa.

"No, I'm okay. I just need some water." I looked at him through the slits in my eyes. But my body gave up the fight, although my eyelids continued the battle. I lowered myself to the couch. I stayed awake long enough to see Ethan start lighting candles around the room. I think I counted six, one at my head, another at my feet, and two on each side of me before I drifted off to sleep.

I was awakened by his voice, with him brusquely patting the side of my face. The strong scent of cedar and other pungent fragrances filled the air, and candles flickered around me illuminating the darkened room. The air felt thick, stifled by a preternatural energy different from anything I had ever felt.

"Sky, open your eyes. Look at me," he said as he lifted my chin until my eyes met his. They fought against opening and eventually closed again. The pats against my face came harder; I opened my eyes and forced them to stay that way for a few moments. Ethan chanted in a low voice. Leaning against my ear he said, "Repeat this." Then he said four words, foreign but easy to repeat.

I repeated what he said, paying very little attention to detail. I blurted out the words in a random sequence so that I could go back to sleep. Holding my face in his hands, he said, "No Skylar, you have to say them exactly as I did."

He repeated them.

I said the words exactly as he did. His lips brushed lightly against mine for just a second, then he exhaled and blew out a breath. He had me repeat the words three more times and each time his lips were over mine for just moments. "Go to sleep," he finally said quietly. It didn't take a lot of convincing. I closed my eyes and drifted off.

CHAPTER 3

The next morning, I held my head, trying to calm the somersaults it was performing. Sliding against the headboard, I drew my knees to my chest. A hangover? No, this wasn't a hangover. It felt different, like I was waiting for the world to relax and slow down so I could jump back into it. I waved my hand across the sheet trying to draw it closer to me. It didn't move. I tried again—nothing. My hand sliced across the air as I beckoned the neatly folded jeans stacked on my dresser to me. Once again—nothing. I waved my hand in front of me to perform the most minuscule magic and I came up empty each time. Nothing.

What had Ethan done to me?

It took me less than a half hour to shower and dress. I was still high on anger as I sped to Ethan's house.

He answered the door before I could finish my knock, a look of smug indifference draped casually over his face as he took several steps back to let me in. I was so angry the words didn't come easily, and eventually he just became bored with us standing across from each other in silence. He leaned against the wall, arms crossed and lips drawn into a thin, rigid line, waiting impatiently for me to speak.

There were things that define a person's character and I had a list of them that I would never do because I considered them histrionic and beneath me. The first was slapping someone: it was a tacky and melodramatic act that only had a place in late-night dramas, reality shows, and soap operas. You really wanted to make your point, you didn't slap them—you punched them in the face. The second was throwing something at someone—another gauche act. Unless you were a pitcher in a baseball league, you were probably going to miss. It was just an overzealous expression of anger and tacky. Another was telling someone you hated them. If you had gotten to the point it needed to be said, your actions probably showed it more times than necessary. Did it really *need* to be said? Actions always spoke louder than words.

As Ethan stood there swathed in his smugness, I wanted to abandon all my beliefs and slap that haughty look off his face, throw the vase on the console next to me hard enough that it smashed against his body, and yell at the top of my lungs how much I hated him. Instead, I remained calm, taking several slow breaths before I spoke. "What did you do to me?" I asked.

He sighed, rolling his eyes. "You know what was done. Don't ask silly questions. Why don't we get on with it? Throw your tantrum, yell, and tell me how hurt and violated you feel. Call me whatever creative insults you've come up with and when you're finished with your little show—go ahead and let yourself out."

His trite indifference just fueled my ensuing rage. My jaw ached from being clenched so tight, my nails pierced my skin as my hands balled even tighter. "Why?"

The gentle timbre of his voice didn't match the scowl. "Why do you think? If you can't stop indulging every childish urge that overtakes you, then we have no choice but to intervene. If it is any consolation to you, I do not enjoy cleaning up your messes."

"What you did was cruel and unnecessary. You could have just asked."

"Would you have agreed?"

I thought about it too long because I didn't know. But he was right. I felt violated and probably never would have agreed. I had convinced Josh it was the right thing, and I would have tried to do the same with Ethan.

"That's exactly why I didn't," he said.

But it wasn't his choice. I snapped, "You had no right to do that to me!" My cheeks burned and nothing I did seemed to subdue my anger. "I know that somewhere behind that monster you put on display at every given moment, there has to be a real person. A person who balks at the way you treat people."

His attention remained on me, unyielding and harsh. "Josh's affection for you has compromised his reasoning. It is unfortunate, because there is no way in hell you should have ever been allowed to keep that form of magic. So I had to clean up his mess and yours before things got out of hand. A situation that should have been avoided in the first place. You need to get over it."

Allowed? Get over it? You wanted to make a point—you punched them. And I did. With all the force I could gather, I hit him in the face. Bones crunched under my knuckles and blood moistened my skin. It felt good. I punched him again. He spit out blood and wiped trails of it away with the back of his hand. I was about to hit him again when he grabbed my hand and backed me into the wall. His body was so close I didn't have enough space for a front kick. When I attempted to sweep his leg from my awkward position, he blocked me with his hip.

Panting hard, he took several long breaths as platinum waves rolled across his cerulean eyes. I hadn't hurt him enough. He spit out blood, then his tongue rolled over his teeth, I guess checking to make sure I hadn't broken any. I wanted to cause him more pain and make him feel vulnerable and excoriated the way he had made me feel. The only thing I had to battle him with were my words. "You hide behind the false dogma that your actions are necessary to protect the pack. That's a load of crap! You do cruel things simply because it brings you pleasure. You are a sadistic, cowardly, self-absorbed asshole that enjoys behaving this way simply for the hell of it. And you are too much of a coward to admit it to yourself. You aren't controlled by your wolf and your commitment to the pack. You are ruled by your narcissism and malice, and there isn't anything humane about you. We might as well keep you in the zoo with the other animals," I barked.

He was quiet as he listened, his face impassive and detached to the point he seemed apathetic. "Are you finished?" he asked softly.

If I had hurt his feelings in any form it was overshadowed by his anger; usually it felt like a fiery inferno, now it was arctic cold. He dropped his head so that his cold gaze could meet mine. "I asked a question. Are. You. Finished."

I steadied my eyes on his. If I could have thought of anything else cruel to say, I would have thrown it out there, too. I tugged at his hold, but he had me secured and fixed against the wall. I assessed our positioning, looking for a possible opening, because all I wanted now was to bring him unthinkable pain.

"If Ethos is actually dead, you didn't think it wasn't going to throw up flags each time you used his magic? It's so strong I can feel it miles away. Whatever is going on between you and Josh has made him complacent regarding your careless whims and irresponsible behavior. I do not have that problem. I will not allow you to destroy this pack because you lack impulse control."

I had used all my good stuff and didn't have anything venomous to spew back at him. He shook his head, his lips kinked into a wrought frown. "But you are too naïve and self-indulgent to understand the repercussions of your stupidity. There isn't anything entertaining about it—it's pitiful. You're pitiful. Don't worry, I won't be pulling your ass out of the fire anymore. The next time you fuck up, and undoubtedly you will, I will let you burn for it."

"Let me go."

He was quiet, trying unsuccessfully to control his anger. Lips tightened to a sharp straight line, eyes wintry cold, face flushed to an odd color as his hand pushed into my chest forcing me back against the wall. "Do you really understand the effects your actions have on things? The problems aren't just yours anymore. You are … no, *we* are dealing with things that we have never encountered, and the only thing you can do is screw up," he snapped. He lost control.

Ragged breaths escaped through his clenched teeth, perspiration dampened his skin along the brow as his face grew increasingly tense. Before I could speak, a dull throb gripped my chest, my heart slowed, dragging to the point it was a sputter, dwindling as it struggled for each beat. I gasped in a breath, trying to force it to respond.

What was he doing to me?

My head felt light, my body weighted, and my senses dulled to the point I didn't feel like me anymore. I gasped for another breath as I tried to push him off me, but his body felt like reinforced steel against me. With each passing moment I grew weaker, feeling the results of a heart that hadn't beat in minutes.

I opened my mouth to speak, but the words got lost. "Get … off … me" was all I could manage through rough, scattered breaths.

Ethan stumbled back, his mouth parted as he stared at me, wide-eyed. He tried to speak, but the words seemed trapped, "Sky, I am so—"

What was that? I pushed him away and ran out the door.

It wasn't until I was at home that I actually took a moment to consider what Ethan had done. He had stopped my heart by just touching me. We weren't alike. He was worse and something totally different.

~

The chips tasted like sawdust, but I kept eating them to keep from gnawing my nails to nubs. Ethan could kill me by just touching me. I just couldn't get over that. Everything felt bitter on my palate but I kept chomping away on the sour cream and onion chips because I needed a distraction, anything that would keep me from spiraling into a tailspin. I was so far out of my depth that I was swimming in mortar.

My suitcase was packed and placed at the door. It was an impulse reaction, something I did the moment I walked through the door. I had calmed down, but running didn't seem like too bad of an idea. Pack life really wasn't for me. Yeah, I would miss Steven, but he had been gone for over four months. And Josh, well, I would miss him and the magic, but now the messiness of that craft was something I wanted to keep my distance from.

My phone rang again. I already had five missed calls from Ethan that I didn't plan on returning. One from Winter, yeah, like I didn't see that bait and switch. And another from Josh. He had left a message, but I didn't care what he had to say, either. What would he have said: "Hey Sky, sorry my brother tried to kill you. It's kind of his thing, let's have lunch and pretend he's not a dangerous freak."

When my cell phone rang again, with an unknown out-of-state number, I grabbed it. "Hello."

"Is this Skylar?" said an unfamiliar female voice.

"Yes."

She was silent for a long time. "You've been looking for me—for us." She didn't sound very happy about it. When my adoptive mother died, I had hired someone to look for my birth family. Initially the private investigator called me weekly telling me about his progress. After a year, he sent me a refund. "Who am I speaking with?" I asked.

"I'm your cousin. Senna. Senna Nunes." She said it with pride, as though it meant something. Senna was my birth mother's name. I wondered if this woman had been named after her or if it was just a common family name.

"And you are Skylar Brooks? Sky Brooks?" she asked, her tone laced with condescending amusement. I wanted to point out that I didn't name myself. It wasn't my fault that my adoptive mother was a pseudo-hippie and thought it was a practical idea to name her daughter air and water.

She didn't say anything for a long time. "What do you want with us?" she finally asked.

I guess we weren't going to exchange pleasantries, just straight to the point. "I recently found out who my birth mother was and I wanted to meet my family."

"Where is your mother?"

"She died giving birth to me." I wished I could have given that news a little better and perhaps even shared the truth, but I didn't know her and based on her curt behavior I was sure it was going to stay that way.

"I'm sorry for your loss." Her voice dropped to a low sympathetic drawl, practiced and automatic. The same way people always did when I told them that.

I heard her whispering to someone. "Why are you just now contacting us?" she asked, her voice strained with suspicion.

"I just found out the name of my birth mother." Keeping from her the fact that that information was acquired from a spirit shade that inhabited my body.

Silence again, but this time there was a sharp back and forth with whoever she was talking to. Part of it was in English, but most of it was in Portuguese. She spoke so quickly I couldn't make out the words. All these years I'd thought I knew it well, but now that I heard it with an authentic accent, I could only translate half of it.

"This is an Illinois number, is that where you live?" she asked.

"Yes."

Her voice softened, but not by much. "I would like to meet you," she admitted.

I tried not to seem overenthusiastic, but it was hard. "I would like that." Then there was another awkward silence. We were definitely related: maladroit and socially stunted people who often stumbled over the intricacies of social normalcy. "I can come there if you would like," I offered.

After another exchange with whoever she was speaking with, she finally returned and agreed. When she hung up, I thought of all the questions I should have asked. Why did they want to meet me now? How did they find me? Why were they able to avoid being found by my investigator? I knew something had strongly urged him to give up the search, but he didn't return my phone calls and his assistant was a great gatekeeper that would never let me pass and simply took down my message on her tacky blue Post-it in fluorescent pink ink.

How did they find me? I decided I would make sure I asked them. But it really didn't matter. I was happy to really meet them.

I guess if the shoe were on the other foot, I would not have been happy with an investigator snooping around trying to find out about me without knowing the reason.

They were in Virginia, just an hour outside of D.C. It was a good thing they agreed to let me come. The pack seemed to know everything that went on within the confines of the Midwest. I liked the idea of meeting a family that they knew nothing of. If things went well, then I would have a place of refuge and people to confide in who weren't part of the pack and didn't dwell in the otherworld. The thought of it was a welcome relief and I felt the soothing joy that came with options. I knew I was getting ahead of myself, but the notion of having family, real blood family, was exciting. It didn't make what my adoptive mother and I shared less special. But I never knew what it was like to actually have a family, similar genetics—a common lineage.

I was excited.

. . .

As soon as I hung up with my cousin, I booked a flight. Within hours I had unpacked my "running away bag" and repacked it for my two-day visit when Quell knocked on the door. I watched him from the peephole like always. His eyes, once a fluorescent green, were midnight. And his face always had the typical vacuous appearance absent of any emotion.

He was another complication in my life. When I had first met him, he fed from *Hidacus*, a plant that, for vampires, was nutritionally the same as human blood. Even its chlorophyll reminded me of blood, but Michaela had destroyed his plants in a fit of rage and forbade him to ever use them again. Now he alternated between feeding from animals and me. Animals didn't seem to slake his lust, and in the end if he sought human blood, he killed the donor. By some sick twist of fate and vampire politics, he was unable to kill me because I was as much his creator as his vampire sire, Michaela, the Northern Seethe's Mistress. I never tried to understand the odd relationship vampires had with their creators. They revered them without reason, treasured them blindly, and protected them. To me, it was a tragically misdirected and undeserved reverence.

For now, I continued to feed him to keep him from killing. After his first taste of human blood, he had become an uncontrollable monster. In three days, he had killed five people. I couldn't have that on my conscience, so I had agreed to be his primary donor.

Now, as I watched him, I wondered if he knew I often just stood on the other side of the door watching him. From his appearance, you wouldn't think he was such a lost soul. His ash brown hair was neatly trimmed, not a single one out of place. The defined features of his face found an odd place between masculine and delicate.

When I opened the door, his lips twitched a little, making an effort to smile. He sat on the sofa and waited for me to grab my usual—an orange, sliced pomelo, and a few crackers. It seemed to do a better job helping me recover after he fed than just drinking juice. Most times we would talk for a few minutes because it seemed downright churlish for him to feed from me without so much as a "How was your day?" Today I didn't feel like talking.

"What's wrong?" he asked. Of course, on this of all days he decided he wanted to be social.

"Nothing," I said. I wasn't ready to talk about what happened between Ethan and me.

I took a seat next to him and extended my arm to him, but instead he ignored it. "You seem sad and angry; which one is it?"

"I had a rough day," I admitted as I dropped my head back against the sofa and washed my hands over my face.

Aware of his gaze that lingered on me, I lifted my head, and was met with his concerned eyes as he waited patiently for me to continue. When I didn't, he asked, "How so?"

"Do you ever wish you could go back to the way you were, before becoming a vampire and being pulled into this world?"

In a sweeping graceful move, he came to his feet and began to wander throughout the room. He finally stopped and studied me in his peculiar way, and I started to repeat the question when he answered, "No, I feel better off. Michaela saved me from a world far worse than this one."

How bad was his life that this was nirvana to him? "Sometimes I feel like I don't know you as well as I should. How did you meet Michaela?"

"You are always so curious and endearing. It is a trait that I feel is wasted on me," he said.

"Is that your way of saying you don't want to talk about it?"

"It is my way of telling you that my past isn't worth discussing."

But he was wrong. The more he evaded it, the more I needed

to know what had occurred in his life that had changed Andrew Fletcher to Quella Perduta, the lost one.

I attempted to read his blank expression. "Why?"

It was a simple and kind smile, but it aptly told me that discussion of his life had ended. What event or series of events occurred that were so tragic that he didn't want to be part of humanity? So disenchanted by humans that vampirism was a welcomed escape. His obsidian eyes went to a place that seemed to provide solace but provided me with absolutely no answers.

Instead of questioning him any further, I placed my arm on the sofa. It wasn't long before he was next to me and sharp enamel pierced my flesh. Most times I diverted my attention elsewhere, either by reading a book or watching television, but today it hurt a lot and the only thing I could tolerate was waiting until he finished. He seemed more ravenous than usual. After nearly ten minutes, I had to pull my arm away.

"You don't taste the way you used to," he said as his hands wiped across his lips, removing the small trails of spilled blood. The hungry look on his face confirmed my thoughts; he wasn't amenable to stopping.

"I was different?"

"Before, it tasted"—he stopped, searching for the right words—"off. Like food that was left out unsealed."

I chuckled. "I tasted stale?"

It took him a long time before he answered. "Yes. Odd. Not like you do now."

Not only could you feel the difference in dark magic, but apparently there was an undesirable taste, too.

He started for the door but stopped. "When will you be back?" he asked, his back to me as he opened the door.

I often forgot that vampires could read your thoughts while they fed from you. Most of the time I didn't care. The thoughts that went through my mind were probably too dull to be of any interest to him. "I leave Thursday. I only plan to stay two days."

"Why such a short time?"

"I have things here I need to attend to." I shouldn't have worried about Quell the way I did, but it was a selfish interest. Each murder committed in an effort to feed was my burden to bear. I still harbored the guilt that he would have been perfectly content dead if it weren't for me. It was my desire to save his life, and now he was my responsibility.

"Stay as long as you need. I will be okay."

Yeah, right.

"Perhaps we should try using someone else again," I suggested.

He nodded, but a look of apprehension crept over his face. The last time we tried it ended with me pulling him off the poor girl and calling Dr. Jeremy, the pack's physician, to tend to her. I spent the next hour taking numerous questions from Sebastian, which ended with him reminding me that I needed to end whatever was going on with Quell and me soon. Which I quickly pointed out that I was, and that is why Dr. Jeremy was at my house trying to save the life of a woman he almost killed.

"I know you can do it." I smiled. I sounded more confident than I felt. There was something innately dark about Quell. Now I questioned how far he had descended from his humanity. He was a misanthropic vampire that hated most humans for their vile ways and slow moral descent from what he considered true humanity.

He smiled gently in agreement, but he didn't seem very enthusiastic about doing it.

"Have a safe trip," he said, then he vanished before my eyes.

I tried to put my curiosity to rest, but it was left restless and unsatisfied. I wanted to know about Quell. How bad had his human life been that vampirism was a welcome escape? What atrocities did he see or endure that caused him to turn his back on humanity?

CHAPTER 4

The small historic district made getting around in a car difficult. The cab driver dropped me off a few blocks from the restaurant. I arrived a couple of hours early. I needed the extra time to calm my excitement. I was an only child, raised by an only child. There weren't any cousins, aunts, or siblings to bond with. Twenty-six years later, I was finally going to have a familial connection. I wanted that connection. Even when they were fighting like they were ready to rip each other apart, Ethan and Josh had an undeniable link that I envied. Something that only a common bloodline could provide. I wanted that.

I browsed through the small historic district in Virginia. The cobblestone sidewalks slowed me down enough that I could peruse the cute boutiques, specialty stores, and bakeries before heading to the French bistro where Senna had chosen to meet. The red velvet cupcake would ruin my appetite for lunch, but since I doubted I would be able to eat, I wasted a half hour sitting at a table outside a small bakery admiring the mature charming gardens and neatly manicured landscape while I nibbled on the treat. The area held a certain old-world charm, probably the reason why it was so crowded.

My hand gently pressed into my stomach. I wasn't sure if it was the cupcake or my anxiety that was making me queasy. The moment I walked into the restaurant, the host greeted me with a wide, practiced smile. Just as I was about to ask to be directed to my party, I saw them. To the left of the hostess was a brunette, maybe twenty. Her stern appearance matched her brusque attitude over the phone. It was like looking in a mirror five years ago. Her hair was an untamed voluminous mound of curls that cascaded over her shoulders, her eyes a deeper green, nearly jasper in color, cheeks not as defined as mine, giving her a rounder and more youthful appearance. The family resemblance was there. She was with an older gentleman, his eyes a deep brown that complemented his olive tone and graying dark brown hair that formed short loose waves against his scalp. Broad cheekbones made his rather unremarkable appearance distinguished. When he smiled, you could tell his personality was a contrast to his frosty, curt companion's.

"Sky Brooks?" asked the young woman, coming to her feet at my approach.

"Skylar," I interjected, shaking the extended hand she offered. The older gentleman stood as well, greeting me with a quick nod before shaking my hand.

My mother had three siblings, and I had expected more people. I took a seat. The man in front of me, I assumed, was Uncle William.

Our food sat in front of us as we sipped on tea. William's smile was earnest, shattering any apprehension I had. His conversation was warm, inquiring, but nothing more than light banter to break the icy barrier that Senna's question had erected. He asked me more personal questions: what did I do for a living, if I had children, where did I live, what college I attended, whether I liked sports. The conversation even steered toward how the city's football team was doing. Senna spent most of her time interjecting more probing questions: Why did I just start looking for them?

Where was my adopted mother? Did I have other siblings? And finally, what did I want with them?

For such a young woman, she was full of skepticism and was about as warm and cuddly as a cactus. She made Winter seem downright hospitable and nurturing. I felt like it was an interrogation rather than a meeting. She took on the role of gatekeeper to determine if I would meet the others.

"Please excuse Senna, she can be a little abrupt at times. We knew we had a cynic on our hands when she was three and grilled her babysitter before agreeing to stay with her. Fortunately, she wasn't very threatening then, trying to interrogate a sixteen-year-old with her thumb shoved in her mouth." He directed his attention to her. "Now Senna, why don't you just put a thumb in it," he joked.

The scorn didn't falter for one moment. She was all business, with little room for congeniality.

"Don't apologize. I understand her apprehension," I said politely. Since joining the pack I had a higher tolerance for terse behavior. Being polite seemed like an unnecessary hassle for most were-animals.

"I want to know where I came from," I finally stated, once she had asked her questions several different ways. Her eyes narrowed as she chewed on her lips. I suspected she anticipated another answer. The questioning continued and I answered them, giving only as much information as necessary. I guess I wasn't so different than the pack members.

When we finished brunch and neither of them initiated plans to meet again, I guessed I hadn't passed the gatekeeper's criteria.

It was surprising the next morning when I awakened to my cell phone ringing at seven thirty. It was a Virginia number. I cleared my throat, wiped the sleep away before running my hand over my face as I answered it. It was Uncle William, and I could hear his inviting smile through his words and his voice was just as mild and warm as it was in person. He invited me over for dinner. He put me at ease and filled me with high hopes that the rest were as kind as he was.

A little after six, I walked through the large white cottage home, whose style stayed true to its motif. Pastel walls were decorated with vintage art, and brass lamps were placed randomly throughout the cluttered space. There were several books similar to the ones in the pack's library on the small bookshelf in the living room. The small talismans placed throughout the room caught my attention. I recognized the statues from visiting London, one of Josh's friends whom I had met a few months ago.

Senna was there as well, with the same distrustful look from yesterday. My aunts Caitlyn, Beth, and Madalena were there, along with cousin Suri, Senna's mother. Her mousy auburn hair and round features made her seem dowdy and plain. Aunt Madalena's amber eyes were hard to pull your gaze from, and the broad smile that covered her face at all times made it difficult to not give her my full attention.

My family didn't give me much space or time to wander throughout the house, quickly directing me to the kitchen. For a few minutes I sat in awe, gazing into the faces of the very people I had been trying to locate for over two years. When I wasn't staring at people who resembled me at various stages of my life, I was peering down at my untouched tea. They didn't seem to care whether or not I drank it, but were hospitable enough to offer to warm it up when they noticed I hadn't. After my incident with Ethan, I just didn't want to drink anything someone gave me. I was paranoid. Instead, I took sips out of the bottle of water I had brought, despising Ethan for making me like this. I directed a little of the anger in my direction for allowing him to.

Aunt Caitlyn seemed very curious about me being a were-animal, asking questions about the pack that I tried to evade, but I hadn't mastered the art of redirection and lies of omission. Since I had never mentioned it, it made me cautious that they knew I was a werewolf. They knew my father and had been at the wedding. I remembered seeing them when Maya had given me a brief view of my mother's life. "Are you aware of the Midwest Pack there? Have they approached you?"

I nodded, but didn't elaborate. She continued probing, unable to drop the subject. "Which is it? Did they approach you or not? Are you part of them or not?"

"A couple of years ago I had a situation, they helped me out," I admitted.

Aunt Caitlyn's eyes narrowed. "What type of situation?"

"It's a long story."

"We have time." Her lips strained to make a smile. "Did it have anything to do with Maya?" she asked.

Crap! They knew. I nodded and gave them a very abbreviated version of the actual events along with a beautiful editing job. I didn't want to seem so dangerous and weird. Based on the books, talismans, and their information about me being a werewolf, I didn't feel the need to edit out the weird things that inhabited this world. In the end, I told them that because I hosted Maya, the vampires assumed that I would be able to survive the ritual that would remove their restrictions. I didn't mention that I was linked to the vampires because of the ill-fated attempt of a vampire to change me and my mother. Nor did I tell them I was now a freak with strange magical ability. I wanted them to like me, but despite the smiles plastered on their faces, they gazed at me with rueful apprehension

"Are you part of the Midwest Pack?" asked Suri. She was just as unfriendly as her daughter, Senna.

"It doesn't matter," Senna snapped just as a sharp, blistering shock pulsed into my side. I fell to the floor, grabbing her by the wrist and pulling her with me. There was a mad scramble to grab the Taser. Aunt Caitlyn took hold of it and pressed it to me again, my body seizing into convulsions. "Help me. Grab her arms," she ordered as she moved to her knees. I kicked her, and the heel of my shoe clipped her square on the chin. She cursed as she tried to grab my legs again. Someone tugged at my right arm and another at the left. I yanked them out of their grasp and elbowed one of them with the right arm hard enough they wailed in pain. A heel strike went into the person on my left. I fought them off, jabbing, punching, and kicking, making contact with any body part I could. A sharp strike into an ankle landed someone on the ground next to me. I hooked my arm around her neck and held a firm grip around it. Using my wrist as leverage I squeezed harder, and she gurgled for breath.

"Leave me alone or you will be responsible for what happens to her," I said in a garbled voice. I tried to get a tighter grip when another sharp shock ricocheted through my body. I couldn't fight it anymore, the pain was excruciating. I collapsed back, releasing my hold on my aunt.

I woke up in a bed, my arms and legs outstretched and bound to its posts with handcuffs. They rattled but didn't give as I jerked on them. The steel strained, cutting into my skin as I tugged at them. "Let me go."

"We can't," said Senna, and for the first time her voice was soft, a saddened resolve laced into her words.

I tugged again, yanking hard, the silver handcuffs jamming into my skin as I pulled at them with all my might. Silver didn't bother me like it did most were-animals, a benefit of hosting Maya. I weighed my options. Could I slide out of them? Probably not without breaking my wrists. Then what? I was going to be useless without the ability to use my hands.

"Stop, you're going to hurt yourself," said someone. I didn't even bother trying to figure out who. As if they cared about my well-being. People who care about your welfare don't Taser you and handcuff you to a bed.

"Where is it?" one of them asked.

"Where is what?"

"The third book."

"I have no idea what you are talking about." I yanked at the cuffs again.

"You have the third book," Senna said.

Third book?

"Your mother took that third book. There is no way you do not have it," someone asserted.

"She will not tell us. Just like her mother, she will turn her back on this family," one of my aunts hissed.

Before I could ask any questions, they started chanting at once, then stopped in unison. A knife swiped across my right forearm, spilling blood. They continued chanting, then the blade sliced deep into my left forearm.

The first cut hurt like hell, but I was prepared for the second and bit back the scream. I pulled at the cuffs again. "What are you doing?" I asked as I tried to free myself.

They continued speaking in unison, chanting over me; crystals were laid at my head, on each side of me, and then a final one at my feet.

I remembered Josh using a similar incantation a couple of years ago when he tried to exorcise Maya. It would have killed me, but at that time, he thought I was going to die anyway and it was a long shot to save my life.

The handcuffs clanked as I jerked at them trying to break free. "You exorcise her—you will kill me!"

The cuts kept sealing closed. Someone made an irritated sound and commented that I was a were-animal and the wounds wouldn't stay open. A thick liquid was dripped on my skin. Whatever it was, it burned. They resumed the spell. This was a lot different than what Josh did. Same chant, different process. I doubted something like that would be of concern to them. Another candle was lit, then they spilled my blood again. Everything had failed. I screamed as loud as I could. William attempted to cover my mouth with his hand, but before he could, I sank my teeth into him. I held on until he yanked my hair hard enough to temper my grip. I tore skin; he glared at me as he grabbed a towel off the dresser and wrapped his hand. I hated the taste of blood in my mouth, but the satisfaction of his glare made the taste a little less bitter.

The house shuttered, lights flickered, the candles blinked erratically, and everyone was pushed against the wall, held there firmly by an unseen force. Then they were released, power rushing over the room. Josh. I knew his presence—it was undeniable and all-consuming. You couldn't be within a foot of him without feeling the intensity of his magic. But it was Ethan who came through the door. His hand covered each candle, extinguishing the flames, before he shoved past anyone who stood in his way. He knelt beside me. "Unlock her." His icy command caused goose bumps to run along my arm. No one moved. "Now."

Still no one moved.

He pulled at the cuffs on my left hand, ripping the bedpost free. The other three received the same treatment. He looked at the blood that swelled from the cuts. "Unlock the damn handcuffs," he demanded through clenched teeth.

Uncle William stepped forward cautiously, moving past Ethan to unlock them. He took a moment as if he was trying to calm his anger before taking hold of my arm. Ethan examined the cuts with a groan. His grip tightened, and it hurt worse than the actual cuts. He dropped my arm quickly once he noticed the wince. "Sorry," he said.

He stood when Josh walked in with Sebastian behind him. Ethan handed him the two books that lay on the table. Sebastian didn't need to announce his presence or tout his position; his ineffable power did it for him.

"Where is the other one?" Sebastian demanded.

Silence.

He went to William, his face just inches away. "*Where* is it?"

William made a feeble attempt to hold his gaze, but inevitably it dropped to the floor as he exhaled. "It was stolen from us by her mother." The same disdain that colored his language when he spoke of my mother was transferred to me.

What were these books that everyone had to have, and why did my mother take one?

Sebastian asked a series of questions. He regarded William intently, studying him as he spoke, seeking the truth behind the answers he received.

"When were they taken?"

"Thirty years ago?"

"And you are just now noticing?"

"Not at all, we've been looking for them all this time," William said.

"Why? Can you use them?"

"No."

Sebastian continued to study him; he closed his eyes for a second, concentrating. "Lie," he asserted.

William took a long breath as he held his words. It had to be a huge annoyance to know that you couldn't dance around the truth when dealing with a were-animal. And if you were skilled enough to be able to, you were still no match for most of them. "We know someone that can," William admitted.

As a show of solidarity, they all seemed to cross their arms, lips tightening into firm lines. Just as I had, Sebastian realized that he wasn't going to find out who it was. He studied each face, a long, persistent gaze that would ensure that he would recognize them if he ever saw them again.

When he spoke it wasn't to William but to Senna, my hostile, tetchy cousin. "We are taking these. You shouldn't have them and aren't in a position to keep them safe. However, if it is found out that you can read them, your family will not be able to protect you. You are welcome to call me." He handed her a card, but it dangled at the end of his fingers as Senna looked at it with contempt. I suspect she wondered, as I did, how had he known?

"Take it," he urged. "I can assure you that one day you will need it."

After a long pause, she finally took the number. "Thank you."

With a quick nod of his head, he left and we followed behind. Sebastian wasn't out of the house long before he had called the East Pack Alpha. He didn't give him a lot a detail, just instructions to watch Senna, and to keep her safe. The safety of the rest of my family didn't seem like such a priority. When someone tries to kill you, it's hard to feel protective and warm and fuzzy toward them.

Sebastian drove away in another car while I sat in the backseat of my rental, with Ethan in the driver's seat. Occasionally his empathic eyes met mine.

We entered the gates leading to a small private airport a couple of miles away. Ethan left my rental car with a uniformed man who met us at the plane. Another one greeted him as we boarded.

The spacious plane made their obvious attempt to ignore me easy. The setup of two seats in a row and enough space between the next row made it quite easy to pretend the other row just didn't exist. Space was good—distance was even better. I took a seat in the far corner near the window and kept my attention on the people outside. Sebastian and Josh sat in the middle of the plane where there was a desk, two seats on each side. It was obviously set up for meetings.

"Let me look at your arms," Ethan said. He declined the flight attendant's offer to assist. The calm, placid look was quite unexpected. But he wouldn't look at me; the seat behind held most of his attention.

He opened the first aid kit, took out antiseptic, and started cleaning the cuts. "I just wanted to meet my family, I didn't expect—"

His tranquil distant gaze lifted briefly to meet mine. "Please don't talk," he requested softly as he focused on the task of bandaging my wounds, handling me with gentle, clinical detachment.

"If I thought this would happen, I never—"

"What part of that request are you having difficulty understanding?" he snapped before he clamped his mouth shut. He dropped my arm and stood. He took several steps away from me. After several controlled breaths, he came back, gently taking hold of my arm again and finishing the bandaging. Usually I healed fast, but whatever they had doused me with seemed to prevent it. The wounds wouldn't close and continued to bleed.

Still in silence, he finished covering my arm, packed up the rest of the kit, and went to the bathroom. Self-righteous indignation got the best of me and I met him outside the door. "Do you think that if I suspected anything like this was going to happen, I would have come here?"

He seemed terribly distracted by everything surrounding me, but the waves of his frustration and anger weren't something easily missed. The gunmetal eyes held mine for just a few seconds before he sidestepped me. "I don't care to try to figure out what actually goes on in your head. I do believe there are children far more responsible and equipped with better survival skills than you. Sky, your—" Then he just stopped, shook his head, and took a seat next to Sebastian and across from his brother.

Sebastian hadn't moved since we entered the plane, and maintained the same profile. Jaw clenched tight, muscles twitching mercilessly along his cheek and neck. Josh's attractive features were skewed by a frown.

The friendly voice and ebullient personality of the flight attendant was a welcome distraction. I ordered water, a turkey sandwich, and chips. They all wanted the same thing—Jack and coke. I wonder if they drank as much before I came into their lives, and if our pack meetings would eventually become a series of interventions. As we made our way back home, I couldn't take the side glances. The two drinks that Sebastian had tossed back eventually relaxed the frown that had become a fixture on him.

While eating the sandwich, I couldn't help but feel disheartened about the lost hope of ever having a real family. For a fraction of a moment, I had one, and it was a nice feeling. Now my life had reverted back to the unsettling reality that the pack were the only people I had in my life. And I suspected, like my family, they cared more about the books than me.

What was so special about those books? I wasn't naïve enough to think that the pack's special forces—the Alpha, Beta, and their secret weapon, a very gifted witch—came just for me. Nope, I wasn't under any delusion that the power trio chartered a plane to fly across the country for just me. I was just an incidental. This was about the books. It was made all the clearer by the way Josh's attention was split between me and them. He looked like he was just minutes from proposing to them. I really wanted to get a peek at them. What was in them?

Josh's brows furrowed, and when he opened one of the books, he leaned over to say something to Ethan. Then he opened the other, and the conversation between the two of them continued. Before long, the power trio were huddled together discussing something. I watched their lips move with the urgency of their words. Even an expert lip-reader would have had a difficult time. It was impossible for a novice.

Josh waved me over and I took the seat next to him, across from Sebastian and Ethan. He placed the books on the table in front of me. "Open them both to the same page," he instructed.

I did. When I opened the book, I could feel all three of them become tense. They leaned forward in their chairs and looked at the pages. Really? Were they checking my work? *What, now I am so incompetent I don't know my numbers? Seriously? Can you be more insulting?*

They watched me like a specimen under a microscope.

"Read the first two lines of each page," Josh instructed.

It wasn't in English and it was a long stretch from Portuguese, which I could read better than I could speak. "I don't understand it," I admitted.

"It doesn't matter, just read," said Ethan.

I did, fumbling my way through the two lines like a child learning to read. They stared at the book, then looked at me—waiting. "Read the next two," Josh instructed.

And once again, I clambered through the wording.

Ethan's and Sebastian's faces remained portraits of stoicism, with intense eyes that pierced into me. Josh looked relieved, and a smile beamed over his face from ear to ear. "Absolutely amazing," he said, giving me a quick peck on my cheek. If we weren't in flight I was sure I would have seen his happy dance.

"Yeah, yeah, I'm great. The best there ever was. The cat's meow. Now tell me what's going on."

Josh took the books from me and opened them. The moment he did, the letters disappeared off the pages.

"They're protected, and there doesn't seem to be a rhyme or reason about who can and cannot read them," he admitted.

But I was sure they were going to figure it out. We knew of two people now, Senna and me.

Sebastian was quiet, his intense gaze focused on me in an ineffable way. "That will be all, Sky," he said coolly.

Did he just dismiss me?

I didn't move. Instead, I looked both Ethan and Sebastian in the eyes, putting more iron in my gaze and bravado in my voice. "Well, since so few people are capable of reading the damn things, it seems like you would be a little nicer to the one person you know who will be willing to do so. I can almost guarantee Senna will not be as easily coerced into helping you. Either you all tell me what this is and what's going on, or I will wish you good luck with your adventure finding someone else, because I will not do anything with these books until I know what is going on."

Sebastian smiled. It was something he did rarely and there was something so mesmeric about it, I was glad he didn't do it more often. The defenses dropped and for a brief moment you forgot that you were dealing with a predator. The very worst there was. His voice was like silk as he spoke. "I strongly advise you against pulling this card again. First, so that we understand each other, I am giving you this information because I don't see any harm in you knowing it. Second, if I were you, I wouldn't underestimate Senna's willingness to help us, which kind of makes you superfluous. Am I correct?"

I didn't bother to answer. I was sure Sebastian could be quite persuasive if necessary. "What are the books?"

"It is two-thirds of the Clostra."

The Clostra was one of the protected objects that literally meant *key* in the debased Latin that witches used to record their spells, but I had absolutely no idea what they opened. Since most of the protected objects were connected to inimical things, part of me didn't want to know. There was still that part of me that maintained that ignorance was bliss. "Someone else is a Moura Encantada in my family?"

Mouras Encantadas were responsible for guarding protected objects. To the best of my knowledge, they were only women. The responsibility was passed down to their first female child upon death. That is how I ended up with the task of protecting the Aufero. It was originally my mother's job to protect it, which Ethan told me in the only way he knew how—cruelly—as he showed the picture of the Moura for the Gem of Levage, who had been killed. We didn't know who did it, but I had been sure it had something to do with her losing it and allowing it to be destroyed by us.

"No, the best I can tell, your family took it. I am not sure what their goal was in doing so. I assume to sell it. They can easily command a high seven figures," Sebastian said.

"And the Moura for it?"

"I am sure she is dead."

"You don't know that. I haven't had the Aufero in my possession, ever, and I am still alive."

"For now," Ethan pointed out.

"Great, just what this story needed—a narrator!" I snapped back. Then I directed my attention back to Sebastian. "How did my family get it?"

"That is a great question. I wish I knew the answer," he said.

I had gone through the journals of my adopted mother with a fine-toothed comb in order to find out what I could about my mother. Except for the incident that led to my mother's death, there wasn't a lot of information about her.

"Did your family say anything to you?" Sebastian asked.

I shook my head. "They just wanted to know where my mother put the third book."

"Hmm, I suspect she took it because she knew that no one should have all three in their possession, even a Moura," he said.

"What's in them that is so important?"

"Spells," Josh and Ethan offered simultaneously.

Seeing the confusion on my face, Josh elaborated. "As long as I can remember there have been rumors about these objects that were so strong they could do things that sheer magic couldn't. We always wrote them off as fables. But once we discovered the Gem of Levage existed, and then the Aufero, we started to speculate that maybe the Clostra existed as well. The idea that there were books of magic so powerful that they were guarded by a ward that would only allow only a select few to read them brought out our curiosity. When the rumors persisted along with those stating that Marcia was trying to find them, we made it our goal to try to find them first. Apparently, the spells are very unique and dangerous, unlike anything witches, fae, or elves can do."

"The one that concerns us is one that can 'lay the beast to rest,'" Ethan added.

Lay the beast to rest? It didn't sound like a bad thing at all. In fact, it sounded like a wonderful idea. We wouldn't be were-animals anymore. Why the morose mood?

"Is that what this is about? You want to use it to cure us?" My heart was beating fast at the idea that we were one book, one spell, away from being normal.

Sebastian's brow furrowed. "The beast will be laid to rest along with the person who shares its body. If the rumors are correct, the spell exists to kill us all."

A spell that would kill all the were-animals—we needed those books. Or did we? As long as they weren't all together, it was better. Let the missing one stay gone, that was my opinion. But I knew that wouldn't be good enough for Sebastian; he had to control the situation.

As Ethan drove me home, I couldn't tell what thoughts occupied his mind. Usually I could sense his emotions; they were like a brushfire, wild and hard to ignore. Now there was a controlled calm that I assumed was for my benefit. He played jazz loud, providing much needed noise where there should have been conversation. Now the car was filled with the sounds of saxophones, trumpets, bass guitars, and pianos. The deep crooning of the artists spoke to me, a deep sorrow from a place of pain where few people could relate.

When we drove up to my house, Quell stood at the front door, pacing. How long had he been waiting? Did he do it yesterday out of habit? I had arrived several hours earlier than expected. Had he been there since the break of dawn, waiting for me?

"Your vampire is here," Ethan said.

My vampire. Were there ever truer words? His dark eyes were bright as I stepped out of the car. He frowned at the bandaging on my arms and without an invitation followed us into the house. Ethan didn't put on any pretense of not knowing how to disable my ward. Once I opened the door, he whispered the key word and held it open for me. Quell slid in behind us and stopped in the middle of the room between Ethan and me as I took a seat on the sofa. Ethan leaned against the wall, fully aware of the barrier Quell had made between us.

Quell's gaze cruised in my direction and remained on the bandages for a long time. "Did you do that to her?"

Ethan balked at the accusation before finding a comfortable place of dismissive contempt, disregarding Quell's question with a roll of his eyes.

"I asked a question: did you do that to her?" A slight threat trailed over his words.

Ethan wasn't going to answer, and when the muscles along Quell's neck tightened and he drew back his lips, exposing his fangs, Ethan pushed himself from the wall and assumed a defensive position. The tension became a little difficult to bear, heightened testosterone stifling the room; it was only a matter of time before one of them allowed it to control their actions.

"He had nothing to do with my injuries," I said softly. I hated trying to placate them, but I figured breaking up a fight between the two would have been a lot worse. I picked the lesser of the two evils.

Eyeing the bandages again, Quell fixated on them as though I had an amputation rather than a couple of knife cuts. He came closer and knelt in front of me. "Are you okay?"

I nodded.

"Who did this to you?" His attention went back to Ethan, who had returned to his position of casually resting against the wall. His mere presence irritated Quell and he didn't try to hide it.

"I don't want to talk about it now. Maybe later." Quell looked more feral than usual. I doubted if he had had anything to eat since I left. It's peculiar how someone that needed blood to survive could be so finicky.

"Have you fed?" I asked.

His gaze kept drifting back in Ethan's direction. "I can wait," he responded, momentarily returning his attention back to me.

But he couldn't. I could see the hunger in his eyes. He would leave tonight and somebody or somebodies would die. Before I could say anything, Ethan spoke up. "No, she'll do it now. The responsibility she takes on doesn't stop because she had a rough day." Then he shifted his attention to me. "Isn't that right, Skylar?"

I glared at him, the king of jackasses. He simply smiled. They knew about my arrangement with Quell, but them knowing about it and seeing it were two different things. Ethan's sole purpose in life seemed to be to embarrass me and throw my mistakes back in my face at every possible chance. I wouldn't have denied Quell in the first place.

"Go ahead," I said, keeping a defiant gaze on Ethan the whole time.

Quell moved with hesitation toward me, giving Ethan one more look, over his shoulder. "Are you sure?"

I tilted my head, giving him better access. He moved slower than usual, cautious as he inched closer to me. His lips brushed against my neck. He paused for a few moments. "Are you sure?" he asked again, softly. I nodded, and his fangs quickly pierced my skin. A hiss escaped through my clenched teeth. It hurt; my wrists were used to the constant invasion. I waded through the pain and kept my focus on Ethan.

Quell stopped often, checking my response, gauging my reaction. While he was concentrated on me, I focused on Ethan, whose glower was clinched into a tight line. His nose flared several times, but he held my gaze, his arms folded across his chest. His glare was so intense it was hard to hold, but I did. I cradled Quell closer to me, sliding my hands down the nape of his neck.

A rose tint spread over Ethan's face and neck. I felt a shameless sense of delight and a vindicating victory. His frown was pulled tight and for several minutes, the rigid composure wouldn't ease. After much effort, he relaxed his arms, pushed up from the wall, and went into the kitchen.

Eventually Quell pulled away, and his tongue slid across his lips and my neck, removing the trail of blood and closing the opening. His lips were cool against my ear as his breath brushed against them, and he held my face close to his. "Did it bring you acceptable pleasure to upset him like that?" he whispered.

Of course, but his look of censure and disappointment caused the moment of self-indulgent pleasure to quickly wither away.

"Please do not do that again," he said as he rose, a lot more graceful and lithe than before. A restored vibrancy that was always missing when he hadn't fed for several days had returned. I couldn't allow him to do it more; it took so much out of me, but because he was so finicky he didn't have a lot of options.

As he started toward the door, I stood, too, when Ethan came out of the kitchen. They kept a careful eye on each other. Ethan tracked Quell's every movement until the vampire let himself out.

With a spark of derisive amusement, Ethan said, "You do manage to get yourself in some very compromising situations, don't you? Michaela's favorite is enthralled with you—how cute. It will be interesting to see how this will play out."

"It can't be any more interesting than you sleeping with Chris, when she was obviously Demetrius's mistress. I can assure you, it was quite interesting watching that train wreck," I said in a tepid voice.

Things were at an impasse, linked by unspoken deception and animosity. There was an unresolved issue between us and neither one was willing to broach the situation as we should have. "Are we going to talk about the elephant in the room?" I finally asked.

His light chuckle dawdled in the silence. "Of course. Should we talk about how you held on to dark magic? Or discuss how you were attempting to run away to be with your family—or anywhere just to get away from us? Perhaps the topic should be Quell and how your actions will adversely affect this pack when Michaela decides to take notice. Yes, let's discuss the elephant in the room."

Well, I wasn't talking about that baby elephant. The one I wanted to discuss was a big horrible brute of a beast that was more than just a series of bad decisions. "No, I would rather discuss what you did to me the other day. What the hell *are* you?"

"You know what I am. Do you really think your panic attack is discussion-worthy?"

Was he kidding me! A loss of words struck me so seldom that I didn't know how to react. The confidence with which he delivered this pile of compost made me relive that night again for a microsecond. Did I have a panic attack? Could I have overreacted that day and exaggerated what actually occurred?

"Do you really believe I don't know the difference between a panic attack and what happened to me at your house?"

A slight shrug brushed off my question. "I don't care to try to figure out what goes on in your mind. It is simpler that way."

"I don't trust you," I blurted out before he could make it to the door to leave.

"Good." He turned to look at me once more. The cool gaze sized me up in one sweeping move. "Because I don't trust you, either." Then he was out the door.

CHAPTER 5

I hit the floor for the fourth time as Winter swept my leg. I was off today. My face had smashed into the mat more times today than it had in the past five months, when Winter had finally given me a slight smile of approval and a terse "You're not bad."

I wasn't going to get anything more than that. That simple phrase was like her handing me a gold medal in the Olympics, because most of the time she was telling me that my skills were laughable. Sparring with her and my continued instruction in Krav Maga had changed that quickly. They were skills that I hoped I would never have to use. I knew how to kill someone with my hands; it should have made me feel confident. It didn't. It made me feel dangerous.

With a quick flip I came to my feet just in time to block Winter's strike and moved to the left to avoid a jab she threw. A quick step to the right gave me the positional advantage for a hip toss that landed her on the ground for just a few seconds. She moved too fast. It was always her advantage, something I was still having a hard time adapting to. My advantage was strength, and—so she said—a predator's instinct that came from being a werewolf. But I didn't feel like I had an instinctual advantage. My wolf was a dud.

On the ground again, I tried to get out of a hold that Winter had me in. I had the advantage, her grip was off, and when I broke it, my elbow jabbed into her stomach. We came to our feet about the same time. A full onslaught of kicks, punches, and tosses ensued, then one left punch caught me in the jaw. Winter stopped, took a step back, and frowned. "You're off and making amateurish mistakes."

When I failed to block a punch and stumbled back, she scowled and asked, "What's wrong with you?" I massaged my throbbing face.

Damn, she hit hard. "Do you ever wonder about Ethan?" I asked.

"In what way?"

"He's different."

Winter's eyebrows rose with amusement "Really? *He's* the peculiar one?"

"You all know about me and what makes me different, but you can't see it. He drops wards with ease. That doesn't strike you as odd?"

"Most were-animals can break wards" was her swift rebuttal. "I can break them, but I still need to improve."

"He broke Josh's protective field. Were-animals can't break protective fields, only other witches."

"Ethan's mother was a witch. It isn't hard to assume that he has some magical ability," she said as she grabbed her water bottle, took a drink, and plopped down on the mat. Even drenched in sweat that made her tawny skin a little too shiny and her hair in a messy ponytail, Winter looked better than most women did on a good day. "It isn't something we want to advertise. The witches are odd about stuff like that. The very idea that we are immune to their magic while in animal form makes them a little nervous.

They seem to forget that in human form we are just as vulnerable as anyone else."

I went on to tell her what happened at Ethan's after he had stripped me of the dark magic, but she seemed stuck on me holding on to that magic rather than Ethan damn near killing me by just touching me.

"Why would you do that?" she asked, exasperated.

I didn't feel like a lecture. "I shouldn't have, that is beside the point. He touched me and my heart stopped."

And she was silent for a long time. When it came to Winter, I never conflated silence with deception. It wasn't in her. I am sure that if she needed to, she had the ability to allow people to see her reality, but she didn't have the patience for it. She was more inclined to tell you it was none of your damn business or challenge you to make her tell you. Which is why I figured she probably didn't really know the dark pack secrets. No, it seemed like Sebastian and Ethan had the position of "guardian of the secrets by any means necessary" taken care of. They were good at their job.

"I don't know, Sky, but sometimes, it's better to be oblivious. I know you don't want to accept it, but it is. When someone can tell whether you are lying by your physiological changes and behavior, or compel...best weapon you have against it is not knowing the truth." It was an earnest response.

"Who can compel you to truth with a touch or spells?"

"Fae can do it, and stronger witches can cast spells, but Josh says it is so draining they use it is a last resort. You know I can do it on a smaller scale."

Yes, I knew that Winter could charm people, which was equivalent to compelling, but it was easy to forget. It was something she chose not to do often and she never considered it as one of the weapons at her disposal. I assumed she considered it cheating. Winter was a lot of things, but she would never be considered a cheater.

"Is there any way to stop a fae from doing that to you?"

"Of course, there is always a way. I generally tell them that whatever part of them that touches any part of me will not return in working condition. Most of them will only require one demonstration and then we are fine." Her clear hazel eyes always held a tinge of menace, in clear contrast with her gentle features and the tawny coloring that highlighted her delicate cheeks and winged out just slightly to accentuate her narrow face.

We usually practiced on Wednesday and Saturday, but she didn't mind adding today, Thursday, when I called and asked. If it were up to Winter, she would live in the gym, sparring every chance we had. A few months ago, she was injured badly and nearly killed by a creature and she went into survival mode. She trained too much, but no one could tell her otherwise. As a were-snake she was considered a lesser species, a title she wore with unnecessary shame. The greater species had more to do with the felidae and canidae, who were larger and had the ability to heal faster. If anything, she and her kind were the greater species. They weren't called by Mercury or the moon and were only forced into their animal form during a solar eclipse. They could virtually live a normal life, reaping the benefits of being a were-animal while only acknowledging its existence every year and a half. That was great as far as I was concerned.

She relaxed back on her elbows and looked up at the window of the gym. It was still hard getting used to the changes between Winter and me. It was less than two years ago that she was the president and founder of the "let's kill Skylar" club. Now we were friends. Well, I considered us friends, but I wasn't sure what we were. We rarely talked on any other days except when we sparred, those two days a week when she tried to beat me up. It was a dysfunctional friendship at best; nevertheless, it was a significant improvement from its origins.

"Besides the threat of bodily harm, is there a way to stop a fae from compelling you to truth?" I asked between drinks of water.

"Not really. Only if they break contact before the effect is complete. But it happens so quickly it's difficult to do so. There's an enigmatic pull that makes it nearly impossible to break. The stronger fae will bind you with a kiss, which they can release in the same manner. Honestly, the best thing you can do is to keep your distance."

"Well, I'm sure the binding kiss is a little easier to ward off than touch," I said, amused.

She shrugged. "For some it is harder than you think. Most of them are rather pretty, the men and the women alike. Most people don't mind the kiss so much." It seemed like she was speaking more from experience than simple knowledge of fae. "It is not something they do often. More like a last resort. They aren't renegades running around making people fall in love, feeling them up, and kissing all that come in contact with them. As with the witches, stronger magic is draining on them and requires extensive time to recover from afterward. If they are compelling you to truth, I assure you they need the information."

"Making you fall in love with them, that's necessary?"

"You get the same results. The emotion of love causes that indomitable need to please that person. I am sure it is easier to achieve your desired results if the person's only desire is to please you. I think I would prefer them to force the truth out of me than to feel an insatiable adoration that can only be soothed by making the fae happy. In fact, I would prefer them to compel me to commit suicide."

Each door I opened in this world made me want to slam it and pretend it didn't exist, and this was another one. Something as simple as a touch. How many people did I touch on any given day? A slide of my hand against their back as I passed them, a good-natured handshake during a greeting, a light touch on someone's knee as I squeezed past them in a row. How easily such a dangerous power could be executed without much thought.

Sensing my ensuing discomfort, Winter said, "Of all the people in the world to fear, a fae is not one. They are usually the good-willed, annoying type, but they are not immune to getting pissed off, too. It is when the happy clappies get upset that you feel like you just went through an apocalypse. If you can help it, don't piss off a fae."

Wasn't that the general rule for surviving in this world? Keep them happy and your world doesn't come crashing down on you. "People can compel me to tell my secrets and fall in love with them, but the lesson I should walk away with is 'not to piss them off,'" I said with credulous doubt.

"I assure you, it's good advice."

We both looked up at the gym's window to see the bulbous nose of Teddy, a very fitting name for the large gym manager. He wasn't fat. He was solidly built, but with a roundish shape. His OCD just wouldn't allow anyone to go over their allotted sign-up time, even if there wasn't someone waiting. He tapped three times at a steady rhythm and Winter responded with a shake of her head in the rhythm. Next, the dark beady eyes narrowed, the paper-thin lips pressed in the window as he called her the b-word. *Brat.* He believed that most of the guys that used the dungeon, a less attractive dank part of the nice gym, gave us preferential treatment, allowing us to skirt most of the rules. Yes, they were a little nicer to us, but it didn't cross over the threshold of the room we sparred in. Once we hit it, the chivalry and be-nice-to-ladies bit was left at the door. They didn't spar as much with us anymore. They were tough guys with fragile egos, and no matter how progressive a man is, getting beaten by a woman stung.

We dressed quickly, and since we had both skipped breakfast, brunch was the only reasonable post-workout thing to do. I hopped into her new monstrosity of a vehicle, and frowned. She grinned. "I don't care, judge away."

"It's an unnecessary gas guzzler. It's just right for you! You might as well move into the darn thing," I joked, my hand waving over the large backseat of the Range Rover, a replacement for the Navigator I destroyed when I backed into the creature that had attacked her.

"I'm sorry. We all can't drive Tonka toys," she smarted back. My poor Civic was the recipient of ridicule every chance she had.

"So where do you want to go?" she asked.

The words had just barely passed my lips when she turned the car around and headed east to our favorite restaurant, Lily's. It was a quaint little Caribbean place we had discovered about eight weeks before and we'd been there at least nine times since.

We were nearing the restaurant when Winter's phone rang, a different ringtone than her typical one. She let it ring until it stopped. The second time the phone rattled, she sent it to voice mail. When it rang the third time, she hesitated before she answered, taking a deep breath. "What do you want, Abigail? I thought we agreed that once we broke up, it was over. No communication—remember? That is what *you* wanted."

Winter's annoyed expression changed at the sobs on the other end. "Will you come to Gideon's house, please?" asked the distressed unfamiliar female voice. Winter listened to her for a few minutes before she took the next exit and turned around. Fifteen minutes later we pulled up in front of a ranch home. Dark clouds crowded the sky, shadowing the white siding and making the house look dark and gloomy. Thunder crackled and rain, hitting just the house and a small portion of the surrounding area. The branches of the trees that neighbored the house folded under the torrential rainfall.

Winter jumped out of the car and headed for the house. I soon followed behind her.

Yeah, go into the only house that has been targeted by Mother Nature's wrath, I thought. *Great idea.*

Winter walked into the house without knocking. Pacing in the middle of the living room was a tall, thin blond woman, whose appearance mirrored Winter's. Abigail's long blond hair was pulled back into a French twist, her features narrow and striking. The distress looked eased slightly when we walked through the door. She hugged Winter, clinging to her as she buried her face into Winter's neck. Winter stiffened, standing motionless for a long time before she relaxed into the embrace, wrapping her arms around Abigail and gently stroking her hair. When Abigail lifted her head, Winter wiped away her tears then kissed her lightly on the cheek.

"Abigail, what's the matter?" she asked.

She opened her mouth several times, but the words just wouldn't come out and once again the tears welled in her eyes, spilling down her cheeks. She quickly brushed them away and asked us to follow her.

Abigail walked us through the house that definitely wasn't hers. The owner should have invested in a housekeeper. Game controllers and a headset were tossed on the sofa. The unflattering light leather armchairs had water stains on them. The area rug was positioned at an odd angle, which I assumed was to hide stains in the carpet. Empty beer cans and potato chip bags filled the garbage cans. In the bedroom, lying on a king-sized bed, was her counterpart. It was apparent they were related. In fact, they looked exactly alike. His hair was mussed, and like Abigail's, his face was thin, features sharp and keen, skin a light dusky color that contrasted with his platinum blond hair. He lay in a comatose state.

"How long has he been like this?" Winter asked.

"Two days. I took him to our doctors and no one seemed to be able to do anything for him. He's getting worse. At first there was some movement, a slight wiggle of his finger and things like that." She knelt down, gently stroking his face. "And now—nothing," she whispered.

"What do you want me to do, Abigail?"

"Dr. Jeremy can help him. I know he can," she entreated softly.

"You want me to have Jeremy treat Gideon? You know Sebastian will never allow that."

This was Gideon? Josh had mentioned him as a potential resource when we were looking for the culprit responsible for attacking and killing the vampires and were-animals. Known as the "master of mischief," he wasn't liked or disliked. But he was an elf, and Sebastian didn't like to get involved with anything that didn't involve the pack. This had nothing to do with the pack.

The blonde stepped closer, taking Winter's hands into hers. Her eyes glistened with tears that she fought back. "I can't just let my brother die without doing everything I can to help him. If I had other options, I would have used them. Please."

Winter sighed a ragged breath as she nodded. She stared at Abigail for a long time, and her habitual moue hardened, unlike her eyes, which were the gentlest I had ever seen. She pulled out her phone, then glanced at me before planting her eyes on the floor. "Jeremy, it's urgent. I am bringing in Skylar. I think I injured her pretty bad," she said.

I heard Jeremy over the phone chastising her about whether she actually knew anything about self-control. She mumbled something and then hung up.

I wanted to say something, but the words just wouldn't come out. I was still seething when Winter picked up Gideon with Abigail behind her. I lingered in the house for just a moment as I composed myself, trying not to let my righteous anger dominate the situation. Winter was trying to save her friend's brother and I was just caught in the cross fire of the horrible politics that existed in this world. I exhaled a long, deep sigh and slid into the front seat. I couldn't look at Winter. Just because I understood the reason I was brought into this deception didn't mean I had to like it.

"I'm sorry, but there was no way Jeremy would have shown up if I told him it was Gideon," she explained.

"I know, but I would have liked a heads-up or something," I said.

"Sorry."

Ethan's, Gavin's, and Josh's cars were already there when I arrived at the house. Gavin, the resident problem child, opened the door, and when he saw Winter carrying Gideon he looked as though he was ready to slam it shut. His eyes narrowed and his frown deepened as the sky suddenly became dark and cloudy. Hard rain fell, drenching us as we made our way to the house.

Gavin directed a stern look in Abigail's direction before turning to Winter. "What are they doing here?"

"Not now, Gavin," she said, walking past him and heading back to the clinic and laying Gideon on one of the beds. We waited in an odd silence for Jeremy. It didn't take long for him to come in and when he didn't seem surprised to see Gideon lying on one of the beds I knew Gavin had warned him. "He shouldn't be here" was all he said after watching Gideon for a long time.

"I know but—"

"No." It was the first time I had ever heard Jeremy sound angry. Each word grating and acrid. "There are no excuses. He shouldn't be here," he repeated, cutting her off when she opened her mouth to protest. "What you have done is unacceptable, and you know that."

He was having a much harder time controlling his anger. I knew there was a staunch rule that everyone took care of their own, punished their own, which was only deviated from on rare occasions. Were-animals had been known to kill a vampire if their bloodlust drove them into psychotic killing. Vampires and others have been known to hire a Hunter to track down rogue were-animals. These things occurred so rarely they were exceptions, not rules, and it was done to maintain our anonymity from the rest of the world.

Dr. Jeremy inched closer to Winter, and his attention moved slightly in Abigail's direction before returning to her. His voice low, tone firm, he said, "You've never been able to deny her, which has always been your problem. That weakness cannot become our problem, and you promised it wouldn't."

"He's here now, will you please just look at him?" she asked quietly.

"I will see what I can do." He patted her gently on the shoulder and the stern mask dropped, an understanding of the difficult situation she was in. Winter followed the rules—that was her thing—often setting aside her own feelings to do what was necessary, and doing this had to come with some effort and humbleness.

He turned and walked over to Gideon, opening the lids of his eyes. He looked and then systematically began to examine him. "When did this happen?"

"It's been about two days. We were supposed to meet for lunch, but he didn't show up. You are aware of my brother's reputation, and it isn't unusual for him to sleep in and miss our lunch if he had a very active evening the night before. But when the hard winds and rain started in our neighborhood, I knew something was wrong with him."

Oh, what a delightful way to say my brother often stands me up when he's drunk off his ass from partying.

"Your doctors have no idea what's wrong?"

She shook her head. "We've already lost four to similar symptoms. They were only alive for five days once it started." She brushed away the tears that rolled down her cheeks, and his face softened. Unlike the other were-animals, who seemed to frown upon any displays of maudlin emotion, especially tears, he seemed impassioned by it.

"No one seems to be able to help him. Some didn't even try. I just couldn't sit back and wait for him to die," Abigail admitted, her voice breaking as she spoke. Her fingers brushed over her face, smearing her mascara as she wiped them away.

"The four that died, were they potential candidates for leaders?" asked Sebastian. He had not slipped in unnoticed. A man like him can't enter a room undetected; there is sense of command that he exudes, wearing his power and predacious nature like clothing. He never had to introduce himself as the Alpha; his ascendancy served as his title. He moved closer to Gideon and looked at him.

Abigail watched him. Her hands slipped over Winter's, holding them as she eased closer to her. "Three of them would be ones I would consider potentials."

"You don't think this is a coincidence?" Winter asked Sebastian.

"Coincidences do not occur as often as people would like to believe, and almost never in situations like this," he said.

He watched them carefully in silence. I was sure he was weighing the situation, trying to decide if helping Winter's friend was worth whatever problems might develop between the pack and the elves.

"You are aware that last month the witches and elves became allied?" he asked Winter.

Her eyes didn't falter, although she failed to hide the same concern that lingered on his face. There was a shadow of hopelessness, as if she expected Sebastian to send them away.

The witches were not ones you messed with. I wasn't sure why, but people seemed to go out of their way not to have to deal with them. It didn't help matters that Josh was an ally of the pack, which had already caused unnecessary strife more than once. His loyalties were split, and most believed that such a thing couldn't exist because in the end you always had to choose. There hadn't been a situation where Josh had to—yet—but there wasn't any way he would pick anyone over his brother. The same was true with Ethan.

Sebastian's attention wavered between Winter and whatever garnered it behind her. Taking a long breath before he spoke, he addressed Dr. Jeremy. "Examine him. Do what you can, but we cannot be involved for more than twenty-four hours. If he cannot be helped within that time, then please accept my condolences for the loss," he said before heading toward the double door. Abigail tried to hold it together, but a cloud of desolation cast a dark look over her face.

Sebastian hadn't made it past the doors before his phone rang. He looked at the number, his brow furrowed as he answered it. "Yes, Mason," he said in a deep voice, just cordial enough to hide his annoyance.

The tone on the other end was a light, raspy Australian brogue. "You should worry about yours, and let me deal with mine. Aren't you tired of poking your nose where it never belongs? Send her away."

"Obviously, if she is here, you aren't taking care of your own." His full lips curled into a reproaching smirk that remained as the chastising voice on the other end continued.

"As usual, you have found your way into a business that isn't yours. I am asking this time. But if I were in your situation, I would consider the request thoroughly and do as I ask."

Had this man ever dealt with Sebastian? He barely responded to polite entreaties and he damn sure wasn't going to respond to an unsubtle threat.

Sebastian's voice had a gentle cool resonance as he responded. "Of course, I will give it as much consideration as I give you." Then he hung up the phone. He turned to Dr. Jeremy. "Take as much time as you need. I want Gideon alive."

The weight that had bound Abigail seemed to have relaxed; a hint of a smile wavered along her lips as she rested her head against Winter. Winter responded by gently stroking her cheek;

she gave Abigail a light kiss on the lips seemingly to comfort her. Winter comforting? I felt like I had been dropkicked into *Bizarro* world.

The thought of leaving the house crossed my mind, and I would have, especially when I saw Gavin slouched in a corner, his delineated features sharpened by a scowl. His hair had grown out too long and the thick straight mass eclipsed his face, covering his eyes, which were his most alluring feature. They were deep cocoa and crescent-shaped. It was like staring into a chasm, getting easily swept into them no matter how unpleasant he was, which was often. "I have better things to do than babysit Winter's girlfriend's brother," Gavin said as Sebastian started toward his office. Sebastian was so used to dealing with the hostile and uncooperative were-panther, he seemed bored with him anytime he had to.

"If I cared, that would be a different story, now wouldn't it? You're here. If Mason decides to act on his threat, I need you, but most importantly, you'll do it because I requested it," Sebastian said in passing, before closing himself behind his door.

If it was directly related to pack affairs, even the unnecessarily agitated Gavin might have found a sliver of interest in the situation. But if it didn't involve the pack directly, the were-animal's interest went down to nil. Gavin sank back into his corner and looked moderately interested as the door opened and a hard click resounded against the floor, announcing Kelly's arrival. The high strappy black heels continued to tap against the hardwood floors until she stopped in the middle of the room awaiting Gavin, who had pushed himself up from the wall.

She smiled. Her limpid wide walnut-colored eyes were coated in dark mascara, thick liner, and deep shades of shadow that gave them a smoky appearance. Her high cheekbones were highlighted by deep coral blush and her lips colored with a similar shade. She slipped off her coat. Underneath she wore a champagne-colored wraparound dress that clung to her frame, accentuating the curves that were normally hidden beneath her ill-fitting scrubs. Hair that was often pulled into a puffy ponytail or back with a headband was a thick corkscrew halo that framed the face.

The stern charcoal eyes burrowing into her didn't seem to bother her. Instead, she stayed planted in the middle of the room, and amusement traveled along her face before settling on her lips and in her eyes. Whether she was willing to admit it or not, she gained a certain pleasure from irritating Gavin, a skill which she had perfected.

"Why are you here?" he asked in a crisp, even voice.

"Dr. Jeremy called me" was her immediate response, and as with everything she did, it was accompanied by her broad smile.

He scoffed. "He calls and you come running, no questions asked. That's a fool's response."

Kelly never let Gavin's behavior or his harsh tone bother her. She shrugged. "Yeah, but it's kind of our thing."

He blocked her advance toward the door, closing the limited space between them. "How many times must I tell you that you don't belong here? When he calls, you can ignore it. They got along just fine before you, and I am sure they will continue to do so." His voice never matched his mood. The low purr always held a slight hint of peril, even when he spoke with her. The dynamics of their relationship were confusing. He didn't dislike her, which made her one of the few people who held such honors; but he didn't seem to like her around, either.

Last year he had been tasked with protecting her after she had foolishly allowed Demetrius, the Master of the Northern Seethe, to feed from her, giving him the ability to call her thereafter. It was for her protection, but also Sebastian's less-than-subtle way of punishing her. For nearly a week I watched their comically torrential battle of wills. By day two, Gavin was frustrated and had threatened Kelly numerous times, which she simply responded to by spritzing him with a spray bottle and calling him a "bad kitty." On day four, he quit, saying that whatever the vampires did to her she probably deserved. "She is an overindulged brat, you deal with her," he said. His meltdown had provided Sebastian with a well-deserved amusement as he pointed out that Kelly had bested him, but that he had lasted longer than he expected. Jeremy teased that since she had made him submit, maybe she should have his position.

Gavin refused to quit afterward, and for the remainder of the week, the battle continued and was too funny to ignore.

Now they found common ground and pleasure in just riling each other, although Kelly seemed better at it.

"Aw, how sweet, you're concerned about me." Her bright, cloying response just added fuel to the fire that was starting to ignite. It was odd how most of the were-animals, especially the higher-ranked ones, didn't respond well to being ignored. From them, a suggestion was simply a pleasantly worded command with an expectation of compliance.

Kelly's only advantage was being wholly human. It seemed barbaric to threaten her with violence because she wouldn't stand a chance against any one of us. No one prided themselves on subjugating someone that was defenseless. It lacked dignity, which was something Kelly seemed to exploit quite often. Mouthy and obstinate far more often than was acceptable, she quickly found restraint and humility the moment she crossed the acceptable line of defiance, but she came too close to the line too often for Gavin's liking.

"I am quite concerned. Concerned that you were given more curiosity and tenacity than common sense," he responded before turning on his heels and leaving.

Multiple times Kelly had professed that underneath Gavin's tough exterior was a sweet person. I wasn't buying it. I believed that behind his coarse overcoat, which he displayed, was an even crueler acerbic person who was going to be a little pissed off that people kept tampering with his top layer. "He's so darling, you just want to pinch his cheeks," she said, loud enough for him to hear.

"You'll probably pull back stumps if you do," I murmured just loud enough for Kelly to hear. I didn't gain joy from irritating him. In fact, I made it a mission to stay as far away from him as much as possible.

When she laughed, it was a distinctive ebullient sound that resonated through the room.

Dr. Jeremy popped his head out of the clinic "What are you doing here so soon? I thought you had a date."

She reached into her purse and pulled out a bejeweled pink phone showing the text he had sent her. "You texted: 'an elf is here.'"

"There wasn't a hurry."

"You call, I come. That's how it works, remember?" It was hard to decipher if her loyalty and availability was a result of her dedication to Dr. Jeremy or her avid curiosity about the otherworld. She had a sordid interest in all the dark things that occurred in this world.

"You ended your date for me?"

She shook her head. "That date was *so* over. Please tell your wife not to fix me up with any more of her clients' children. It never works out, and it's starting to make me feel like she's pimping for real estate sales. Tell her my dignity is worth more than a four-bedroom, two-and-a-half-bath Colonial with walk-in closets and an unfinished basement."

Dr. Jeremy frowned. "He is a single physician, with a condo in the city, a lodge in the country, and a stellar military record. And he's a Rhodes Scholar!" he said, washing his hands over his face. While Dr. Jeremy vetting her date to such an extent appalled me, she didn't seem either surprised or upset that he had. It was something she probably had gotten used to. The level of screening they did often struck me as unnecessary and evasive.

She shrugged. "Wow, he sounds great. Maybe you should date

him." Once again, big dimples and a wide smile tempered her words. She dismissed the guy with a wave of her hand. "I could never love him more than he loved himself."

The frown lines deepened.

She simply smiled. The soft, whimsical voice and infectious smile was her strength, but one that seemed to only work on Dr. Jeremy. She shrugged off his curiosity. "I prefer to hang out with an old physician with the God complex than a young one with an unwarranted one."

"What you call a God complex is rightful confidence, don't confuse the two." For a few seconds he just looked at her, his mouth twisted to the side. "Okay. No more fix-ups."

"A promise I am sure you and your wife will keep like the one you made four weeks ago, three months ago, and again last year," she said.

The grin widened. "We will attempt to keep this one."

"I'll accept your well-intended lie in the spirit it was given," she conceded before she ducked into one of the rooms and reappeared looking like a life-size Skittle, dressed in lime green scrubs, loose and comfortable.

CHAPTER 6

Waiting with Winter and Abigail to hear about Gideon made me feel uncomfortable, although their affections extended to nothing more than Winter stroking Abigail's hair as Abigail leaned against her. I felt like I was intruding on a private conversation, gawking at two people at their most intimate moment. And waiting in the living room wasn't any better. Gavin anxiously paced through the house like a caged animal.

With more pressing things to tend to, like finding the Aufero, I'd locked myself in a room and pulled out my paper with the pictures of the items that would help guide me to the right place. Scrolling through the Internet in an effort to look at the inside of the shops through their web pages, I realized this approach was too limited in scope. I needed to go on-site. Since Marcia had it, I knew it was somewhere in the city. But how close? Would she keep it in her home? Or were witches like the were-animals with a common home where she stored it? Josh was a witch, but because of his alliance with the were-animals, so many things about the witches were kept from him. He was a better resource about the magic than about the ins and outs of the Creed.

As I started out of the house to check out another shop, the sound of Josh's voice coming from the library caused me to make a U-turn. He was sitting at the large walnut table across from his brother. Each time I saw them together the similarities and differences were always apparent. Both had stunning blue eyes: Josh's were clear like a deep tropical ocean, Ethan's held a hint of gunmetal gray, a constant reminder of the wolf that he shared his body with. They were both slim, Ethan a more muscular build, the benefits of not being wholly human and his love affair with the gym. Josh's frame was a result of good genes and his daily runs with his brother. Modesty was an attribute that neither of them possessed and I had seen both of them nude or partially naked more times than I could remember. Josh was usually in his boxers when I came to practice magic, and only after some encouragement would he get dressed. Ethan, like most were-animals, wore clothing because it was dictated by society and laws. If it were socially acceptable to be naked in public, nearly all of them would not have a problem with it. And it didn't hurt that most of them had bodies that were worth seeing in the nude.

"Just the person I wanted to see. I was just about to come get you," Josh said as he pulled out a chair. I sat across from Ethan. Well, at least one of them was glad to see me. Josh plopped the Clostra in front of me, opening them both to the first page. "Please start reading."

"Read what?"

"All of it. We need to translate it," he said.

Each book had to be at least two hundred pages. Then add the complexity of having to read one line from one book and then the next from the other. This was going to take days.

Josh took out a recorder and a notepad and scribbled on it as I spoke. "Do you understand any of this?" I asked after he asked me to repeat certain words. Fumbling my way through each word was hard enough, but each time one of them leaned in close to the book, the words vanished.

"It's Latin; I understand most of it, but the rest we will figure out later."

Who was the "we," I wondered, because *I* couldn't help. As I continued to read, I tried to ignore Ethan, whose eyes remained on me. Each time I finished a spell, I asked Josh what it was for. Every explanation was a guess, because each line held just a minuscule amount of information. Whoever created these books was as cryptic as possible.

As I read one line, Ethan leaned forward, listening attentively. I knew *bestia* meant *beast*. Another word caught my attention.

"What is *ripiso*?" I asked.

"Rest," they responded in unison.

"The beast will lay to rest," I whispered. But we didn't know what the other part was. It could very well say that "when it awoke, it lived happily ever after."

Several pages later, another line seemed to capture Josh's attention: "*Magia rescet.*"

Magic will wither. Josh paled as I read the line. Afterward, he wanted to take a break and left for a while, returning with three cups of coffee. It was going to be a long night, and I realized they weren't going to rest until we had gone through the entire book.

Two hours later, my eyes were tired and dry. I needed a break from reading. I rested in my chair as Ethan's narrow gunmetal gaze followed my every movement as though he was peering through a sniper scope. I leaned back, watching him as he watched me. His words "I don't trust you, either" replayed repeatedly in my head. Did he in fact see me as an enemy? Was he waiting for me to answer for my crimes of betrayal against the pack? I guess at face value I didn't seem like a strong asset to the pack. Being able to read the Clostra probably wasn't of as much value as I believed. I was one of the few people in this world who could read the spells that could ultimately kill the were-animals.

"Do you know who can do these spells?" I asked, turning to Josh, but I could still feel his brother's eyes on me.

"There seem to be numerous safeguards for the spells. Not only do you have to be able to get past the ward; you also have to be strong enough to perform them." He looked down at his notepad. "These seem to be very strong spells. I wonder if even I could perform one." He ran his fingers thoughtfully over the arcane books.

Well, that was encouraging.

We read through nearly thirty pages in an hour when fatigue started and I kept fumbling over the words so much that Josh couldn't understand me. If he came anywhere near the book to help me out, the words disappeared from the pages. Ethan was quietly sipping a cup of coffee. Each time I looked up, I was met with his deep, inquisitive gaze. It was different from before, apprehensive and suspicious. I was glad when he stepped out to get another cup. I read a couple of lines and then took a break, resting my forehead on one of the books. It smelled funny: sage, metal, and sulfur. At some point, blood had been spilled near it, and the sulfur was probably from a spell. I wondered how many spells had been cast over them in an effort to unveil the words.

The battered midnight blue cover with simple gold script to distinguish book one from two didn't necessarily scream, "Hey, I am a kickass spell book." The most bizarre thing about it was the odd picture on it, similar to the Rod of Asclepius' orb. The books were powerful, but without all three, they were useless. And without someone that could read them and had the power to perform the spells, they were useless.

Josh laid his head next to mine; a little devious spark brightened his eyes, his finger twirling around strands of my hair, as he grinned. "Want to go downstairs and practice?"

Practice what? His brother had stolen my magic. I could feel the anger coloring my cheeks. There was a change in his look. Guilt by association was molded across his face. I am sure he knew what his brother had done, but I wondered if he knew before or after it had happened. His hand was gentle as it stroked my hair, then he planted a kiss on my cheek. Guilt. It was as though he was asking for forgiveness for his hand in things.

I wasn't sure why I needed to hear him admit it, but I did. It was as if the question was scrawled across my face in bold letters because he said, "Don't. Let's not talk about it."

I nodded. The stretch of silence was galling. The seams of our friendship felt strained at that moment. "Let's practice," he said.

The gym was empty. I hated the way it smelled. Blood and sweat overwhelmed the air, and the matted floors felt odd under my feet with shoes on, so I slipped them off. Personal space meant nothing to Josh. "What do you want to work on?" he asked.

"Protective fields?"

"You're a pro at those. Offensive magic," he suggested, taking out a small knife from his pocket. It had been a long time since I had borrowed magic from him. I had forgotten what it felt like to possess it. He quickly ran the knife over our hands, then clasped mine and stepped closer. The warmth of his breath feathered against my lips as he recited the spell.

"I need to be able to do a bigger one and cover someone else," I said.

He nodded. "Try one now." When I attempted to step back, his arm slipped around my waist. "If you can do one with the two of us, then you make a larger one. Try it."

I did, and with ease the translucent oval covered us, and then Josh started to step back. The wall expanded, widening and keeping us covered. He returned to his position next to me, and the wall slid in with him. "Am I doing this?" I had to ask because it came with such ease, I couldn't believe it.

"It's all you," he said. "What else do want to try?" He was

annoyingly close, his lips brushing mine as he spoke. *Personal space, learn about it.*

"How is London?" I asked, dropping the field and moving a few feet away.

London was his friend and sometimes lover, but he seemed to value the friendship more than anything. Last year when he had involved her with finding Ethos, it seemed to have caused an irreparable rift.

"She blocked my number," he said softly. He turned his back to me so that I couldn't see his expression, but I could hear the sorrow in his words. "What do you want to try next?"

"A field that covers you while you are there," I said.

"Those are hard. You're talking master level. Plus, I don't know if you have enough magic to do that." Loaned magic was weaker. I held it, but unlike anyone who was innately magical, I didn't have a limitless supply of it. The ineluctable problem with borrowed magic was that it was easily depleted. There wasn't an indicator that showed a "low on magic" signal. It just stopped.

"I need you to be able to use offensive magic. Not the small things like making your clothes dance across the room," he said.

Did everyone know I did that?

He clasped my hand, the one he used to bind us. "Feel what I'm doing."

It was a small pulse that snowballed into strong thumps of power coming off him, off us. I felt it race through me in jolts and I needed to get rid of it. When he let go of my hand, I did. With a wave of my hand, he went back, too hard, slamming against the matted wall. "Sorry!" I said.

He grunted, but remained pinned against the wall. "Release me," he instructed gently.

I tried to pull it back slowly, but it was a jerk and he went forward fast onto his hands and knees.

Kneeling down next to him, I couldn't stop apologizing. "Try another protective field," he said.

I did. The shadowy wall formed over me, but it lacked power, just a glamour. "Offensive magic requires a lot of power. You will have to use it sparingly."

I missed it. And longed for the ability to have magic at my fingertips once again. The strong immutable desire was a constant reminder of magic's enthralling effect and how easily it could become an addiction. It drifted off him as a heavy mist, incessantly present. Now I was the one invading *his* personal space. My undeniable affinity for it was just short of destructive. I leaned into him, my head resting against his chest. He pulled me closer.

The emptiness was there. For months I had full access to it. Yes, it was dark magic—and I probably wouldn't have been able to control it—but it didn't make the void any less. If anyone could understand, it would be Josh.

"I would, too," he admitted, as perceptive as usual. I didn't have to express my feelings.

I was just about to ask to borrow more when Ethan spoke; his gaze jumped from me to his brother. Then he glowered. "Playtime is over, we need to go back to work."

Josh glanced over his shoulder, then quickly dismissed his brother. "Okay."

"Now," Ethan insisted.

Josh sighed, but he didn't move for a few moments and when he did it was to shoot his brother a glare.

This battle for control between them could go on for hours. In the end they would find out they were equally stubborn and had just wasted time. I moved and started up the stairs past Ethan. When Josh didn't move, Ethan jerked his head toward the door. "Come on."

Josh grinned. With a slight movement of his hand Ethan went back against the rails. It wasn't hard, just enough to be annoying. I rolled my eyes, and couldn't help but imagine them with their fingers in each other's face, childishly saying, "I'm not touching you." I laughed loudly at the image, and they both looked confused. Ethan was the Beta of the pack, but Josh continued to have to remind him that he wasn't in command of *their* two-man pack.

Another hour and twenty more pages read, I had started to hate Latin. Indecipherable riddles filled Josh's notebook, spells that meant nothing without the third book.

Josh just looked at the scribbled words on his pad and frowned.

"Anything?" asked Sebastian from the door.

Josh looked down at his paper and shook his head. "This is a riddle within itself. There is absolutely no way to tell what the spell is for without the third book. Like this one: The first book reads 'I will that the undead walk among'—then it continues in the second book—'The living will hear my request—'" He slid the pad away. "And freaking what? Then do *what*, a dance? Bake me a cake? Sing me a ballad? What will they do?"

There was an indecipherable look on Sebastian's face as he stepped into the room. He stroked his chin and started to flip over what now had become blank pages. If he was disturbed by it, there wasn't any evidence of it on his face.

He turned to me. "Senna, what's her deal?"

The mention of my cousin's name brought the bitterness and loneliness back as I was reminded that I didn't have a "real" family. The spark of anger made me feel vengeful—I really hated feeling that way. I shrugged, he probably knew more than I did. "With how meticulous and obscure this world is, I am surprised that someone else in my family would be so closely linked to an object of power."

Sebastian paced the small space, engrossed in his thoughts. "I don't think she is true family," he finally said.

"We look just alike. She's a teenaged version of me."

"No. She's a dark-haired, olive-colored woman; other than

that there wasn't anything that similar in your appearances. I don't believe she is a Moura Encantada. There has to be a link between you and her as to why you two can read these things. I need to find the link."

"Why, so you can find others?"

"Yes," he said simply. "Do you see something wrong with that, Skylar?" His silky baritone voice contrasted with the hard edges of his words.

"Yes. If they are as dangerous as you all say. I don't think *we* should have these books at all, let alone try to find the other people who can read them."

"I prefer to know those that are in a position to hurt this pack and handle things as necessary," he said. "As far as the books are concerned, I would love to destroy them."

He went to one of the cabinets and took out a lighter, ignited it, and then touched it to the book. It flashed. Blazes of orange, red, and blue engulfed the book, and for several minutes, bursts of flame spread over it. Biting cold air filled the room, and a brisk frigid wind breezed over us as oxygen was siphoned from the room. Ice crept up the table and slowly immured the book, snuffing out the flames. The fire extinguished, the ice melted, the book remaining perfect and undamaged.

"As you see, they can't be destroyed."

I lost my focus on Sebastian and placed it on the books. Something this dangerous should not have a fail-safe and the ability to protect itself from destruction.

"I want to know as much as I can about the Clostra. I prefer to go on facts and not rumors," he said. "Once you have translated them, they will be separated."

Just as he started to leave, we heard a crash and Kelly shrieking, "Get it off of me!"

Sebastian rushed out of the room, Josh, Ethan, and I right behind him. We spilled into the room to find Kelly on the ground.

The tray and table were tipped over on the floor as she clawed at her leg.

"Get it off of me!" she screamed repeatedly, her hands scrabbling over her body.

Dr. Jeremy knelt in front of her, his hands running along her arms and leg. When he didn't find what he was looking for, he ripped open her scrub pants. He scanned the area. He cursed under his breath and tore the pants even higher, skimming over her leg with his hands.

"What am I looking for?" he asked, his fingers slowly gliding over her skin.

"It looks weird … a bug, small legs … tan, no brown," she said scanning her lower extremities.

"I found it," he finally said. We leaned in to look at it. I could barely distinguish the creature from her skin. As it lay flat, it disappeared against the backdrop of her flesh. He took tweezers, plucked it off her, and placed it in a jar, where it quickly changed, merging into the clear background and becoming nearly invisible. The only things distinguishable were the light brown legs that couldn't blend entirely.

"Are you okay?" Sebastian asked, taking in the distressed look on her face.

She shook her head, slowly. "I can't move my legs," she said, the tears starting to brim at the edge of her lids. Her legs splayed to the side, immobile. Sebastian bent them and held them in place. When he released them, they flopped out to the side.

"What happened?" he asked as he lifted her and carried her over to one of the beds. She wrapped her hands around him and seemed like she didn't want to let him go when he lowered her to the bed.

"I found it on Gideon, at the nape of his neck," she said in a strained voice as she continued to try to move her legs. "It jumped on me when I tried to remove it. The next thing I knew it was biting and clawing its way up my leg. I couldn't get it off me." Her eyes stayed closed as she calmly recapped the events. "And then I fell. I tried to stand, but my legs wouldn't move."

Dr. Jeremy was calm the whole time, until he took out a box of tools. Using cold and warm instruments, he asked her to describe what she felt. His calm mask faltered when she said she couldn't feel anything.

His face was withdrawn and guilt-riddled throughout the entire examination. He tried the instruments on various parts of her body, but she didn't feel anything until the cold tool touched her abdomen. I wasn't sure what that meant, but it couldn't have been good. There was a worrisome scowl on his face. He took a box of microfilaments, touching one to her skin. She stared at him the whole time. When his eyes lifted to meet hers, he quickly dismissed his worried expression to replace it with a stolid one.

He went to his desk and looked at the jar. "I've never seen anything like this," he finally admitted. Dumping it into a deep petri dish, he took several pictures of it and then did a database search. Nothing. The desolate frown started to reemerge when he looked in Kelly's direction.

Gavin entered the room, nearly unnoticed. He surveyed the broken glass that no one had cleaned up and the table that was still tipped over and then slid past Sebastian, who stood next to Kelly. Placing his hand gently on her leg, he asked softly, "What happened?"

Realizing she couldn't feel him touching her leg; he moved his hand to her arm. His thumb stroked lightly across it.

Dr. Jeremy spoke up before she could, telling Gavin everything. Jeremy gave him detailed information the way he would have if he'd been speaking to a patient's family. Gavin listened quietly.

"Are you in pain?" Gavin asked, moving her pillows around her and adjusting the settings on the bed until she was in a more comfortable position.

She shook her head. Her voice quivered too much to talk;

instead she just responded to Gavin's questions with nods and shakes of her head. Occasionally she looked around at the faces in the room, which were now those of everyone in the house, including Winter and Abigail, who had slipped in and taken up a place right next to the bed where Gideon lay.

"We will fix this," Sebastian assured her with a level of confidence it was impossible to doubt.

We will? How were we going to do that since no one knew exactly what bit her and how it had affected her?

Gavin walked over to the desk, studied the creature for a long time, and against Dr. Jeremy's protest, dumped it out into his hand. It crawled up his arm, flattening its body against his tawny skin, and fading into it to the point it was imperceptible. With small winding movements, it slinked along the length of his arm. Then, without incident, it inched its way back to Gavin's hand where it stayed.

"It's a sleeper," he said softly, examining it closely.

Dr. Jeremy inspected the critter closer with unparalleled interest. "I've never seen one before. I assumed it was a myth. Weren't they supposed to have been destroyed?" he asked as he rubbed his temple. When he spoke again, I assumed he was talking to himself, working out something that at that moment seemed to change things drastically. "The elves created this creature…." He frowned.

Gavin added, "They created it is as an undetectable elimination tool. It releases venom that paralyzes the body, eventually infecting the organs, rendering them ineffectual. Once you're dead, it slithers away, taking along all evidence, leaving the cause of the person's death inconclusive and the murderer blameless." Controlling his temper was no longer in his grasp; his hands were clenched, teeth bared. "Why is an elven creature that should have been destroyed in our house, Abigail?" His austere gaze bore into her, his anger uncontained and uncontrollable as it overwhelmed the room.

It was Sebastian who spoke, briefly taking his eyes off Kelly to look at Abigail. "You all created this thing that causes death, but don't have a problem killing your own people who happen to be capable of the same thing?" Sebastian said calmly and with tremendous effort, keeping his ensuing anger and frustration at bay.

I guess it wasn't an urban legend. They had killed all the dark elves. Most elves' magic was innocuous. Elemental elves, like Gideon and Abigail, could control weather within a certain radius, magic skills equivalent to those of a lower-level witch, but they were known for using theirs for mischief and a tame level of diablerie. Erde elves' magic linked to the earth. To the best of my knowledge they were hippie types, in touch with the earth, able to make any living thing flourish. Hexerei elves' skills mirrored those of mid-level witches and fae in their ability to perform spells, but they weren't able to perform defensive and offensive magic.

Dark elves were a totally different thing. They weren't innately evil or dark, but their gifts could not be considered anything but malevolent in nature. They could cause death of the body and mind with merely a touch. The elves weren't able to contain it, counter it, or control it. Realizing the magnitude of the dark elves' power and the danger of being able to do that type of damage with something as simple as a touch, with the help of the witches, the dark elves' kin had *contained* them. That was the nice word used for *genocide* in all the books. And a covenant between the fae, elves, were-animals, and vampires was established to contain this problem. It left a sordid taste in my mouth knowing that a person, due to no fault of their own, was sentenced to death because of what they were. Because they possessed magic so powerful and deadly that they were deemed too dangerous to exist.

Kelly had turned an odd shade. "If it released venom, even if you can make or find an antivenin, whatever damage is done will be permanent," she said in a tight voice.

"That's for snakes," Winter offered in consolation. But it didn't help. Maybe for a layman that would have been enough, but Kelly was an experienced nurse.

"When is your election?" Sebastian asked Abigail.

"In four months," she said softly, but she was unable to focus, her attention drifting back to her brother.

"And they will select the candidates in probably a month," he said with a sigh. "What happened to your brother wasn't a coincidence, nor was what happened to the other potentials."

Abigail's skin blanched as she pulled in a ragged breath and she started to walk the area, nervous energy causing her to fidget. "As I said before, my brother has no interest in leading. That was my father's dream for him, not his," she said.

Sebastian regarded her for a long time, his eyes narrowed to slits. Then his attention slipped in Gideon's direction. "But eventually he will mature and will accept his responsibilities. Maybe not now, but sometime in the future, he will want that position, and due to your father's legacy, it will be his without opposition. This is not a coincidence."

Abigail rested against the bed her brother lay in, distracted by her thoughts; when she finally spoke it was barely a whisper. "Someone tried to kill my brother." She gripped the table as her color quickly faded.

"Is there an antidote?" asked Dr. Jeremy. Like everyone else, he didn't seem to care about the elves' politics.

Distracted, she simply shook her head. "Not that I know of, but we need to find one."

"We should call Mason to see if he knows anything that can help," Dr. Jeremy suggested to Sebastian.

"He will not offer us assistance," Sebastian responded.

"Call him anyway," Dr. Jeremy entreated in a low voice. Gideon stirred and Sebastian's attention went to him before he could respond to Jeremy. At first, it was minor movement, a slight jerk of his foot, then he slid his legs up and down and before anyone could move closer, he moved sluggishly to the edge of the bed. Brushing his hands over his head as he cautiously peered over the room, his body remained rigid until he found his sister, who was just a few feet away from the foot of the bed. He relaxed into the smile that slowly covered his face. She quickly moved to his side.

He kept his attention on Sebastian as he leaned closer to Abigail, speaking softly in a language I didn't understand. She responded, at first in English, but quickly changed. Josh squinted, leaning in as he carefully listened to her speak. "I don't know what they are saying," he admitted.

Gavin watched them carefully and then he started to translate for us. Abigail recapped everything, conveniently leaving out that someone had tried to kill him.

She stopped talking for a long time, as Gideon made a strong effort not to look in our direction. "Abigail is afraid of us," Gavin offered.

Rightfully so, given the fact that Gideon was up and about seemingly without any lingering side effects, while Kelly lay in the bed a couple of feet away from him, unable to move from the waist down. It didn't bode well with anyone.

"May I use your bathroom?" Gideon asked eventually, for the first time giving us his full attention, his eyes roving cautiously over everyone's face. Dr. Jeremy was the only one to move and escort him to the nearest one, on the other side of the room several feet away.

"He can't find out that someone tried to kill him," Abigail said the moment he stepped out of the room.

"You think it is wise to keep such information from him? He can't protect himself from an enemy that he doesn't know exists," Ethan said.

Really! Mr. Secrecy had a problem with hiding the truth. This man would lie about the color of the sky if it suited the pack's or his interest and now honesty had somehow clawed its way to the surface as one of his priorities.

"At this time it would be best," she said softly with a sigh. "He will respond irrationally. Right now is not the time."

"I don't care what goes on with the elves and what truths you hold from him," Sebastian said curtly. "You keep whatever secrets you like. We need to find a way to fix Kelly."

Kelly's lips parted, but quickly closed as her gaze dropped to her hand. Usually she was enthralled by this world, far more often than she was appalled by its depravity; apparently, it had lost some of its fascination.

"If he's awake, then I should get better, too, right?" she asked hopefully, optimism brightening her wide-eyed gaze.

Dr. Jeremy was slow to answer, and when he did, it was with a noncommittal shrug. The hope that she held to faded as she relaxed back on the pillow. Truth was the very thing that linked them and I doubted he would lie to her, even if it was to unburden her. "If you don't, we will find a way. You will not stay like this," he pledged.

CHAPTER 7

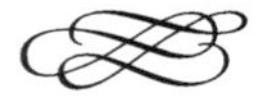

The same hour's time it took for Gideon to recover once the sleeper was removed was a long and arduous wait to see if Kelly would as well. Periodically she attempted to move her leg without success, and each time her spirits dampened. The final time she tried, tears welled in her eyes, which she blinked away. When one finally spilled, it was Sebastian who was the first to look away.

"Why isn't she better?" he asked Abigail.

Aware that she would be held accountable for everything that happened to Kelly, she was careful with her response. "I'm not sure. Is she wholly human?" Sebastian nodded. Often he wore his emotions like a badge, easy to read and usually undeniably hostile. Now he seemed withdrawn and concerned, glancing over at Dr. Jeremy, who had kept watching Kelly carefully, waiting for something to happen. The minutes passed and she still lay there immobile. Magic helped us to heal, but it was something that Kelly didn't possess being human. She was at a disadvantage.

Abigail frowned. "Hmm, usually you all are fanatical about limiting exposure," she said softly. "Why is she different?"

"That's not your concern. Concern yourself with things that

matter. How can we fix this?" said Sebastian. "What do you know about this sleeper?"

She considered the question. "It is new to me, just as it is to you."

"Yes, but it is an elven creature," Gavin interjected angrily.

"No, it's a *Makellos* creature," she corrected.

"To me, it's the same thing," Gavin said. "Whether they consider themselves elite to you all or have skills and powers stronger than yours, at the end of the day they are still elves. You all knew they were creating creatures foreign to us. Things that are so vile they keep them hidden, and when they manage to escape, no one can fix the problem."

"They are not the same; they consider themselves pure-breed and do not associate with the likes of us. We know as much as you do about what goes on with them."

Dr. Jeremy finally spoke, his voice sharp and grating. "Then you need to play nice and find someone to help her."

"We will see what we can find out," she said as she linked her hands with Gideon and started to head out of the room.

"No," Sebastian said. "He stays. You will work better without him."

I didn't trust that she would come back and I was sure Sebastian didn't, either.

"People will respond better to him," she admitted.

Sebastian smiled. "Then during your drive you should work on your people skills."

"I'll go with her," Winter offered.

"No. It will be difficult to get information with any outsider, but it will be even more difficult with you present," she said apologetically. She kissed her softly on the cheek and then looked at her brother.

"I'll go with her," Josh offered.

Abigail considered his offer for a moment. "Okay."

"Me, too," Ethan said, but it wasn't an enthusiastic offer. It was obvious that he was going for Josh's sake.

She studied Ethan, taking in the inhospitable person with the infamous reputation. Her attention lingered on the stern grayish blue eyes and features that never seemed to relax. Her voice was light and pleasant as she refused the offer. "That will be unnecessary. Josh will be just fine." He had an advantage that extended further than his charismatic personality. Josh was a witch, a very powerful one. Most people desired to curry favor with him.

Gideon had stayed on his bed for some time, quiet most of it, but occasionally he would question Kelly: "How are you?" "Are you in pain?" and "Are you usually this quiet?"

She answered the questions with much effort, perpetually distracted by her legs that remained splayed out and would only stay straight because of the meticulously placed pillows around them.

"I'm hungry," he announced an hour after his sister left. I wasn't sure who he was talking to. The only people left in the room were Dr. Jeremy, Gavin, and me. Sebastian, Winter, and Ethan had left minutes after Abigail had.

"And I should care?" Gavin asked.

"I doubt my sister is going to be forthcoming with any information if she comes back to find me starved and mistreated." He grinned, and then took a whiff of himself. "And I could really stand for a shower. It's been a couple of days." He looked in Kelly's direction. "It's going to get a little ripe in here, and I don't think she's going to appreciate that."

"Come with me," Dr. Jeremy said, more amicable than Gavin as he escorted him to another room across from the clinic. He would keep him close, in order to watch him and restrict access to the rest of the house, but it was obvious he really didn't want him near Kelly.

After he had showered and been given something to eat, he stayed in the room across from Kelly for just a few minutes, with the door wide open and refusing to allow anyone to close it. He surfed TV channels for a while before becoming bored with that and found himself in the room with her. She didn't mind the visit, but for some odd reason Jeremy did. Each time he entered the room, Jeremy met him at the door before promptly asking him to leave.

The lord of mischief didn't let a thing like inhospitality stop him; he cruised throughout the house, going into rooms that weren't locked, and simply freezing and breaking the locks of the ones that were. He'd done it about four times before he found himself face-to-face with Gavin. "I don't find you amusing at all. Break another lock and ..." The threat lingered, but his searing dark gaze easily finished the sentence.

The miscreant smile stayed on Gideon's lips and eventually worked its way to his eyes, which seemed a little too mischievous. He spun on his heels a little too theatrically for my taste, and headed to his assigned room and plopped on the bed. His hands resting behind his head, the door open for all to see, he watched a show that barely held his attention.

Just like everyone else, I had gotten my fill of Gideon and Gavin, but I was reluctant to leave the house until Kelly was better. I found Winter downstairs in the media room, staring at the soccer players on a television that resembled a cinema screen. Well, the television was on, but she was clearly distracted. Standing at the door, I watched her for a long time trying to come up with the right opening sentence. Everything I came up with seemed obtrusive and unnecessarily nosy.

"Gideon is really pushing his luck with Gavin," I said to Winter. Gideon's rumored deviancy was in rare form. "Gavin doesn't like getting a dose of his own medicine."

"Gideon's an ass and so is Gavin. Either they will end up falling in love or killing each other, who knows? And honestly, who cares?"

We usually didn't have long, obtuse silences, but now it was there, permeated by the many questions I had that I was sure she wasn't going to answer.

"Ask your question, Sky," she finally said, "or do you plan to keep standing there breathing like a rhinoceros with a sinus infection for the rest of the day?"

"Abigail isn't back; it's been three hours."

"Her brother is here, she will come back. For him, she will do anything," she said softly. But it was the things that she didn't say that drew my attention. If it were to save her own standing with the pack, I doubt she would have the same confidence in Abigail's return.

"How's Kelly?" she asked.

"Pretending to be fine?" And she was: the smile remained, bright eyes and a rehearsed platitude of "I'm fine" came so easily it was starting to sound recorded.

Winter stood and slowly started to walk throughout the room. "I shouldn't have brought them here. I shouldn't have gotten us involved," she finally admitted, after pacing for several moments in silence.

"Of course you should have. He would have died without our help. Could you have lived with yourself if he had?

"No."

"If it were you, she would have done the same," I said confidently.

She looked grim. "I am not as confident as you are that she would have." Then she turned her back to me and continued pacing. Lithe, swift, predacious movements that only reaffirmed my comfort with our friendship—or whatever it was—and the knowledge that I would never be on the other side of those silent steps coming after me. "In every relationship there is always someone that cares more and is more invested," she said, looking up briefly. "I was that person in my relationship with Abby. She can be callous and cruel sometimes."

Callous? Cruel? Coming from Winter, a person who once tried to kill me in cold blood, I couldn't imagine what atrocities Abigail was capable of: did she snatch the walkers away from the elderly, rip away toddlers' pacifiers just to see them cry, trip people just to laugh at them as they crashed onto the ground?

"Do you really think someone tried to kill Gideon because he is a potential ruler of the elves?"

"Underestimating people can be a fatal mistake. Typically, elves aren't malicious or unkind, but power can corrupt even the mildest person. They choose a new leader every ten years, but Abigail and Gideon's father led to nearly sixty. If Gideon is in that position, I am sure, even doing a mediocre job, he can ride on his father's legacy for a while. He may not want it now, but once in there, I doubt he will be willing to give up the position so easily," she said, shrugging off a thought that brought a deep frown to her face. "I think power can be addictive to anyone, even Gideon. Abigail wants it for him. The elves aren't progressive in all things, and a woman will never be their leader. If one could, Abigail would have jumped at the chance."

There was something troubling behind her eyes before she turned her attention back to the television, and she was too distracted to really care what was on. "Will you check on Kelly? I am sure she would like company instead of having Dr. Jeremy mothering her."

The boundaries of our friendship had been established long ago. We weren't going to sit in front of the television chomping down on chocolates while watching absurd reality shows. But it had changed significantly over the years and this was about as close as I was going to get to having a girls' night with Winter.

. . .

At the four-hour mark everyone was getting more agitated. Josh hadn't returned any of our calls and neither had Abigail. Tension was running high, and staying in the house was more difficult with every minute that passed. But leaving wasn't an option until I knew what was happening with Kelly. I was struggling to remain optimistic, so I just looked in on her from the small window in the door. Dr. Jeremy wasn't being overly nurturing. In fact, he was at the desk, ignoring her, and looking at the odd creature that had left her paralyzed. After searching the computer for several minutes, he went to the library and continued that cycle of going to his desk in the clinic, pacing, and then returning to the library. He did that for nearly an hour. The frown lines deepened and the tension formed an unappealing scowl that didn't relax. The last time he went to the library he took his laptop with him and a picture of the sleeper. His frustration turned more to agitation, but it had a lot to do with Mercury rising tonight. The felidae gravitated to it the way canidae were drawn to the moon. He fidgeted too much, took too many breaks, drank too much coffee, to the point where Sebastian came out of his office and met him midway between the library and the clinic.

"Are you okay?" he asked.

Dr. Jeremy, whose eyes were usually warm and expressive, was now distant and withdrawn. He nodded absently.

"You should go and change now, it will do you good. Just go for an hour or so. It will calm you. Relax the mind. It isn't helping that you are worried about her," Sebastian said.

Some were-animals were so in tune with the nuances of that which called them that days before they lay in anticipation of it. Steven was often distracted and on edge days before a full moon. The call was a tender ballad that they answered willingly. We knew it was coming but we could feel its presence hours and sometimes days before. For most it had a calming effect, a gentle reminder of our relationship with it. Some went into their animal form hours before they were forced.

For years it was a scream to me, and there was nothing calming about it. It wasn't a gentle reminder, but a siren that left me on edge. I never thought I would get to the place where I was now. It didn't calm me, but now the relationship was amicable. Twelve years later, I still didn't have the same affinity for my animal that the others did. I didn't hate her or sedate and lock her in a cage anymore, but we weren't one. I waited until I was forced into my change. My wolf was one of the things that I begrudgingly accepted, like the pimple that showed up on my cheek once a month and the dying hope that there was ever going to be an M&M diet.

I stood on the patio and watched as he changed in a swift movement. I liked to watch the felidae when Mercury rose and they changed into their various forms. Dr. Jeremy morphed into a ravenous, massive tiger that was diametrically opposite to his thin frame and aristocratic appearance. He was a beautiful creature. Deep stripes highlighted his silky coat and the majestic way he commanded the area with long graceful strides made him look like he was performing an elaborate dance. The beautiful, predacious creature quickly made me forget about the gentle, kind-hearted physician who hosted his body.

For fifteen minutes I watched Dr. Jeremy run through the bosk, disappearing often behind the crowded trees and thick, viny grass while I entertained the idea of leaving. But I just couldn't until I knew Kelly was okay. I never understood why she was so enthralled by this world, and now she was a casualty of it.

Gavin sat on the edge of Kelly's bed, offering her a sandwich.

"I'm not hungry," she said, and pushed it and the cup of water to the far end of the tray table. She had refused to eat or drink ever since I had taken her to the bathroom nearly two hours before. When I'd left the room to give her some privacy, I could hear her sobbing from the other side of the door.

"If I go and get you Albert's, will you eat that?"

She nodded.

With a wry smile, she relaxed against the pillow after he left. "Good, that should take him at least an hour, I need the break. I appreciate the concern, but ..." she admitted. Most of the were-animals' concern seemed overly intrusive and overbearing. On the surface, it appeared to be innocuous, kind, and benevolent, but you pulled back the curtain and found an overenthusiastic obsession that toed the line, very closely, to psychopathic and possibly stalker-like behavior. It wasn't done out of malice. They just didn't know how to rein it in. Everything was always extreme.

"Have you seen him drive? He'll be back in about a half an hour," I said. He drove like he was trying to place in the Indy 500. Once he was behind the wheel, all you could see was just a glimmer of the dark blue Lotus as it sped away.

"I may stay like this," she whispered after moments of silence. The troubling thoughts had added years to her appearance and her eyes had lost all glint of hope.

I wouldn't lie to her, but what I could say with confidence was "If it is at all within Sebastian's ability, you will not stay like this." I had accepted long ago that this pack didn't care about titles. They didn't want to be the "good guys" nor did they care if they were considered the "bad guys"; they were the people who got things done. They never really cared which guy actually achieved the goal as long as it was handled.

"But it's not within his power, is it? This is an elven creature. He doesn't have any control over that. No one even knew what it was. How is he going to fix this? How is anyone?" The sob caught in her throat.

Please don't cry. Please don't cry. Ugh. When had I become that person? She was sad and scared; tears were appropriate. But she didn't cry. She inhaled a deep breath, relaxed the frown lines that marred her face, and plastered that genteel infectious smile that had become her mask. You couldn't see it without reciprocating.

~

"You can come in," she said, lifting her eyes to meet Gideon's as he rested against the doorframe, where he had only been for only a few seconds. I sensed him when he first moved, and I think Kelly saw him.

He nodded, bowing his head in a histrionic gesture. Kelly, like me, seemed to be intrigued by Gideon's looks and those of his sister. The only difference between them was of his hair, which was shorter and lighter. His lips were too fine and bowed, and the thick, long light hairs that veiled his eyes were too delicate. His narrow face and long, straight-edged nose were identical to his sister's. Although an average height, he was thin, just a couple of meals away from being considered a waif. Three days without shaving and there still wasn't a hint of a shadow on his face. He spoke in a light tenor and was very calming.

"We haven't officially met, I'm Gideon." He extended his hand to Kelly and she shook it.

"Kelly." She didn't seem to mind that it took him too long to release it.

"You fixed me," he said, moving closer to her. He was a space invader, but it bothered me more than it did Kelly.

She shrugged. "I guess I did."

"Thank you," he said, keeping his firm hold on her hand as his smile broadened.

Staring at her legs, he asked, "Do you mind?" his hands hovering above them.

She tensed as he moved closer. The sky crackled once and the gentle drizzle of rain was a soft drum against the window. The soothing flow of rain falling at a slow rhythm had its intended effect; Kelly relaxed comfortably against the pillow, listening to nature's ballad, one created for her by Gideon.

His fingers brushed over her leg. "You can't feel this, can you?"

She shook her head.

"Doesn't really matter, I have a light touch anyway," he admitted, his lips curved into a smile.

I thought, *Are you freaking kidding me? You're flirting now? Really?*

"Are you going to get to your point soon?" I quipped.

"Is she always this impatient?" he asked, grinning and sliding closer. Sparks formed along his fingers, and Kelly focused on the flickers of light that intensified causing his fingers to tremble. "May I?" he asked.

Desperation had made her devoid of logic and common sense and I felt I needed to intervene. I grabbed his hand. "What do you think you're going to do, jump-start her leg? No, it's not going to happen."

With hopeful desperation, she said, "We can at least try. I've seen odder things happen here."

Perhaps there were remnants in her of an optimistically naïve person who was able to have hope in the impossible. I released his hand and stepped aside.

The colors sparked in his hands, brighter than before. I suspected some of it was for melodrama, and at her assent he touched her legs. They made short spastic movements for several minutes, but when he moved his hands the movement stopped. Her legs lay out to the side as immobile as they were before.

He repositioned them with the pillows. "I'm sorry," he said softly, taking a seat on the edge of her bed. "It was a long shot." His smile melted into a dour look of regret.

Regret or not, it wasn't going to help make the red welts go away before Dr. Jeremey came back. He noticed them seconds after I did. His brow furrowed, his hand extended and soon I could feel the frost chill the room as it formed on his hands. The temperature dropped so much that my lips started to tremble. He rested his hand against her leg. She couldn't feel his icy touch, but after nearly ten minutes, when he removed his hands, some of the redness lingered but the welts had gone away.

There was something unsettling about him and his skills. I had to admit, I didn't like elemental elves. They were freaks. I understood the hypocrisy in my feelings; after all, I changed into a wolf every month and on some occasions just for the heck of it. But there was something odd about controlling something as forceful as the weather. The ability to have nature at your control and manipulate it at a whim was disconcerting. How powerful were he and his sister to be able to perform such acts?

He made himself comfortable once again, with an incessant focus on her. "You're not a were-animal, so how did you get yourself mixed up with this lot?" he asked.

She shrugged a response

"Oh come on. I'm sure it's an interesting story," he said with a smirk.

"Not as interesting as you probably imagine." As if she had been trained by the best, she dismissed his curiosity quickly.

I couldn't deny it, I was curious as well. The story of how she had become involved with Dr. Jeremy was rather hushed up. There was a unique bond between them, usually forged by either a secret or going through adversity. The curve of her lips was genial and welcoming, but her face was firmly set with determination. Whether she was sworn to secrecy or not, there must have been confidences in the story that she wasn't willing to disclose to an outsider.

"I'm sure the reason you declined the position as the elves' leader is far more interesting." Dismiss and redirect, it was as if she had read Sebastian and Ethan's "how to be evasive" handbook.

He brandished a coy smile, but his curiosity was hard to ignore. "You tell me your story and I will tell you mine," he teased.

Maybe it was the time that she spent around were-animals, and being plunged into a world that had more than its share of violence, domination, secrets, and power, because her intimate relationship with it was starting to show. Her ebullient, wide smile remained. "I already know your story, Gideon Mercle, son of Darion, who ruled longer than any of his predecessors and was one of the most respected elven leaders. It was expected that his death would lead to his son's succession into leadership. I suspect that you don't want the position because of the fear that you will never live up to everyone's expectations. That's understandable."

His forced pleasant smile didn't hide the flickers of irritation. "I am his son, not he; their votes would solely be based on their desire to have him back."

But it was the things that he didn't say that resonated. He would never live up to the legacy his father left behind, and although he attempted to hide it behind a charismatic smile, the insecurity was there.

"Ill-placed adulation and foolish votes are better ways to become a leader than the ways others have." The tinge of disgust that laced her words made me fully aware that she knew the rules of the pack. She knew that the leader was chosen based on dominance, which was usually determined by a fight, often to the death. I could see how it would have left a dank taste in one's mouth. And it should have in mine. Once upon a time it did. Perhaps I had bonded too much with the animal that dwelled in me, but I understood and respected the need for the superior person to be in charge. It guaranteed survival.

"Yes, the elves would have supported you and voted for you because your dad was a good leader and every supporter wished your mom was theirs. But it is up to you to replace his legacy with your own. You set the elven world aflutter because you decided to be—well, let's use a nice word for it—a rebel and turn your back on the politics. Some say it's admirable; most think it was selfish. Ten years have passed and now it is time for a new leader," she said.

I glared at the side of her face, but she kept her attention firmly on him. She was itching to tell him of the assassination attempt. Would she betray us again because of her overzealous ethics? "Well, it's up to you, but you don't seem like the type that responds well to others leading. You have the opportunity to lead, not follow, and I don't understand why you won't take it. If it were me, I would at least try it. You buck against traditions and rules anyway. If you don't like it, quit." She glanced in my direction with a smirk.

He chuckled. "I feel like I'm at a disadvantage. You know so much about me and I don't know anything about you. Sebastian is quite invested in your well-being, but it seems to be tied to Dr. Jeremy's affection for you. If he is half as good as he is rumored to be, I guess Sebastian will do whatever it takes to make him happy. You make him happy," he said, watching her intense amusement with every moment of the Q&A. "The question is, why are you so important to him?"

Dr. Jeremy liked most people, but his adoration of Kelly was the apparent result of something more than her exceptional clinical skills, bright personality, and witty sense of humor. There had to be a story—a good one. And I wanted to hear it.

"He likes lasagna. I make really good lasagna," she mocked dismissively.

He grinned. "Of course."

Gideon's curiosity was no longer a blithe inquiry; it was intense thirst for the information that she was purposefully withholding. Everything was always a game of power. Find the person's Achilles' heel, exploit it, threaten it, control it if necessary. Kelly was important to Jeremy; that was good information to know. Sebastian would do a great deal to protect her—even better information. There was a story behind the adoration and for some reason Gideon was hell-bent on finding out.

He seemed determined to be there until she was willing to answer any questions, but Dr. Jeremy peeked his head in. "Gideon, I need you."

"For what?"

"Please come with me" was his only response. Usually paternal and friendly, Dr. Jeremy didn't seem to have it in him to be either just then.

Gideon moved, but it was slow and measured and the moment he was out the door, I turned to Kelly. “How did you get mixed up with us?” I asked.

She grinned. “Dr. Jeremy got me suspended from work.” Using her arms, she pulled herself up a little more. “Well, I got myself suspended, but it was because I helped him.”

I waited for her to continue.

“I worked in the ER two years ago with Dr. Jeremy. He worked at the hospital a few days a month. I assumed he was semiretired, now I know he probably did it to keep his skills sharp. You guys may get injured more and in worse ways, but you heal fast and have an advantage that we don’t.”

“But how did you know he was a were-animal?”

“I didn’t. But he made me feel strange. You all do, but not in a bad way. Dr. Jeremy was quite impressive in the ER. It was like he was working on a different level than the others. Once, we had a gunshot wound and the guy’s assailant came in to finish the job. He didn’t get past Dr. Jeremy. He had him disarmed within seconds. The whole time, he seemed off. Feral, instinctive and dangerously primal. If I hadn’t pulled him off the guy he would have killed him. That part didn’t bother me. If you have the gall to come in a hospital and risk the life of fifty people over drug territories, I can’t find the compassion to care if someone kills you in the process. I just didn’t want Dr. Jeremy to get in trouble for beating the man to death in front of a room full of eyewitnesses. He couldn’t even plead self-defense. I was able to get him to follow me out, but he looked weird. Really weird. His eyes had shifted to an odd brown and he seemed savage, like an animal. It’s really hard to be afraid of him. He’s such a cuddle-bear, but that day I was a little afraid.”

Okay, there wasn’t anything cuddly about any were-animal I’d met. Did she know what *cuddly* meant? Bear, yes, and just like one, they are likely to rip you to shreds.

“He thanked me and I didn’t see him for months. I thought he had quit. Then one weekend, the ambulance brought in a were-animal, but I didn't know what he was at the time. I don't know what attacked him, but he was barely holding on, and the only thing he would say was Dr. Jeremy's name. I didn't know if he was a relative or what. But when he opened his eyes, they were just like Jeremy's ... um, like Dr. Jeremy's were that day. Then his hands did something really gross."

"He was about to change?"

"Yeah, I know that now, but I didn't then. I put him in another room and called Dr. Jeremy. He and Sebastian came and got him. But as far as the staff were concerned, I lost a patient. They suspected it was drug- or gang-related, and even in his condition, he didn't want to be there in case the police were called. But as far as they were concerned, I had lost him."

"You weren't fired?"

"Nope. But I was written up and given a couple of days off. Dr. Jeremy came by my home a couple days later."

"Then he offered you a job here?"

She shook her head. "No, he came up with some bogus story about it being a friend with a rare blood disease. Maybe if I was a naïve person off the street I might have believed him. But I wasn't buying it. He stuck with the damn story for a long time—months. He eventually returned to the hospital and continued to work as though nothing had happened. Can you believe that?"

Of course. They would change in front of her and convince her that she hadn't seen it. So yes, I could believe it.

"Then one night while I was jogging in the woods—" She stopped and cast a look in my direction. "I don't need a lecture from you about how stupid it is to jog in the woods at night, I got the same one from Dr. Jeremy two years ago." She smiled fondly as though she remembered him chastising her, which I knew from experience was a little comical. His voice always has a smooth, soothing inflection to it, and even when raised, it was still there.

"There was a woman lying on the ground. I thought she was

unconscious but when I checked her, she was dead. On the side of her neck were two puncture wounds. I had to call the police, but by the time I had retrieved my phone, she was missing. That night I thought my mind was playing tricks on me because I swore I saw a figure move in front of me, but it was so fast I could barely register the movement. That night I ended up at Dr. Jeremy's house. I told him what I had seen. I wasn't crazy, but he treated me as if I were. He asked about medication, my history with illicit drugs, alcohol, family medical history, and so on. You know the drill. I was so angry."

There was a long lull as she retrieved the memories to give me an accurate account. "By the time he finished with his fake questions, I'd resigned myself to staying right there until I had answers. I knew I wasn't going mad. In a span of six months I had seen him display what could only be described as supernatural speed and strength, feral animal eyes on a human, and an odd patient that kept calling for him, and to top it off, a dead body had just vanished in front of me. I knew it was connected and he knew about it."

"I guess he really didn't have any choice but to come clean, huh?"

"You would think, but of course he didn't. You all are so stubborn. It is a wonder anything gets accomplished here. He went on and on about some nonsense as though I was stupid enough to believe it. I was finally fed up. I sat on his sofa and refused to leave until he gave me answers."

I could imagine her doing just that. Pouncing over to it, plopping down, arms crossed and face screwed up in defiance refusing to move until he came up with something that made sense.

"It was stupid, because with his strength he could have just thrown me out. But I pointed out that I called him when the injured were-animal came to the hospital and that I got in trouble because of it. He wasn't aware of the suspension. He took me outside and started to strip. I wasn't expecting that at all. Then he changed." She was quiet for a few moments. "I guess I should have been scared, but I wasn't."

Her curiosity belied good sense.

"I had to pet him. How often do you get to touch a tiger?" she said excitedly. "Here I am. I still work at different hospitals to fill in as needed; but it's just to keep my connections there. Who knows? If another were-animal shows up, I can make sure to get them out in time."

The desolate look returned when she attempted to move her legs. I wonder if she wished that she had never gone to Dr. Jeremy's home that day. I wished it for her even if she didn't wish it for herself.

She fidgeted with her hands, and it only made me feel worse. I didn't know what to say to make things better.

"You will not stay like this," I said with more confidence than I really felt. I hated doing that, but I hated her sorrowful look even more.

The smile was forced and fake, but she tried her best to pull it off. "Of course."

Getting kicked out of places was starting to get a little annoying, but at least Kelly saying she was tired and wanted to rest was reasonable. I could use the reprieve. Watching her try to be optimistic made me feel bad. A house this big and I still felt like there wasn't a place to go. I decided to go back to the library and see if I could try to translate the Clostra. I searched through it, but the books were nowhere to be found.

"What are you looking for?" Ethan asked from the door.

"My glass slipper, have you seen it? What do you think? The Clostra. I want to finish translating."

He closed the door behind us and then moved the rug back. Slipping his finger into a small space in the floor, he slid it back, revealing a lockbox. Then he unlocked it and handed me the books from inside it.

"Sheesh, it's just us, don't you think this is a little over the top?" I asked, taking a seat at the table.

"Apparently we are now running a shelter for misfits," he said as he took a seat in front of me. "We have enough carelessness here; I will not add to the problem." The dark eyes lifted in my direction.

Why battle with Ethan? I didn't have the energy, and honestly, it was just a waste of time.

I laid out the book, grabbed a tablet from one the shelves and placed it on the table. Ethan moved the tablet over toward him and pulled out a pen. "Start."

"You know Latin?"

"You don't have a mother who's a witch without learning Latin," he said, barely making eye contact.

"And yet you made Josh do all the work," I said in an attempt at a half-hearted joke.

There was a glint of annoyance as his attention went back to his notepad. "Josh is the only one who finds your little quirks entertaining. Can we start?"

Josh and I were more compatible, but Ethan and I worked better together. There wasn't any joking, breaks that extended too long, or even inside witticisms, which for someone on the outside could be annoying. The more we translated the more complicated things were. There were spells about fae, elves, and those who controlled magic. Nearly a third of the way through, I stopped. The words *spiritus umbra* jumped out at me. Spirit shade. Since I had discovered I hosted one, I was familiar with the word in almost any language. I read the sentence: *"Et non consurget a umbra spiritu militia …* What does it mean?"

Ethan studied the sentence for a moment. "The spirit shade will rise from its host and no longer …" His lips pressed into a sharp line.

"There are spells for spirit shades, which mean that there has to be more than just the one in me," I said.

When he didn't answer, I asked the question again.

"I don't know," he said.

Dealing with Ethan was frustrating because I didn't know where the truth lay between his answers. He operated on a need-to-know basis. He and Sebastian acted as gatekeepers of sensitive information. "If you are lying to me, then stop it. Despite what you seem to think or believe, we are on the same team." I pushed the book aside. I was getting tired and I had a feeling that dealing with him was about to exhaust whatever energy I had left.

His glower always held a look of mistrust and contempt. "If I knew the answer, I would give it to you. For now, we are on the same team; but I am under no illusions that you will be anything but the undoing of this pack. Unfortunately, the feelings people have for you will cause them to ignore affronts and tolerate things longer than they should and only deal with them once there is irreparable damage."

"I am sorry, are we talking about *this* pack?" I seemed to remember when Sebastian threatened to kill Winter for disobeying him. Ethan and Sebastian had to be talked into a calm to stop them from killing each other after a disagreement about Josh. I wasn't under any naïve delusions that the affections of this pack extended further than loyalty and their notion of each member's perceived value. Perhaps we were somewhat like a family, a sick and twisted one that had one another's backs because we shared that same bloodline. We were a family that would fight off the bullies on behalf of our lineage, keep the skeletons deep in the closet where they belonged, and overlook one another's shortcomings. But, unlike family, it was conditional. In return, the pack expected blind loyalty, and anything less was considered betrayal. Sometimes I felt like it was a bad trade-off, but if it weren't for this psycho family, I doubted I would be alive.

Ethan sat back in his chair eyeing me with the same curiosity he had when we first met. The veil of all the things that made me an anomaly had been exposed: I was a host to a spirit shade, my mother had been a low-level witch, and although most were-animals can't, I am able to bring a vampire back from reversion, their form of death. Because of the death of my mother, I am a Moura Encantada, responsible for protecting the Aufero. I have a pack family that doesn't really trust me and a real family that couldn't care less if I lived or died. He had his answers. It wasn't pretty or nice, but it had been handed to him in a messy, complicated box.

The more Ethan studied me, the more indignant I became. He wasn't exactly a simple little box, either. It was just that he and Sebastian were very good at keeping the skeletons at bay. And if one of those bones fell out of the closet, all they did was make you see *their* "reality." Dark things found Ethan's presence abhorrent and withdrew in aversion. He could not only break wards, but protective fields as well, something that were-animals cannot do. And I was convinced he was connected to the fifth protected object that he and Sebastian seemed to want me to forget was mentioned once. If anyone deserved not to be trusted, it was him.

"People make mistakes, it happens. No one sets out to do anything to jeopardize this pack." My thoughts quickly went to Winter's situation with Abigail and the guilt she felt over it. She wasn't wrong. Why should she be made to feel bad for helping an ex-girlfriend in need?

I relaxed back in the chair and studied him with a purpose. "If I am not mistaken, your relationship with Chris compromised this pack quite a bit. You sleeping with the Master of the Northern Seethe's mistress wasn't good for the pack. Yet, you continued to do so without reservation."

It was just a spark: anger flashed, then faded just as quickly. "She's not his mistress. My relationship with Chris was never a question of compromise when it comes to this pack. We had no illusions about our roles and the boundaries of our loyalty to each other. If she was a problem or ever became one, trust that she and the situation would have been handled without hesitation."

"Oh, you were handling the situation just fine. You seemed to *handle* each other every possible moment you could. So you can take your hypocrisy and shelve it, and while you're at it, put the attitude and the arrogance there, too."

There was a moment of silence, but the sharp glare continued. I took his silence as a small victory, a short-lived one. He returned to the notepad. "Go through the book and read off all the spells with spirit shade in it," he said. He flipped over toward the back of the notepad and I began to read all the ones that I could find. In the end, there were twenty-eight out of nearly three hundred spells. Cryptic spells that, without the third book, meant nothing. I felt the same frustration that Josh had earlier. It would take days before I could go through the whole book to translate it, but skimming through it, there were only three spells regarding were-animals. As I stumbled my way through the translations, Ethan, not possessing the same patience as his brother, let out several irritated sighs and we became resigned to me spelling out everything.

"Twenty-eight spells," I said, sitting back in the chair.

Ethan's eyes lifted, studying me as I fidgeted.

"There have to be more spirit shade hosts than just me out there," I said.

The long stretch of quiet contemplation was starting to annoy me. *Say something!*

Instead, he rested his head on his hands, carefully watching me. "And?"

"Don't you wonder if there are, and their purpose? For years Maya remained dormant, and all of a sudden, she is making a grand appearance. I can hold magic, manipulate it into dark magic, feed vampires and—" I stopped abruptly. I was about to tell him about our venture to the dark realm, but I didn't want to discuss it or the fact I saw something there that resembled him.

"And what?" he asked.

"And I feel like something is off."

He frowned at the lie, his arms folded over his chest as he leaned back in his chair. The cool platinum eyes studied me for a few minutes before he spoke. I had his attention, and it wasn't the best feeling. "I guess you are more dangerous than we even speculated."

I shook my head. "Just different. There are twenty-eight spells for spirit shades. We are nearly a third of the way through the translations and there are only three regarding were-animals. Are the were-animals so innocuous that so few spells are needed for us, or are the spirit shades so complex that more than three spells are needed to subdue them?"

"There isn't any way we can find out if there are any more spirit shades. Maya is hundreds of years old and just now coming to light. It would be difficult to find one, especially if they are hosted," he said. But he seemed intrigued by the idea of finding more.

"Well, it would be limited to a smaller number than the masses. They can only exist where magic does, so the host will either be a mage, witch, were-animal, elf, or fae. That definitely brings down the numbers."

"Not enough; there are millions of us," he said.

"Then we follow the origin and talk to Tre'ases," I suggested. The thought of finding more intrigued me because I was curious about Maya and had vowed to find out who had murdered her and why. Finding others would help that. Why would someone murder a child? That was one of the many things I hated about the otherworld—amoral and unscrupulous behavior arose from the desire to keep it stable and as safe as possible in a world full of monsters. I suspect most enjoyed the seedy, dark, unscrupulous underbelly of this world and others deemed it a consequence of living in it. I had been pulled—no, I was really dropkicked—into it and held under the swamp-like surface until I screamed uncle.

And sometimes I was ready to scream it again at the top of my lungs.

Ethan's gentle smile seemed foreign. Far too often, it was done to distract from a venomous deed. "That is an idea," he admitted. "The problem is we only know of one; she is dead and so is her son. We have no way of finding out if other Tre'ases exist."

I stood, examining all the books on the shelves. A plethora of information and yet we were still clueless about so many things in this world. Last year we were able to source the magic and find the Tre'ase's son, but it was a familiar relationship. Tre'ases were trickster demons that had a long history of causing trouble. They were infamous for providing their services to the highest bidder or those that could wreak the most havoc.

"I am more concerned with the link between you and others that can read the Clostra," Ethan said.

"We need to determine if it is just my family lineage, being a Moura, or hosting a spirit shade that allows me to read the Clostra. If it's because I host Maya, then that can be a start. I suspect it has something to do with my family since Senna can read them, too," I said, pacing the floor. I returned to studying the books, pulling out a few that caught my attention and scanning over them. I could spend weeks in here reading from sunrise to sunset and never finish all the books in the library. Without Josh, who was the unofficial librarian, it was even more difficult. The various languages were a challenge, too. Most of them were in Latin; intermingled among the ones in English were other languages that I needed Google Translate to figure out.

"It's not your family," said a melodious baritone voice behind me. I turned and looked up from the book in my hand to see Sebastian leaning against the doorframe. It was always troubling how a man his size moved so silently and undetected, with quick stealthy movements.

"Senna isn't a blood relative. Her hair isn't naturally dark like the others in your family; I could smell the chemicals in her hair."

That was a horrible skill to have. I was sure he was just wonderful on a date as he told her he couldn't stand the smell of her chemically colored hair.

He continued, "When she speaks, her Portuguese isn't fluent. She stops too often to think about her words before she responds, which means she learned it at a later age. The small cleft in her chin is another sign. There was a picture on the mantel of the fireplace of her and a woman who claims to be her mother along with a man, who I assume is the alleged father. A cleft chin is a dominant trait; one of them should have one—they don't. They are not her parents."

That was a sore subject for me. "If they raised her, then they are her parents," I said in a sharp tone.

"Semantics. The issue still remains; she isn't related to you. Her ability to read the Clostra isn't linked to your lineage. Your family are low-level witches, but since she is the only one able to read it, I assume it isn't linked to that, either." He slipped into the chair next to Ethan, and they pondered this. "There has to be a link between you and Senna since you two can read them."

What did he want from me, to play nice to get information? That was something I knew I couldn't do. Resentment pricked at me each time I thought about what my "family" did to me and the blatant confirmation that I didn't have any relatives I could depend on. No, I didn't care to know any more about the people who tried to kill me.

Sebastian studied Ethan with astute intensity, taking a long moment before he spoke. When he finally did, he was careful with his words. "Chris knew a lot about Gloria, right?" he asked. Gloria was the first Tre'ase I met, over two years ago, when we were trying to find out more about my past and my odd abilities.

Ethan's head barely moved into the nod.

"She knew about her son, as well?"

Again, the nod was negligible.

"She seems to be privy to information that we aren't. Sometimes ahead of us by steps."

"She is good at what she does … or rather what she did," Ethan responded, cool and stoic.

"We should see what she knows."

"Of course."

Sebastian watched him cautiously, but Ethan didn't offer much for him to read. He was stolid as usual and would never show how he felt about visiting his ex, whom he had been willing to let die.

Ethan didn't object when I offered to come along. The looks he shot in my direction didn't bother me. I was so used to them that if he didn't give me one every now and then, I would be concerned.

Sebastian was right, Chris had a lot of information, which she wasn't always willing to give, and it was often accompanied by her trying to obtain just as much information from the questioner. As a Hunter, her lack of implied loyalty to anyone made her the go-to person for most things that occurred in the otherworld. Nearly two years ago, she had been contracted to kidnap me for the vampires. I had every right to hate her, although I knew to her I was just a job, nothing more or less. And she was good at her job.

When she lay in the pack's hospital near death, there was a part of me that didn't want her to die. I didn't like her, but I respected a person who managed to survive in the otherworld, and she got a few extra points for doing it as a human. But that wasn't the case anymore. Now she had been a vampire for almost three months.

CHAPTER 8

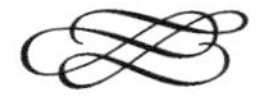

The ride to Chris's home was uncomfortable and teeming with tension. I wasn't sure what to expect: anger, violence, the intense sexual tension that often marked every moment that Chris and Ethan were near each other.

When we pulled up to her postmodern home, a large coppice surrounded most of the area, giving sufficient privacy to the few homes on the block. I guess when your life consists of catching and killing malicious things and socializing with creatures of the otherworld, privacy is needed.

It took her a while to answer the door. I wondered if she stood on the other side debating it. Eventually the door opened; an assessing look stayed on Ethan for several moments before she stepped aside, in near silence with nimble, graceful steps.

Dressed in a black tank and a pair of jeans that had to require feats of acrobatics to get into, she looked different but the same. Her skin had maintained its pecan hue, with a pale undertone. She slid her fingers through her sable hair, refocusing her dark eyes, which were veiled by long lashes and thick eyeliner, on us.

Her soft features no longer displayed relaxed confidence; instead, she looked guarded and dour.

"What do you want?" she finally asked, walking away to stand near Demetrius, the Master of the Northern Seethe, who was seated on the sofa.

Ethan focused on him. Demetrius's dark hair was chin length, a lot shorter than it was when we first met. He came to his feet, like an elusive wave nearly imperceptible to the eyes. The black marbles narrowed and he stood taller, focusing on Ethan. The coolness of Demetrius's ire drifted throughout the room.

I guess there was going to be violence after all.

Chris quickly stepped between them and then turned to Demetrius. "I need you to leave," she requested softly.

His eyes widened at the demand before he shot us a baleful glare that landed and remained on Ethan. "I'm not going anywhere."

When she spoke, it was firm but gentle. "This is business." She turned to address Ethan. "Right?"

"Yes, I need to ask you something," Ethan said, but he hadn't taken his eyes off Demetrius. Their resentment toward each other was so deeply ingrained that it had become the norm. They would each gather great satisfaction from standing over the other's dead body. Sometimes I wondered if it was really about Chris. I had a feeling their animosity predated even her. It was the same when Demetrius and Sebastian were in the room. Could two powerful males ever coexist in a space without feeling the need to assert their dominance and power?

"It will be quick, I can assure you," Chris said.

"Then you will not mind if I stay," Demetrius protested.

"He will not speak to me in front of you."

"Then he should leave," Demetrius said with a look that implied he was prepared to assist Ethan in doing so.

"Please," she said. "It is not his request, it is mine."

He split his attention between me, Ethan, and Chris before he said, "I will be back in half an hour. It will be best if he is not here when I return."

The simple noncommittal shrug seemed to be enough for him. He leaned down to kiss her, and she turned, offering him her cheek. Demetrius's departure was a performance, a kiss on her cheek that lingered too long to be chaste; then he nestled his face in the curve of her neck, his hands roving slowly along her shoulder, back, and waist, a casual display of ownership. He kissed her again on her forehead. This time she leaned into it enough to comfort him. Shooting another strident look in Ethan's direction, he vanished without another word.

Really! Not his mistress. Ethan, welcome to denialville, population: one.

The tension wasn't nearly as thick as I anticipated, but there was an air of animosity. The large open floor plan wouldn't be an issue if the situation became violent. I had no doubts that the desk in the corner, with her laptop on it, probably had at least two guns in it. If I looked in the closet, I was sure I would find a baseball bat, a sword of some kind, and probably a rifle. The lovely pristine white room off to the side with the ceiling-to-floor windows, covered with thick light-filtering off-white drapes, surely had a couple of weapons stored in it. And the small circular ottoman sitting in front of the urban chic sofa, an odd burnt tangerine color, probably had a gun, knife, and maybe rope or handcuffs hidden in it. The clay sculptures meticulously placed throughout the room could be used as weapons. The dark V-shaped television stand had four drawers, and I imagined at least a couple of them stored weapons of some sort. I knew this because I had stumbled on all this in Winter's home. Even though Winter and Chris hated each other, I suspected it was because they were so similar. I was curious to see if I was right. I stepped back to look in the closet whose door was ajar. Well, there wasn't a bat, but there was a nine iron. I peeked into the umbrella holder, and bingo, exactly like in Winter's home, I found a sword sticking out of a scabbard.

I watched her carefully for any quick movements toward her weapons; but would it really matter? She was a vampire now; her movements would be too fast for me to really do anything to stop her. The only option would be to defend ourselves.

"What do you want, Ethan?" she asked

"How many Tre'ases do you know of?"

"Hmm." Her interest was piqued. "I am sure I am not your first stop. Who did you go to first, Ann or Sean?"

"Sean."

"Did he know anything? Or did he just flounce around like a self-entitled twit, demanding payment upfront for information he didn't likely have? He's a piece of work, isn't he? A true shyster." She scoffed, "He considers himself to be my replacement since rumors have it that I'm dead."

"Well, technically—" Ethan started.

"Don't."

Had Sean's reputation preceded him, or had she gathered that from dealing with him in the past? It had happened almost exactly as she stated. An arrogant young man answered the door of an expensive town home in downtown Chicago. Dressed unnecessarily in combat fatigues with a gun holstered at his side, a knife at his waist, he was smug when he answered the door. He kept us waiting, knocking at his door, and I was sure he stared out at us from the peephole. When he finally acknowledged us, he didn't know who Ethan was. Usually I would have dismissed it as Ethan being arrogant, but this guy was supposed to be a Hunter. The one that had touted himself as Chris's replacement. After three years at this, and attempting to build a name for himself, how could he not know who the Beta of the Midwest Pack was? Sadly, he didn't know who the Alpha or the leader of the elves was, either. Ethan could barely hide his disgust and disappointment. Forty-five minutes later, we were standing at his ex-girlfriend's house.

She sneered, "He is absolutely useless, more arrogant than competent." She continued to pace, but this time the focus of her attention was me. "Terait, odd magical ability, a connection with Ethos, unusual ability to stop a vampire's reversion, and let's not forget the connection you had with the Gem of Levage, you are a very *unique* little wolf."

"And?" Ethan said.

She shrugged. "Usually an anomaly like her would have the Midwest Pack siding with others to rid us of a potential problem that could get out of hand. I guess times have changed." She considered him for a long time, the moue deepening with each passing moment. "I always thought the fall of your pack would be something far more cataclysmic than a doe-eyed brunette."

Shaking off the idea, she moved to her desk and turned on the computer. For several minutes she browsed it, and when she addressed Ethan, she didn't give him the courtesy of her full attention as she kept her focus on the screen. Her voice was soft as she spoke. "Ethan, you don't need to worry. Your little anomaly has no effect on my life, and until she does, she is safe from me. But I would make sure she is never my problem." She glanced in my direction and quickly dismissed me.

"Oh wow, thank you. You mean you aren't going to kidnap me and try to give me to the vampires to be murdered? You're so sweet. Do you like gift baskets? I should send you a gift basket. Such largesse should be rewarded," I responded.

Fine. If you aren't going to play nice, I won't, either.

She chuckled. Her fingers moved swiftly over the keys and a few times she tapped at the screen. "So, Bambi, is it safe to assume they need this information for you?"

"It's Skylar, and no, I am just here with Ethan."

She looked over, skeptical. Although it was the truth, I guess she was so used to so little of it existing between her and Ethan that she dismissed it as being another lie. "I really would prefer to stay out of things like this, but I kind of feel like I owe you, Bambi."

Now I had to laugh. "It's Skylar, not Bambi. Do you really think our past—you know, the whole thing of you trying to kidnap me to give me to the vampires—will be squared by this information?"

She stood, the smile cordial, although the way she looked at me was far from it. Dismissive at best. "You don't like me, I get it. It isn't undeserved." A slight smile played at her lips and made its way to her eyes. Once a gentle brown, they now had eclipsed to charcoal, a sign that she was a vampire that fed well. As a human she had been dangerous; I could only imagine how lethal she was now. "Now if only I could find it in me to care. Like I said, I feel like I kind of owe you. But whether or not you like me just isn't something I can care about. It's probably better if you don't."

Well, she got her wish. I didn't like her, but I just couldn't hate her, although I had every reason to. I understood we worked on a different code of ethics. She was a mercenary, and expecting anything else from her was really naïve of anyone. Although Ethan had given her a pass on such behavior, which I am sure had a lot to do with his libido more than anything else, I just wouldn't. I understood it, but I didn't accept or forgive it.

Handing Ethan a piece of paper, she said, "This is how much this information will cost you."

He glanced at the paper and handed it back to her. "Try again. I asked for addresses and names, not for you to organize a meeting with them on a private island."

"That's what the information costs. If you aren't willing to pay, that's your problem. You can let yourself out," she said as she jerked her chin toward the door.

"You're being unreasonable," he said.

Whatever feelings she was managing to suppress erupted. "You want reasonable from a person you chose to let die!"

"I didn't have a choice!"

"You had a choice. It just wasn't the choice you wanted. You can't always have things your way!"

Ethan was perceptive about many things, but his narcissism made him blind in this situation. They were now dealing with the product of their dysfunctional relationship. Often on opposite sides, for once they had been working on the same team, and she was disappointed that he hadn't done whatever it took to save her. But did she have the right to be? She wore her bitterness and anger hard on her face. And adding injury to insult were the speculations that she wasn't injured during battle against Ethos and his creatures, but by Michaela, the Seethe's Mistress, as an act of retaliation against Demetrius. The pack didn't care enough to investigate, but Josh was certain of the rumor.

Their emotions often danced between primal lust, keen dislike, and distorted variations of both. Now there was just discourse that I doubt would be resolved, because no one but Ethan really knew why he chose to allow her to die. Was it to permanently rid himself of the woman whom he would never admit was a weakness? Or was it truly an act of compassion to rescue her from a world where she really didn't belong?

She shoved the paper into his chest. "You want the information; this is how much it will cost. This isn't a rummage sale. We aren't going to haggle."

"No, it is more like extortion."

Her gaze shifted to the door. "You are welcome to leave."

Now they stood glaring at each other, their anger palpable as the complexity of their relationship came back to bite them, and I was afraid things would erupt in violence before we could get the information. They were victims of a horrible situation that they had created, both of them too arrogant to acknowledge that their dysfunctional relationship didn't work. Whether they would ever admit it, their commitment could never truly be to each other, their loyalties were devoted to other people. His was to the pack and his brother, and hers to whoever was paying her. Their union in any form was an uncontrolled, convoluted mess and even the Arrogant, Great, and Powerful Ethan and Chris couldn't make it work and overcome the self-inflicted obstacles placed upon it. How could they think a relationship, no matter how shallow, could survive when they both knew they would sacrifice the other to serve their own best interests? They had failed; their relationship was a failure. It was a victim of their own nescience and misjudgment. Neither one of them humble enough to see it for the devastation it was and admit failure. Instead, they lingered in a perpetual stalemate, accepting nolo contendere rather than defeat.

I wasn't sure what she expected, but she wasn't getting it from Ethan. With untainted indifference, he crossed his arms over his chest, his gaze shifting to the wall behind her, his tone cool. "What? Do you need an apology? If you need one, I will give it to you."

Chris might not have realized it, but she had changed the rules of their relationship while Ethan had stayed the course. He despised vampires and wasn't going to create any more, even to save her.

But he would give her that apology, a half-hearted statement of insincere platitudes. He would give her a simple unemotional obligation, if that was what she needed. "Either you take the apology or—"

For all that is good in the world, please do not say "get over it."

Ethan loved to tell people to do that and right now we just didn't need his brand of derision.

"Deal with it," he said.

Not much better, Ethan.

Chris swallowed and then started chewing on her bottom lip, and for a long time there was nothing but cold hard silence. I could feel the tension in her emotions: anger, disappointment, vengeance. But the unresolved anger remained the most dominant. Did she want revenge? The idea seemed to linger as she continued to look at Ethan with contempt. Eventually she dismissed it and relaxed. Maybe a person less skilled at denying her emotions would have given in. I almost wanted them to punch each other just to get it out of their systems.

"Why don't you deal with this? This is my fee for the information. Either pay it or get the hell out. If you don't make a decision in the next minute—yes, I mean sixty seconds"—she looked at her watch—"starting now, the price doubles."

He pulled out his phone. "Is the account the same?"

She nodded.

After a few punches of the keys, he said, "Done."

She went to her computer and printed out a page and handed it to me. Her finger ran down the list of six addresses. She checked one with her pen. "This one. If you tell him I sent you, he is a lot more amenable." Her finger slid lower down on the list and she placed a dash by other names. "They will help, but there will be a price and it may not necessarily be money. And these two—well, I can't help you on this, but I strongly advise you to leave my name out of it, or they will never talk to you and will likely try to kill you."

We were out the door when Chris called to Ethan. "You should hope that Ann or Sean get better at their jobs, because I won't help you or your pack again, so please don't ask. We are done."

We had lost her as a resource and I wanted to get as much information as I could. "What do you know about spirit shades?" I blurted before she could close the door in our face.

She stopped. "Is that what you are looking for, Bambi?"

I nodded. She took the paper from my hand and she circled two names on the list. "Then you will only need to speak with them."

I looked at the names: one was the Tre'ase that she had a friendly relationship with; the other was her foe.

For whatever reason, she was giving out information generously and I was going to obtain as much as I could. "What do you know about protected—"

I was silenced by her finger pressing against my lips. "No, Bambi. You are part of the Midwest Pack, so *you* have no more business here with me."

I was just seconds from finding out what the tip of a vampire's finger tasted like and her learning to live with that part of the offending finger missing when she removed it.

Addressing us both, she said, "Don't come here again. Don't challenge my request. I mean it. That includes you, too, Bam—Skylar." The cool voice drifted off behind the door.

Once in the car I said, "I guess that is one source we no longer have."

"For now," he said confidently as he pulled out of the driveway.

"You can't seriously believe she is going to change her mind?"

"Yes, but out of necessity. She was created by Demetrius. People will assume she has an intrinsic loyalty to him. No one will hire her again."

I watched him for a few minutes. "And you don't believe that blind loyalty exists?"

"Did you see how she responded to him? A new vampire would never do anything to displease its creator. As they age, it becomes more obligatory than compulsory. Did you sense any of that between her and Demetrius?"

"I don't think she is capable of fealty, and displeasing people seems to be her thing."

He answered with a half-smile and that odd appreciation he always seemed to have for Chris's unorthodox behavior.

"Hmm, so that is the way to your heart, a person who actively tries to displease you? Pardon me for considering that the behavior of an insane person," I said as I looked at the list of names. Only one lived near, two lived nearly four hours away, and the other one was in Texas. The one in Texas was one of the two that would know about spirit shades.

His smirk fanned over his face as he shrugged. "She gets the job done. Always. Whether she makes enemies or friends in the process has never been a concern. I don't know of any job given to her that she didn't complete."

"The number of maimed, murdered, and betrayed that she leaves in her wake doesn't matter?"

"It matters that she always completes the job," he said in a low, tepid voice.

On the drive home we went over the list and decided to visit the Tre'ase closest first.

He asked, "When do you want to leave, tomorrow?"

I fidgeted in my chair. I didn't know if he had paid for the information or if the pack had, but I didn't want him to go. For some reason Tre'ases didn't respond favorably to him. His presence annoyed them.

"I don't want to leave until tomorrow when Kelly is better." I was trying to be optimistic, although we hadn't heard from Abigail and Josh. But I couldn't go four hours away without knowing that she was okay. Stifling the image of her sobbing on the floor earlier was getting more difficult. I didn't want to go so far away without knowing her fate.

I convinced Ethan to take me home to get my car. I hated being chauffeured around. Well, that was the excuse I gave him. I wanted to visit the friendly Tre'ase that Chris had recommended. He lived close. Maybe he would know about more than just spirit shades and could tell me about protected objects, Maya, and why she was killed as a child. It was at least worth trying, and I knew I wouldn't get anywhere with him while Ethan was present. Once he pulled into my driveway, I said, "I want to go visit the Tre'ase with Josh instead of you."

"Just because you and my brother can't stay away from each for longer than twenty-four hours, you will not put him in a dangerous situation. I am going with you," he said firmly.

"My relationship with Josh has nothing to do with it. Each time you encounter a Tre'ase, they respond poorly to you. One of them already isn't going to be friendly, why agitate them or the situation any more by bringing you?"

"Fine, if I need to stay outside I will, but I will be close and Josh can come as well."

I hopped out of the car. "Thank you, your majesty. Whatever would we have done without you granting our approval to leave the city?" I said in a saccharine tone.

I did not need to look back. I could feel his virulent glare on me as I went to the house.

I had decided to pay the "friendly" Tre'ase a visit, but I had no idea what Chris's idea of friendly was. Could it be someone that only tried to kill her half of the times she visited? She was odd enough to think that was friendly behavior.

Pulling slowly into the spot where the GPS had led me and where the Tre'ase's home should have been, I found myself on a gravel road with a roadblock marked "Private Property." Willow trees, a thick coppice, and high grass made looking past the immediate surroundings difficult. I was going to have to go in blind.

Unaware of what I might encounter, I had a Ruger LCP holstered at my waist, concealed by a light jacket. But unless the person was standing three feet away, they were safe if I had to use it. No matter how many times Winter took me to the range, I couldn't hit anything. The knife secured to my leg was large enough to do damage if needed. I really wanted to bring a sword or my trusty golf club, but how did you explain showing up to someone's home with something like that? You just couldn't explain that away.

As I started to get out of my car, an oversized SUV pulled up behind it. I didn't have to look at my rearview mirror to know who it was. Ethan.

The grimace remained on his face as he walked toward the car, and didn't ease even when I greeted him with a bright, wide smile. "Hi," I said when he opened the door.

"Hi," he said, doing a horrible impersonation of my voice. "You're so predictable it's not even a challenge anymore."

I got out of the car. As I headed up the path, he sidled in closer, his steps matching my quick pace up the trail.

"Skylar," he said in an icy soft voice. "I am only going to say this once so I need you to listen carefully. For whatever reason, Sebastian wants you alive. I couldn't care less if the Tre'ase rips you to pieces the moment you walk through the door. But for now, our responsibility is to keep you alive. Your behavior is making it more difficult to care whether or not we succeed. Perhaps we may find it easier if you weren't alive." He stopped and took hold of my arm. "Do you understand me?"

I pulled away. "I don't need a babysitter, and I'm sorry that you feel that I do. I need answers and I am going to do what it takes to get them. You've made 'babysitting' me your job; no one gave it to you. Either you learn to love it or quit. I hope you quit. Regarding the pack no longer caring to keep me safe or alive—big deal. If I don't get the Aufero, I am as good as dead anyway; so you won't have to make that decision." I started the hike up the long gravel walkway. The path was narrow, and the large florets of trees hung low, blocking the path, darkening the long obscure route. As we got closer to the small cottage that was heavily cloaked by the forest that surrounded it, I begrudgingly admitted to myself that I was glad that Ethan was with me.

I stopped just short of the stairs. It was quite a few hours from dusk, yet the surroundings near the house were stygian. I clung to the fact that Chris considered this Tre'ase a friend. Ethan placed his hand at the small of my back. "I'm ready when you are."

I wasn't ready yet. For a minute I stayed, checking how easily accessible my weapons were, then I inhaled a deep breath, and the smell of pine and oak prickled at my nose. I stepped forward, and before I could knock, a deep mellifluous voice said, "Come in. I was wondering how long it would take for you to get to the door."

He wasn't what I expected at all. Gloria, the first Tre'ase I met, was a wide, stout woman with salt-and-pepper hair. Her son Thaddeus was a horrid-looking thing with horns, hooved feet, and fur. This one was different. He had a broad and muscular build. Deep russet coloring was complemented by the short chestnut-colored hair that waved at the scalp. Intricate body art ran up his sinewy arms. His eyes didn't match his appearance, either; they were an odd lavender blush, something I had never seen before. He looked past us, so I wondered if he was blind.

But eventually the odd-colored eyes settled on Ethan, hard. *Here we go again.*

He stepped closer, his head tilted, and then he smiled. He started to touch Ethan, but stopped and continued to examine him with interest. Ethan remained motionless as the Tre'ase slowly circled him, getting closer and closer with each step. He eventually stopped. "Remarkable," he said as he continued to study him.

"Logan?" I asked. I had to, because he didn't act like any Tre'ase that had encountered Ethan.

He shifted his attention to me for merely a second. "Yes, how may I help you?"

But Ethan reaped the rest of his consideration. He reached out again slowly, his fingers tracing an invisible line around Ethan. "May I?" he asked.

"No."

"Just for a moment. Please. I will be a better host if my curiosity is satisfied."

Ethan looked in my direction and considered the request for a long time. Probably, contemplating, as I did, whether or not Logan would be helpful if denied. After several moments of thought, he nodded. Logan stepped so close to Ethan that if he hadn't been a couple of inches taller, their lips would have met.

Overly excited by the anticipation, he had several false starts before he placed the palm of his hand on Ethan's cheek. The glamour he presented fell for just a second, enough for me to know it was gone, but not long enough for what I saw to register.

"Please have a seat," he said as he walked into the living room and sat sideways in a tuxedo chair with his legs dangling over the side.

His strange comfort with us there felt eerie. How strong was he that two were-animals showing up at his home didn't send up any alarms?

"Do you want something to drink?" he asked.

Ethan and I declined at the same time as we took a seat on the overstuffed sofa, an odd shade of red that contrasted with the geometrical design of his chair. I looked around the little cottage that didn't maintain the image on the inside. It was a hodgepodge of eclectic modern and cottage-chic that was just as odd and unsettling as his personality.

"How may I help you?" Logan asked.

"You don't want to know how we found you?" I asked. He lived in the middle of no-man's-land, two strangers show up at his house, and the only thing he did was offer them a beverage. I knew there had to be a whole lot of crazy going on in his head.

He shrugged. "Very few people know I am here. The ones that do, I know and trust that they wouldn't send harm my way. And if they did, I am confident I can protect myself," he said casually.

"Chris sent us," I said.

He smiled. "Ah, Chris. I adore her. She's a delightful little misfit with a temper to match. It is a pleasure to watch her. How is she faring these days? Still causing trouble?"

"A vampire," I responded.

He sat up in the chair and his eyes widened. "Really? How did that happen?"

"A long story." It wasn't that long, but I didn't want to spend the visit talking about Chris. "She thought you would be able to answer some questions for me."

The gentle smile remained, his demeanor relaxed and kind as he periodically glanced in Ethan's direction. "Of course. I will do my best. May I ask that once I answer your questions, you offer a favor to me in the future?"

The pupils were expanding so much that they overtook the eyes. The variegate markings of the tattoos moved like scrolls revealing distinctively different markings just as foreign as the originals. The room pulsed with enough strange magic that both Ethan and I gasped in a breath, suffocating under the power of it.

"No," Ethan blurted. "No favors. If you answer our questions, there will be no debts, no favors. We will pay you cash if necessary, but nothing more."

Then I remembered Josh's warning from a couple of years ago to never make a deal with a Tre'ase. It was so easy to forget as the hospitable demon trickster sucked us in, weakening our defenses.

His interest in our visit diminished significantly and he didn't hide it, but he still maintained his pleasantness. "I don't require your money, just a remembrance that I helped you when you offered nothing to me."

I didn't answer; it seemed like a convoluted way of asking for a favor.

"We acknowledge the assistance, but offer nothing more," Ethan said.

He sighed. "Very well."

I was glad Ethan had come, and when I looked in his direction, he simply smiled. Yep, I was out of my depths and it was getting more annoying each day. Just when I thought I had this crazy world figured out, another wrench was thrown into the machine. There were too many rules and too much trickery.

The smile had lost some of its warmth, but it was kind enough. "What information do you seek?"

"Spirit shades: what do you know about them?"

"They are nothing more than unsettled souls cursed to walk the earth without a body. Nothing special."

"Do you know how many there are?" I asked.

"I am sure there are still spirit shades, but not nearly as many as there were in my youth. We are becoming extinct, maybe less than a thousand of us exist, and most do not live here in the States. No one really requests that we create spirit shades anymore. It is such a taxing effort that the offerings for us to do it are considerable. I assume those that do know of our abilities aren't willing to pay the cost," he said, shrugging it off.

Chris's list was grossly inaccurate. Maybe a thousand?

"Perhaps it is better that people do not request that of us. I have not created one, and I doubt that I will."

"And why is that?" Ethan asked.

"Except for a few humans who were made shades as punishment, it is far crueler than death for them—"

"Because of being immortal," I offered.

"No, because they are alive but unable to live without a body to experience life through. They usually have a problem finding hosts. No shade with great powers would consider a human because humans have nothing to offer. Most shades were killed for a reason. To give them a chance to exist again is a very unwise decision. I am sure there are many types of powerful shades: witches, elves, mages, and even demons. Of course, no one could change a vampire for obvious reasons, and your kind"—he paused and studied us for a long time—"back then weren't the pretty little things you are now. Then you were more animal than man: gruesome, vile creatures." He cringed at the memory. "Animals cannot become shades."

Ethan snorted in derision.

Really, that's your line in the sand. He basically sexually harassed you and made out with you—and calling you a "pretty little thing" is where you take offense?

"What about the fae? Are they immune to such a fate?" Ethan asked.

Logan's eyes widened. "It was mutually accepted that we would never help them, but of course there are some of my kind that enjoy the anarchy and destruction that only a fae can deliver."

"Really? Fae?" Ethan asked, surprised.

Logan laughed. It was a gentle rumbling sound and his odd eyes held an amused twinkle at our avid curiosity. "Yes, you all call them fae now, which is quite fitting since they are mere fractions of their ancestors, the Faerie. What this world considers fae"—he rolled his eyes—"are what I consider demi-Faerie, if not quarter-Faerie. Their mere tricks and poor execution of their pitiful little spells are just a minuscule representation of what Faeries can do." He did a comical gesticulation of his hand. "Oooh, my magic can make you fall in love with me. Look at me, my magic can force truth with a kiss." He stopped, becoming very serious. "Whatever little spells they manage is nothing compared to those of their Faerie ancestors."

He stood to get himself a cup of coffee. His movement wasn't as smooth as it should have been for someone of his build; he rather lumbered about. I wondered if he used his glamour body so infrequently that he had very little control of it. We declined coffee. But when he came back with a large cup of French vanilla flavored coffee, the scent made me want to reconsider. They were such tricksters that I was suspicious of anything they offered to eat or drink.

"Where was I? Oh yes. Faeries, the original, were powerful beings, masters of chaos and violence. They were so powerful in strength and magic that they were feared by most in this world. No one bothered them. The only thing that stopped them was the limited number of them that existed. Too few to be the threat that they could have been. They possessed the strongest and most nearly unstoppable form of magic that I had ever seen. They had the ability to manipulate the world with the same ease with which we blink our eyes. They reproduced with one another, but their progeny were so few it was only a matter of time before they mated with humans. You want to retain power, you don't reproduce with the weakest.... it never turns out well." He caught himself and looked in our direction and the smile widened. "Well, sometimes it works out. Were-animals were dreadful creatures. I still find it difficult to believe they found willing human mates." He shrugged. "Perhaps they weren't all willing. Or maybe they were; we all have our own little perversions. Faeries made us look like docile little peddlers of magic. No, you definitely didn't want to make a Faerie a shade. Doing so would likely ensure your death."

"Why?" I asked.

"We all like magic and power. Even death has its appeal." He smiled in Ethan's direction. "That is why I am enjoying this visit so much. It can be cleansing, whether it's yours or someone else's, and it settles well on the palate."

Ethan didn't seem nearly disturbed as I was with Logan's fascination with death. He kept the indiscernible look on his face.

"How does creating a Faerie as a shade ensure the death of a Tre'ase?" I asked.

"You create a shade, you are linked to it indefinitely, which has its advantages. But as I stated before, usually shades were formerly powerful beings, and that craving to have possession of it again doesn't die with the loss of their body. They are very selective of their hosts, seeking ones with the ability to use magic. They pick hosts that are weak enough that the idea of hosting them is a benefit. The longer it is hosted, the closer the bond becomes and then one begins to wonder if the actions of the host are truly their desires or that of the hosted. I can imagine that it can become quite the dilemma. The hosted lives past the life of its host. Once the host dies, it moves on to find another one. And they will continue to live until the Tre'ase that created them dies. Now you see why I don't want the hassle. What if the shade is a terror and needs to be stopped? Well, you can kill the host, but the shade lives on and will just find another body to inhabit. You kill the Tre'ase and you correct that problem."

My stomach crawled into knots, but I did everything I could not to react. I kept a simple smile on my face. Logan considered both Ethan and me for some time, finding me less interesting. Flecks of mischief played in his eyes and wandered onto the smile that hadn't wavered since we first arrived.

He relaxed back on the chair. "This visit has been quite nice for me. Please come again, under a different agreement." When he stood, we knew the conversation was over. He hadn't gotten anything out of it other than being in the presence of power, magic, and death, which seemed to appease him during our visit.

He directed us out of the home, but reiterated several times that we were welcome to return.

His door would always be open to us. Of course it was. It was open to anyone willing to strike a deal with him.

I tried to keep pace with Ethan as we walked back to the car. Distracted, he seemed to have forgotten I was even there. "What was that about?" I asked.

He stopped abruptly. "What?"

"The Tre'ases, either they love you or hate you. The one that claims to have an obscure fondness for death was quite intrigued by you," I pointed out.

The placid blue eyes with the hint of gunmetal, which were difficult to read, fastened on me. He shrugged. "Make up your mind. Are you concerned that they like me or dislike me?"

"I'm concerned with both. Why is one who professes an adoration for death so intrigued by you?"

"As with you, I try not to concern myself with what goes on in the mind of someone that I will never understand. It makes life simpler that way." And with that he ended the conversation.

I wish I could be as dismissive about it all. What was Maya? I knew she had power, but what was she really: Witch? Elf?

Demon? Faerie? I didn't know her age, so she could be a fae, a weaker descendent of the Faeries. That didn't make sense. Who would go through the trouble of killing a fae? She had to be worse because she was stronger now. It scared me that at one time she was dormant, but was now becoming increasingly more active. Who was it that desired Ethos's magic: me or Maya? Was I slowly being crowded out into nonexistence, just a shell used to do her bidding?

I sat in the car for a long time before I could even drive, remembering Winter's words of concern about Maya's increasing presence. I can manipulate magic and change dark magic to natural magic—something witches can't do—and bring a vampire back from reversion—something were-animals can't do. Silver doesn't affect me, I have a peculiar bond with protected objects, and I can borrow magic. It didn't concern me then because I was used to being an anomaly. Before, I wondered who would kill a child, but now I wondered what about the child made someone want or need to kill it.

The only thing that I was sure of was that Gloria, the first Tre'ase who was able to sense Maya's presence, was dead. If what Logan told us was true, I would have died when she did if she had been Maya's creator. I needed to find the Tre'ase that created her. Its death meant mine. The thought made me sick—the acts of someone that I didn't know could lead to my demise. I considered going back to Logan but decided against it. If it wasn't for Ethan, I would have made a deal with him.

CHAPTER 9

Ethan's car was already parked in the driveway when I pulled into the pack's home, but Josh's was still gone. Standing in front of Gavin's car was the peculiar and deviant vampire Sable. Her voluminous dark hair framed her small round face. Her deceptive wide-eyed innocence, chocolate eyes, and cherub appearance belied her infamy as the psychotic little vampire that most feared for a reason.

The petite brunette didn't look the same as she did a couple of months ago in the pack's living room, fawning over Gavin. Sable was the Seethe's little problem child, and she had developed a fondness for *our* problem child. Her skin, usually parchment, was now grayish, a side effect of coming out before dusk broke. The older vampires were not as limited, and if they fed from a fae they had the ability to move that timeline up a couple of hours. So close to six o'clock—it was several hours from sundown—someone Sable's age should be resting.

"Is he here?" she asked me in a small voice.

"I think so," I said. Like her creator, Sable had an odd inclination for feeding from were-animals. Were-animals couldn't sustain vampires, and the craving was more of a limbic desire that

I believed was rooted in the need for domination. Were-animals weren't known for feeding vampires, and if a vampire ever tried to feed from them, their efforts were usually met with violence. Most vampires held a similar dislike and disgust at the idea of feeding from a were-animal. Sable and her creator were definitely anomalies. This strange infatuation with Gavin was something no one could understand.

"Will you let him know I am here for him?" This was how her victims succumbed to her. She was so docile and gentle, it was hard to believe that she was the infamous vampire who as a human had been in all the newspapers as the perpetrator of one of the most heinous crimes ever committed in Illinois. No one would ever believe the young woman with the large eyes was capable of the nine murders she committed when she was human. Two of them were vengeance for the killing of her family. The others were family and friends of the people who murdered her family. As a vampire, her cruelty had reached a new level. She was the vampires' weapon of destruction, so far removed from humanity people often wondered if she had ever possessed it.

I nodded and started toward the house with more of a desire to distance myself from her than to get Gavin. Before I reached the house, Gavin came out. Her face brightened at his approach. That odd longing that draped so heavily over her disappeared.

She smiled and watched him with as much adoration and intrigue as she had the first time she'd seen him and described him as beautiful. Describing him in such glowing terms was a stretch because his personality marred him. If you could get past the jackass that housed the slender build, tawny skin, and piercing, crescent-shaped eyes and the generous supple lips that were often twisted into a sneer, then you might have been able to consider him attractive—very attractive. He kept fidgeting with the anthracite hair, unsuccessfully trying to tuck it behind his ears each time it fell into his face.

"I waited for you to come visit me," she said, her smile quickly turning to a pouty moue.

He focused on the forest behind her, a yearning for it that he wasn't able to ignore. Mercury rose tonight, forcing the felidae into their animal form.

"And?" He barely made eye contact as his arms crossed over his chest.

"You haven't been home all day," she pointed out, frustrated.

He shrugged. "So." He looked bored and her grilling seemed to be of no interest to him. He focused on her for just seconds before he returned his attention to the thicket.

He stared at it, distracted; Sable touched his arm to redirect him. "Are you here with her?" She frowned. "Is Kelly here?"

"Yes, she is here." Again his attention floated back to the woods.

"I don't like it."

He leaned down, his stern gaze meeting hers. He spoke softly but in a tone that commanded compliance. "Go home," he said before he turned and started for the house.

"I will kill her and take her from you!" Her hands clenched into fists, and her lips trembled as she hissed her venomous threat. She might as well have dropped to the ground with her arms flailing about because this was nothing more than a tantrum. A fit because the vampires' little princess didn't get her way.

He stopped midstride, his lips pressed into a stern line as he inhaled a deep, slow breath and exhaled it even slower. Then he returned to her. She was rendered speechless by his presence, his indomitable gaze holding hers for a long time in silence. When he finally spoke it was soft and steeled. "You will never touch her. Do you understand me?"

She dropped her head and nodded.

He lifted her chin gently until her eyes met his. "I need to hear it."

"I won't touch her," she said with a regretful gentleness.

The stern look remained as he brushed her hair away and then kissed her gently on the forehead. "Now go home." Then he turned his back to her, something I wouldn't have done, as angry as she was. But she didn't move. Once he made it to the house, he turned from the door and simply mouthed "Now." Lacking the ability to *travel*—and simply vanish like Demetrius, Michaela, and Quell could—she scurried to her car, and quickly sped away.

Both Ethan and Sebastian waited for Gavin as he approached. Little sparks of gold rolled over his chocolate eyes and he seemed tense. Trembling hands ran through his hair, distant eyes were barely able to focus on them.

"Gavin," Ethan said just to his right.

Gavin turned but he looked unusually agitated. Gold shimmered briefly and then dimmed, smothered by his dark natural eyes. His breaths were measured and slow, but his heartbeat was erratic.

Sebastian, watching Gavin closely, spoke in a mild tone. "Mercury is rising and you need to change. Shouldn't you be outside preparing with the others?"

"What do I need to prepare for? It peaks. I change. Then I run around in panther form for a couple hours, and then I'm back. Preparation isn't needed," he shot back.

I wondered if Sebastian and Ethan ever grew tired of dealing with such an antagonistic, ill-tempered person, or did they encourage the challenge? Most were-animals submitted easily to them—they were a force that most wouldn't dare defy, but Gavin didn't seem to mind taking on the task.

"I'm not going to leave her here alone while *it* roams through this house unchecked."

"We will make sure she is okay," Sebastian said.

"Of course, because you all did a great job before," he said, rolling his eyes.

"She'll be fine. He's more of a nuisance than a threat," Ethan added.

Gavin scoffed, eyes narrowed to small lines. "She can't move her legs. He's not just a nuisance; he's a problem. It is because of him she is like this."

"It was an unexpected event," Sebastian, said firmly, his patience thinning with each word.

"And that makes it okay with you?"

"No it's not okay, but you not changing and being an irrational ass isn't going to help, either. You want to protect her, so do we—"

"If you really wanted to protect her and this pack, we wouldn't have gotten involved, damn it! So what if Gideon had died? He's not the ruler and probably never will be. What did saving him do for us?"

He attempted to toss off the anger, but it was still there, radiating off him. Sebastian and Ethan remained surprisingly calm. "I don't think I am going to change this time," Gavin said.

'I don't think I am going to change?' Are there choices? Okay, I choose not to change, either, from now on.

"Just because you *can* do something doesn't mean you should. She's scared and you seem to comfort her. She needs you at your best. You're a jackass when you don't change. Go change so that you can be there for her, because she needs you better than you are now."

Sebastian was trying to appeal to him without it becoming physical. He had found his Achilles' heel; Gavin's anomalous friendship with Kelly had given Sebastian leverage and he wasn't above exploiting it. We all had one. Ethan's was Josh, and although he would never admit is, so was Chris. The pack was Winter's. Abigail had her place, but if at any point Winter felt it would have compromised the pack too much, I doubt she would have helped.

Oddly, being someone's weakness had its benefits. They were protected as though they were part of the pack. The moment Kelly was injured, it cemented Gideon's safety even if he hadn't recovered, because they had to fix Kelly. There was a certain comfort in it. Because I saved Winter last year, despite my declining an invitation to join the pack, Sebastian had protected me. His protection bordered on extremely psychotic, but it was his way. It was like yanking you out of the way of an oncoming car, but breaking your arm in the process. Yes, you were safe, but you had a fractured arm.

He stepped closer to Gavin. Everyone needed him better than he was now. You could feel his tension; it was like an over-stretched cord that if barely touched, would snap.

"I'll be fine."

Sebastian was about to lose it. Gavin had pushed him to the end of his patience and it was starting to show. He stepped closer to Gavin, his voice a low rolling thunder. "You will change and you will do it now. There will not be any more discussion about it. Do you understand me?"

Gavin attempted to hold his gaze, a subtle challenge, as the amber rolled over Sebastian's eyes, his body tensing as he reared back slightly, prepared for what was inevitably about to end in violence. Gavin retreated, slowly turning and moving in graceful strides to the back of the house.

Gideon was perched on the edge of the bed talking to Kelly when I checked on her. She had eaten about a fifth of the burger and was nibbling on the fries Gavin had brought her earlier. The veil of optimism had dropped and she had succumbed to the idea that she was going to remain like this, a paraplegic because of an unknown elven creature. Abigail and Josh had been gone for hours and it was nearing eight o'clock.

I had just decided to stay with her, when I heard the gentle padding of paws against the tiles. I peeked out the door and saw a panther with clothes gripped in his teeth, walking toward the room.

Yeah, that's sanitary.

When the panther made his way into the room, he nudged his

way between Gideon and Kelly and propped himself up on the bed, nearly laying over her legs. She stroked his midnight fur, and a deep rumble reverberated in his chest as he licked his lips. Occasionally he presented his sharp fangs to Gideon, who got the message and took a seat across the room, making my presence there unnecessary. I left.

CHAPTER 10

Winter must have felt the same level of desperation and uselessness as I did, because when I asked her to go with me, she agreed without any questions. It wasn't until we were nearly fifteen minutes away from the pack's house that she inquired about where we were going. When I told her it was to visit a Tre'ase, I expected a little more of a reaction and a lot more questions; but instead she simply shrugged and sat back in silence on the passenger side of the car.

When the extended quiet continued, I thought she was rethinking the idea of going to see Logan, until she spoke. "If things turn out badly for Kelly, it's my fault," she said with a glower. Her emotions had worn heavy on her, hardening her features.

She cradled the jar that held the sleeper close to her, occasionally looking down at the small creature that had caused so much damage. It lay pressed against the glass, with the exception of its legs barely visible.

We pulled up to the little enclave, the borders separating it from the rest of the world. Just like our last visit, the world on the other side of the barrier was dark and gloomy. I couldn't convince

Winter to leave her sword behind. Instead she handed me the jar, which I placed in my canvas purse.

"You will not need it," I said.

"But if we do, you'll be glad that I have it," she said as I led the way to the house. The air changed, the presence of a strong and toxic magic diffused into light waves in the air becoming heavier at our approach. Winter didn't seem to notice, and if she did, it didn't bother her.

The door was open when we arrived. Logan leaned against the counter, and the welcoming smile persisted even after he realized that Ethan wasn't with me. "Another visit so soon," he said, his brow raising slightly with interest. Pushing up from his position against the counter, he approached Winter.

"Hmm, this isn't a social visit I presume." He eyed the sword at Winter's waist. Minimally concerned with the weapon and her, he quickly dismissed her and turned to me.

"Do you know what this is?" I asked, presenting the jar from my purse.

Once again, he was by the counter, relaxing against it, the odd eyes fixed on me. "I will help you as much as I can as long as you accept that you will owe me a favor," he said, his eyes widening, the art on his arms moving around, aligning and realigning. Cool brisk air pricked at the tip of my nose as stifling magic swept through the air.

"No." I took out my wallet and pulled out money, searching through the hidden pockets in my purse for more. Then I handed the money to him. Winter offered more bills, several hundred dollars.

He frowned, then handed it back. "I have no need of your money."

"What do you need?" Winter asked, her voice a low, clear, mesmeric tone. Her eyes changed, vertical slits narrowing and expanding in slow beats. Logan's eyes remained fixed on hers as he moved closer. His breathing was thick, wispy and rushed. He leaned in, following her movement in an odd trance-like state.

"You will help us," she said softly. "Identify the animal and tell us what it is." Her voice held a beseeching request that he seemed unable to deny.

He remained close, concentrating on her eyes. Holding them, allowing the power of her words to linger, draping over him as she waited for him to respond.

There was a stretch of silence before he spoke. Then he laughed, a loud, boisterous sound. "I assure you that someone as young as you are possesses neither magic nor skills strong enough to control me." He laughed again, ebullient and jovial.

"A snake." His look of mild interest stirred into a newfound appreciation as he studied her. "Your kind didn't look like this before, either." His finger slid playfully over the bridge of her nose. Then he tapped the tip of it.

Did he just tweak her nose? This meeting was going to go downhill very quickly. But it didn't. Winter had put aside her inimical tendencies in order to help Kelly. Instead she smiled, pleasant. A kind reflection of his coltish behavior.

He grinned. "Very pretty. Nothing like your ancestors, scaly disgusting things meandering about using their tails like legs to stand. They spoke as humans, but maintained the form of their animal. There were so many then. Are there more now?"

"No, there are very few," Winter admitted.

He smiled in understanding.

I didn't know if it was Winter or her answer that pleased him, but he relaxed as he turned to face me. "I will help you. Not often am I gifted with such a show." He glanced over his shoulder at Winter again. "What can I help you with?"

I handed him the jar. He examined it and then started to pour it into his hand.

"It bit one of our friends, now paralyzed," I warned.

"I appreciate your concern, but there are very few things that can harm me." He dropped it out into his hands. His face became somber as he examined the creature. "I don't know what this is," he whispered.

When he looked up, disappointment spread quickly over his face. "I don't know what it is," he repeated, the discontent replaced by frustration. "How did you get it?"

"It was found on an elf," I said.

He stared off. "I'm sorry. I am old, but at times I feel young and new. Things are changing so much around me."

"Change is overrated," Winter offered sympathetically.

He nodded graciously, but his drab look remained as he walked with us toward the car. It was odd that Logan strolled leisurely next to Winter, seemingly forgetting about my existence as he talked to her. Their conversation was too low to really hear, but Logan was deeply interested in what she had to say. He stopped just a few feet from the barriers and took her hand in his. "I am sorry I wasn't able to help. I hope you do come to visit again."

When she gave a noncommittal answer to do so if she could, he was ecstatic. She maintained the same gentle smile until we drove away. She relaxed back against the seat. "He can't leave past the barriers. It's probably a curse or a ward he can't break."

"What makes you believe that?"

"You didn't hear his breathing change along with the coloring of his face. The closer he got to the barrier, the more erratic his heartbeat became, his skin flushed, and I could feel the warmth of it coming off him."

I focused on the road, feeling inept in my skills. I hadn't noticed any of that. How and when did she? Just when I had started to feel the apex of my failure, she said. "It's not easy for me, either. I have to try. Ethan and Sebastian don't. Steven is pretty good at it, too, and Gavin is better than them all."

"I should be better at it," I said. No matter how confident I started to feel in my abilities, I was constantly reminded that I was just a novice in this world. Even Winter had the ability to charm me into following her commands, which she did two years ago when I found myself bound to a book. It was the same thing she tried to do to Logan. I had given in freely while it had done nothing but provide him with a few moments of amusement.

I could feel her eyes on me. "What?" she finally asked.

"I was just thinking how easily I was able to be charmed by you, yet it didn't have any impact on Logan."

"It wasn't the same thing. When I did it, you were already in an entranced state. I just interrupted the source and redirected it. Pretty easy to do. I am not sure if it is my skill or my ability, but it isn't consistent. I've practiced on many of the pack members, even on Abigail and Gideon. It only worked on Gideon, a few lower-level pack members, Steven, and Gavin. It was a long shot with Logan." The smile she gave me was weak, and I pretended that it relieved my insecurities, but it hadn't.

It was close to nine when Abigail and Josh returned. Abigail fidgeted with her long braid as she spoke with Sebastian and Ethan. I could make out what she and Josh said; both of them having only normal hearing forced them to speak at a normal volume. Sebastian and Ethan always spoke too softly, barely moving their lips, which made reading them difficult as well.

Both Winter and I had the same idea, and walked over to them.

"So you have nothing?" Sebastian asked.

"Mason didn't take my request for assistance to help you at all well. And he must have put the word out because no one would give us any information," Abigail said.

Josh shrugged, his hands running through his hair several times. "Most people claim they didn't have any idea what it is. I have a hard time believing that so many people were killed by this thing and no one knows anything."

Abigail watched Sebastian carefully, aware that this wasn't the end. She would not be able to leave with her brother until Kelly was whole. "Even if Mason could help, he will not. Now that there is an alliance with the witches, he has a renewed sense of power. He feels invincible and no longer fears you as an enemy.

Sebastian scoffed, "Invincible? It will only be a matter of time before he no longer has any control; he has foolishly rendered Marcia too much of it. Your people will not be any better off. Instead, they will become victims of her thirst for even more power. She will destroy you from within."

"I know, but he was chosen to lead and most follow him blindly. I share your feelings and have voiced it too many times, that now, I have lost favor with him and most of my people," she admitted, dropping her head.

He was so angry, the natural color of his eyes disappeared in a sea of amber, exposing his wolf eyes. When he pulled out his phone, Ethan, anticipating his actions, spoke up first. "There will be no reasoning with him."

"Who else will have any information on elven creatures?" Sebastian asked.

Abigail shrugged. "Maybe the witches. I doubt they would enter any alliance with anyone blindly. They will know enough about us, maybe more."

That didn't make Sebastian happy. His frown deepened and the little line that formed around his chestnut eyes resurfaced. He cursed under his breath.

"Marcia will not help without an offering." Josh said, worried.

We all knew what that offering was—to break Josh's alliance with us. I doubt it had anything to do with Josh but more with the fact that he had proven to be one of the most useful assets we had. Losing Josh would weaken us.

"No," Ethan blurted. He pulled out his phone. "Give me a minute," he said and he ducked into the office.

. . .

It didn't take long for Ethan's phone call to manifest something, Claudia, his godmother. Dressed the most casually I had ever seen her, she wore a pair of dark slacks, a white short-sleeved button-down, and a multicolored scarf draped over her shoulders. It was close to eleven o'clock; the gallery had closed hours ago, so these were her lounging-around-the-house clothes. Behind her stood a tall, slight man, his lips pressed into a thin line and his eyes drifting over everyone in the room. His flushed cheeks against his goatee were the only things that stood out on his unremarkable features. His deep-set hazel eyes were hidden well behind a pair of dark rectangular tortoiseshell glasses. Nervous fingers ran over the brown mass that was starting to prematurely thin at the crown. Dressed in a tie, vest, jacket, and slacks, he looked as out of place as Claudia for a casual meeting, and he clung to a well-worn satchel. Even accompanied by the two tall, bulky men who probably could handle themselves in any situation, he still didn't seem comfortable in the house.

"He is one of the Creed's assistants, I think he will be helpful," Claudia said to Sebastian.

"Claudia, thank you," he said. "I owe you."

She shook her head. "No debts. It was my pleasure." She looked in Ethan's and then Josh's direction, and the gentle maternal smile remained as she insouciantly slipped her gloves off and grasped Sebastian's hand. He tensed, but allowed her to hold it for a long time. She smiled.

He moved closer to her and kissed her lightly on each cheek, then whispered something, but it was too low to hear. As she released his hand, he said, "It is good seeing you again."

She nodded. "And you, too." Before she crossed the threshold, she looked back at Sebastian, studying him with interest before giving him another faint smile before leaving.

The gentleman cleared his throat, pushing his glasses up his nose before clutching the satchel closer to his chest. "You are in need of my assistance. What can I help you with?" His speech was so sharp and formal, it surpassed scholarly and found a nice place near haughty. For whatever reason, he was here and not happy about it. He looked around the room at everyone, his brows raised slightly at Abigail, then he frowned at her before returning to Sebastian.

"Yes, follow me," Sebastian instructed him.

Dr. Jeremy was sitting at his desk, looking through the microscope, books sprawled around him on the floor and desk and a vial of blood next to him, when we walked into the clinic. He looked up at the stranger and hope gleamed in his eyes. Kelly eyed everyone suspiciously, while Gideon sat in a chair in the corner, a place where I am sure Gavin had not-so-politely extradited him to. Gavin stood next to Kelly and stepped even closer and frowned at the arrival of the stranger, which was quickly returned.

"Bernard." Gavin greeted the stranger with a sneer.

"Gavin, it is good to see you here. The new city must be a welcome change," he said with a smirk.

It seemed like Gavin was thinking of the many cruel ways he could respond, but after a quick glance in Kelly's direction, he chose silence.

Sebastian pointed to Kelly, and Bernard looked disinterested as he approached. His indifference continued as Sebastian explained the details of what had occurred. Dr. Jeremy added that the paralysis was progressing and that the same creature had rendered Gideon comatose.

"It was on you first?" he asked.

Gideon nodded.

Bernard looked puzzled before he turned to Kelly. "Madame, did things happen as they report?" he asked.

Madame? Did they let him speak with other people? Or was he only allowed out of his cave for jobs like this?

Once Kelly confirmed their story, he walked over to the table and looked at the jar that contained the creature. He examined it for a long time in silence, showing a growing appreciation for it with each passing moment.

"It's a sleeper," Gavin offered.

"Yes, a Tod Schlaf," he responded, keeping his attention on the creature, briefly but shifting his attention to Gavin, "but the boorish translation would be sleeper."

Bernard's attention focused on the wall as he relaxed into his thoughts, his arms placed in front of him as his thumbs rolled methodically over each other.

"Madame, you are not cursed, are you?" he asked, his back still to her as he addressed her.

Her brow furrowed, she shrugged and then looked at Sebastian, confused.

"No, she isn't a were-animal," Sebastian stated.

Biting down on his bottom lip, Bernard looked at everyone in the room briefly. "But you consort with the cursed. Would it be too much to ask why?" he said, finally giving her his undivided attention.

"I work here," she said softly.

"Are you indentured?"

"No."

Pushing his glasses farther up his nose, he seemed befuddled. "If you work here, I doubt your skills are substandard. Could you not find employment among the civilized?"

Her soft voice and limpid eyes tempered her harsh words. "I chose to work here because I like them and I like my job."

He made an attempt at a smile, crooked and forced. "You seem wise, but your choice in associates has shown a true lapse in judgment. I hope once this is over that is remedied and you find that your love of this job isn't worth what you will endure by sheer association"—he shot a disparaging look in Sebastian's direction —"with certain people."

Maybe she had grown tired of justifying her association with were-animals or she, too, was questioning the downfall of choosing to be part of this world. If she had dwelled in the world among the insipid, she wouldn't have been in this predicament.

"And your connection to Claudia, may I ask the particulars?" he asked.

I was positive Kelly didn't know Claudia, but without missing a beat, she smiled pleasantly. "Does it matter?"

His curiosity was snuffed by his irritation. "Yes, I am curious why a woman of such power and means, who chooses a position of abject neutrality, is so interested in your survival. Why have you been given such favor?"

I didn't bother to look at Ethan, whose face was probably expressionless, or Josh, who probably attempted to display the same.

Hmm, I guessed there was in fact more to Claudia than art, high tea, fancy gloves, tailored suits, and a soothing maternal attitude.

I added finding out what she was to the top of my list of things I needed to know.

Bernard waited for a while, and when he didn't get an answer from Kelly he turned to Abigail. "Do you know how to get to Elysian?"

Her face flushed red as she shook her head.

"You've never been considered worthy of an invitation?" he asked derisively.

Her lips were pressed closed as her gaze dropped to her hands, which she had wrung so roughly they had red marks on them.

He handed her a piece of paper. "These are the directions to Elysian. There, if granted admission to the dark forest, you should find what you need to help her. I can't offer any more than this, but it should help you. Whether or not you will be allowed entrance will be up to you. It would be in the interest of both parties that you choose the one among you all that would be considered least offensive to ask for admission."

"I will go with her," Gavin offered.

Our self-righteous helper laughed, a deep, hearty sound that would have been musical if it hadn't been doused by his derision. "If you wish to receive cooperation, I advise you not to flaunt the more unflattering aspects of their history to them. He would not be a good choice."

Gavin's gaze narrowed. "Why didn't they just get rid of me instead of sentencing me to the bowels of the world and holding a grudge that will outlive my existence?" he snapped, his Brooklyn accent thickening with his anger.

Okay, Middle America wasn't New York, but "bowels of the world" was just downright offensive.

Bernard smiled. "You hate it here? Perhaps the intended justice has been served."

Gavin ground his teeth so hard I waited to hear them crack. "Screw. You."

Gavin bumped his shoulder as he left the room. Bernard's lips were spread so wide into a grin he looked comical. "So eloquent and refined, I see why Jessica was so enthralled by him. Worth the shame her betrayal and infidelity caused Conner."

"Yes, Gavin should have been penalized for the loose morals of the New York council head's wife. Gavin is truly responsible for him not choosing a more suitable and monogamous spouse. And it definitely is Gavin's fault that elves are so simple that the actions of their spouses reflect upon their ability to remain on the council. No, it's not their flawed system that should be held accountable, it is definitely Gavin's libido that is responsible for the crumbling government of the New York elves," Dr. Jeremy chimed in, far more irritable than I had ever seen him. His face flushed with each word that spilled through clenched teeth. "Are you going to offer assistance or continue to pass judgment, Bernie?"

"Bernard," he responded with tension.

"Okay, *Bernard*," Dr. Jeremy responded.

"Your phone, sir," Bernard said to Sebastian.

When Sebastian handed him his phone he rummaged through

a binder from his satchel and took a picture of a photograph in it. "Find this and you will find the cure. It often camouflages itself among the trees, but will find shelter behind what it perceives as the vilest predator. This is how it survives because its defenses are weak in comparison," he said.

He pulled out a pen and paper from the satchel. He scribbled something on it, then handed it to Abigail. "I wish you success in this endeavor," he said, and then he looked at Kelly. "It was a pleasure meeting you. I hope you maintain your favor with Claudia; it will serve you well in the future."

The curiosity that I saw in Gideon had been ignited in him as well. I wasn't sure why they didn't understand that everything revolved around one thing—guilt. It was the catalyst for all that had occurred. An emotion that worked better than a threat, promise, or even passion because it gnawed at your very being until you exhausted all avenues you had just for the chance to relieve it.

"Thank you for your help," Kelly said genuinely.

We all should have shown some form of appreciation because we were further than we ever would have been on our own, but it was really hard to be appreciative of a man who was such a raging ass.

CHAPTER 11

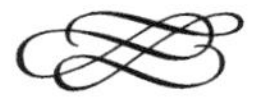

The next morning Abigail and Gideon led us through a wooded field. Thick, mature trees and bosk crowded the area. Twenty minutes we had traipsed through the thicket, following the directions that Bernard had given us.

"Why do they live separately?" I asked as we continued through the secluded, desolate land that would need severe construction before it could be habitable.

It took her a while to gather her words, and when she spoke, it was slow; each word was chosen with great consideration. "They are different than those of us that populate this world. Most of us are products of a relationship with someone other than an elf. Gideon and I are among the few that are considered 'unchanged' that do not live in Elysian."

"Unchanged?" I asked.

"They are full elves, from a pure line," Sebastian offered.

There was a hint of envy in her voice, as though she had been deprived. Had she been spurned and never invited to live in Elysian?

Gideon snorted. "They're snobs, the strongest of our kind, and they do not care to descend from their ivory towers to ever consider associating with the likes of us. A world of only self-professed royalty. They are arrogant, narcissistic jerks that my sister and I would never join no matter how sweet the offers were. They make the vampires seem humble."

So they had been invited, but it must have been a package deal, and Gideon couldn't be persuaded to join them.

We stopped in the middle of the woods. The trees looked dull, unkempt, and barely alive, the greenery and soil spoiled as though someone had salted the land so nothing could truly flourish. There was no way this was Elysian—the celestial land, their nirvana. No one would willingly live here, let alone a society of people. The sky paled, smothered by the clouds that filled it. All noise seemed to cease, silence—immense, bleak silence. Abigail began to read the supplication on the paper. Whatever it was—which I assumed was a very extravagant glamour—dropped. A slit in the area opened wide enough for a passage of one body at a time, forcing us into a single file line.

As soon as we were in Elysian we received a king's welcome, or rather a king's mortal enemy's welcome. Ten uniformed guards met us at the entrance, faces impassive and cold. They moved in unison, a well-regulated militia, dressed in blue button-down tunics with large single-breast pockets similar to Swiss Army jackets, complete with epaulets on the shoulder.

They parted, forming a pathway as a gray-haired gentleman came through. His intense silver eyes complemented the color of his hair. There weren't any signs of aging on his deep taupe skin. Standing nearly six-five, he was slender but solidly built. His attire was a little too gentle for his stern appearance: a tailored two-button ash gray linen suit that hung neatly off him and would have washed out his appearance if not for the contrast of a striped pear-colored shirt. Gideon hadn't exaggerated about the snobbery. If he had looked any farther down his nose at us, his eyes would have crossed.

"Sebastian, what brings you here?" the shrewd man asked.

"He is here on my behalf. I am humbly requesting entrance into the dark forest," I said in the politest and most reverent tone I could manage, just as Abigail had instructed me. She said he would take offense if we didn't acknowledge his importance and that he was the only person who could allow us entrance.

He laughed. "You? Who are you, little one?"

Please, be more condescending.

"I am Skylar Brooks."

He smiled at my effort and repeated my name several times. It lost its intensity with each vocalization. By the time he finished, my name sounded flat and dull. As I suspected, he decided I wasn't anyone. Being polite was getting a little harder. I was getting tired of people assuming I was defenseless, incompetent, and innocuous. No one would dare question Winter wanting entrance to the dark forest. "They will accompany me," I said, pointing to Ethan and Sebastian.

"Perhaps he should go instead of you. The dark forest is not fit for someone like you," he said as his gaze cruised over me in flagrant disregard and fixed on Sebastian.

"Liam, I do believe that would be best," Sebastian stated diplomatically.

I forced myself not to shoot him dirty looks, but one slipped by. Was that my purpose? To have Liam scoff at the ludicrous notion of me going into the dark forest only to suggest that Sebastian save me from my delusions of grandeur and protect me from myself by going in my place? I was itching to say something and nearly sliced my tongue in half trying to bite back my words.

"So *you* will be the one requesting entrance into the dark forest. May I ask why?"

"My friend, a human, was bitten by a Tod Schlaf," I said.

His eyes narrowed and I was sure he wondered how this had happened and, more importantly, how a human had come in contact with it. But I doubted he would ask because then it would reveal that either he had a traitor among his people or someone had slipped into Elysian without his knowledge. People like him would never admit to such a flaw.

"Then it is *you* who is actually asking for entrance," he said as he directed his attention to Sebastian. A newfound interest accompanied his Cheshire cat smile.

Sebastian nodded.

"Excellent." He whispered something to the man next to him, who left and returned with a scroll—a contract. "If I allow entrance, then you must acknowledge you are indebted to me."

"Of course." Sebastian looked down at the scroll. "We usually use an honor system. It is widely known that if you renege, there are severe consequences."

With unnecessary pomposity, Liam sneered. "The honor system among those that have proven to have very little. How trite. You will not be offended if I choose something a little more official."

Poor Gideon; he obviously didn't know the difference between a snob and a condescending jerk—Liam was definitely the latter.

Liam handed Sebastian the scroll and he read over it carefully. "There is no way in hell I'm going to sign this," he said. "You do not think we have honor; however, no one I've ever been indebted to would dare ask these things, nor would I of someone else. You want this signed, then take these things out." His hand pointed to several things on the list.

Liam looked at them carefully and glared. "You are requesting a favor of me and yet you make demands of what you are willing to do to fulfill the subsequent debt," he asserted incredulously.

"What you are requesting is beyond reason." Sebastian stood taller as he met Liam's austere glare with derision.

Sebastian stepped closer to him, his features as hard as stone, amber rolling over his eyes in waves. The man who initiated this deal had stepped aside, and allowed the predator to finish it. "I will gain entrance. The only question now is whether it will be over the dead and badly injured bodies of your people or on more amicable terms. I would prefer on good terms. But the choice is up to you."

Liam considered him for a long time. The sour look on his face would not relax. "Save your energy for the forest, you will need it." He whispered a few words, his finger ran over the lines, and the letters vanished from the scroll. "Better?" he asked as he turned it toward Sebastian, who looked at the new contract and nodded.

One of Liam's guards handed Sebastian a knife. He hesitated, his grin spreading the length of his broad face. I was sure he was imagining shoving it into Liam's chest, but instead he pricked his finger and signed the blood contract.

Liam said, "You do realize you will have more than just cross words to contend with if you ever default on this."

Sebastian simply nodded, brushing off the implied insult in a manner that only he could—by making someone he had obligated himself to seem inconsequential.

"Very well, a guide will be by to escort you."

I could have stayed there forever. The trees were tall and so green they looked artificial. I touched several of the leaves to make sure they were real. Many of the trees around the vast area bore fruit and avocados. The thick grass was neatly manicured. Small scenic lakes were surrounded by stout trees. I really hated to admit it, but this place *was* a nirvana, perfect right down to the temperature: just a couple of degrees warmer than outside. A herd of animals that were a cross between a horse and an okapi trotted toward us, guided by two riders, a male and a female.

The woman dismounted first. "Abigail, Gideon," she welcomed with a smile. Like staring through a contrasting mirror, our guides looked like Gideon and Abigail. The fact that they were twins was undeniable. The male features were soft—effeminate—and the female look was striking and androgynous. Her long titian hair was pulled back into a French braid, his hair a neatly cut coif that looked like he had taken a great deal of time making sure every strand was in place. They looked out of place dressed in their finest J. Crew. Their apparel was just a little too trendy for this place. He wore a white shirt, pin-striped tie, and dust gray chino pants. She wore a deep gray cardigan sweater, pink camisole, and light gray slacks. It wouldn't have been my first choice of clothing for riding bareback on a pseudo-horse.

Abigail was quite friendly when she greeted her elite twin counterparts, but Gideon didn't care to be bothered with such niceties. His eyes rolled in their direction—his frown hardened his appearance.

It had been nearly twenty years since my mother thought it would be adorable to photograph me on a Shetland pony. She never got the picture of me happily riding the animal, but instead settled for a photo of a red-faced girl scrambling as fast as she could to get off the pint-sized menace. I had planned to go a lifetime without ever reliving that experience. The creature didn't have a saddle, just a long mane that draped along its elongated neck. There wasn't any way I was going to be able to ride it without a saddle. "I don't know how to ride," I admitted.

"She can ride with me," Ethan suggested. I looked around the group for options. Ethan and I were playing nice, but I didn't want to cozy up to him while galloping through elf land. The male guide smiled. "She will be fine, they take very little skill." He patted one of the animals, then made a simple command, and the odd okapi/horse bowed down so that I could mount it. Once seated, it shifted until I was placed squarely on its back.

We rode for a long time before we stopped abruptly at a line that clearly delineated Elysian from the dark forest. The forest wasn't just dark: it was stygian and gloomy. The apparent ward that separated it from the mainland was strong; the hairs along my arms stood on end. The elves possessed strong magic, and I had underestimated them.

Our female guide got off her elven horse. “This is as far as we go.” She handed Abigail a small scroll. “This will allow you entrance and exit. The words can only be spoken twice, don’t lose it or … well, you know what will become of you.” She smiled politely.

She stroked her okapi/horse before she got on the animal her brother was riding. “My animal will guide you on your return.” Her brother patted the horse and it galloped quickly away, traveling double the speed it had with us. The animal’s stride increased to a speed so fast it looked airborne as it whisked them away.

Standing next to the line that separated us from the dark forest, there was an imperceptible discomfort that was hard to deny.

“You’re with me,” Sebastian said to Gideon, who simply nodded at an invitation that most people would have declined. Then Sebastian turned to Ethan. “No matter how long I am in there, don’t come after me. Okay?”

Ethan shook his head. “I will give you an hour.”

“Ethan, don’t come after me,” he said firmly.

Ethan frowned at the request.

“Understand?” Sebastian asked.

After a long moment of silence, he still hadn’t answered. Steven often said the strength of the pack rested on the fact that it had two Alphas. Ethan was strong, resilient, and a true leader. Sometimes I wondered if he never challenged Sebastian because he didn’t think he would win or because he couldn’t lead as well. Sebastian waited patiently for him to come to whatever terms he needed before he agreed. Reluctantly, Ethan nodded.

Gideon’s lips pressed gently against Abigail’s forehead. He read from the scroll, slowly, having more difficulty with the language than his sister. The earth that separated Elysian from the dark forest waved in deep convulsions before it opened, forming a small tear in the fabric big enough for a single person to pass through, as with the opening leading into Elysian. Sebastian entered first, then Gideon slipped in just as it started to seal.

It suctioned closed and the self-protective urge to reduce the chances of being swallowed up forced us to take several steps back. Ethan stood close to the barrier, eyeing it in anticipation. Eventually we both were standing near the spot where the rip had first occurred. The earth bulged in sporadic ripples, expanding and reaching out toward Ethan. He tensed as the waves stretched out farther, grabbing out for him. He closed his eyes, taking rough, sharp breaths that were soon reduced to sharp gasps. Perspiration glistened along his brow, his lips quivered, and the muscles of his body clenched and relaxed spastically. He dug his heels into the ground, each step heavy and labored as he stepped back. He lumbered until his back was against the large willow tree near us. Panting, he slumped against the tree until he was fastened to it. He then dragged himself around it until he was as far as he could get from the wall. The activity of the barrier stopped and came to a calm as he settled against the tree.

He wasn't recovering. His eyes withdrew into a glazed cloud. I touched his cheek; it was pallid and damp. "What's the matter?"

"I need your help," he gasped. His skin was icy and clammy. Sweat drenched his hair and matted it to his skin. Unfocused eyes tried to hold mine, but wavered often and periodically rolled back.

"What do you need?" I asked, clasping his face between my hands, but he was too far gone to focus.

"Help me change," he said in a weak voice. He leaned farther into the trunk as he struggled to take off his clothes. Frustrated that a simple task had become an extraordinary feat, he collapsed back against the tree. I helped him remove the rest of his clothing, ignoring Abigail's curious gaze. Stronger were-animals could help with the change of a weaker one. Ethan, who was dominant to me, now looked like if I touched him too hard he would keel over. When he slid to the ground, I crouched over him.

I wasn't very proficient at changing myself. It often took too long, and by the time I finished, I was sometimes too exhausted to be of any use. He leaned into me, resting his head against my shoulder. I had never considered doing this and had no idea what to do. Placing my hand over his shoulder, as both he and Sebastian had done when they helped me change, I tried to change to my wolf in the hope that it would facilitate a change in him. It was getting harder to concentrate as Ethan's fingers crushed into my skin. He started to change, and for the first time since I had met him, it wasn't a smooth, controlled transition. The bones cracked, making a keening, crunching sound. Shrill screeches filled the air as soft tissue was pulled to its tensile point, barely holding the limbs together. Then there was the sound of hair puncturing through the skin, which seemed to cause him a great deal of pain. He winced and groaned through the whole process.

After several painstaking minutes, Ethan lay on the ground, panting, in wolf form. Trembling, he moved just enough to drop his head into my lap. Stroking his fur gently, I looked back at the invisible wall that had now gone dormant.

Abigail started toward us. "He's okay," I said quickly.

But she continued toward us. "He's fine, stay there." My tone gripped her midstep and she quickly reversed. I added a "thank you," but the damage was done.

He moved closer and then drifted off to sleep. When he awoke, he didn't move, lying stilled against my leg, his massive body rising and falling as he took deep, labored breaths.

The dark forest where the elves hid their creatures of destruction really wanted him. Why did it want the were-animal that had the ability to break protective fields and perform minor magic? He had stopped my heart by just touching me. He was something dark.

The moment we entered Elysian, the screen on my cell phone went blank so I had no idea how long we had been there. I suspected just a couple of hours, although it felt like nearly five.

Gideon emerged first; his typical smug look of indifference had been replaced by shock and trauma. Dusting the dirt off his pants only caused it to blend more into the blood and dark liquid that covered it. As Abigail approached him, he tugged at his shirt, making a futile attempt to cover the long scratches on his leg and smeared blood on his pants. There were thin cuts running along his hand and forearm. Sebastian's shirt was ripped, and deep claw marks ran along his shoulder and back. A couple of puncture marks were indented in the top of his arm. No one was brave enough to approach him. He was on high alert and defensive, any wrong move and I was sure he would have attacked.

For a long moment he stood motionless, taking long, calming breaths, trying to find symbiosis between man and animal that would allow him to proceed. He was in a dangerous place and I didn't know how to help him. Several moments passed before he seemed to embrace any part of humanity. His eyes were still a deep amber as flickers of brown fought their way to the surface. He didn't seem surprised to see Ethan lying near the tree, but if he were, I would never have known. I never really knew what was going through his mind unless it was what he wanted. He approached Ethan slowly, wincing with the slightest movement. Fatigue now slanted his appearance, but he seemed more concerned about Ethan than himself.

Gideon's gaze fell somewhere between intense trauma and apparent esteem as he watched Sebastian. The more time anyone spent around Sebastian, the more it was apparent why he was the Alpha. His carnality and dominance radiated and enclosed him like a graphite shell. But like so many, Gideon must have fallen victim to believing the stories about him were just whimsical embellishment. Sebastian was a beautiful monster and so were most of the were-animals. Often it was realized too late to do anything about it.

If we weren't supposed to draw attention to ourselves on the way out, we failed. We trotted on the elven creatures at lightning speed across the plains with a wolf in tow. The moment we neared the wall separating us from Elysian, it opened wide, an unsubtle request to leave as a bastion formed blocking all but forward movement. We dismounted our odd horses and they quickly ran away. We started out of Elysian. The moment Gideon, the last of us, slipped his leg onto the ground, the opening sealed.

CHAPTER 12

"Where is it?" Gavin asked, meeting us at the door with Dr. Jeremy on his heels.

Sebastian handed the jar to Dr. Jeremy, who eyed it with disbelief. "This?"

He nodded. "It will draw out the venom."

"Then there has to be contact with her?" Dr. Jeremy asked, studying the jar closer, his lips pulling into a disapproving straight line at Sebastian's affirmation.

He then moved in slow motion as he prepared Kelly, cleaning her skin and explaining what had to be done. Kelly listened, nodding slowly. I doubt she cared; she just wanted it to be over.

Please let it work. I said it over and over, a supplication to anyone that could help.

If this didn't work, we didn't have a lot of options or even another viable lead. We had already lost a day looking for this and more of Kelly's body would become paralyzed bit by bit. Dr. Jeremy held the container and looked inside it, reluctant to proceed.

"Jeremy," Sebastian urged in a low voice.

He nodded, but still didn't move. When he finally did, it was with slow burdened steps in Kelly's direction.

Gavin turned to her. "Don't look," he said. With a gentle touch on her chin, he guided her attention to him and repeated his request. She nodded, took a deep breath, and closed her eyes. But it was a promise that she was only able to keep for a few seconds. "Don't look, okay?" he said again in a concerned whisper.

Dr. Jeremy's shoulders slouched as he proceeded, exhaling a long, measured breath. He looked at the small creature again before finding the ability to unleash something that had once resided in the dark forest on his protégé.

He placed it onto one of her legs and we waited. The minutes crawled by and we continued to wait for the little critter to decide whether or not it was going to get off its creepy-crawly ass and do something. Instead, it lay there for a few more minutes as though it was sunbathing in the heat of her skin.

Kelly's curiosity once again bested her and she looked back at her leg. With his fingertip on her chin, Gavin guided her face back toward him. "Eyes up here, young lady," he said with a grin. For a long time her gaze stayed fixed on his. But as each minute passed, she struggled to stay engaged.

It finally moved. First the pale blue creature sidewinded along the length of her leg, then stopped near the top and like a leech bored into her. Blood spilled as it waddled deeper in and out, then it inched farther up her leg and did it again. It was a good thing she couldn't feel anything.

Gavin's hand was flat against Kelly's face blocking her view, pressing her into his chest. He frowned as the creature continued to burrow into her. We had one of the strongest witches on this side of the country at our disposal, two elemental elves, and the finest doctor in the world, and we were reduced to using a magical leech to treat Kelly.

As the thing continued to slog up her leg, dipping in and out of it, leaving pools of blood in its path, Kelly screamed—it was bloodcurdling. She could feel it now. Dr. Jeremy looked relieved, but we couldn't stop it until it was finished. Another agony-filled scream pulsed through the room as she sobbed uncontrollably into Gavin's shirt, her nails clenching into his back. Her right leg snapped up and attempted to kick it off. Dr. Jeremy grabbed her leg to stop her and held it to allow the little leech to finish. Each time she wailed, he winced.

"How much longer?" Gavin asked. It seemed like an hour, although I knew it was just minutes. But hearing Kelly's tortured cries and knowing there wasn't anything we could do about it was a personal hell.

"I don't know, this is my first time, too," Dr. Jeremy lashed back. He exhaled and stepped back, tightening his arms around his chest. The long breath he managed to take calmed him, but he still kept his distance, probably ensuring that he didn't stop the creature. Would we have to start over and subject her to this torture again?

He couldn't give her anything for the pain because he wouldn't have known if it worked.

"Maybe she should take a break," Gideon suggested softly. Still shell-shocked from his adventure to the dark forest, it was the first time he had spoken. I thought he and his sister were trying to melt into the background, eventually leaving unnoticed after Sebastian forbade them to leave. Dr. Jeremy's finger pressed on the belly of the leech, holding it in place.

Kelly sobbed uncontrollably, unable to focus; Gavin held her face between his hands and waited until her eyes eventually connected with his. "Do we need to stop?"

She tried to speak through the sobs. He rested his hands on her shoulders as she heaved erratically. Her head dropped, and she couldn't stop crying. Her usual unshakeable persona was nowhere to be found. "Look at me," he commanded softly, forcing her head up. She just couldn't compose herself. He waited patiently. "Kelly." His tone was harsh enough to force her attention back to him. He leaned into her. "I need you to answer me," he said in a firm, gentle voice. "Do we need to stop?"

She closed her eyes, biting down on her lips as she gulped down the last sobs. "No. Go on," crackled her weak voice.

He smiled and she struggled to return it, but a subdued grimace was all she could offer.

"Continue," Gavin said.

Dr. Jeremy hesitated, studying her, and just when her breathing was normal again, he released it. The parasite continued, burrowing its way through her, drawing out the venom. Dr. Jeremy was the one who finally broke: he started to grab the creature as it resurfaced, but it was finished. Lying flat against her skin, barely able to blend against the backdrop of the legs, it remained immobile.

She pressed closer into Gavin, clinging to him. His shirt was stained with her tears as he calmingly rubbed her back. Dr. Jeremy quickly collected the creature.

"You okay?" Gavin asked, his full lips twisted into a grin.

"Piece of cake." Her voice was low and rough. She was still panting, eyes red and glistening with unshed tears. She sucked in her bottom lip, which was red and raw from her biting on them.

"It looked like a cakewalk," he joked.

His thumb swept gently over her face, wiping away the remainder of her tears as he waited for Dr. Jeremy, who moved quickly to clean the exit wounds left by the creature. It was hard to be gentle and quick, and he seemed to work at hiding the marks before she could see them because they looked worse once the blood was removed. He quickly slathered on a cream he pulled from the cabinet and spread it over the marks before bandaging them.

She winced. Gavin leaned in closer to her, his head relaxing against hers as he brushed her coarse ringlets that were now drenched with sweat from her face. His lips rested just inches from hers. For a brief moment he lost himself, inching closer to her. He was about to kiss her when he moved back with a powerful jerk. It didn't seem like he could gain the distance he needed between them. Busying himself with helping Dr. Jeremy, he wrapped her legs; he kept his head down. Her brow furrowed in confusion and faltered into disappointment as she kept looking in Gavin's direction, waiting patiently for him to look at her again. He only glanced up once he was finished wrapping her leg. "Jeremy will take great care of you," he said before leaving. She kept looking at the door long after he disappeared through it.

Her legs weren't ready for the quick thrust of weight placed on them as she attempted to stand, and they gave. Sebastian moved quickly to help steady her, but she pushed his hand away and used the bed to pull herself up and stabilize. She stood for several minutes before she hopped back on the bed looking as though she had filled in for Atlas and now the world wasn't hanging heavy on her shoulders.

"How does it feel?" Jeremy asked.

"Good," she said. "I'm okay."

Fifteen minutes later, Abigail fidgeted, ready to leave while Gideon skulked in the corner where he had stayed the whole time, quietly observing everything.

Gideon only stayed around long enough to say good-bye to Kelly. I guess I expected more than just a wave of his hands and an indolent "thanks" as he left.

Abigail watched him leave. "I think he knows," she said with a frown. "He needed to know." She looked to me and Sebastian nodded graciously to us. She kissed Winter lightly on the cheek, and then pressed her forehead against hers. "Thank you so much for your help. I don't know what I would have done without it."

"Of course," Winter said, but she seemed distant. As though

she accepted that this was the end. This hadn't rekindled their relationship.

Abigail backed away, just a couple of feet from the door when Sebastian asked, "When did you decide to try to kill your brother?"

She jerked her head back as though she had been slapped. "What?"

"Please, we both can do without the performance and the pseudo-ignorance. When did you decide you were going to try to kill your brother? When did you realize it wasn't as well thought-out as you anticipated?"

Her face was blank, her lilac eyes devoid of anything readable. "I don't know what you are talking about."

Winter's eyes widened as she stared at Sebastian, who glanced in her direction, giving her a moment of consideration.

"You murdered your own people to keep up this deception," he added.

"I did no such thing! I didn't have anything to do with that, but I saw an opportunity and I took it." She turned to Winter, who was flushed, her mouth slightly parted. Her face gave away her various thoughts although she seemed to have lost the ability to express them. It was when the anger manifested that she lunged at Abigail. Sebastian moved in time to grab her around the waist and keep her at bay. Winter struggled at first, but soon relaxed against his vice-like steel grip into a calm.

Sebastian held Winter securely against him, speaking to her in a soothing, low voice. After several moments, she had settled into a quiescent state, and he released her. The anger was gone, replaced by a bitter indifference directed solely at Abigail. I wondered if the opposite of love was indifference, instead of hate.

Abigail appealed to her. "Winter, it was only a matter of time before it was done to him. I controlled the situation and made it work to our advantage. It doesn't diminish the love for my people, but proves the depths of it. My brother should be the leader. He has the potential to restore us to what we were. How can you not understand that? It wasn't my intention to hurt you. You have to believe me."

I didn't believe a thing that came out of her mouth and Winter didn't seem to, either. Once you attempted to kill your brother to push him into power, it was hard to have credibility. Winter's lips furled as she looked at Abigail and then she dropped her eyes, refusing to look up again.

Abigail continued with her impassioned speech, dividing her attention between Winter and Sebastian. "He needed an incentive. He squandered his life, wasting time on trivialities and behaving as though he was ever meant to have this life as his own. My father wanted a predecessor to continue his legacy. The sole purpose of Gideon's existence was to continue the name my father established. Do you understand what he went through, the debts he accumulated, the favors he called in, just so he could have a child, a son? And Gideon has just made a mockery of a life that was expected to accomplish far more," she asserted, raising her voice. Finding calm, she stepped closer to Winter. She went to touch her cheek but Winter jerked away. "Mason did it to the others. I didn't have a hand in that. Gideon was a threat to his position and it was only a matter of time before he came for him. I am protecting my brother and in the process making sure something good comes out of it," she continued.

Winter's frown softened, but was devoid of forgiveness. She simply shook her head. "You knew I would help and that I would bring him here. You didn't just risk Gideon's life, but Dr. Jeremy's as well."

"I didn't use you, Winter," she said softly. "You know if I were ever in a position to help you in any way, I would. My feelings for you didn't end because the relationship did."

"How convenient that mine didn't, either. The difference is that I would never ask you to help me betray my family or my pack. You haven't changed at all. Power over everything. You care nothing about your father's legacy or fulfilling his dying wishes. You want to be the sister of the ruler of the elves. You know that you can never rule because of their antiquated sexist laws, so you plan to do so by proxy. Gideon listens to you and will do anything you ask of him. You are a piece of work," Winter said as she walked away. She pushed her way past Abigail and left.

I expected a lot of vitriol from Sebastian, but there was nothing. He was calm and professional, as though what Abigail had done wasn't a horrific act of betrayal. He was unequivocally composed and placid. I wasn't sure what to make of it.

With an unexpected confidence, Abigail turned and approached him. "There is no doubt who will rule us by the end of the year. You saved Gideon's life. His memory is long and it is something he will not forget."

Draped in passivity, Sebastian didn't respond. Everything made him angry, yet this paramount betrayal didn't seem to bother him. Then it dawned on me: he wasn't angry because he knew. He had known all along and her confession was just a formality.

He stepped closer to her, his striking appearance dulled by his pensiveness. It took a while for him to respond, and when he did, it was soft, intended for her ears only. "A group divided will never prevail. That is something that Gideon should make a priority, don't you think?"

She smiled. "I agree."

Gideon would become the leader, and Abigail and Sebastian would ensure that there was a civil war among the elves. If Gideon won, great, Sebastian would have the elf leader as his ally. Someone that felt indebted to him because he had saved his life. If he lost, the war would leave them weak, no longer an asset to the witches, who would quickly sever their alliance. The witches wouldn't have the strength in numbers that they hoped the alliance would give them. They wouldn't want to be allies with a people going through a civil war. Best-case scenario, Gideon would get a taste of power and his disdain for Liam would work to destroy them. It was a win for Sebastian in any case. In one sweeping act, Sebastian and Abigail had ended the alliance with the witches and orchestrated a civil war.

Abigail was careful with her words as she spoke. "Kelly interests him, and it would be a good match. She is untainted by—" She stopped. Manners wouldn't allow her to say *impurity*. "She would be easily accepted as his companion and her commitment to you would be advantageous."

Was this really happening? Were they bargaining with her like she was property, a pawn in their sick little game of power and manipulation, to use as needed, sacrifice if necessary, barter when fit? I was just about to voice my opinion, even though I didn't have to. If Kelly ever gained knowledge of this situation she wouldn't have had a problem telling Sebastian or anyone else her thoughts in the most scathing way possible.

He chuckled, but any amusement was absent. "Let's get this straight. You fumbled your way into success with this, and it came with a big cost. Instead of possibly killing Dr. Jeremy, you put Kelly in harm's way." The fuse of his anger was lighting quickly. "I will not forgive that." His icy tone caused her to take a step back. "You were willing to sacrifice your brother, I don't care. But she is not part of this, and you will never involve her again."

"She was a casualty of this situation and it was not my intention for her to be hurt," Abigail rebutted quickly.

"But she was."

A woman who masterminded her brother into power while giving an award-winning performance didn't strike me as one that would scare easily. But the ominous look on his face made her stand up a little taller. The cloying look on her face faded. "If I am not mistaken, you having her here in any capacity put her in harm's way. I am not to blame for her predicament; you are. If she continues, I doubt this will be the last time her safety will be compromised. Your only hope will be that Gideon values her enough to protect her life, too. You seem as though you may need some assistance in that matter," she stated, matching his tone.

"I assure you I will not need your or your brother's help with this," he said confidently.

Once again, her voice was casually soft and entreating. She started to slowly walk the space in front of her, and the cruelty that Winter had spoken of peeked through. "My brother is easily distracted. The women he has entertained himself with lately aren't fit to run their own lives, let alone be responsible for others. She would offer the needed stability for him. They would be a good pairing. She cares a great deal for your pack and I believe would steer him toward decisions that would greatly benefit it."

She had it all figured out. Her brother was nothing but a puppet that she controlled with her strings of manipulation. He would rise to power, thinking that his sister was his number one advocate, ignorant of the fact that she was the puppeteer. He would get married, a union arranged by her with the person she felt would best suit her cause. There was a hungry glint to her. She didn't do it for her brother, for her people, or because she thought her brother was the best choice—it was for power. Who was I kidding? It was always for power.

I couldn't believe that all this time I had been naïve enough to believe that empires were built by hard work and strategy, only to discover that they were built the same way they were destroyed—from within, through backhanded dealings, manipulation, deceit, and secret alliances.

"They will be a good pairing for us both," she said. Her unrelenting gaze was a subtle threat that she could easily deny.

Sebastian's eyes shifted to the floor for so long that it seemed like he had forgotten she was there.

Was he considering this? Was this what happened? Were people's futures handled like commerce, discussed and exchanged for favors? Sebastian was silent, giving her his undivided attention. I was just seconds from voicing my enraged and unsolicited opinion.

He stepped closer to her, straining to keep the pleasant look on his face. "Your brother will stay away from her, and you will stay away from Winter," he said firmly.

"I can't stop his attraction to her. And as far as Winter is concerned, I do still care for her. I always will. But I care about my people and my brother's positon as leader more. It is unfortunate that Kelly was hurt in the process. If I could have had it any other way, I would have."

Sebastian's chuckle lacked warmth; in fact, it was dark and portentous. "I'm sorry. I didn't make myself clear. That wasn't a suggestion, it was a command. The topic isn't up for debate."

A gentle bend played at her lips and moved effortlessly over her features. "I am not part of your pack, so your commands mean nothing to me. But I can see how you would forget that. Today has been quite a trying day for us all." She looked directly at me then back to Sebastian. "Especially for Ethan. It has been exceptionally trying for him. Will you give him my regards?" she said as she headed for the door. "But today, and all that has transpired, should be forgotten. Don't you think that is a good idea?"

Snuffing his anger seemed impossible; the veins bulged on his neck as the muscles tightened. He simply nodded in agreement. Yes, Sebastian had benefited from the deal, but the clear winner in this situation was Abigail.

CHAPTER 13

Ethan answered the door and stepped aside to let me in before I could complete the knock. A half-empty box of pizza, several mystical books, and his laptop covered the large cognac-colored ottoman. He pushed it aside, giving me more room as I negotiated around the crowded space near the sofa. The floor was cluttered with more books and stacks of paper with messy script scrawled on them. Usually his tailored clothing flattered his physique, but now he didn't look like himself. His well-worn jeans and loose t-shirt hung off him casually and he wore the trials of the day heavily on his face.

Taking a seat across from him, I sat comfortably in the oversized chair and waited for him to speak. After nine minutes of silence, I realized that if it were up to Ethan, Mercury would rise again and we would still be sitting on the sofa with less than five words spoken between us.

Where did I start? A bastille for the creatures the elves created that were too heinous to live among the general population wanted him. It was where their mistakes were sequestered and hidden from the world and was attempting to retrieve portentous creatures. It had tried to break open just to claim him. I always considered Ethan dangerous, but on a smaller scale. I truly had no idea.

"What are you?" It felt odd being the one asking that question when Ethan had asked me the same thing so many times.

He sank back into the sofa, and his lips formed a severe line. It took a long time for him to speak. His hands roughly washed over his face. "My grandmother was a dark elf; she died eight days ago."

You didn't just blurt something like that out. You eased into telling someone that. You said something like: as of eight days ago I became death. Witches', fae's, and elves' magics are never destroyed; the gifts are passed on through bloodlines. Wolf magic often prevented things like that from happening, but obviously it wasn't an exact science because Ethan had inherited some of his mother's witch magic upon her death, although most of it was passed on to Josh. Since Ethan and Josh were only half-brothers, and the dark elf magic affected Ethan only, it must have been his paternal grandmother who had died.

"Do you have any aunts or uncles?"

He shook his head. Which meant he had inherited it all.

She was lucky to have been allowed to live long enough to see her grandchildren. How did she live her life? Did her life imitate Ethan's childhood in that she was forced to live with an absurd amount of iridium on her, or even pumped into her to suppress the magic? Was it in constant fear that she would be discovered? Was it a solitary life because she was too afraid to let anyone in? Living in constant fear that a simple uncontrolled touch could cause someone's death?

How much control did she need to make sure she could touch someone without killing them? To interact with Ethan without hurting or killing him. She had to know how to control it to some extent; after all, Ethan had learned to control it in just days and she had lived with it all her life.

"The other day, with me, was an accident, wasn't it?"

He looked down at his hands, watching his fidgeting fingers.

When he finally looked up from his hands, his steely titanium eyes were distant and indecipherable. "I am not as strong as she was, the wolf part of me controls some of that." He shrugged. "It gets better each day."

Well, maybe he believed it, but his words lacked the confidence to make me believe it.

He slumped back onto the sofa. He looked so defeated, like a wounded animal just moments from being put down. Now, he was forced to battle constantly with how he interacted with people and trying to contain his new power. Making sure he had control in even the most minor situation. At any given moment, he could have killed Josh.

"What happens now?" I asked. Well, I knew what was supposed to happen. Based on the agreement, he was supposed to be "contained." The idea of it made me sick. It was a stupid rule initiated by the elves and it needed to be overturned. "Does Sebastian know?"

"Yeah, he is the only one that does." He smiled weakly in my direction. "*Was* the only one that knew."

I didn't know what to say. Things had changed. If anyone else found out, then they were obligated to adhere to the covenant. Of course, anyone in the pack would honor the secret, but eventually something would slip, someone else would find out. Maybe Abigail would use it to blackmail the pack. Or what if someone like Demetrius found out? I was sure he was itching for a way to get back at Ethan. But I found some comfort that soon Gideon would control the elves and maybe he could change this.

"Does it work?" I asked, pointing to the iridium-cuffed band around his wrist.

He shrugged. "I don't know. I had it on in Elysian and it didn't seem to work."

I looked over the mass of books sprawled over his sofa, table, and ottoman. The witches could remove magic from witches as punishment. Could the same be done with elves? I'm sure we would need more than just Josh, and the witches would rather "contain" the situation than help Ethan. To them it would be just one less were-animal in the world. With Ethan out of the way, Josh could be easily persuaded to end his alliance with the pack.

"We need to get the Aufero," I said.

He nodded thoughtfully. "I thought about that, but I have no idea where it is."

"I do," I blurted. "Well, not exactly. I have an idea where it may be." I grabbed my purse and pulled out four pieces of paper and laid them out in front of him. The sketches became more detailed, focusing on different parts of the room. "I saw this room that year I was in the in-between."

"These were done at different times," he said, inspecting them. "Why?"

His deep inquiring gaze made taking creative liberties with the truth impossible. "I visited it again, recently," I admitted.

He frowned. "With Josh, I presume."

I nodded.

"You have indeed become one of his weaknesses." His voice was rough with disappointment. He sighed, then returned his attention to the paper in his hand.

"Better me than anyone else. I will never hurt him, betray him, or point a gun in his face," I said, reminding him of when Chris had done just that when we first met.

"You say that now," he mumbled under his breath as he studied the sketches.

He placed the laptop on the ottoman. His fingers clicked away on the keys, preoccupied by whatever was on the screen as he kept glancing up at me. Several times, I caught him watching me. From the printer, as he retrieved the pages he printed.

"Are you sleeping with him?" he asked, the deep gaze demanding a response.

"With who?"

"You know damn well who. Are you screwing my brother?" he snapped.

I am not sure why I didn't just give him a straight answer; it would have made life a lot easier. "It's *your* brother; maybe you should ask him about his personal life."

"He wouldn't tell me."

"Probably because it isn't any of your business," I pointed out as I reached for the list. He held on to it. My gaze didn't waver as it fixed on his.

Damn, he is intense. Okay, let's just make this easy. "We can sit here all day while you speculate about what goes on between me and Josh in the bedroom, but we both need the Aufero. Don't you think we should dedicate our energy to looking for it?" I took the papers from him and laid them on the ottoman so that we could get a better look.

"What is this?" I asked, pointing to the odd symbol from my picture.

"It's a protection symbol, most people have them simply for the esthetics. If enchanted correctly, it weakens all magical beings that enter the shop. Marcia would never have a real one where she keeps the Aufero, because it would weaken it and her as well. I've seen them in all of these places, but I am not sure which ones are real. We will have to go to them."

I took a pen and marked off the ones that I had gone to. He looked at the list, now slashed by a third, and smiled.

When he extended his hand to help me off the sofa, I hesitated before I took it. He pulled me up and he stood close. Leaning down, he pressed his forehead against mine. Then his lips brushed lightly against mine. It wasn't a kiss; his lips just remained there, warm and inactive. He smiled, then stepped away. "It's getting easier."

Oh great, he had decided to practice his death touch on me. *Glad I could help, buddy!*

I pulled my hands back. "What does it feel like?"

"Chaos. If I'm calm, I can control it better. It's harder with you around," he admitted.

He reached out and touched my arm and held it again. The tension relaxed and the weight he had carried since I entered his house lifted. There was a buoyancy to his smile. "It's a lot better."

During the day, we went to each place. Ethan didn't hide his ability or even care that I knew that he could detect magic, something that were-animals shouldn't be able to do. Even when I hadn't borrowed magic, I could still detect it. Since our visit to Logan, I wondered if my skills were a "Sky" thing or a "Maya" thing. We walked through each store, inconspicuously looking for secret rooms, eyeing the protection spells to determine if they were authentic. Sometimes, if the owner watched us too long or became suspicious, we purchased something. After we visited each store, we'd narrowed the list down to three.

It was eleven o'clock and all the shops were closed. We could go through them undetected to look for the Aufero. Ethan opened the door and gave my outfit a once-over: a bright fuchsia modal t-shirt with a panda bear on the front, jeans that had seen far too many tumbles in the washing machine, and muted silver slippers. I wasn't exactly dressed for a heist, but neither was he in his work jeans and wrinkled button-down. He made a quick change out of his clothes into a black shirt, dark jeans, and boots. Still not heist wear, but a step up from his sloth appearance.

He gave my attire another look and frowned.

I said, "We are about to commit larceny. If we are caught, who will look like a criminal and who will look like an employee who came back to the store to pick up her forgotten bag?" I tapped my head and winked. "You have to think outside of the box."

"I assure you, no one will believe someone would hire you knowing this is your manner of dress," he said with a derisive smirk.

"Well, I plan to get them to 'see my reality,' while you will be seeing the inside of a precinct."

"Let's not get caught."

Ethan sped through the traffic, once again taking the speed limit as a mere suggestion. I sank into the soft leather of his car, gripping the dashboard and pumping on my imaginary brakes. Deep in thought, he was more than happy to maintain our comfortable silence and for a while, I pretended to be as well. "What do you do for the pack?" I asked.

"What?" he asked, shifting gears and whizzing even faster through the traffic. My nails dug into the leather as I pressed back farther into the seat wondering if this overindulgent sports car could survive a crash with the Tahoe we barely missed as he darted around it into the next lane.

"It's harder to kill us, but not impossible. I am pretty sure going through the windshield is going to hurt like hell and put a dent in our plans."

A sly smile played at his lips, but eventually he slowed down. The silence continued. It wasn't like when I was with his brother. There was rarely silence between me and Josh, and when there was, it was different.

"What do you do for the pack? What is your job besides Beta? Josh manages the pack's club." I was using *manage* in the loosest of ways. Whenever I visited the overcrowded hot spot in the city, Josh was "managing" his way to the nearest table full of barely clothed beautiful women with a tray of shots, which he usually helped them finish. During one of his *managing* duties, I found him escorting a group of drunk men and a soon-to-be groom, and two scantily clad women who I was sure were exotic dancers, to the VIP section to help the group celebrate his commitment and monogamy with liquor and a lap dance. When he wasn't *managing* his way to partying with the local rap artists, pop princesses, boy bands, and up-and-coming musicians, he was with the "it crew" ensuring that the club remained on the list of places to party. The charismatic witch had perfected that part of managing the bar. It was a good job for him, allowing the flexibility he needed to be available to the pack.

"Sebastian is a day trader and owns real estate, Steven's a student, Winter is an IT consultant. I'm still not sure what Gavin does, and I don't think anyone else is, either. What is your job?"

After receiving my first quarterly check, I envisioned the pack's homes being swarmed by a SWAT team or some overly dramatic sting operation. Where did they get money to own safe houses, buy state-of-the-art jammers, and pay people off? There had to be a source, and although I hadn't traced the foundation of most of the money, it was comforting that it wasn't coming from the seedy underbelly of the world: human trafficking, drug trade, and organ acquisition. It was odd how that was where my mind went in regard to that being their source of income.

"I'm an attorney," he admitted without taking his eyes off the road. The smirk flaunted the absurdity of his admission.

My gut started to hurt from suppressing the laugh. If I didn't let it out, I was going to have irreversible damage. I laughed, wiping the stream of tears from my face. Why was this so wrong? Oh, right, because he lied for sport and there weren't too many laws the pack or he wasn't opposed to breaking, and he had a general disdain for human beings, which was probably made worse because of his close dealings with the corruption of the human spirit.

"Criminal law for two years, then I switched to corporate," he said as the amused grin lingered. It was a much-needed break from the stressors in my head. I didn't think about how we were going to somehow sneak the Aufero out of a locked building, or how we were going to thwart the wrath of Marcia once she found out it was missing. And once we had the Aufero, how would we do the spell? And would it actually work?

Instead, I fixated on Ethan as a criminal defense attorney and the baleful glare he had to give every time someone lied to him. How many times did he threaten to kill someone just for ticking him off? Corporate law probably didn't bother him much. Hiding behind torts and contracts, he probably interacted with people minimally, and the venality must not bother him, either.

I should have known the first two shops would be a bust, because things never were that simple. Neither of the quaint buildings would be the chosen safe house for the Aufero. The cramped metaphysical bookstore we visited first didn't require much of a detailed search. It was easy to detect that there was nothing there except overpriced books, crystals, and incense.

The second store was larger, which gave me hope. Ethan's frustration was starting to escalate. We were easily camouflaged in the dark alley and the Dumpster we parked behind adequately kept us hidden and close to the back door. Ethan pulled a tablet from the glove compartment, powered it on, and his fingers worked quickly over the screen. "The alarm shouldn't go off," he said.

Lawyer. I chuckled to myself. But it wasn't like he was a policeman, with a job to uphold the law. He just needed to be able to defend himself or others when they were suspected of breaking it. He took out a small case from under his seat and quickly got out of the car. By the time I had joined him at the door, he had it unlocked.

I shot him a dirty look when he turned on the lights. "You draw more attention when you are fumbling around in a shop with flashlights."

"Seems like you are speaking from experience."

Small bottles of colorful oils ranging from yellow to turquoise filled the shelves closest to the cash register. Next to them were various herbs, powders, henna, and metals. Candles on the far end, and books on Wicca, spirituality, and Tarot reading were stacked along the tables in the store. The largest shelf held an assortment of alchemist's and wiccan protection stones. The tranquil yellow walls were covered with symbols of protection, prosperity, and wisdom. There were other symbols, but I couldn't remember what they were for. Now I cursed my poor study skills, because Josh had gone over them at least a dozen times, but the subtlety of the markings made learning them even more confusing and they had all started to just merge together and look alike. But I did remember that you couldn't pair certain symbols; that would make them ineffective. I just couldn't remember which was which, and that's why I had a cheat sheet in my phone.

Ethan was efficient with searching the place and after we had gone over every inch of it, we went to the next location on our list. We entered the third shop. I walked around the large store, the symbols were on the wall, just like in the picture and in the three other stores. The other ones held magic, weak magic. This one didn't. Marcia wouldn't want her magic weakened under any circumstance. "It's here," I said.

"Are you sure?"

I nodded as I moved quickly toward the back of the cluttered space that had more things in it than the other two places combined. I was drawn toward the door on the other side of the store where the smells of the oils were more potent, and the powders tainted the air with a caustic aroma. The symbols on the wall were mixed with blood and henna, and Ethan smelled it as well. There was magic at the other places, weak, negligible, almost missed. But strong magic was performed here, and the people who possessed it had used it recently, leaving their magical imprint throughout. Josh said that when magic left a fingerprint, the owner of it, if necessary, could be traced. Here it would be undistinguishable. Too many fingerprints marked the air. I didn't know whose magic it was, but I definitely knew it had been performed excessively here.

With a quick jerk, I tried to break the lock, but it was sturdier than it looked. When it didn't budge, I shoved my shoulder into the door, and after several hard hits, the lock gave as the door splintered at the frame. This shop was a front, because the back room was the real attraction. From the outside it looked like a small extension of the building, but the large beveled mirrors on the back wall gave the illusion of a larger space. There was a mahogany conference table with five chairs placed against the opposite side. Across from the table was a large wooden chair, with sigils placed on the back frame. Leather restraints were on the front leg and arms of the chair. Silvery-white colored links were attached to the restraints, which I was sure were laced with iridium that would render anyone with magical ability helpless.

The strum of magic floated from an armoire in the corner. I moved closer to it. Through the glass I could see talismans and books on the first shelf. Ebbs of light reflected from the glass, and with each step closer, the light pulsed harder. An object on the second shelf shone brighter, illuminating its deep mahogany house. My scribbled drawings could never have prepared me for the presence of the Aufero. Its power was a combination of magic left by the many witches that had fallen victim to its misuse. A miscellany of various levels of magic that cumulated into a power far greater than anything I had experienced. But there wasn't any purity to it, the way Josh's magic felt to me. It felt similar to Ethos's magic, a muddled dark force that could never truly be wrangled into control, something that used its purveyor as its servant.

When I was inches from the armoire, the shuddering increased. Then the doors thrust open, revealing it. It looked just as it had when I had seen it in the in-between: a diaphanous silhouette enveloped it, and it pulsed waves of magic toward me. I opened my hand and it propelled itself there, molding to it for security.

As I cradled the Aufero, the door of the room blasted open. Ethan skidded hard through it, his back slamming into the wall. A medium-height, slender woman with oddly frosted short hair came in behind him. I barely noticed the four other people behind her, because my focus stayed on her. Josh was a level one and considered the strongest of their kind, which made me wonder what she was. The magic that came off her in waves easily eclipsed his. I didn't need an introduction; I knew I had finally met Marcia.

Ethan attempted to stand. "Stay," she said with a quick nod in his direction, and he collapsed to the ground. Then she turned her attention to me. "Give it to me," she demanded.

I pulled it closer to my chest. "No."

The Aufero glowed, pulsing energy that seemed to hold her at bay each time she dared to approach it.

"Now!" she barked angrily. The walls bulged, straining against the force while the floors trembled underneath. I struggled to stay upright.

"No."

She sucked in a breath, cold charcoal eyes echoed back at me just as they did when Josh called upon stronger magic. I braced myself for her worst.

Nothing.

Her lips moved quickly, her arms spread wide, the room rumbled again, the lights flickered, and Ethan was pinned against the wall, wincing in pain.

I stood unaffected. The Aufero shone and shuddered, which only fanned the flames of her anger. An indomitable shield of magic protected me from anything she could dole out.

She couldn't hurt me. It was hard to keep my ego in check. There was no way in hell she was getting it back. Intoxicated by indestructibility, my intention was to get Ethan and me out of there.

The field that now surrounded me protected me from her wrath, but I couldn't perform magic while enveloped in it. I concentrated as I had done many times with Josh and broke the field. Shattering it in pieces, I stood just feet from Marcia and the others. The magical energy was strong and now all I had to do was use it to my advantage. My finger moved against the crisp air and the four witches pounded hard into the wall. They struggled to get free but I held them there. I had magic at my disposal, but not the skill. If I had, I would have made them vanish. Instead, I thrashed them against the wall until they were nearly limp.

"Let him go," I said.

"You are way out of your league. If you want to walk out of here with him alive, you will relinquish it to me." Her wave of magic tugged at me. Like a storm, it ravaged the room, easily dominating anything that Josh had exposed me to. It thrashed against me, slamming me into the wall. Her finger clawed at the air, then moved toward her as she tried to pry the Aufero from me. It clung to me. Marcia was relentless, calling on stronger magic, yanking at it.

I pushed back and forced her into the wall, harder than I had anticipated. Her eyes were totally black, and the room rumbled from her rage. No matter how strong the Aufero was, I lacked the ability to rival any of her attacks. Two of the witches had already released themselves from the wall. I wasn't going to win against five powerful witches. I erected another field, just in time. A force slammed into it, and waves rolled over it. It collapsed inward, but the shell continued to hold.

Her attention quickly turned to Ethan, and with a wave of her hand, all the other witches, who were secured against the wall, crashed to the floor as he remained pinned, arms outstretched, legs immobilized.

"Give. It. To. Me," she demanded.

I didn't respond. She glared at me, then went back to Ethan. The mirrored glass wall shattered into pieces. Shards of glass sped toward him.

"Give it to me," she said, her voice strained as she concentrated, keeping the glass at bay.

I closed my eyes for just a fraction of a second. I tried to erect a protective spell, push it in his direction—nothing. The Aufero shed a light radiance; its magic felt dormant as though it had served its purpose, which was to protect its Moura.

She grabbed one of the larger pieces of glass from the mass that floated in the air. Her features were taut, eyes narrowed to lines as she concentrated. She was quite powerful, but this was a task that required a level of skill that was not easily accessible to even the most powerful witch.

"I've always been curious how much a were-animal body can endure before it shuts down from shock and dies," she said, inches from Ethan.

"Relinquish it to me," her strained voice demanded again.

When I didn't, she shoved the glass into his stomach. His eyes shut and he winced, biting into his lips. A deluge of blood spilled when she removed the shard. He struggled, but without success.

"Stop struggling. You'll need your energy," she said in a sadistically calm voice.

The fingers moved just a hair through the air and the fragments of glass moved back several inches. Enough of a distance to accelerate, inflict more pain, and cause more damage.

"I didn't realize you all had a Moura. That explains quite a bit. Your pack has been quite busy. Do you have any others?"

Gasping for breath, Ethan ignored her question.

She waited a moment, his silence sparking more anger in her. Smiling, she swiped her fingers across the air, and several pieces of glass embedded into him. He cringed but did nothing more. Not a scream, a howl—nothing. When she did it again, I screamed, though he endured it in silence. Then he slumped down, pinned against the wall by her magic and the pieces of glass shoved into him. His clothes were sodden and crimson with blood.

I dropped the field. "Here."

"You know I can't have it once it is in your possession. You need to relinquish it to me. Give up ownership," she demanded heatedly as though I had intentionally disobeyed her.

"Fine, I relinquish the Aufero to you," I snapped.

She exhaled a sharp, annoyed breath. "*Praeditos,* the Aufero is relinquished to you. Say it."

I repeated her words. The Aufero pulsed, heating to the point it singed my fingers. I tossed it to her, hoping it would burn hers, too. The orange and yellow light that pulsed in it smothered to gray, then black. Death. I waited for it to glow again, which it did after just a few moments.

"I accept," she said softly and then she disappeared along with the four people who'd accompanied her. I doubted they had gone far; probably waiting around to ensure that we left. I moved toward Ethan and pulled out the pieces of glass two at time. There were seven in all; three were fused into his legs, one in his chest, and the other three in his shoulders.

He moved unexpectedly well for a person who had been stabbed by thick pieces of glass, and refused my assistance, hobbling his way to the car. He was agreeable to me driving home, which was the worst decision. It was a manual shift, and it was a bad time to learn how to drive one in a car that cost more than I made in a year. He tried to instruct me the best he could and each time he winced, I wasn't sure if it was from pain or the fact I was driving in the wrong gear. It stalled just four times, but by the time we arrived at his home, I was sure he probably would need his car serviced.

The pain had increased enough that he willingly accepted my help to get him into the house. "A manual transmission is stupid," I said as we went up the stairs.

He managed a weak smile. "It's the only way to go."

He plopped onto a leather seat, leaving a trail of blood behind him.

"My Civic has an automatic transmission and a cool little camera that keeps me from running into things. You would think that BMW would catch on," I said with a hint of amusement as I looked under the cabinet in his kitchen, then his bathroom, in search of a first aid kit. I knew he had one.

I couldn't have cared less about automatic or manual transmission, but I wanted him to concentrate on more than his injuries. As I gathered the supplies from the bathroom, I tried to prioritize them. The ones on his leg looked bad, and I definitely thought it would be a good idea to call Dr. Jeremy, but he declined. It didn't dawn on me until I was kneeling in front of him helping him out of his pants that looking for the Aufero might not have been supported by the pack. It would surely change the dynamics of the relationship between the witches and Josh.

"Wait," Ethan blurted once I started to touch him. He closed his eyes, taking several long, controlled breaths before nodding. "Go ahead."

This subdued version of him wasn't something I could get used to. He was hostile, short-tempered, and in touch with his wolf on a primal level. It wasn't his best attribute and made dealing with him a pain, but it was who he was. This was a manufactured version of him I didn't like. He seemed restrained, limited and unnatural.

Once the blood was cleaned away, the wound didn't look as bad. "I should have given her the Aufero sooner," I said, my guilt making it hard to make eye contact.

"That wasn't the goal. I didn't expect you to choose me over it."

I didn't know if that was an indictment of his character or mine. Did he think his life had less value than the Aufero to me? Did he think I was cruel enough to allow my self-interest to trump his life? Or was he projecting because that was what he would have done: let me die and walk away with the Aufero?

Instead of satisfying my curiosity, I continued to treat the cuts. No matter how I ignored it, I could feel his keen gaze on me. I glanced up in silence several times, chewing on my lips as I suppressed my questions.

"I would have given it to her, too."

"Well, I hope so; even you aren't that big of a jerk," I said with a half-grin. Relief. It shouldn't have made me feel unweighted, but it did. Ethan and I weren't going to ever be friends, I accepted that; but we were part of the pack, and he wasn't a bad person to have your back.

He glanced down at my patchwork nursing, but it was just a moment. I assumed that if he gave it too much attention the calm that he had worked so hard to achieve would crumble. Marcia's cruelty angered me, and she hadn't stabbed me with broken glass or threatened to slice me into bite-sized pieces.

When he stood, he winced, so I stepped back, giving him room to move. "She knows what you are. She will likely approach you soon," he said.

She could approach me all she wanted; it didn't mean that I had to talk to her or do whatever she asked of me. Or did I? Could she cast a spell on me that would force me into compliance? I doubted it. If that were possible, I was sure that Sebastian would have ordered Josh to cast one on me the day he met me.

"What would she want with a Moura?" But that wasn't the most important question. Why did the Midwest Pack want one?

"Your connection to the Aufero is stronger than hers is. I am willing to bet she thinks she can use it and you to find the other protected objects. More specifically the Clostra. Believe me, if she ever gets a hold of it, we are done. The first spell she will use is the one to kill us." He glanced at the clock. "It's getting late, and I am tired," he admitted softly. Desolation hung off his words. I was reluctant to leave, but Ethan insisted. He wanted to be alone and his mood made that very clear.

I couldn't stop thinking about the look on his face. It bothered me more than the fact that Marcia had the Aufero in her possession again. Sitting on my couch and trying to grab the final crumbs in a family-size bag of Doritos that I had devoured over the course of an hour, I couldn't get the defeatist look that had eclipsed Ethan's appearance out of my head. How long would it take before he would have his abilities under control? But what would his life be like? He was a person controlled so much by his wolf, his normal temperament could be easily described as hostile. How long would it be before he and Josh got into one of their typical fights and he accidentally killed him or someone else?

The more I thought of it, the less contempt I held for the elves and that covenant to "contain" dark elves. In a sordid way, it was a mercy killing. How long would it be before Ethan would require the same fate? My head was starting to hurt thinking about it. If they decided to continue to hide him, what would happen if his existence became known? How would the others respond to the pack's noncompliance to an agreement they had vowed to uphold?

I had to get the Aufero from Marcia, and I knew it wasn't going to be easy.

The light knock at the door was a welcome distraction. Quell's black eyes lifted to meet mine as I looked out of the peephole. I opened the door. He was paler than usual, and his hunger was apparent, but he pushed it aside and took a seat on the sofa. His gaze followed me no matter where I moved. His hand rested across his leg, the pensive look the only thing different about him.

"You're unhappy a lot these days," he acknowledged.

I stopped pacing the floor and took a seat next to him, but that wasn't any better because my fingers continued wringing the bottom of my shirt. I didn't stop until his hand covered mine. "It may give you some relief to talk about it."

Quell wasn't one to confide in. He was the odd vampire so far removed from humanity that he was a peculiarity even among vampires. Not as overtly cruel as the ones I had encountered, but his misanthropy somehow made him even crueler. His inability to connect with the basic nature of humanity made him dangerous. My guilt about being the one responsible for what he was today had me fettered to him in a way that was indescribable. He would never be a confidant because my emotions were something he would never understand.

But I was desperate and he was better than just talking to the wall. "I feel that there is always that line you cross where you can no longer consider yourself a good person. I have to do something kind of bad, and I think I will have to cross it," I admitted.

He listened quietly, and when he finally spoke, he gave each word careful contemplation. "Rules of good and bad exist in the human world, from which you seem to draw your ethics, but they are biased at best. People will act in their best interests, using various means to justify the most heinous of acts. If you are holding yourself to the same standards and ethics seen in the human world, then there aren't many things you should feel shame for. You do what is necessary to survive. I guess we all draw a line, but letting others define yours is futile and can be dangerous. I urge you to set your own boundaries of good and bad, because if you allow it to be set by others, it will lead to nothing but disappointment and self-loathing. Your life will become a pattern of self-deprivation because you fall short of what others have defined as human. Once that happens—" He stopped abruptly and sat in silence, drawn into his thoughts as I continued to wonder about Quell, the lost one. "Just don't let that happen," he whispered.

Sometimes my curiosity about him got the best of me, but he had discouraged my inquiries about his life before he was turned, stating that some tales of darkness should remain where they deserved to dwell. But how awful was his human life that he asked Michaela, the Mistress of the Northern Seethe, to change him from being human?

"I know nothing about you," I said. His vacuous look didn't make getting personal easy. "What was your life like before?"

"There isn't much to tell," he said, dropping his gaze. The cloud of despair rested heavily on him as his eyes stayed focused on his hands that fidgeted in his lap. After a long stretch of silence, he spoke so softly I had to scoot closer to hear him.

"When I graduated from college, I thought I would teach: liberal arts, psychology. Human nature once fascinated me. Somehow I was foolish enough to think I would mold the minds of a generation, and marry Clara, a woman I loved dearly. But fate had its own warped plans. They weren't supposed to draft the remaining child in a family that had lost others; it was a promise that the government upheld. But when my brother died serving his country for what he believed in, I felt that, at least for appearances' sake, I should show the same bravery.

"I felt sorrow for those suffering, but not enough to actively do anything about it. Shame was what drove my actions. So I enlisted." He took a long time before he spoke again. I quickly did the math in my head; he had to be speaking of World War II.

As many times as I had seen the atrocities on the History Channel and read about it in books, I couldn't imagine seeing it firsthand and not being irreparably changed by it.

He bowed his head; ignominy radiated off him, making his skin warm. Not warm like mine, but for some reason his skin didn't feel cool when I touched it. He wrapped his hands around mine. He opened his mouth to speak but all he had was silence. Finally, he found his words. "I was good at war," he whispered.

I didn't push it anymore. My curiosity had to be shamed into silence. But I was left wondering what he had done that now left him still brokenhearted. Did you ever forget the horrid things you had done? Or did you still wake up with night sweats, reliving the night you tortured someone? Did the faces of the people you killed in cold blood still haunt you? Was what he had seen during times of war so disturbing that he'd lost all hope in humanity?

He went on to tell me what it was like to walk over dead bodies that were tortured for an ideology. He said the word with such passionate disdain and loathing. He was less detailed as he brushed over the tales of torture as the recipient and the purveyor.

"I went there with the intention to do good, but somehow things went very bad. Once you see such devastation, you no longer care about doing a good deed—you want to seek revenge. In the end you become the very monster you thought you were fighting against. It is hard to consider yourself human. It is hard to consider others that way. As humans, you live by a code that dictates your humanity; anything that falls short makes you a monster, inhumane, evil. And you battle with that so long that …"

"You feel moral fatigue," I offered.

He mouthed the words "moral fatigue." I think he liked them, because there was a hint, just a wisp of a smile that emerged. "It brings things out of you. In your mind you want to do the right thing. To maintain yourself. It is a constant battle of trying to remain true to who you are and who you need to become to succeed. The more horrors you see, the harder it is to care one way or the other. Eventually, you stop caring."

Now his voice was emotionless. "I was such an idealistic young man. But once you've been in a war, you realize the world is small and limited by so much. It is easy for men to become monsters in the middle of hardship. And for the unremarkable to become heroes. And what you become has less to do with the character of the person and more about the situation. I became a monster. A monster that commanded and trained others to be and do worse than I had. Because I saw horrible things and thought violence and retribution were ways to make it right." He frowned before he looked away.

For the first time since I met Quell, I understood his fascination with being a vampire. They didn't have a standard of humane and inhumane behavior. There wasn't that constant need to stay in the lines of acceptable ethical behavior, because they didn't have any they adhered to. Vampires operated on a pleasure principle. Whatever made them happy was the right thing to do.

Quell had lost hope in humanity. He held them to the same standard that he held himself, and when he failed—he removed himself from it. So many had fallen short in adhering to the standards he set for humans, leaving him in a constant state of revulsion over the nature of humanity. I wasn't sure if I accepted that devolution was the norm or if his standards were too high.

My hand covered his. He stared at it and eventually slid his from under mine. Before I could say anything—he had vanished.

I hated when he did that.

CHAPTER 14

Claudia never looked surprised to see me, and when I showed up at the gallery just minutes after it opened she didn't make an exception. The gentle smile that always graced her lips remained as she said good-bye to the first patron. Her warmth was a pleasant distraction. Nothing seemed to shock her; it was probably from years of selling art at prices that would otherwise make most people flinch. Instead, she welcomed me with an air-kiss near my cheek. "As usual, it is a pleasure," she said with a courteous smile before she informed her assistant that she was going to her office for a meeting.

"What brings you by?" she asked, waving me forward to follow her into her office.

"I need to talk." I needed to do more than just talk; I needed a favor. Claudia was more than what she'd presented and had connections that I needed. I knew that, but I didn't know the extent of her reach and capability. Could she help me retrieve the Aufero from Marcia? At this point, desperation made whatever slim chance it was a viable option.

Once in her office, she slipped off the jacket of her pale blue suit and laid it across a wingback chair. The room was a reflection of her personality. The desk was cherrywood, antique with a matching credenza and an inkwell in the corner. It was a unique look of old world enhanced by the art that covered the walls and the beautiful sculptures that decorated the large room. The hardwood floors looked recently buffed and the brass handles on the drawers and windows were shiny and spotless.

Her expression changed. The smile fizzled and became a businesslike expression. Her lips a thin line; eyes expressionless. She moved to the corner and began to make tea. It was a lot more formal. "How do you take your tea?" "Just milk, please."

She placed the teapot between us and poured the tea. When she sat down with me, she gave me a small appreciative smile as though she had tamed the savage. I like coffee, usually black, and I didn't like tea. During our first "afternoon tea" she had stared in disgust as I dumped four cubes into it and then started to drink from the cup of colored sweet water with the spoon still in it. The look of vapid umbrage had remained frozen on her face. And when I'd dipped the biscotti into the tea before eating it, I'd halfway expected her to press her hand against her forehead as she fell back from a fainting spell, like in one of those old melodramatic black-and-white films.

Now I sat across from her. I stirred my tea, placed it on the table, my napkin already placed in my lap as I took a small bite of the biscuit before taking a sip of my tea while I wished for coffee.

After she had taken several sips of her tea, she sat back in her chair. "Kelly, is she Ethan's?" she asked.

The question nearly made me spit out my tea. *His*? What was wrong with this woman? *Step into the twenty-first century please.* The first time she met me, she had asked Ethan and Josh whose I was.

"No, she's Sebastian's," I blurted out, then backtracked quickly in order to explain. "Ethan requested the favor on Sebastian's behalf because she is one that the pack's protected," I rushed out before tipping the cup to my lips.

She nodded her head slowly. Something was off and I couldn't quite put my finger on it. This was the first time I didn't see her as the nice woman with the broad smile and extensive knowledge of art. Her demeanor was so formal and businesslike. In the past, I'd felt like I was sitting with a mentor, maybe even an older friend. At this moment, I was sitting with the woman who owned the largest and most successful art gallery in the city. The person who bought and negotiated paintings that could go as high as seven figures. This was a woman who had made unknowns into celebrated and revered contemporary artists in the city. The dynamics had shifted into obscurity and I didn't like it.

"In any other pack, Ethan would be the Alpha," she asserted, "but he seems to be content with his position as a Beta. I guess that is where the strength of your pack truly lies: in the benefit of having two Alphas."

She was quiet for a long time, and then she stood, pacing lithely in front of me. Her thoughts preoccupied her more than I had ever witnessed. The little lines on her forehead hadn't relaxed for a while. "Most packs destroy themselves from within," she said, smoothing the hairs in her tight bun. "I guess it is a hard predicament for one to be in when your second-in-command, the one you should be able to count on, is vying for your position the moment you show weakness."

She exhaled a breath, and her pellucid eyes watched me carefully. "Sebastian is a good leader. I like him. Most struggle with trying to attain power and doing what is necessary to maintain it without letting it consume them until they have lost themselves in the pursuit. He is ruthless enough to do the unscrupulous things necessary, but endearing enough for the pack to care and trust him. In his seventeen years of leadership, I've witnessed a substantial change in the Midwest. They are the strongest they have ever been." Her voice was low, just a mere whisper as she assessed the state of the pack.

Listening to someone's perception as an outsider was different. Claudia was part of this world, but considerably removed from it.

I would never consider the feelings that the pack had for Sebastian endearment. The pack was full of people who reaped the benefits of his strong and successful leadership. I wasn't sure if it was him that they loved or the rewards. "He is a good Alpha," I had to admit.

She stopped pacing, her gaze bearing into me hard. "Are they friends? Ethan and Sebastian, are they friends?"

This question was not as simple as it seemed. It wasn't inquiring whether they might go out for a beer, catch a game, call each other occasionally to say "what's up." She was asking whether they were close enough to die for each other. I didn't know how to answer that. When I'd first encountered them, they had had a fight, and if Winter hadn't intervened I wasn't sure if it wouldn't have ended in a violent challenge with one of them dead. But I remembered the concerned way Sebastian had looked upon Ethan when we were in Elysian. And then there was him inciting a civil war among the elves: was it done just to weaken them for the heck of it, or to ensure Ethan's and Josh's safety? Was that his agenda? Gideon in power was their hope to end the covenant that had forced them to kill off dark elves.

"Yes," I finally said.

Her smile was pleasant, a clear appreciation that I had taken time to consider my answer. "If he had to, do you believe that Sebastian could kill him?"

That question caught me by surprise and I grabbed my napkin and quickly wiped the tea that I had spit out off of my shirt. "I don't ... I don't know how to answer."

She took a seat in front of me. "If it was between destroying the pack and killing Ethan, would Sebastian be able to do it?" she asked, the low treble of her voice austere.

"I can't answer that." It wasn't that I couldn't answer it; I just didn't want to.

The searching gaze remained on me for a long time as she waited for an answer that I wouldn't possibly be able to give. Then she gently patted my hand and smiled. "It is a complex world, isn't it? Often hard to find your place."

Brushing off the topic as inconsequential, she asked, "What brings you here, my dear?" And just like that I was speaking to Claudia, the peddler of overpriced artwork. A woman who didn't have a problem selling you a six-figure piece of art as though she was giving you a bargain basement price.

Nope, I wasn't ready to abandon the topic. "In what scenario would Sebastian have to make that choice?"

Her smile was pleasing enough. "A number of things in this world have consequences that are as cruel as the one I just presented, if not worse. It is never a bad exercise to have an idea of where the lines are drawn between acceptable and reprehensible behavior. It is also good to know the potential of those that you consider allies."

Like everyone in this world, there was so much more to her, and for the first time it was a little dark and scary. "What do you think?" I asked.

A demure curl played at her lips and reached her eyes. "If I had that answer, I doubt I would have asked you. But I guess a better question would be: what are *you* willing to do to protect the pack?"

I considered her ability to foresee the future, but nothing was truly destined. There was always something major, and at times trivial, that could change the course of one's destiny. If it wasn't for the betrayal of a Southern Pack member, my life would have been quite different—simple. Now it was something I didn't even recognize anymore. Was I invested in the pack enough to say

"Whatever is necessary"? I didn't think I was. After what went on with me, with Kelly, and even with Ethos, I knew they were important to my safety. Watching Sebastian make a deal with the she-devil confirmed he would do anything for the safety of the members of the pack. What other back-dealing had he participated in to keep me safe, and others? Preoccupied by the madness behind the machine, I forgot to answer the question.

Perhaps Claudia sensed that I wasn't able to because she said, "Now let's get back to the reason for this visit. How can I help you?"

I explained everything to her, well, the CliffsNotes version of it. I left out that part about Ethan being a dark elf. I had a very strong feeling she knew by the tiny smile as I breezed over the information. Honestly, I was there because I felt lost and hopeless and there was a part of me that wanted her to swoop in like she did with Kelly and make it better. I would have been happy if she could just make Marcia give the Aufero to me. Should I have been ashamed that I felt that way? Maybe, but I wasn't. I wanted it to be over without anyone else getting hurt.

"It is yours, compelled to you in a way that magic can't restrict. As far as it is concerned, you are its human counterpart. It has an affinity for you, which is why it broke that ward to get to you in the shop. If you are near, and it senses your presence, it will come to you. Just like at the shop."

"Why now? If the pull is that great, why didn't I wake up with it at my doorstep?"

"Even magic has its limitations. Do you expect that Marcia or even Josh would be able to perform magic hundreds of miles away? The stronger ones have a reach I estimate at about twenty miles."

That wasn't comforting. Twenty miles was a long way for someone to be able to attack you with magic. I could only imagine strolling down the street, then bam! Crazy magic.

My curiosity had me distracted. Who was Claudia? Was she

acting on behalf of her duties as a godmother, or as something more?

"That's great, but I just have no idea where to look. I'm afraid to go back to the in-between, and there is no way Marcia will hide it in the same place."

"Of course she will not. The Creed's weakness has become Marcia. They have given her too much power. She has now become a self-appointed leader and they have bowed to her will."

"I gathered that."

"Unfortunately, like most leaders, her arrogance and thirst for power is her weakness." She scribbled something on a piece of paper. "The Aufero will be wherever she is. I would try her home first."

This was where the almighty witch that headed the Creed lived. It didn't fit the sadistic power-hungry person who had drilled shards of glass into Ethan, a two-story simple white Colonial home, the tan shutters and large backyard overpowered by Norway spruce and Canadian hemlock. Manicured shrubberies surrounded the house, and a small floral garden grew on each side of the stairs. I slid my hands slowly up the rails and was met with a wrought iron mat at the door where most people usually had welcome mats. The house was dark; I had watched it for hours and there wasn't any activity. She had to be gone.

The back of the house was a little darker; a small patio surrounded an uncovered oval pool. The water was nearly translucent with the help of a lot of chemicals that I could smell. Birchwood trees shaded the open area. I was grateful for the large hanging bosk that cloaked me as I slid the crowbar down the edge of the back door and tried to pry it open. It didn't budge. That was plan A, so I wasn't very disappointed. Plan B was noisy and destructive, but it would get the job done. As I prepared to strike the window with the crowbar, glass sprayed and I raised my arm just in time to protect my face from the shards. Small cuts laced the side of my arm.

The Aufero sprang toward me with force, slamming into my chest. It took me a minute to grasp what had happened. Just like at the store, it readily came to me. I shoved it in the bag and starting running from the house.

That was easy.

If I had learned anything in life, it was to never say it was easy or that it couldn't get any worse. I had made it halfway to my car when Marcia emerged from the house. A wave of her hand and I was thrown back several feet, crashing hard on my butt. The Aufero bounced across the ground several feet from me. I scrambled to my feet only to be thrown back again, her eyes eclipsed to midnight. There was something different about Marcia's magic; not dark like Ethos's, but dangerous.

Tree bark dug into my skin as she slammed me into a pine several times. Pressing against the force, I tried to release myself. With a large hunter's knife in hand, she rushed toward me. The Aufero pulsed hard, but nothing happened.

She came closer, gripping the knife, and just as she pulled back to stab me with it, the Aufero punched into her back. She gasped, dropping the knife and turning her attention to the orb. Even the most talented witch couldn't perform magic when distracted.

The orb moved through the air, trying to get to its Moura. It was close, and I moved closer to retrieve it when Marcia's hand sprang open. A bastion enclosed around the orb and it beat defensively against it in an attempt to free itself. I ran closer to it, but a strong force shoved into me, sending me into the pool. I quickly sank to the bottom. Without enough time to take a breath, I gulped water. Pushing myself from the bottom, I resurfaced. With the Aufero in hand, Marcia pushed me under again and held me there. I clawed at the water until I felt her arm and yanked it, pulling her in with me.

We fell back into the icy water. If drowning didn't claim us, hypothermia would. Grabbing my leg, she used her weight to pull me under, pushing me farther down before climbing up my body to get to the edge of the pool. I lurched up, grabbing the back of her clothes and yanking her back with such force she sliced through the water, losing all control. I hurried and pulled myself to the edge and then out of the pool. She sprang up, but I pushed her back under. With a positional advantage, I held her there, coughing up the remainder of water that had entered my lungs. The fight in her slowly died, and the small bubbles that came from her mouth and nose slugged away. Then they stopped.

I had killed Marcia, wicked witch of the Midwest.

Strong hands yanked me back and snatched her out of the water. They rolled her to her side, and she vomited water. The more water she expelled, the more her breaths came out stronger, unobstructed. She dropped back onto the ground, her eyes closed, her breaths now slow and steady.

Quell's disappointed gaze fell on me. I crawled over to the tree and pulled myself up. Pain flared with each movement. I grabbed the trunk for support. Quell's attention had left me and he lifted Marcia and carried her to the house. He stopped for just a moment to look back at me, and then at the Aufero clenched at my side. As if the sight of looking at me was too much, his gaze dropped and he returned his attention to Marcia.

My damp clothes were still matted to my skin, and my eyes stung from chlorine. Adrenaline was still pumping through me like a drug by the time I arrived at Ethan's home. He stepped aside, watching me cautiously as I walked into the room. Before I could sit on his couch, he said, "Wait until I get you some dry clothes."

Thank you for caring about my well-being rather than your furniture. I sat the Aufero next to me and sank back into the sofa. He started to say something but quickly changed his mind when I glared at him.

He glanced at the Aufero but didn't ask any questions, and I knew he wouldn't. The pack cared more about the results rather than the "how" and "why" of the matter. Consequences they considered as well.

Ethan handed me a towel as goose bumps ran over my arms as my body made every attempt to regulate my temperature.

"Is she still alive?" he asked.

I nodded, but I couldn't read how he felt about it.

"She'll want it back," he said.

"I want red velvet cake to be part of the food pyramid. We can't always get what we want. She may as well learn it now. "

Reading Ethan was always a difficult task; nothing ever betrayed him, and he remained expressionless. I expected him to be a little enthusiastic about me having the Aufero. Instead, he left and returned with a teal t-shirt and jeans and handed them to me. They probably would fit fine, but I really didn't want to wear any of his conquests' clothes.

"So do you have your own little women's consignment shop back there?" I jerked my head in the direction of his bedroom.

He shrugged. "People leave things here."

"People, or women?"

"People."

"Fine, then you can go back there and get me a guy's t-shirt; they're more comfortable." I shook out the cotton/Lycra blend t-shirt with the plunging V-neck, then tossed it to him. He didn't bother to try to catch it, but instead glanced down at the bundled fabric at his feet.

The arrogant smirk returning, he crossed his arms over his chest. "You're the one that's wet; I didn't think you would be so picky."

We had somehow reverted back to our comfy little place of battling wills and snarkiness. Fun times.

After several minutes of verbal fencing, I stood by the dryer, wrapped in an oversized towel, as we waited for my clothes to dry.

"She will not come after you for it," Ethan said confidently.

I didn't believe that for one minute, yet he seemed very definite about his assertion.

"Being a Moura will offer some protection, because you all are enigmas. We know there is a bond between you and the Aufero, but she doesn't know how strong. You now possess the power to do what she has done to many other witches. She'll stay away because she doesn't want it done to her."

He had pointed out something that had gone through my mind several times since I had arrived at his house. I wanted to render her powerless. How easy would it be to divest her of her power? Remembering what Josh had said, I knew that the spell required a great deal of power from other witches. But I wasn't sure how it worked with the Aufero. It held the magic that had been taken from witches as punishment over the past twenty-five years. And soon it would be used to remove the dark elven magic in Ethan.

"It shouldn't be hard. The Aufero should do most of the work," he said once I was dressed and on the sofa as he reached for the Aufero placed in my lap. It pulsed, and a diaphanous shimmer surrounded it, protecting it from him. The wall thickened until it was devoured by it. He inched back, and after a few minutes the wall slowly dissolved.

A tight smile clung to his lips. "I guess I will walk you through it," he said. Pulling out a paper from a locked drawer in his desk, he handed it to me. Each step to the spell was laid out so meticulously that anyone should have been able to do it, but I was still nervous.

"Shouldn't Josh be here?" I asked. We were about to perform a powerful spell and I wasn't entirely comfortable doing it with Ethan, the bootleg witch. Most of his life he had denied his magical ability, so I was sure he hadn't mastered it.

"You can do it," he said confidently. The ability to embolden people and make them feel like they were invincible and able to meet all demands was a gift that he and his brother shared.

"When you read, it must be continual; you can't break the invocations. If you stop, then you must start over. Okay?"

I still held on to my twinge of doubt that I would be able to rip the death out of Ethan.

Confident eyes foolish and desperate watched me as I placed the candles on the oversized ottoman as the paper instructed. Ethan was as meticulous as the spell, readjusting them to make sure they were an equal distance apart. He handed me a knife, which I would use to draw blood.

Why is it always blood? Why not a strand of my hair, a tear, a flake of dandruff, or something?

The gentle tenor of his voice pulled me from my thoughts, firm but confident. "You can do this," he repeated.

Just because you say it a bunch of times doesn't make it true. I bit down on my lip, coaxing my self-doubt back.

I smoothed out the papers that were already lying flat on the surface, then I fidgeted with the candles and repositioned the knife several times, but ended up placing it back in the same position.

"Whatever happens, you can't involve Josh. Understand?" Ethan said.

There was no way I was agreeing to that. The phone was discreetly placed next to me so he was just one button—specifically number four—away.

"Promise me you will not involve him."

"Your constant protection will form the resentment that will eventually destroy your relationship with him."

"I didn't ask for your advice, just your compliance."

The bitter silence was all I could offer as he waited patiently for a response. He leaned forward to touch me, to get my attention I assumed, but I lunged back, too far, jamming my back into the sofa a few feet away. I winced, a sharp pain shooting through me.

He slowly reared back, his cheeks flushed, as he looked away, speaking in a barely audible voice. "There are many things in my control, but far more that aren't. I protect him because the things that I can't control are the things that could hurt him the most. You may not see the point of what I do, but there is one. I ask that you respect that. Please, don't involve him," he said softly, the concern barely masking the pain of me moving so quickly away from him.

I didn't want him to touch me. I was afraid of him, in a very different way than usual. He was death, not just the threat of it. But it wasn't his fault. Once again, I couldn't help but think the sanctions held against the dark elves weren't an act of cruelty but of grace. It was to save them from a life of restrictions and limited possibilities. I wanted to apologize, but I wasn't sorry. His agitation could have led to my death.

Ethan was one who had difficulty controlling himself because of his animal, which he had years to learn to control. He had only had days with this new power and I doubt he had mastered it.

I moved slowly back toward that ottoman and then knelt in front of it. He took his position at my side. I stretched my arms out until my hands were flat against the ottoman and in front of me. He hesitated before he moved closer. His eyes closed, he inhaled a deep, slow breath, and he extended his fingers to touch me. When he was just inches from me, I fought the internal protective urges that he triggered. He needed this. His hands lingered over mine before his fingers intertwined with mine. "Please, don't get Josh involved."

I nodded, but we both knew it was a half-hearted commitment.

He smiled. He held my hands for a long time. This had to work because he couldn't live like this. He was afraid of himself, unfamiliar with the body he had controlled for so long.

With the Aufero in hand, I started to recite the invocation on the paper, following it word for word. Ethan rested back on his heels with a confidence I wished I possessed. The knife sliding over my flesh only stung for a moment. It was a feeling I had become accustomed to. I continued whispering the invocation and waited for him to do his part. It didn't seem difficult for him to inflict himself with the cut before touching the opposite end of the Aufero.

I could feel it, a shift in the air, an angry burst of wind engulfing the room, a keening howl. Objects moved around us in fury, glass shattered in the distance, and the room filled with magic so strong waves of it prickled and lingered on my skin; the Aufero expanded, stretched so far I raised my arm in anticipation of it shattering. It rebounded with force and when it expanded back, the power of it sent us across the room. Ethan crashed on top of me, the bookshelf collapsed to the floor, objects slammed into us. Ethan was my shield and soon everything came to a calm.

He remained close, his breath warm against my face. He moved his head slightly, and his lips brushed lightly against my skin. It seemed like a million years ago when him being this close would have made me uncomfortable, and now I relaxed against him. His heart was beating erratically. "Are you okay?" he finally asked, as we remained stilled against the floor, our ragged breathing finally slowing to normal. We lay in silence, his body enveloped around mine, his lips brushing against the nape of my neck. I was vividly aware of everything around me, the sound of his breathing, the warmth of his body, the way his lips felt against my skin.

By the time we were standing, the Aufero was pulsing against the ottoman, the sunburst coloring smothered by a dark fog. It throbbed for its survival, expanding to the brink of destruction, then relaxing.

The Aufero wouldn't stop moving. There were erratic bursts of color as it attempted to regurgitate what we had forced into it. As though it was resolved to its fate, it calmed, but lost its vibrant color, now a burnt orange. What type of magic had the Aufero pulled from Ethan that had devoured it, leaving an eclipsed version of its former self?

For nearly five minutes we stood in silence until I couldn't deal with it anymore. "How do you feel?" I finally asked. It wasn't what I really wanted to know, but saying "What the hell was inside of you?" felt downright rude. So I picked the alternative.

"Fine," he admitted, his gaze shifting to the changed Aufero.

Once again, we were standing across from each other, the unspoken words screaming in the silence. He moved slowly as he started to clean up, starting with the candles that had been extinguished. It was nearly an hour before everything that wasn't broken was put back in its original spot.

The Aufero had accomplished something that no one could—it saved someone from being "contained."

"If your grandmother was able to hide, I'm sure there are others. We can use this to convince the elves that they no longer need to 'contain' the dark elves, but instead remove their magic," I said.

The small smile he gave me was encouraging, although it was to placate my idealistic views. It was done in that same encouraging manner in which a parent urged their talentless child to pursue their dreams. He might as well have patted me on the head, and said, "Of course you can catch the rainbow, you just have to try harder." And he would continue with his small smile at my failed endeavor.

"I'm serious."

"I know. You want to save the world, but realistically, you can't." He stopped and looked up. I couldn't read his expression:

not quite blank; there was a hint of something. Admiration? Nope, that wasn't it. Pity? Maybe I was getting close. Concern? I thought that was it.

"No, not the world, just people given a death sentence for being born into something they can't help. Maybe we could work out something with Mason and save the lives of these people." Or Gideon. Based on what I had experienced of Mason, he didn't seem willing to work with Sebastian under any circumstances, which only made me appreciate the potential change in leadership.

Ethan's smile of amusement and condescension remained. But I didn't care, I rambled on about the possibilities and what this meant for the elves and everyone. No longer faced with the obligation to commit manslaughter the Aufero had opened a new door for me. I wasn't going to be discouraged.

"Letting everyone know you have the Aufero and what you are capable of doing with it isn't a good idea. You are part of this pack; just by association people will be reluctant to trust you because they will not believe your motives are altruistic. They will assume that you have ulterior motives."

"Then you all need to do better about improving your public image. Doesn't it bother you that people have so little trust in you all?" I paused. I was now part of the *all*. "We need to do more about our image. I don't like people fearing us."

He nodded again, just another placation. "Perhaps you're right. We should work harder at making people see us as docile and ineffectual, deny what dwells in us, and work on people seeing us as soft and cuddly pushovers. Easily subjugated by anyone who would choose to dominate us. Sounds like a brilliant plan."

"I realize the importance of a strong pack; there isn't a need for you to be such a jackass. But what's wrong with helping others? I can assure you that possessing the ability to restrict those that have the ability to kill with just touch will work in our favor. I think Mason would appreciate that, and if he can't, then whoever is chosen next might."

He smirked. "You mean Gideon."

Of course he knew.

He continued to feign interest in my plan, his titanium eyes distant and intense. "Contrary to what you choose to believe, we are not monsters. Less than a century ago, others felt they needed to contain us, so we are more understanding of the situation. The three times that we abided by the agreement were unavoidable situations and we didn't find any joy in doing so."

When he looked away, I remained focused on the defined features that hardened as though something dreadful occupied his thoughts. Ethan's movements were always too quick, sharp, and predacious even when he wasn't trying. I stiffened when he took a seat next to me. He said, "Mason is unnecessarily difficult. He will not trust such an altruistic gesture because it is easier to believe we are incapable of such acts. When Gideon is in power, then we will visit this again." Was he serious, or just pretending consideration to quiet me?

He looked out the window, then at the clock. "It's getting late. You should go home, get some rest."

It was nine forty-six. Yeah, that was late. I was living like a rock star. Hanging out into the wee hours of nine o'clock.

"Of course, I can't continue to live this party lifestyle." There were too many things unanswered and I couldn't leave. "Tell me about the fifth object?" I asked, sinking back into the sofa, an act of defiance. A subtle way of saying I wasn't leaving until I had answers.

Ethan was back to his typical persona, stoicism eclipsed his face, supple lips pulled into a firm line as a frosty gaze held mine. "It's late, we will talk about it tomorrow," he said as he opened the door.

"Promise?" The long day had drained most of the fight in me.

"If possible, we will talk and I will answer whatever question you have to the best of my ability. No more secrets."

That was worded so perfectly that a novice in dealing with Ethan would have let it slide. "I expect more than answers 'to the best of your ability'; I expect the truth and real answers." I gathered my things, including the Aufero, and headed out as he watched me from his front door.

"I'll be back tomorrow at nine," I said. Then I let his keys, which I had swiped earlier, dangle around my index finger. "I'll let myself in if you're not awake." Then I fiddled with several of the keys on the ring. "Is this one for the office? Oh, let's not bother with such trivial things. I will just snoop around until you get up. Okay?"

He scowled, but there was still a hint of amusement to it, just a glimpse that danced around the corner of his lips as he worked at the frown. Then things changed. Titanium rolled over his pupils as he focused behind me. He inhaled a deep, ragged breath and spoke as he exhaled. "Skylar, come here." I heard growling behind me, rumbles like deep rolling thunder. Chains clanked as they loosened, only to be yanked taut again. Padded footsteps sounded closer, just inches from me. Snarls cut through the air, vicious rumbles. Magic whipped at my back, different from Josh's, but not the same as dark magic. It weighed against me, freezing me where I stood. "Skylar, come here," Ethan repeated in a low warning voice.

Quick hard steps pounded nearer toward me. I pulled the Aufero closer, and charged toward the door. Once I was close enough, Ethan pulled me into the house behind him, shielding me from the stranger who was behind us. The tall man was barely controlling the monsters he had confined to a thick chain leash. Nothing else would have been able to restrain them. His sand-colored hair was just a shade darker than his skin. The broad, sturdy body was enough to control the six hounds he had tethered in front of him. The animals must have been dogs in their previous lives. Magic had defiled them into what was before us, just fragments of their former selves. They had mutated into malformed monster hounds. Their floppy maws could barely close over mouths full of canines sharpened to dagger points. Thick legs supported their long sinewy flanks. Dull stubby variants of black and gray hair covered their bodies.

The stranger was a statue moving ever so slightly to constrain the feral hounds. The breeze made his chin-length hair flutter around his face, obscuring it as the wind hit. As the long blue coat parachuted behind him, it was unable to hide the concealed sword and rifle he had with him.

"Samuel," said Ethan in a rough, strained voice.

Samuel looked past him, focusing on me. His head tilted slightly. A light smile formed when I finally met his gaze. "Can you read the Clostra?" he asked.

I didn't bother with an answer. I was sure he already knew.

"Give them to me," he demanded. As he stepped closer, the hounds became more restless than before, lunging and jumping toward us. He whispered a command and they stilled.

"What are you doing here?" Ethan asked.

"Give me the books," he requested again in a very gentle voice.

"You know that will never happen."

"Of course it will." With a simple command, the chains that kept that hounds at bay disappeared and so did Samuel. The largest one led the pack.

Their heavy paws stampeded across the ground, causing it to rumble as their pace continued. One lunged at Ethan. He charged at it with force but it only went a fraction of the distance I expected. It snarled and Ethan's growl matched its menacing sound. They charged at each other again. Ethan slammed into the creature, holding it as it clenched down on his arm. He pounded into its flank, gaining the advantage as he slipped to the side and twisted the massive skull.

Came through the door and pounced at me. Pressing the

Aufero to me, I waved my hand through the air. The hound crashed into the other side of the wall, but another attacked me from behind, biting into my leg. I struck into it with my fist, but it clung to my flesh, gripping deeper into it. Blood dampened my pants. Using magic to push it back wasn't an option because it would have ripped away muscle. I needed it to release. Drilling into it with my elbows, I finally freed myself from its hold, then I used magic to back away and hold it at bay. The Aufero glowed bright orange and black, pulsing erratically as it had during the spell with Ethan. It still hadn't recovered from the odd color it had changed to.

Ethan took the third creature down even quicker. His eyes didn't resemble anything remotely human. I backed up closer to him until we were touching, then I formed a protective field around us. He was injured, bite and claw marks wept blood, and he panted. He looked as feral as the animals that had attacked us, his eyes sharp and gunmetal, the color of his wolf. Keeping my hands in close contact with the Aufero, I kept the thin shield covering us. It was no longer the sheer diaphanous color that I was used to; it was a thick smog that enveloped us and sucked the air out of our bubble and even Ethan noticed. The hounds snarled, chomping aggressively at the restriction. They thrashed against the field. It quivered, but held. The malformed creatures jumped onto their hind legs to claw at the barrier. Then the growling came to a halt. A single growl, then they fell back. Dead.

I dropped the field and considered doing the same with the Aufero. Something was wrong with it. The magic felt off, distorted. I looked at Ethan. He was too distracted to care about the dead hounds lying at our feet and the fact that the protective field had done that to them. I had done it to them.

He grabbed my hand and ran toward his garage. Its doors had been ripped from the hinges and all five of the cars had been rendered inoperable. I tried to keep pace with him as he ran, not allowing his injuries to slow him down. He darted through the thicket behind his home. Overcrowded by trees, bushes, and tall grass, there wasn't a clear path as we navigated deeper into it until we came to a Jeep Rubicon. Behind it, enough of the area was cleared away to allow passage away from the house to the streets. I was sure that was the way he intended. If the situation were different I would have made a snarky comment about this being unnecessary. But his doomsday preparation was exactly what we needed.

"Do you have your phone?" he asked after we were both seated in the Jeep.

"Not with me, I left it in my car."

He reached over me to open the glove compartment and pulled out an old-school flip phone. I had one, too. They were more durable and held a charge longer than the new smartphones because the only thing they could do was make phone calls.

He pushed one button. Josh picked up on the first ring.

"What's wrong?" he said.

"Samuel's in town and he has the third book and wants the other two."

There was an extended silence and then a rumble of curse words from Josh, and then another temporary silence before he spewed another string of them.

"You need to get out of there. Go to the cabin."

Cabin?

"Okay," Josh said, then there was a thunderous boom over the speaker followed by a loud crack and then a thud. The sound of struggling went on for a while: grunts, crashes, glass shattering against a hard surface, and then silence. Cold hard silence.

Ethan dialed again and the call went straight to voice mail. He darted and weaved through the traffic, and I kept checking the rearview mirror for the flashing lights of police cars. Slamming the car into the driveway of Josh's house, he jumped out and approached at a pace that had me running to keep up.

The front door dangled off the hinges, fragmented glass was

sprinkled over the floor, furniture was tossed around the room, the sofa lay flipped over, and the remnant of powerful magic was a dense fog in the air. Josh's distinctive imprint. The permeation of a foreign imprint, strong and overwhelming, cluttered the room as well.

Ethan stared at the splattered blood for too long and the knife, just a few inches from it. "It isn't his," he exhaled in relief.

"But this is," I said about a trail of it leading into Josh's bedroom. The window's glass was gone, the dresser embedded in the wall. The mattress was tossed off the frame. I wasn't sure what a fight between powerful witches was like typically, but this one had been very violent.

I had to run to keep up with Ethan as he left the house. Minutes later, we were speeding down the highway. He focused intently, but not on the road, as he maneuvered in and out of traffic, and twenty minutes later we drove up a gravel driveway to a farmhouse. It was deserted. He grabbed a flashlight out of the car. We searched through the house. Samuel had been there at some point, and had performed magic. Its vestige crept throughout the room as did the odd scent of the hounds. Ethan cursed under his breath and snatched a piece of paper off the counter. Gritting his teeth, he left the house.

By the third semi-deserted home, Ethan's search became more frenzied and desperate. There wasn't a method; he was just trashing each house, going through the rooms, tossing things around, checking the walls for hidden rooms. But Samuel hadn't been to any of them. The distinct trace of his magic was missing. Ethan's gaze was erratic, lacking the control I was used to.

"Ethan." I said his name softly, but there wasn't any calming him.

A vacant look bathed his face, and he grew pallid as he accepted the circumstances.

"He's gone," he whispered. He left the house, and I made a quick sweep trying to clean up what I could in an acceptable amount of time. I wasn't totally confident that he wouldn't leave me.

One call was made to Sebastian, but I wasn't surprised to find him along with Winter, Gavin, and a few other were-animals at the pack's house. The moment he walked through the door, Sebastian started with the questions.

"It was definitely Samuel?"

Ethan nodded, and handed over the paper he picked up from the other home.

Sebastian looked at it, and tension formed sharp lines on his face. It was a long moment before he was able to get them to relax. "He thinks we are stupid enough to drop the books off at some disclosed location and trust that he will release Josh. How arrogant."

Ethan nodded. "I don't know how he knew we had the books. I am sure he thought Josh had them in his possession. The house was trashed."

Sebastian contemplated the situation, keeping a careful eye on Ethan, who was pacing the area like a trapped animal. Unrestrained energy rebounded viciously through the room. His hands clenched into fists, and the ragged breaths he took didn't seem to help.

"Ethan," Sebastian said quietly, "we cannot give him the books for Josh. I can't let that happen."

Sebastian's hand washed over his face a few times, and the weight of the situation placed a worrisome scowl on it.

As Sebastian watched him, it was a long moment before Ethan spoke. When it came to Josh's safety, Ethan worked on impulse, not logic. I took my cue from Winter and positioned myself between them. They were now working on separate agendas. For Ethan, getting the other book came second to Josh's safety. Sebastian had vowed years before that he would protect Josh's life as though it were his own. And I was sure, in theory, he meant it. But if the Clostra was so dangerous to the lives of thousands, if not tens of thousands, he couldn't risk it for Josh. He couldn't for anyone.

Although I figured Ethan knew it, when Sebastian said it, you could see the wounds of his words. He wouldn't meet Sebastian's eyes. "I need Josh back," he said in a low voice.

Sebastian simply nodded. "I know."

"Samuel has elven hounds with him," Ethan informed him. I was pretty sure that wasn't the actual name, but I guessed anything freaky and weird created in this world was the result of the elves' genetic engineering. Great. They were mad scientists as well—how could this get better? Could they control the weather? Right: dammit, they could. Or at least some of them could.

"Maybe we can track the animals. Their scent should still be in Ethan's house. It is quite strong and very distinctive," I suggested.

"We can, but that will take time; even with our best hunters that could take days. We may not have days. Samuel isn't known for his patience," Sebastian said.

"There is no way he's in town and Marcia isn't aware of it. She makes it her business to know where he is. Power like that can't go undetected very long. They can find him," Winter offered.

"Are you sure she will know? Our surveillance lost him three months ago."

"If anyone will know of his whereabouts, it's her," Winter asserted.

Sebastian nodded. "I will arrange a meeting." He excused himself to his office. I didn't think she would help. Josh was a witch, but he was so far removed that they didn't consider him theirs. They would not put a lot of effort into finding him or protecting him.

Before Sebastian could leave, I said, "When you call her, tell her that if she helps us find Josh, she can have the Aufero."

He stopped abruptly, regarding me with narrowed eyes. I could only imagine what was going through his head, how many strategies and simulations were done. “Sky, are you sure?”

“Positive, but I want to meet with her, too. I have some conditions.”

CHAPTER 15

Trust is a two-way street and it was blocked on both ends. The witches didn't want to come to the pack's home and Sebastian was hesitant to meet them at an undisclosed location. But in the end, he had to put aside his apprehension and an hour later he, Ethan, Winter, and I were in the back of a windowless passenger van. I didn't have a problem with cages—for years I had willingly allowed myself to be locked in one—but the others were claustrophobic. If the ride were any longer than twenty minutes, the drivers, the same guys who had come with Bernard to the pack's house, would have had to deal with some very agitated were-animals.

We were led into a garage and followed them down a dark hallway that spilled into a large neutral-colored room. We were directed to the left into another dark room. We collectively gasped the moment we crossed the threshold. Foreign magic bound us like a shackle. Runes covered the walls and surrounded the five members of the Creed, who sat at a long banquet table. Marcia sat in the middle, and each of the others' lips were twisted into identical expressions of scorn. A slight Asian woman with dark eyes nodded in Bernard's direction. He stepped out, closing the heavy door and locking it behind him. Marcia looked comfortable sitting in the oversized chair, which had carved designs running up the ornate arms. If one doubted for one minute who was the true leader of the witches, one look at her ostentatious chair and there wouldn't be any doubt.

The gas lamps behind each of them barely illuminated the room and the scent of various metals, henna, and tannin diffused in the air.

"You will not be able to change, we've assured that," she said, as she waved toward the wall. "Perhaps that will ensure our safety and prevent us from being accosted by animals that do not respond to our magic."

Our minor immunity to her magic while in animal form was really a thorn in her side.

The uncomfortable silence lingered, not quite fifteen seconds, but it felt like an eternity. Limiting my ability to change didn't bother me, but Ethan and Sebastian had such symbiotic relationships with their animal halves that restricting them in any manner had to be torturous.

She extended her hand. "You promised me the Aufero if I met with you."

With a heavy sigh, Sebastian rolled his eyes in her direction. "No, you said that you wanted the Aufero in exchange for meeting with us. I applaud the confidence you have in your presence; however, I made it clear that it is yours if you help us," he said. "Are we going to have a discussion, or should we leave?"

She could barely focus on him. Her yearning eyes kept drifting in my direction, looking at the Aufero. With great effort she was able to peel them from it. Power and the anticipation of it was an addiction that most didn't want a cure for. Marcia was not exempt from its allure. Even someone as powerful as her still wanted more.

"What can we do for you?" she asked in a crisp, dismissive tone as she clasped her hands in front of her.

The tension held strong, a barrier constructed by their mutual dislike and distrust. "I need your help," Sebastian said.

She exhaled an irritated breath. "I figured that much. At some point do you plan to offer specifics?"

Sebastian's lips spread into a full smile, his deep baritone voice as soothing as a waterfall as he spoke. "Samuel is in town."

Marcia and the rest of the Creed didn't seem surprised or concerned by the information. "Yes, we are aware of this. I am sure when he has acquired whatever he came to town to retrieve, he will leave as quietly as he arrived," she said. At this point she had dismissed Ethan and me, not even giving us the courtesy of a flippant glare.

"He has Josh and is threatening to kill him," Sebastian said.

Well, at least it wasn't just me. Sebastian never disclosed more than needed to be to anyone.

Marcia rested her hand on the table, and her eyes started to droop from boredom. "Well, that hardly seems any concern of ours," she said.

"He is a witch. It is your concern. Do you not have a duty to protect your own?" he inquired.

"Josh is no more a witch than you all are Homo sapiens. The world sees one face in the daylight, but when the moon is full, Mercury rises, or the world is eclipsed, your true being is exposed. He is not one of us. When I was being brutalized by that"—she dragged her scornful glare in my direction—"where was Josh to muzzle the rabid dog?" Her cruel words danced past her lips as though they were from a sonnet she was reciting from memory.

Oh come on. Surely I can't be the first person to ever try to kill you. Her personality warranted such assaults daily. I tried to shrug off the insult and remained quiet, but the Aufero quickly came to my defense. Perhaps I thought about it too hard, or wished for it too strong, but it used magic that I didn't know I possessed. Their chairs slid to the side, and the stout, heavy walnut wood table slammed into their stomachs, pinning them against the wall. And for several moments they were trapped in that position. Simultaneously, they waved their hands over the table, slicing through the air. Dark, entranced gazes zoned over to me as the table flew in my direction. I barely ducked in time.

Marcia gasped, clinging to the anger that had ignited into something so fierce that it could not be contained. "That is unacceptable," she hissed at Sebastian. "You come here for favors and you allow one of your were-animals who is able to control magic to come here. Now you see what happens when an animal is given gifts that belong to those that have a civil nature," she spat out angrily. Her cheeks flushed ruby; her hazel eyes darkened with anger.

Oh crap, this is going to go downhill fast. I needed to do some damage control. "I apologize. That was unintentional," I admitted. "Please do not let my poor manners be a death sentence for Josh. I am sorry." I lowered my head and waited. I hated pandering to the egotistical bitch.

While the others had returned to sitting, Marcia continued to stand, her fingers clenched, cheeks fire-brushed with anger, a glare that pinned me where I stood.

"This meeting is over," she said as she returned to her seat.

"Samuel has the Clostra," Sebastian rushed out before Bernard could escort us out.

Frozen for just a mere second, Marcia seemed genuinely surprised. The spark of interest quickly wilted to apathy. "That isn't an issue we care about. According to my knowledge, the spells in that book don't affect us."

Ethan spoke up. "That is where you are wrong. We have it on full authority that the book has spells that will strip magic from all that hold it. You do not believe that with the books in his possession he will fail to seek to control you all as well. You want him dead as much as we do."

"We will stand against him if needed. His grievance isn't with us, but the existence of your kind. I assume you have the other two books. Once he has them, I am confident we will not hear from him," she said, relaxing back into the chair. The idea of Samuel killing off the were-animals seemed to bring her a level of comfort. "So tell me, why should I help you?"

"You want the Aufero," I interjected. "It's yours if you help."

That was what she wanted to hear. I wasn't sure why she was beating around the bush.

She didn't answer immediately. And for five minutes, thirty-two seconds, we waited in silence. Sebastian was expressionless, the set of his jaw rigid, gaze empty, his heart at a calm, resting beat.

"It is a difficult decision, but one you need to make quickly," I said impatiently. We were wasting time. She wanted the Aufero and we wanted Josh.

"Let us discuss this for a moment," she said.

And I was foolish enough to believe she would do it in front of us, so that we could hear. Instead, they chanted together, a quick wave of their hands, and the world fell silent. Their lips moved, some more fervent than others as the debate continued. What was the problem? Did the idea of getting rid of the were-animals trump even her lust for increased power?

Eventually the silence ended. And she said, "Okay, we will help."

I needed to get everything I could out of this bargain. "First, you will help us find Josh. As you stated, he isn't one of you; therefore he can no longer be governed by your laws. You are not allowed to sanction him under any circumstances. He now belongs solely to the pack."

"No, that is not acceptable," she responded quickly. "In the event Josh requires discipline, I doubt that the pack will ever do it justly. He is coddled because he is the brother of the Beta and you all need him."

This one I refused to budge on. "Well, I worry about the fact that you conveniently and often punish those whose powers mirror if not exceed yours. I am not confident that he would not be punished far too severely for a minor infraction."

"No," she simply said, her face so stern that I could see the small lines that formed around her lips and eyes.

There wasn't a doubt that as soon as she could manage it Josh would be on the receiving end of a wrath intended for the pack; if she weakened him, she weakened the pack.

"Fine, all possible sanctions must be agreed upon by you and Sebastian," I added. Punishments by Sebastian would be handled with leniency, while those from the Creed would be done with the utmost severity.

The moue remained on her lips. "He and I would never come to an agreement. You are wasting our time with your unreasonable request," she said sternly, her agitation becoming something that needed to be quelled.

I said, "Then all sanctions will be handled by you, Sebastian, and an agreed-upon third party." It was a decision that would work in our favor. Josh would never receive any mercy from Marcia, but Sebastian would willingly give it. Sebastian was connected enough that the third party would side toward leniency. I was confident in that. I suddenly saw he was right: the very things I hated about him, I needed. It was what I—no—what *we* needed to survive.

She nodded slowly in agreement.

"And you have to help us find Samuel and retrieve Josh. If he isn't retrieved safe and unharmed, then the agreement is void," I added.

"We can't guarantee that he is unharmed. That isn't in our control."

"He's been gone for two hours now. The longer he is gone, the greater the chance that he will be harmed or even killed. If I were you, I would agree, climb down off your high horse, and go find Josh to make sure this deal isn't voided."

A collective gasp filled the room. The members mumbled in protest, and were silenced just as quickly when Marcia raised her hand. "We will need a minute of discussion," she said. Once again we were enclosed in silence.

Soon, she said, "Agreed. However, a restriction will be placed on the Aufero. The Aufero is drawn to you therefore it will continue to seek your ownership as long as you are near it. You must agree to stay away from it and allow us to place a restraint that will force it to return to us even if it must be over your dead body."

"Restriction?"

She nodded. "A curse that will not only sever the tie, but if you are ever in possession of it, will return it to me."

"But not without killing her first," Winter added.

She nodded once.

Was this when I should have run from the room screaming? But I didn't. Instead, I exhaled. "Okay."

Marcia's flat eyes settled on Sebastian. "Very well. My final condition—I want Samuel. You are not allowed to kill him; preferably, I would like him unharmed."

Anger clouded Ethan's and Sebastian's eyes. Marcia didn't care about Samuel's safety. She had lost Josh in the deal and wanted to make sure they both left this meeting mutually dissatisfied. Placing a curse on me just didn't seem to be enough. Taking away their ability to seek revenge had left them truly discontented.

~

The witches walked throughout Josh's home, looking at the splatters of blood. The knife with Samuel's blood was still where we had left it. "That's Samuel's blood, and that is Josh's," Ethan said. He paused before he said his brother's name, nearly forcing the words out. Sebastian's attention often went back to Ethan, assessing how he was doing. It was better than expected, but not by much.

"I am aware," Marcia said dismissively.

"Although Josh is our priority, if we find Samuel, I am confident Josh will be near."

Marcia stood over the knife, and pulling out a pouch, she scattered tannin over it. Then another white substance was dropped over the knife. Watching someone find the magical source like some supernatural GPS was still amazing no matter how many times I saw it done. She whispered a couple of words, and her fingers waved gracefully over the knife. A golden smoke formed, and a blurry image of a house appeared. She chanted more and the home enlarged. Just as it was visible enough to the see the address and the surrounding area, it vanished.

Cursing, she smiled, an odd look of pleasure. Contrary to what most people think, powerful people didn't like dominating a weaker opponent. There wasn't any pleasure or value in it. But dominating one whose power paralleled theirs was an adrenaline rush.

She performed the spell again. It fizzled and died without any more information than the first time. "His skills have improved," she said to the others. They clasped hands, and the spell was performed again. Shimmers of color flared in rolling waves, then gold clouded the air, and as plain as a photograph in HD, the house showed along with the address. Lines along the house displayed side streets leading us to our destination.

We never would have found Samuel in the middle of "nowhere"

and "go the hell away" in a million years. Large fields of barren soil, poorly cultivated farmland, and pilfered agriculture surrounded the nondescript house that blended with the other homes around it. You didn't have to be magically inclined to feel the power that surrounded it. It strummed against the body, captured the air in a manner that made breathing difficult. How could Marcia not want Samuel? He was stronger than the five of them combined. The ward he used defeated Marcia's magic and required the assistance of the others to counter. The knowledge that one person possessed that type of power made me uncomfortable.

Five witches and twenty were-animals, half of the latter staying in human form, came. As we approached the house, a wave of energy hit us hard, sending everyone onto their backs, but when another one started, a large field shielded us. Each force placed on it rippled over its surface, and occasionally a huge indent appeared, stretching it to the point it looked like it would tear, but it held. It was good having five witches.

Samuel finally came out of the house. The long coat was gone, but his ominous appearance wasn't diminished by his new attire: t-shirt, canvas pants, and boots. His chin-length hair was in dire need of shampooing. "Marcia, this isn't your fight. I urge you to not make it yours," he said.

"Samuel, release him," she said.

"Of course, when I have the books, you can have the witch. I can see why you were so distraught over losing him to Sebastian. But you should find comfort in the fact that he will never take your position in the Creed, although with more practice he will make your little dog and pony show look like mage magic."

And I was happier than ever that we had secured his fate. Josh was strong. Marcia would find any excuse to punish him with the Aufero.

The banter was nothing but a distraction. The field shattered, then six hounds pounded toward us. Soaring through the air, one of them quickly latched on to Marcia's arm. She screeched, beating against it. Gavin's sharp fangs dug into the flank of the animal. It released Marcia's arm, leaving deep punctures before it turned and snapped at Gavin, who was even faster as a panther than in human form. Gavin's sharp claws slashed over its face, then its chest and back before ripping its throat out with one swift lurch. The head twisted at a weird angle, then it collapsed. Gavin attacked three others in a similar manner.

As the fighting escalated, Sebastian and Ethan approached the house to retrieve Josh. Winter took pleasure in taking down two more of the hounds. With her sword in hand, she charged one creature, and when it sprang at her, she plunged her weapon into it, yanked it out, then severed the head with one quick strike. She dropped to one knee, spinning around in time to catch the other in the abdomen with an arc swing. Its claws struck her hand, knocking the sword out of reach. Retrieving the dagger from her ankle sheath, she came to her feet in a powerful burst. The animal circled her, baring its dagger-like teeth, lunging to snap at her and then retreating before she could attack. It played this game for some time: lunge and retreat, lunge and retreat. On the final lunge, Winter flipped over it and then embedded her blade into its spine. It immediately collapsed to the ground.

Fanned out into a V, the witches advanced toward Samuel. The smug arrogance remained as he brought down the field each time, only to have it replaced by another. The final time he brought it down, a fog engulfed him as a silver band formed around his body, binding his arms to his sides. The witches' bodies quivered as they worked to keep him bound in position. Someone shackled an iridium leg brace around him. He howled like a wounded animal. Was it painful, or was the idea of being magicless as harmful as an injury?

"Let me go!" he demanded.

Even through his anger, his gaze remained diametric to it, soft and gentle. But I was sure that if released, he would not only hurt them, he would probably kill them.

He stared at me, and I started to feel sorry for him. Behind the scruffy beard, just a shade darker than his sandy hair, there was a gentleness to him. *Stop it, don't feel sympathy for the devil.* But was he the devil? He didn't seem like the devil; his topaz eyes reflected something different from his actions. Soft and lucid, there was a tacit entreaty for understanding.

"Do you have the book?" Marcia asked.

Sparks of anger flared from his once gentle eyes. "We are now enemies," he said through clenched teeth.

"Now, Samuel, we will have none of that. We are going to go into the house, get Josh, and continue as though none of this ever happened. We play nice from now on. Understand? This is not personal and I don't want it to be."

His gaze didn't offer any forgiveness as his eyes met hers. Hard, ragged breaths slipped through his tightly clamped teeth.

The tenor of Marcia's voice was coercive and genteel. "This was one of the more distasteful dealings I will have to live with. I doubt you will ever understand my position, and I realize that. I don't want to hurt you, but you will have to let this go. I need more than your word. We will need to perform a *pacem fœderis mei* to ensure that you won't retaliate against us. We need a binding of peace."

He turned away from her, clearly disinterested. Clawing at the shackles was a feckless endeavor, yet he behaved like a trapped animal willing to sever a body part to get out of a trap.

Marcia pulled out a knife and held it to his throat, pressing hard enough that small trickles of blood ran down his neck. "Do you really want it to end like this? Defeated by Sebastian and his pack because of your tenets? Agree to the *pacem fœderis mei* or we say our farewells now. Understand, I do not want you dead. I needed to do this for reasons you will one day understand. It is not personal. Do not make it so," she said softly.

She lifted the knife slightly until it no longer pressed into his skin, but it remained close enough to cause damage if needed. "Will you agree?" she asked in a grave, thin voice.

And with great pain he managed a rigid "Yes."

Cautiously, they released him from his shackles, and just as I expected him to run away, so did they. They held the cuffs close enough to re-shackle him if necessary. But he stood straight without any inclination that he planned to break his word. The witches whispered several urgent invocations; first blood shed for the bond, and the final step was for Samuel to repeat his part in it. He recited it in a low, detached manner, refusing to make eye contact with any of them. He seemed to have found an interest in me and regarded me for a long time and smiled. Okay, it wasn't a smile; it was just a slight lift in the frown that had been etched on his face since he had been captured.

As the witches turned to walk away, he said, "May you receive the true peace that you all deserve."

Marcia stopped and turned. "If we find it, at least it will not be at your hands. Now we are bound in peace you can't hurt us."

It was a good thing, because Samuel looked as though peace was the furthest thing from his mind.

Samuel nodded in my direction, then vanished. I hurried toward the car, following Ethan and Sebastian. Josh's shirt was stained with blood, a bruise on his cheek, and numerous cuts on his hands. The look on Ethan's face made it seem as though he was bringing out a mutilated corpse. Sebastian drove, Winter sat in the front passenger seat, and Ethan and I sat next to Josh in the back. Like Samuel, he kept clawing at the brace on his arm, the scowl growing increasingly intense with each failure. His skin was raw from him trying to slip out of it.

"Does it hurt?" I finally asked.

He shook his head, clawing at it more aggressively. "I just don't like it on," he said.

"Josh, stop," Ethan said. Josh desperately tried to get out of it.

Ethan exhaled an irritated breath as he watched his brother become overwrought with distress. “Sebastian, will you pull over?” he said.

Sebastian did and opened the trunk. Ethan took out the tool box and came back. After a few minutes of tinkering with it, the brace slipped off Josh’s arm. He relaxed back against the seat, calmly rubbing his excoriated skin.

CHAPTER 16

Josh hadn't spoken since Ethan explained the details of getting the witches to assist in retrieving him. Now he stood on the opposite side of the room from his brother, his arms folded over his chest in quiet defiance. He refused to accompany Ethan and me back to the witches' home. And for minutes, they stood in silence looking at each other. They continued to deny they had a telepathic link, but they communicated in silence better than most did with the benefit of words. Josh looked just short of pouting, his lips drawn into a pucker, eyes narrowed, and his nose flared each time he exhaled.

Ethan shrugged off his annoyance. "Perhaps it is better if you stay here," he said. Josh simply glowered at him as he guided me toward the door.

Josh closed his eyes briefly. "I know you didn't have a lot of choices.... I hate that I am the cause of this," he admitted.

I stopped and went over to him. "If the situation were reversed, what would you have done?"

He didn't answer immediately, but I knew the answer. More than anything, I think that the idea that I was in this situation because Samuel had dominated him left a bitter taste in his mouth. The guilt only added to it. Guilt, I was tired of seeing it, feeling it, and dealing with it. He took another look in our direction and then frowned. There wasn't anything Ethan or I could say to relieve the guilt. It was a burden he wasn't ready to release.

Bernard and his personal bodyguards looked as though they were as sick of seeing us as we were of them. They led Ethan and me into a different building than earlier: a cement bunker. Bernard instructed us to stay in the long, narrow anteroom. When he exited, the clank of steel locked us in. A thick bolted door kept us in, while the door on the opposite end locked us out. Each breath I took was a little shallower than the one before. My bravado had shed away and I couldn't put up the facade any longer.

"Are you afraid?" Ethan asked.

"No." I exhaled my lie. Maybe it wasn't a lie. I didn't feel anything. I didn't know what to feel. Fear? I was too numb to interpret fear. Concern? The adrenaline pumped too much for thoughts like that to linger. Anxiety? It was probably the closest thing I could think of to describe my feelings. I just wanted this to be over.

His eyes narrowed, but I doubted he would call me on the fib. Even with enhanced vision, the dimmed lights made it difficult to see him as he rested against the wall. But his eyes stood out, deep blue with hints of gunmetal. The air felt thick, breathing was becoming difficult, and each time I considered what was about to happen, my heart thumped too loudly against my rib cage. I was glad it was dim, it made it harder for Ethan to read my face, even though I was sure the poorly hidden camera at the end of the corridor was able to see it just fine.

Wrapping my arms around my chest, I found a gentle rocking from heel to toe had a calming effect, and for a moment I closed my eyes and welcomed it. It came from a place of satisfaction, because Josh was alive. I did that and whatever consequence occurred because of it, I found solace in preserving Josh's life. But Marcia's words replayed in my head: It would return to me over her dead body. My hand ran along the long strap of the bag that held the Aufero close to my hip.

Each time I looked up, I found Ethan watching me, expressionless. I was sure his mind was fast at work. I started to pace. Nearly fifteen minutes had passed and I was getting anxious. Was this a scare tactic, some weird psychological thing? Because the longer we waited, the more my anxiety increased, converting to fear. It wasn't until he spoke that I realized Ethan was so close. My natural impulse was to step away, but instead I stood still.

He asked again, his tone grave. "Are you okay?"

I nodded.

"If you want to leave, we will."

I shook my head and stepped away, turning my back to him as I returned to pacing the floor. When I turned around, he was leaning against the wall, and his gaze roved slowly over the room, to the dimmed lights, the door in front of us that led to the witches, the exit, and the walls. He paid close attention to the seams of the wall, probably more cameras.

Marshaling a look of pseudo-bravado that I was sure wasn't fooling anyone, I said, "I can't leave." His relief was apparent as he relaxed farther into the wall. I wished I could say it was honor that made me stop, a sense of virtue that wouldn't let me break the promise I had made to the witches, but it wasn't. I was bound by the consequences that would accompany the revocation of our agreement.

He held my gaze for so long that I thought maybe he was trying to entrance me or something, and then he inhaled deeply. It was an odd thing about predators: they were drawn to the alluring fragrance of fear, no matter how they denied it. The primordial part of them held an odd infinity for it. I wasn't looking forward to when I, too, would be ruled by the predator that dwelled within. Maybe that was why I fought it so much.

We continued to wait for nearly twenty more minutes. I hugged the sling backpack with the Aufero close to my chest. Ethan stood behind me. Usually his presence was a little overwhelming and off-putting, but now it was a welcome distraction. Comforting. The gentle beat of his heart against my back beckoned mine to join in unison. My heart easily complied, pacing to something that didn't make me feel like I was about to go into cardiac arrest.

If making us wait this long was a tactic to make me come unhinged, Marcia succeeded, even with Ethan present. I was terrified by the time Bernard stepped in and waved me forward.

"Ms. Brooks, please follow me back," he said.

Ethan followed me, staying extremely close as if he hadn't heard Bernard ask for me specifically. The candles offset on each side of the dark room provided just enough light to see the six cloaked witches in front of us. Blood was fragrant in the air, along with the smell of salt and sulfur and a strange acidic odor that I couldn't place. Each one of the witches remained hidden behind the cloak concealing everything, including their faces and hands.

Decidedly it was for theatrics, and boy did it make a presentation. I would have rather seen *Stomp, Cats, Wicked,* or even *Jersey Boys* than this over-the-top production.

"You are not welcomed," Marcia said to Ethan.

He simply smiled, baring his teeth ever so slightly to make his point. "Then I will remain here unwelcomed." He shrugged.

Bernard started toward him to escort him out. When he reached for Ethan's elbow, Ethan said in a deep rumble, "I wouldn't."

Marcia waved Bernard away.

"Come closer," Marcia instructed me.

Her command elicited the opposite effect. I stepped back so far I bumped into Ethan.

"Now," she said.

Taking slow steps toward them, I tried to find some comfort in the fact that there were so many. At least it took more than one witch to conjure a curse; otherwise they could just go around cursing people at a whim. A lizard laid supine before them, his belly sliced exposing his guts, as they chanted.

They had started chanting the moment I was escorted in, and they grew louder the closer I stepped. Marcia's words were more forceful and fervent as she flicked something into the cauldron, causing fire to spring up in bursts.

I assumed the four in the center were the witches from earlier, but I didn't know the witch at the end. The hood and dim lighting made it difficult to see their faces, but the one on the far right kept turning from me.

Marcia, who stood in the middle, threw off her hood, and her shadowed appearance made her seem more frightening than I remembered. Or perhaps it was knowing that she was the one responsible for sentencing me to such a fate.

She immersed her hands into the depths of the lizard's belly, covering her hands in blood, then beckoned me closer. I wasn't sure when it had happened; maybe when they had lit candles, or surrounded the lizard with salt and sulfur, or sprinkled an odd green concoction in a small cauldron. It wasn't until I felt Ethan against me that I realized I had wandered back again just inches from the door. I didn't plan to make a break for it, but apparently, my sympathetic nervous system, which was all about flight or fight, had other thoughts. I was in full-on flight mode.

"Do you want to leave?" Ethan asked again in a low voice, for my ears only. His arm girded my waist and braced me closer to him.

Hell yeah! But instead I shook my head because there was no way my lips were going to form the words to say no.

"Skylar, come closer and give me the Aufero," Marcia requested firmly. I slipped the bag over my head and took out the Aufero. Had she experienced pleasure greater than this? If she had, you wouldn't know by the look on her face. An immense joy that one might have only seen on a child's first Christmas.

I handed it to her and then she asked for my hand and pulled out the knife. I closed my eyes and waited for the pain of it slicing over my hand. Blood wept from the cut and she held it over the cauldron until she was satisfied with the amount. She tossed me a crumpled handkerchief, which I wrapped around my hand. Perhaps the cloaks served a greater purpose than ceremonial. Maybe they needed anonymity during the curse. Who was this sixth person? It was someone powerful, because after each verse of the chant, they stopped and the unknown person's hands waved over the lizard then waved in my direction. When the unknown finished the final part of the curse, he crept back into the shadows. The movements were odd: slow and laborious. Eventually he disappeared behind a side door.

A curse seemed like something bad that would take you to the brinks of torture, usher you to death, and snatch you back before you could enjoy the comfort of peace that only death could bring. But this was far worse. As they chanted, it clenched my heart until it lost its ability to beat, then it twisted at my intestines until I felt like I would soon relieve myself of everything I had eaten that week. Just as I was going to vomit, Marcia instructed me to start walking away. When I was nearly fifty feet away, my body settled and I felt normal, or as normal as one could be, once cursed.

"See, I gave you a fail-safe. Now you will know when you are too close. It is up to you whether or not you want to preserve your life," she said with a wide smile, showing perfect pearly teeth that conjured thoughts in my head of many brutal ways I wanted to remove them.

The last way I considered made me smile, but instead I used it to my advantage. "You are more considerate that I have given you credit for. Thank you." That was the appropriate thing to say. There wasn't any way to nicely say that thoughts of her slow, painful, violent death would comfort me to sleep. But instead, that demure grin stayed fixed on my face, ornamental and necessary.

I didn't think I would feel different, but I did. The magic coursed through me differently. It was hard, tumultuous and made me feel jittery like I had taken special liberties with chocolate-covered espresso beans. It didn't feel like Josh's and I longed for that calming breeze. It didn't even have the erratic dense feeling of dark magic. This felt utterly, devastatingly different. Inside I was electric, but everything around me felt sluggish and diminished, as though I was just waiting in the midst, ready for it to claim me. Was I going to feel like this forever, or was this just an aftereffect? There was magic festering in me, but its power was dormant. I hated feeling like this.

Ethan watched me more than the road, and by the time he pulled into my driveway, I was glad to be home, but trying to sleep didn't appeal to me.

"How do you feel?" he asked.

"Fine." I hadn't managed to convince myself that I was and definitely didn't convince him. The magic wore heavy on me: coiled and unable to be released. I didn't know what to do. I tried to use the magic to erect a protective field. Nothing.

When I got out of the car so did Ethan. "Come with me," he said, taking my hand and leading me deep into the coppice behind my house. The thick bosk was muted by the darkness, highlighted minimally by the illumination of the moon.

"We should go for a run, you'll feel better." He stripped off his clothes without hesitation, as always, very comfortable with his nudity. I wondered if he would be as comfortable if he had a keg instead of a six-pack. As he approached, each step caused the muscles of his stomach to tighten, and delineated lines ran along his chest and legs. I dropped my gaze once he was in front of me. He waited until I lifted them to meet his. With a reassuring smile, he slipped my shirt off over my head and then knelt down to unbutton my pants and waited until I stepped out of them. When he stood, his hands wrapped around my back, and with a simple slide of his hand he unclasped my bra. I grabbed it before it fell to the ground. "Go ahead. I'll catch up."

He backed away and effortlessly switched to his animal form, then disappeared into the thicket. It took me a little longer to change, but when I did, I found him in the middle of the trees, plopped down on the grass waiting for me. I ran past him, absorbing the pungent scents of oak, pine, fresh grass. The cool night air was cleansing to the senses as we sped through the grassy plain, darting around the trees. I felt invigorated, the trials of the day stripped from me, the magic dulled by euphoria. I ran faster and Ethan kept pace with me. I whipped around the trees, stopping short to go in another direction. I needed a few minutes alone. Not long, just a few minutes to enjoy that feeling that seemed so rare to me, joy. Sensing my need, he hung back.

I ran at top speed, the ground pounded into my paws, broken branches pricked at my skin, and the strong crisp air cleansed me. Finally, I stopped. Peace. I hadn't felt it in so long. I could stay like this. Immune to magic, unrestricted by the obligation of being a Moura, recluse from the pack and from civilization. I plopped on the ground, closed my eyes, and gave in to the fantasy. I wasn't sure how long I was there, maybe five minutes, perhaps five hours. I would have stayed just like that, but Ethan nudged me with his nose. My head lolled to the side, looked at him, then returned to my position. He lay next to me, close, half his body over mine. When he licked my face, I jumped up. Gross. That was something I just couldn't get used to.

He headed for the house in a slow, lazy trot and I remained

several feet behind, walking gingerly back to my life and all the complicated troubles that came with it.

Ethan was dressed, leaning against the house when I got there. I waited for him to turn around so I could change. He rolled his eyes, exhaled an annoyed, exasperated breath, and walked around to the front of the house.

I changed quicker than usual and found him leaning against his car.

"Do you feel better?" he asked.

I was afraid that if I said yes, he would leave. The buzzing stopped and I had relaxed significantly, but I was a victim of my imagination and it was as paranoid as they come. Constant flashes of the many things that could go wrong with that curse haunted me incessantly. The relief was immediate when he followed me into the house. Ethan and I weren't friends. Our relationship had limitations and constraints, unlike what I had with his brother. I wouldn't have had a problem asking Josh to stay, but with Ethan, things were different.

He looked around, walking slowly through the space as his gaze swept over the area. It had to be hard to be him. Did he ever just walk into a room, relax, and take a seat or did everything require recon?

"I need a shower." But I didn't move. Would he leave in my absence?

He relaxed back on the sofa, his arms outstretched, an indecipherable expression on his face, but his eyes were always expressive. Far too often I saw the deep gunmetal; now they were soft cobalt. "I'll be right here when you get back."

Hot water and steam usually relaxed me, making me feel renewed. But a half hour later, thoughts of the curse still remained fresh in my mind, unable to be cleansed, replaying in my head over and over—the consequence of possessing the Aufero was now death. The morbid thought clung to me in a manner that forced me back against the tiles, inhaling steam that felt like smoke. Breathing didn't come easy anymore; sharp ragged breaths just weren't deep enough. The calming effect of the run was undone and thoughts of everything came rushing with a fury. Things were bad.

It took some time for me to return to something that resembled calm, and when I came out of my room, I found Ethan in the kitchen. A plate of bacon and a stack of waffles were on the counter, and the eggs looked like they were almost done. His hair was damp and disheveled from being towel-dried and he'd changed clothes.

"I used Steven's shower," he said.

"Steven doesn't have a shower, that's the guest bathroom." It was an ongoing debate between Steven and me. I refused to have a housemate, but somehow he had managed to sneak his way into being one. Every time I said I didn't want a housemate, Steven shot back the same response: "Good, because I don't live here."

Ethan grinned. "Of course."

"And the clothes?"

"I always keep some in my car? Don't you?" Then his lips lifted into a crooked grin as he gave my outfit a once-over.

I looked down at my gray modal pants and matching tank. "What?"

He shrugged. "Cute outfit. Maybe for your birthday you can get some grown-up pajamas."

Ignoring his snide remark, I grabbed a couple of strips of bacon off the plate and took a comfy spot near the food. I wished I were the type of woman who owned sexy sleepwear. Cute sexy pajamas that were hard to sleep in. Give me a t-shirt or tank and comfortable pajama pants. Most of the time, I took them off and opted to sleep in the nude instead of the binding clothing. *What's wrong with comfortable clothes, and how is my outfit not adultlike?* I caught a glimpse of myself in the window. Okay, maybe I could have worn a plain t-shirt instead of the gray one with a wide-eyed owl in a sleep hat.

We devoured the food in no time standing at the kitchen counter. "What happens next?" I asked.

"We find someone to remove the curse. But it will not be anyone here. Marcia commands too much loyalty around here."

"Then what?"

"I don't know, right now there aren't many options. We have friends in the east that may be able to help, but honestly …" He paused. "Finding someone to remove a curse is going to be a task. It's such an archaic practice, the younger ones only know how to do it in theory."

"Your friends in the east, are they experienced witches that can do it?"

"They aren't witches at all. They're fae."

"How are they going to be able to help?" To me it seemed like he was bringing an electrician to a job that required a plumber. Especially after recounting Logan's derisive remarks about them.

"Yes, most fae can do spells. Like witches, there needs to be a certain skill level. I've never needed them for anything of this nature," he admitted.

Despite giving it a good fight, I couldn't ward off the fatigue and yawned several times. But if I went to bed, I wouldn't sleep.

"You need to sleep, you're running on fumes," Ethan said.

"I'm fine."

He stepped closer. He assessed me for a few moments, and amusement played in his eyes. "What? You think you are going to turn into a troll or fall into a deep sleep that can only be broken by a prince's kiss if you go to sleep?" he said with a grin.

"Yep, and where the heck are we going to find a prince this time of night?"

"Go to sleep, Sky, you've had a long day. Things will look a lot better tomorrow after you've rested."

Unless I was going back in time, that was doubtful. How

would things be better tomorrow? Tomorrow: I still would be cursed, be a Moura without her protected object in her possession, and be living in fear of an unknown guardian who killed Mouras if they didn't have their protected objects.

No matter how I tried, I couldn't stop thinking about it. But I nodded absently at his suggestion and helped him clean up the kitchen, just to delay the inevitable: a sleepless night or one riddled with nightmares. I wasn't looking forward to either.

Before he left, he leaned down and kissed me lightly on the cheek. He drew back, but stayed close. I moved closer, my lips lingering over his just moments before I kissed him. Lacing my fingers through his hair, I pulled him closer and his warm lips pressed against mine. He wasn't close enough. I tugged at his shirt, pulling him closer, his kisses more fervent as he backed me into the counter. He leaned into me, his lips entreating for more, his response passionate and feral, all-consuming. The weight of his body pressed against me. I grappled at his shirt, one hand pulling him closer. Grabbing a fistful of hair, he clung to me, and his ragged breaths beat against my lips. His tongue was warm and searching. We were as close as any two bodies could be, yet I needed to be closer. His fingers slid under my shirt, kneading into my skin. Slipping his hands under my legs, he placed them around his waist as he carried me to my room.

He laid me on the bed, reluctant to end the kiss. Pulling away, he moved just long enough to yank off his shirt and toss it aside, and then his pants. Firm, languid fingers trailed over me, and as his lips made warm trails in their wake, he removed my shirt and pants. The weight of his body relaxed firmly against me. I was stripped down to my underwear, and he sat back on his heels as his gaze moved leisurely over every inch of my body before he leaned down and kissed me again.

Threading my hands through his hair, I was reluctant to release him as he eased away from me. His warm lips cruised over my stomach, my panties, and my inner thighs before he returned to me. His kisses were ravenous and his hands made slow, languorous sweeps, exploring my breasts, stomach, and inner thighs.

He slipped off my panties, and I tensed when he sidled in between my legs. He stopped and watched me. Panting lightly, I closed my eyes, and his body rested over mine, melting into me. I was acutely aware of his light touch as his fingers intimately explored me, followed by gentle kisses. I felt him, a gentle pressure against me between my legs. I tensed and exhaled a ragged breath. He pressed harder, his lips moved lightly over mine. I gripped the sheets, taking slow, measured breaths as he gently rocked farther into me.

Then, he abruptly stopped, and when I finally opened my eyes, he watched me for a long time in silence. He kissed me again; warmth lingered on my lips for mere seconds before he nestled his face in the curve of my neck as his languid fingers gently roved over my body.

He pulled away with a tender smile, kissed me again on my cheek, then slipped to the side of me, nudged me over, and then cradled me against him. "You should get some sleep."

What? Are you freaking kidding me? How could I sleep? I was fully aware of his naked body behind me, the restless energy in me that hadn't been sated, the constant reminder of his attraction that poked at me from behind, and his hands wrapped around me, his fingers just inches from my breasts. Rest? How the hell was I going to rest like this?

His body was like reinforced steel. I attempted to nudge him away, but he didn't budge. Eventually, I relaxed against him, and his hold tightened. "I will wake you in an hour. If you don't wake up, I'll go look for that prince for you." He chuckled softly into my ear.

I wasn't going to sleep because I had no idea what had just happened. Why did he stop?

~

The next morning, probably like many women before me, I awoke to an empty bed. Ethan was gone.

I took a long shower and my thoughts were split between the curse and Ethan. Still baffled by what had happened, I wished common sense would take over. Ethan wasn't the type of person you liked, fawned over, or even slept with for that matter. He was the type of person you gave a smile and a quick nod to and went on with your day, aware that he would never be the person to give you "happily ever after." But that wasn't what went through my mind. If his looks didn't captivate you, his primal sexuality did. Why couldn't I just think of all the jackass things he had done to me instead of allowing them to slip to the back burner? And now the only thing I could think of was his lips on mine and the firm but gentle way he touched me.

Shaking off the thoughts of Ethan, I focused on Marcia. What was the game plan? Ethan didn't sound very confident that his contacts could remove the curse. If they couldn't, what was our next move? Who else could we turn to? With the exception of Josh, there wasn't another witch that could help us. For a brief moment, I considered Logan. He had to have some knowledge of the archaic practice of cursing someone. But I wasn't sure of the depths of his power. Could he remove it? But I quickly dismissed the idea. It was still an option—a last desperate option.

The voices on the television were louder as I stepped out of the shower. Pulling on a shirt, I expected to see Ethan. Instead, Steven stood in the middle of the kitchen, scarfing down a large bowl of cereal. I nearly knocked him over when I ran and hugged him. "What are you doing here?"

"Ethan called my mom yesterday and said if she didn't need me, he wanted me back here."

He quickly returned to his bowl of cereal, shoving spoonfuls in his mouth and barely chewing before he swallowed.

"Joan didn't mind you leaving?"

"The transition was easy. No one seemed to have a problem with her as the Alpha. But that probably had a lot to do with the fact that the higher-ranked ones were killed. It speaks volumes that she survived an attack that killed their Alpha." He scratched at his beard, which I planned to tell him later how much I hated. It didn't fit him. He was always trying new things to shake the boyish cherub looks that kept him from ever being considered handsome. He was cute, handsome-pretty at best.

"I'm glad he called because it saved my mom from looking bad once she kicked me out. Apparently, I am 'a messy pig that should live in a barn.'" He grinned.

I looked around the house. He had been here maybe a couple of hours, but his suitcase was in the middle of the living room, a jacket tossed on the floor, I was sure intended for the back of the sofa. There were unrinsed dishes in the sink, crumbs on the counter from a bagel he had half-eaten and placed on it. Trails of cereal were on the counter and so was a carton of milk, the cap removed and nowhere to be found. He was a slob, but I had missed him.

CHAPTER 17

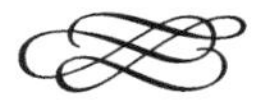

Although it had only been two days since the curse, I felt despondent because I hadn't heard from either Josh or Ethan. I figured they were working on something, but I wished I knew what. I was so desperate that I considered paying Logan a visit. I sent Ethan a text message since he didn't answer his phone: "Are you making progress?"

"Yes."

"Like?"

"I will let you know later."

"Do you think Logan can help?"

"DON'T GO TO LOGAN!"

I typed a text asking why, but deleted it. He didn't want to be indebted to Logan any more than I did. Tre'ases were tricksters by nature, so it wasn't as simple as just striking a deal. But the way things were going, I might have to make a deal with him just to survive.

I sat on my couch finishing up another project for work. I really hadn't wanted to take this assignment, but since I had turned down several of the audits offered to me, I had known I had to take this one. My employer had kindly sent me a copy of the contract, a reminder that I had agreed to take at least one assignment a month. Being a healthcare auditor wasn't a hard job. It was a good job that I liked and it worked for me. All I had to do was go assess a facility and fill out a report pointing out all the deficiencies that would cause them to fail a federal audit. It was the easiest job that I was probably going to get fired from if I didn't stop letting pack business interfere with it.

I finally hit the send button on my finished project. My stomach was telling me it was dinnertime. I looked over at Steven, who sat on the couch opposite me, with headphones on, looking at something on his computer. His stomach had growled less than ten minutes earlier. Foolishly, I thought it would urge him to fix dinner. But he hadn't changed, and he would wait until I gave in and made dinner.

Moving around the chair that for some reason was in the middle of the room, I negotiated around a couple of games that were sprawled over the floor and made it to the kitchen where I was met with bowls and plates from Steven's breakfast and lunch. "Your mom is right, you are a pig," I mumbled.

He looked up, removed his headphones. "What?"

I grinned. "Nothing."

He scowled. "I'm not a pig. It's organized chaos." He snapped his headphones over his ears.

When someone knocked at the door during dinner, I expected it to be my neighbor. He would be just as excited that Steven was back as I was and I knew that a surprise visit was only a matter of time. Ten was a little late for him, he was a brunch or dinner type of guy. Pointing out that his fascination with Steven was technically cheating on his partner was only met with a derisive grin and a rebuttal that noticing the neighbor wasn't cheating, just an appreciation for pretty men. I never got the pretty thing with Steven. Describing him as such was rather misleading; I considered him cute— a description he hated. The jasper eyes with flickers of brown, a result of a very intimate relationship with his animal half, were deep and engaging. Winged cheeks that were too flushed, and dimples that dipped too deep whenever he hinted at a smile, made him look young for his age. The supple bowed lips always took him from that place where he could be considered handsome. Even with the full ginger beard that he refused to shave after my multiple protests over the past two days, he didn't look twenty. When he smiled, he wasn't the hot guy, but the dimpled boy next door.

I couldn't hide my shock at Demetrius, the Master of the Northern Seethe, standing at my door. His hands were shoved deep into his slacks, and the deep opal eyes were a chasm as they looked back at me. It was hard to hold the gaze. The glower tarnished, and when he spoke his tone was as grave as his appearance. There was always a hint of an accent that I still hadn't been able to place. "I need to speak with you. May I come in?"

When I didn't extend an offer to let him in, he said softly, "Michaela is unhappy."

Good, send me a text when she is downright miserable. "Thank you for letting me know, you can give me a call the next time," I said as I started to close the door.

He held it. "She is upset because Quell isn't well. May I please come in?"

Out of my peripheral vision, I could see Steven's objections as he shook his head wildly. He didn't need to object: there wasn't any way I was letting Demetrius into my home. Because of my history, I didn't have the same immunity afforded to others, but Josh's ward kept out most of the undesirables.

"Quell is going to die," he said.

I mouthed the words to drop the ward and opened the door wider for him to enter. Steven stiffened, watching Demetrius carefully. Two years ago, he had stabbed Steven with a sword and twisted it while it was lodged in his gut just to cause more pain. He was a sadist, and now he was in my home.

He sighed and shook his head. "He will not feed. In fact, he will not do anything. I've sent ten people from the garden to his home and he sent them away untouched."

Demetrius could care less about Quell, but since he was one of Michaela's favorites, he had to care because her happiness seemed to be a priority to so many people. Such reverence of her was undeserved, and if it weren't for my feelings for Quell, I would have rejoiced in anything that brought her misery.

"Next time don't lead with anything about Michaela being unhappy, because I can assure you I don't care," I said.

His dark gaze was a smoldering charcoal abyss that could be easily entrancing. Even with the tinges of anger that spread across them, they were still oddly engrossing. It was hard not to be enthralled by the sadistic vampire with the appealing features. His hair was longer than it was the first time we met, but still a midnight-azure color. Thin supple lips did an exceptional job of making one forget the deadly weapons that hid behind him. A defined strong jawline and cheeks hardened his features when he frowned, which he was doing at the moment.

Was he actually upset that I didn't hold the same sense of sorrow that his horrible partner was unhappy? How could I care that the queen of evil was disgruntled? In fact, it brought me satisfaction that she was, and I just hated that it was because of Quell. But at least I knew why he cared. Their odd polyamorous lifestyle didn't stop him from doing whatever it took to make her happy. Quell made her happy for some odd reason. It wasn't anything born of virtue or depth. He was pretty, with the potential to be psychotic. She was drawn to that like an addict. Violence was her drug of choice.

"I've never dealt with anything like it. It's like he is trying to starve himself into nonexistence." He frowned. "I come to you because you have a way with him that I do not understand, but it is powerful. Can you help me?"

"I'll try." I didn't disclose to him that I might be the last person Quell wanted to see.

"Very well." He reached out his hand. "We can go now."

I wasn't *traveling* with Demetrius. The process seemed too intimate. And I didn't trust him to bring me back if I was successful with Quell. I was pretty sure he didn't care how I got home if I wasn't.

"I will be there in an hour," I said.

Entitled and used to the world bending to his will, he had the same look Sebastian got when anyone told him no. I could nearly taste his bitterness at my denial on my own palate. But he made a tremendous effort not to linger on his hurt feelings. "Very well, then I will see you in an hour."

"You can't get involved," Steven said in a stiff voice as soon as the door closed.

"I have to."

"What is your problem? This hold he has on you has to end."

"It's not a hold, I like him. We are—" I stopped, because I didn't quite know how to describe what we were; *friends* was the only thing that seemed to be suitable. But we were far more. We were connected on a level that Steven or anyone else would never understand. I didn't understand it. There was an odd responsibility I felt for him and I didn't know how to shake it. He would have been content dying months ago from a stake through the heart, but I had forced him to drink from me. It was the first time he had fed from a human and now I was responsible for him as he existed because I couldn't let him die, which I think he would have preferred.

He sighed, shaking his head in resolve. "You're setting yourself up. That monster will be your fall."

"How?" My irritation flared. "You keep calling them monsters, but how are they any different than us? If they are monsters, then we are monster-adjacent. We kill. If I'm not mistaken, that is how you got your position. You killed a man for it."

I should have slapped him; I think it would have stung a lot less. He winced. I softened. It wasn't his fault. This was one of the distasteful aspects of pack life—fights for dominance. He had made a challenge, but it was the choice of the challenged whether it was to be to death or submission. Steven's young age seemed to challenge his opponent's ego more than anything. Steven had won the position and his opponent died that day. I understood why it was necessary, but it was still a horrible way to live.

When I spoke again, it was absent the anger. "I am not saying that those of them that kill for the hell of it aren't evil; but you can't group them together, because they are different." He was doing the same thing that Quell had done, grouping all humans into this category of horrible inhumane creatures that had devolved into something that he couldn't bear to be around.

Steven listened, but the deep-seated frown was a true indicator that he wasn't going to change his mind. The were-animals judged the vampires harshly for their arrogance, but there was a level of narcissism that was deeply entwined in the pack's behavior. Both groups were blind to their own faults and cruelty. But I saw clearly despite the clouds of indifference that seemed to exist.

He exhaled a deep breath. "You've changed the rules to absolve him of his wrongdoing. Don't be foolish enough to think we aren't aware of what he is capable of. We know about the five women he killed in a matter of three days. And it did not escape us that they all looked similar to you. He has an insatiable bloodlust; he is a monster in the making. He is worse than a newbie. At least they learn to tame their lust, but he went years without having to and now he is an older vampire, strong and uninhibited. Michaela, due to her infatuation with him, will never choose to control him, and Demetrius will overlook it to make Michaela happy. Isn't it better to let it end this way, to save us all the hassle?" he said in a low wry voice.

Between Steven and me there was an indeterminable understanding. Never as deep or intrinsic as what Ethan and Josh shared, but it was distinctive and functional. I knew when he was trying to ease me into the iniquitous and dark side of pack life. The parts that I needed to be shielded from. "Don't touch him," I said firmly. "I mean it."

"It will not be up to you, but Sebastian. If Demetrius will not control him, and if Michaela encourages it, then we will have no other choice but to intervene."

For some odd reason Steven took on the role of executioner for the pack more often than most. The cherubic face hid a baleful side. Teetering closer to the line between his animal and human sides, he could use force or diplomacy when necessary. But when it came to dealing with vampires, he preferred violence and extermination.

"Don't. Touch. Him," I repeated in an icy, steely voice. "If you do anything to him, I will never forgive you and I will hate you forever."

His eyes were limpid and indecipherable, solemn. "You will hate me for a while, dislike me for a little longer, and then eventually you will forgive me and we will be as we are now," he said softly. "Because no matter how you try to sugarcoat it, you know what he is. At some point you will grow tired of trying to fix him and realize we didn't do it to betray you, but to help you."

"I can fix this."

"No, you're not fixing things. You're applying a bandage to a gaping wound that needs stitches. It's temporary and ineffective."

"I need him." The moment the words came out I wished I

could shove them back in. Steven looked like I had just kicked him in his man parts. The look of disgust and pity disfigured his face like a scar. I might as well have told him I had baby flesh soup for lunch.

His hands scrubbed over his face, but no words would come out. He just stared at me, the gold rolling across his green eyes in waves.

"It's complicated, and I wish I knew how to explain it," I said.

He shook his head. "I don't want to talk about it anymore. You go bandage your vampire and when it finally gets infected and is beyond repair, it will die on its own or we will euthanize it."

I would have killed Marcia if it weren't for Quell's intervention. Was it a necessary evil that needed to be done? Or just good old-fashioned, simplistic revenge? I had been angry because she hurt Ethan, even angrier that she had hurt me. I had the Aufero at the time, the thing I had come for, yet I had been willing to kill her. Was I in any position to judge anyone at this point?

"Can you fault the lion for slaughtering the gazelle for food because it develops a fondness for beauty? The lion needs to feed, and I acknowledged that it comes with consequences."

I couldn't believe I was saying this, either, and Steven's eyes widened at my response. I grabbed my canvas bag, shoved three stakes into it, then pulled out the knife that I kept in the bottom drawer and strapped it to my leg. "There came a point where I decided not to pass judgment, because if I used it too harshly, I doubt I would be able to like myself, let alone you," I admitted.

I was lashing out and it was unfair. For the first time in a while I felt overwhelmed. I didn't have the Aufero, I had a death curse on me, Quell was broken and I wasn't sure I could make it right. It was a lot to deal with and I was holding myself together by a tendril. When it finally snapped, all hell would break loose.

Steven knew me too well not to take it personally. I had told him everything, maybe too much, and he bore my burden without hesitation. He was calmer. He stepped closer and kissed me on the forehead. "Do you want me to come with you?"

He hated vampires. One was responsible for killing his sister, the only person left after his parents were killed in a car accident. He nearly died killing the vampire that had murdered her. He did what he could to stay away from them.

"Of course, but I can't ask you to," I said. "I think things will go better if I go at this alone."

~

Demetrius's dark shadowed eyes looked surprised when I drove up. The smile was unexpected. He walked to the car and opened the door. He extended his hands to help me out, and then pressed my hands against his lips once I was in front of him.

"Thank you for coming." His attention went to Quell's ajar door. "Michaela is in there with him."

Oh great, I get to deal with the Northern Seethe Mistress, whose claim to fame is her cruelty. A few months before, she had punished Quell by locking him in a box, depriving him of sensory stimulation, and starving him. It was how they traditionally punished. It wasn't how she punished him that bothered me; it was the reason. He was punished because he fed on me to keep from dying during reversion after being staked. How ironic: now he was doing it to himself.

She looked deceptively demure and sweet, her long dark hair swept back into a ponytail. Her thin frame didn't look so diminutive next to Quell, whose appearance was gaunt and febrile. How long had it been? Was it the last time he fed from me, which had been nearly three days ago?

Michaela's hand was splayed against his cheek, and her thumb lightly ran along the apex of it. Her voice was always a gentle melody despite most of her acts being direct contrasts. "They are here for you. If you can't stop, it is okay. We will accept the loss."

Three people stood in the corner; I assumed they were of the Seethe's garden. I hoped they hadn't heard how easily she would cast their lives aside as though they were nothing. I asked them to leave, but they didn't move. I considered telling them that if Quell were to use them, they weren't likely to survive and Michaela seemed okay with that. But they probably wouldn't care. I was still trying to figure out what psychological dysfunction led a person to be in the Seethe's garden. To feel that their highest honor was to serve vampires who didn't value their lives at all. They were nothing but pleasure and food to them and odd variations of both.

Michaela finally turned to look at me, not pleased. The leer rolled in my direction and then refocused on Quell. "She is here for you. Do as you please. If you can't stop with her, you will be forgiven and we will accept the consequences that may arise from it."

Then she looked up and gave a small smile as though she hadn't just offered me up like a turkey on Thanksgiving. We were in a good place of mutual hate and I was very comfortable with it.

She stood, beckoning for the garden to follow her, shifting one more scornful look in my direction. She might as well have spat on me with the contempt that laced her gaze. It more than insulted me a thousand times over.

Once seated next to Quell, I waited nearly five minutes before he gave me a clipped glance and spoke. "You shouldn't have come."

"You seem to be in trouble. If it were me, you would do the same."

"Are you confident in that assertion?" he asked, barely lifting his eyes to meet mine.

I nodded.

Michaela once said during one of her many nonsensical tirades that vampires often go through a period where they remember and long for a human life. Was this Quell's bout with it, or had my cruel act of violence and devolution just cemented what he believed—people were horrible and void of empathy and compassion? He didn't speak to me, but occasionally looked in my direction. Then he stared at me for a long time before looking away.

"If I hadn't arrived, you would have killed her. Why?"

"She had something I needed," I admitted. It was the first time I held his unwavering attention. I expected disgust, anger, maybe even revulsion; but instead it was appreciation, a limpid look of avid appreciation.

"The globe?"

I nodded.

"You had it in your possession, yet you continued," he said as he looked away, staring out into space.

Why was I being chastised? He had actually killed five people in three days and he was judging me. It bothered me. Not the judgment, but the fact that he was correct. I had had the Aufero, Marcia had been contained, and yet I had continued to hurt her.

"I didn't expect such things from you."

That ignited an anger in me that I wasn't aware existed. "You killed five people out of bloodlust!"

It was quiet as he looked at me; the dark eyes were opposite of what was shown on his face: a wistful and morose look. "You are better than I am." His voice dropped to a whisper. "I need you to be better than I am. That is why I stopped you." He shook his head slowly. "You should have seen your face, you looked so different—lethal. Of all those that exist here in the otherworld, for some reason you cling to an ideal based on the purity of humanity. I considered it a little foolish and part of me still does—but I am alive only because of the way you feel. I can feed without killing because of the way you are and—" He stopped and worked for a while at a smile that barely curved his lips. "I like that about you. I don't want you to ever become morally fatigued, because then, maybe I can be proven wrong and maybe there is more out there. And I am okay with being wrong."

I've had the experience of being stabbed several times, and they all felt better than this. I slouched into the seat next to him. "Please don't make me the beacon of humanity. Don't judge others by what I do. I'm struggling and probably will screw up a lot. I can't deal with that type of pressure," I said softly.

I could feel him appraising me as I continued to fidget with my hands. "She hurt Ethan," I said. "She tortured him." But was it really an excuse for what I had done?

"You wanted to kill her because she hurt Ethan?"

I thought about it for a long time, and in the end, I didn't have an answer. "I don't know," I admitted. "The pack is all I have. They protect me, and I want to do the same for them."

"You have me."

I smiled. "I am glad that I do." I had become accustomed to him being in my life. His little idiosyncrasies added a unique fabric to it. "But I need them as well." It was the first time I had admitted it selflessly. Before, I needed them to protect me, but somehow it had either evolved or maybe even devolved into a need. I needed the pack.

He nodded. "I understand." And he did. The ignoble relationship he had with Michaela forced understanding. They hadn't created me, and my devotion to them wasn't intrinsic but it was born from a need that they managed to fulfill.

He turned to face me with a quiet resolve that made me relax a little. There was a hint of that peculiar plant-eating vampire lurking behind his dour eyes. I held out my arm. He moved it aside, moved closer to me, and his cool lips pressed against my neck, where they remained for a long moment. I gasped when he finally drew blood, slow, careful pulls from the vein. Pulling back every few moments to make sure I was okay. When he finally stopped, he lingered close to my face. The soft kiss placed on my cheek was also unexpected. "Thank you for coming," he said.

I stood up. He hadn't taken a lot, and probably would need to do it again soon. "Will I see you tomorrow?"

"No." His tone was devoid of any emotion. I couldn't figure out what was going on. "It is time that I start using the garden."

The vampires had a few that they cared about, but some were disposable. How many would he kill before they stopped him or he would have to seek outside sources? I wanted to stay to question him, but he had checked out of the conversation and was focused on something past me.

Michaela stood alone by my car as I walked out of the house. She looked surprised to see me. I barely gave her the enjoyment of my time as I opened my car and started to duck into it, stopping just before I could sit down. "It would be counterproductive to punish him when all he truly wants is death," I said softly.

"Will he survive?" she asked, the compassion in her voice something I wasn't prepared for. Did she really care for him? Was she capable of such feelings?

"I don't know, but you can't keep punishing him like this. He has to be allowed to feed as he did before."

It was doubtful that we had many things in common, but we both wanted him alive, or whatever vampires were. "I will consider it," she said. "His dependence on you is a problem, and I do not like it at all."

Why don't you give me a list of the things you actually like, I am sure it is shorter?

"I really would appreciate it if you did," I said gently. And I was able to keep the malicious thoughts and names that went through my head off my lips.

She stepped closer to me, regarding me with her deep onyx eyes. The demure smile was her most deceptive attribute. "'Appreciate'? It seems as though you are asking a favor of me, am I correct?"

"No. In fact, I came here at the request of Demetrius, who approached me on your behalf. I came here, although I despise you. And let me be clear: I do despise you. But I didn't request that it be considered a favor, although I had every right to do so."

She listened, but the same obstinacy and arrogance that dictated her personality left a little smile on her face that was too alluring for someone so cruel. "I will not forbid him to use you." If the smile had stayed for any longer I wouldn't have had the willpower not to wipe if off. "You can thank me if you would like."

Thank her? I was too preoccupied with thoughts about hurting her.

Her lips pressed into a tight moue. "You're not going to thank me?" She smirked and kissed me lightly on the cheek. I relaxed the clenched fists at my side and made a poor attempt to calm myself. "Let's just call it even, shall we?" And then she vanished.

Each time I dealt with her, the idea of a war between the were-animals and vampires didn't seem like such a bad trade-off for killing her. She was unnecessarily cruel and it bothered me that she received exemption from consequences because she was the Mistress.

After she left, I went back to Quell's home. The door was still slightly open, but I knocked anyway. He was still in the same place I had left him, but he looked better. He barely acknowledged me; he was so pulled into thoughts that held his attention more than I could. He looked at me with an intense curiosity.

"I don't want to leave," I admitted. "Can I stay?"

He simply moved farther down the couch to give me room to sit, which I did in silence for just a few moments before he lifted his gaze from his hands. "Would you like something to eat or drink?"

He had food? "What do you have to eat?" I asked.

When he went to the kitchen, he pulled out a family-size bag of M&M's and a bag of microwave popcorn. "I have these. You seem to have them both at your house a lot."

I nodded at both the M&M's and popcorn. He popped the

corn, then brought them and a glass of water back. When I dumped the M&M's into the popcorn, he made a face.

"Don't knock it until you try it."

He grabbed a few and ate them.

"You can eat."

He nodded. "It doesn't satisfy anything, but I can taste it. And honestly, I don't see the appeal," he said with a slight smile as I shoved handfuls of sweet-and-salty mix into my mouth.

We eventually settled into an odd but comfortable silence. There wasn't even small talk, just silence. "Was your transition easy?" he finally asked.

"Hell no," I scoffed with a smile. "For a while I knew I was different, but I couldn't put my finger on it. The enhanced hearing and smell made me feel like a freak and I always felt uncomfortable in my skin—like I didn't belong. Because I was adopted, I didn't know much about my family and had absolutely no idea I was a were-animal. Then at fifteen, I changed." The memories came back harder than I expected. The doubts, sorrow, feelings of confusion and desolation washed over me briefly and I quickly shrugged them off. I wasn't a fifteen-year-old girl anymore and I had seen too many things and been through so much that it was rather insignificant now. "When I finally changed to a wolf, I did this five days later." I extended my arm: the scars from trying to slash my wrist were faint, and if I hadn't done it so often in hopes of preventing my body from healing, I might have been scar-free.

He looked at the scars for a long moment. He said nothing as his thumb ran slowly over my arm. "Now?"

"I like being a were-animal," I said, taking extreme creative license with the word *like*. *Accepted* or *tolerated* would have been a better choice, but I sensed that Quell needed more. I needed to love what I was. "Once I met the others, I didn't feel like such a freak anymore."

"What did you think before you met them? What were you like?"

I grinned. "A complete and utter weirdo."

"Well, that can't be true."

"I don't think I have said anything more truthful. I bounced between being on the un-dateable and weirdo lists constantly," I said, and it was the first time I could bring myself to laugh. "I wish being on the weirdo and un-dateable lists were the biggest of my problems." I popped a couple of chocolates into my mouth. "And I cemented my position on it when I broke up—or rather my first and only boyfriend, Robert, broke up with me. We'd dated for nearly a year, he didn't know I was a were-animal and I am glad I didn't tell him—he was a huge gossip. But after dating for so long it was time to ..."

Although I thought the implication was apparent, he seemed to want me to finish my statement. The expectant look remained as his head tilted slightly.

"Have sex. He was supposed to be my first, and we had planned it for weeks. We were about to do it when I growled. Not moaned, but growled, like an animal. I darted out of the house with my clothes in hand and drove home."

"Why did you leave? I assure you growling wasn't a problem for him."

"It wasn't out of pleasure, I was about to change. The same odd feeling I get whenever I changed happened. I had to get out of there. A couple of times before my mother started sedating me, I changed and somehow ended in the woods with a half-eaten carcass next to me. I didn't want him to be a carcass next to me."

"So you weren't deflowered, because you were afraid of eating your lover. How noble," he said, grinning, then he put another handful of popcorn and candy in his mouth and frowned.

"Nobility had nothing to do with it. A half-eaten boyfriend may have been quite hard to deal with. I spent most of my teen and young adult years waiting for the torch-wielding locals to find out about me. Then my life became such a train wreck that eating a potential lover became the least of my worries."

He looked me over with a hint of amusement and appreciation. "Hmm, so no lovers? A woman of virtue. That is very hard to find these days."

I took a long drink from my glass of water. "Don't give me too much credit. The only thing that stopped me then was the fear of eating my boyfriend for dinner. 'Virtue' had nothing to do with it."

"So if it weren't for the possibility of eating your lover and your 'train wreck'—I believe is the word you used to describe your life—then what? You would be the city's harlot?"

Harlot? Did people even use that word anymore? "Probably if we were living in the fifteenth century. I just don't want you to place any undeserved flattery on me. I am not a woman of virtue, just one of horrible circumstance."

The smile and his mood change were welcome. He had shed whatever thoughts weighted him into his somber state. "Well, you are indeed one of the best harlots I have encountered." He ate another handful of my concoction and grimaced. "You like the way this tastes?"

"Of course, salty and sweet." I shoved another handful in my mouth. "So now you know my little secret, and it is one, so"—I pressed my fingers to my lips—"shhh … I have a reputation to uphold."

"Of course," he said, his smile broadening.

The elated fun mood was just what I needed—what we both needed. The weight of the curse and whatever had darkened his mood seemed so far away. But my curiosity about the odd vampire that I cared too much for was still there.

"Were you married?" I asked.

"No."

"Did Clara ever marry?"

He nodded. "I am glad she did. She deserved better than the person I had become." As if he had remembered that brooding was his thing, the smile vanished, replaced by a sullen disposition.

Sorrow darkened his eyes and his features held the same pronounced sadness. I inched closer, and when I touched his hand, he linked his fingers with mine. His thumb ran rhythmically along the side of my hand.

He was quiet for a long time and just when he started to continue, there was a knock on the door. I cursed whoever was there, and when Steven peeked his head in, I glared at him.

"What?" I snapped.

"I'm sorry to come by unannounced. Sky, you aren't answering your phone." I had forgotten about the freaking phone that was tucked away in my purse on the floor. I had heard it vibrate, but ignored it. I retrieved it to find that I had three missed calls and five text messages.

"I had it on vibrate."

The gold rolled across his eyes and he tried hard to douse the anger, but what he had to say was displayed prolifically on his face: *How dare you silence your phone while you are here with this monster?* But Steven quickly put on his guise of diplomacy and gave me a small smile, just big enough to expose dimples. "Yeah, that's a habit you really should break."

Then he directed his attention to Quell. "I guess she didn't want her visit with you to be interrupted. But she has to catch an early flight tomorrow," he explained.

That was the first I had heard of this. But when I looked at my messages there was one from Ethan, Josh, and Steven informing me of it. A flight to New York tomorrow at 3:17 p.m., which wasn't an emergency. There was plenty of time. But that was the excuse Steven used to get me out of there. The three hours had gone by too quickly and I still didn't want it to end.

"Okay, I will be home later," I said.

Steven didn't move; instead he leaned against the door, the pleasant smile still on his lips. His eyes wandered over the room. I suspect he was just as surprised by the home as I was the first time I came here. The Tuscan décor that inspired the feeling of an

Italian countryside. The muted oranges and variations of brown and tan complemented the ceramic tiles, the subtle variations of colors on the walls adding a warmth to the home that I'm sure Steven didn't expect.

The room received a quick glance, then the bowl of half-eaten popcorn and M&M mixture, but it was Quell who garnered a great deal of consideration. Steven's smile looked genuine, but he was quite skilled at it even when it wasn't sincere.

"Quell, do you wonder if Skylar's the only one that can stop a vampire's reversion?" he asked.

It was the first time anyone had ever discussed it. The incident had been ignored as though it were a dirty little secret. He was just "my vampire" and I was left to fix the situation. It was a situation I had under control, but I suspected that everyone was tired of finding out more quirks about me. The ability to hold and manipulate magic was one thing, then there was the fact that silver didn't affect me like it did other were-animals, and the occasional *terait,* usually seen in vampires during bloodlust. As a result of a vampire trying to turn me in vitro, I had the honor of having that particular trait.

"I hadn't given it any further consideration," he responded, and the mood we had shared was now gone, the bond broken by Steven's interruption. It was becoming increasingly difficult to keep my irritation from showing.

"Do you mind if I explore my curiosity?" he asked.

The understanding of what he was asking came to us immediately and almost at the same time. "I don't think it is necessary," I said.

"And that is why I am asking Quell." When he spoke his voice was persuasive and gentle. "Quell, you have every right to decline to satisfy my curiosity, but I hope you will consider it. I extend the same trust that Sky has in you. You must understand how vital this information is. I need to know if things have changed and the vampires are now able to feed from our kind and survive."

Quell didn't appear to possess the same curiosity and I was torn between finding the answer and putting him through reversion to do so. My face remained blank as he studied Steven, trying to make his decision. Quell would do a great deal for me. By default, his obligatory feelings for me were easily transferred to Steven, because of the closeness I had with him. I was conflicted. Curious enough not to stop Quell if he were willing, but not so curious that I'd ask him myself.

"Yes," he said.

Steven had the stake in hand and had plunged it into Quell's chest before he could have a chance to rethink his decision. Steven said, "I am sorry, I assure you the anticipation of it would have been worse than the act. This is the best way."

Quell fell back onto the couch, his face twisted into a pained grimace as his legs stiffened the same way they had when he had gone through reversion a couple of months ago. Steven waited a little too long for my liking. I said, "What are you waiting on? Feed him."

With a deep, ragged breath, Steven hesitated for a moment before he gave Quell his arm. It was disgust rather than pain that shaded his appearance as Quell fed from him. But the reversion continued. I pushed Steven away, the fangs slipped across his forearm, and he hissed as blood spurted from the entry point. The reversion didn't occur as fast as it had the first time, and I was sure that since he now used my blood instead of a plant's, he was more resilient.

He latched on to my arm immediately, and for several minutes took long painful draws until the reversion stopped. After a few more, we waited as he became whole again. He rested his head back, eyes closed as he took a moment to assuage the pain from having had a stake plunged into his chest.

"Is there anything you need?" Steven asked. His voice held concern, although I knew it was insincere. Not because he was cold, but because I knew how he felt about vampires and I doubted my friendship with Quell would change that.

"No," Quell said. "I will recover."

"Then we will leave you to do just that."

But he was on his feet the moment Steven suggested we leave. With a voice like gravel, he called my name. "When will you return?"

"I don't know, but I will make every effort to be back in three days."

"Okay." He leaned forward and kissed me lightly on my forehead.

"Then I will anticipate your visit."

He escorted us out the door. His demeanor had changed, and his gait was encumbered and pained. I wondered if he had fed enough to sufficiently heal or had restricted himself for fear of nearly killing me as he had the first time.

Steven quickly started toward his car. "You hesitated," I said. "Did you consider just letting him die?"

"He's already—"

"Don't do that."

He simply looked past me to the odd cornfields behind Quell's home. "I didn't think it would be so hard to lower myself—" He stopped abruptly. "I didn't think it would be so difficult for me to feed a vampire. I thought the information we gathered would be enough for me to overcome my aversion. I was wrong."

"You can't stop a vampire's reversion."

"Were-animals can't, and it's a good thing. We heal faster, and although I don't think a vampire would be stupid enough to do it to someone that is part of our pack, there are smaller packs and lone were-animals that would be abused just for that purpose. I don't care about the ones that have their kinks and quirks about feeding from were-animals; it's purely psychological. They wouldn't feel joy from doing it to a were-animal that they perceived as weak, but it's a perverse pleasure I would rather not try to understand. The Sable and Gavin thing is disgusting and so is what you two have." He paused. "He likes you."

"Of course he likes me. He would like you, too, if not for the things he is forced to deal with regularly."

Shaking his head, he said, "No, that is not it. He *likes* you. What is your endgame here, Sky? What do you plan to do with him? If you get married, does he move into the basement so you can keep him from becoming the inevitable—a murderer? Will you continue to coddle him because you don't want him to have another three-day killing spree where all his victims coincidentally look like you?"

"Don't be ridiculous. That was just an isolated incident. He behaved as any newbie would, and now he is fine."

"Is he? Then we'll see if you need to be in New York more than a few days. Perhaps you'll need to be there for weeks. What do you think will happen then?"

I didn't answer because I didn't have one that would please him. Steven inched closer to me, his gaze soft and sympathetic. "It's best that you distance yourself from him. When he needs to be dealt with, it will make things easier."

"What? Do you plan on murdering him?"

"When he has a heartbeat I will call it murder."

"How about assassination, is that better?"

Sagging into himself, he washed his hands over his face several times. "Do you realize Michaela will be just as diligent in protecting him for extreme misdeeds as you are at trying to save him from himself? It is only a matter of time before we intervene."

"Then promise you'll help him. You'll let me handle things. I will fix it. I swear."

He frowned, turning his back to me as he opened the car door, and said, "I will show compassion. I promise to do it while he rests, so he won't know what is happening. I don't have any desire to do this, especially if it will hurt you. But I have dealt with vampires longer than you have. Take my advice and distance yourself from him." He hopped into his car and drove away.

I looked back at the farmhouse and wondered if Quell would be there when I returned. Fighting the urge to go back to his house, I came to the sour realization that Steven was right. If I was the only thing keeping Quell in check, despite my feelings of obligation to him, it couldn't last like this for much longer.

CHAPTER 18

We arrived in New York too late for me to catch a show, which was on my to-do list. Ethan and Josh went to their rooms, and by the time I was settled, neither one of them was still there.

I stopped by the concierge for a recommendation of a good place to eat.

"What are you in the mood for?" she asked with a painted-on professional smile that remained long after I had started to walk out the door toward the Mexican restaurant she recommended three blocks from the hotel. I stopped and turned in the opposite direction, passing several restaurants, but none of them appealed to me. A jazz restaurant got my attention as I stopped at the door. The sultry instrumental sounds of bass, trumpet, and a mournful, soulful voice kept me engaged longer than the smell of the food. I stood at the entrance and inhaled the fragrant smells of salmon, bison, poultry, rosemary, onions, and ground pepper. It was alluring, but not enough to accept the invitation of the hostess to be seated.

The next place was a nice Italian restaurant. Duck, flour, pasta, oregano, tomato, and basil were enticing enough to be my meal.

The smell of vodka mixed with vermouth lingered throughout the room, yet it wasn't what I wanted.

The yearning was odd and strange; my olfactory sense was unable to be sated by any of the restaurants so far. I walked several more blocks and was coerced into another restaurant by the scent of olive oil, potato fries, beef, peppers, onions, and various other seasonings. The hostess, sensing my hunger and urgency, told me she would send over bread as she guided me to a booth at the back of the restaurant. Before I could be seated, Ethan, who sat just a few seats from where the hostess was directing me, looked up. His narrowed curious eyes linked with mine for a few moments before he waved me over. I slid into the booth, ignoring his attentive gaze as I stared at the double steak-burger, rare, with cheese. My mouth watered and the server couldn't get to the table fast enough. Ethan slid his plate in front of me.

Taking several bites out of the burger, I chewed it enough to allow space to shove a few fries in, too. I finally looked up to find Ethan, who had relaxed back, watching me carefully. "Did you track me here?"

"No. I didn't track you. I tracked down a very good burger and some mediocre fries," I said, taking several more bites from the burger.

"You passed at least six other places that served burgers. Why this place?" I really hated half-smirks, and he and his brother had a fondness for them.

I shrugged. "The same reason you did. I could smell it from the street."

He didn't look convinced. He leaned forward; his thumb slid over my lips to one corner, wiping away the spilled ketchup. He said, "It is one of my favorite places to eat when I am here."

I grabbed a napkin, dabbed at my lips, and looked down at the nearly devoured burger. I probably looked like a savage. "I guess I was hungrier than I thought."

He ordered the same meal again: rare burger and fries. When the server came back to the table, I ordered salad and wings. His sneered at the salad.

"I like salad," I said defensively.

"No, you cling to the idea that you like salad because it makes you feel 'typical.' Like the average woman having an average meal. You do not like salad any more than I do," he said as he glanced at the empty plate.

"You didn't answer my question. How did you end up here?" I wished he would just wipe the smug look off his face. He took a drink, but his attention remained on me.

Even I was starting to consider the situation. Why did I come to this restaurant out of the many I had passed? It wasn't as if I was a food snob. Of all the places I could have chosen, why did I come here?

Our food came and I picked at the wings, taking a few bites, but I made sure I ate my salad.

The conversation between us had been reduced to annoying small talk because we were ignoring the elephant in the room; it was dressed in sequins and dancing the cha-cha.

"Why did you leave in the middle of the night?" I asked.

"It wasn't the middle of the night, we didn't go to bed until morning."

"Okay, I'll play your little game. Why did you leave in the middle of the morning like a tacky jerk?"

The smile didn't quite curl his lips and settled into something between a smirk and a sneer as he took another sip from his glass. "Does it matter?"

"If it didn't, I wouldn't have asked."

Leaning into the table, he asked, "What creative reason have you drafted?"

But I hadn't come up with one. So many things about his behavior left me bewildered. I didn't think I would ever understand him. And more importantly, did I want to?

"I think you are complicated and I will never understand why you do half of the things you do," I said.

His gaze softened and lost some of its focus on me. "I didn't want to be there when Steven arrived." Resting back in his seat, he studied me for a moment, then asked, "You were really nervous with me, why?"

"I wasn't nervous," I lied. At this point, why did I even try?

The crooked smile played at his lips too long to be amusing. "Women are a lot of things with me in the bedroom, but never nervous."

"It's probably because your modesty and humility puts them at ease," I shot back.

He wouldn't drop the subject. Admitting my lack of experience came easy with Quell, but I just couldn't with Ethan. I simply shrugged off the question.

He opened his mouth to speak, but stopped. His hand shot up to signal someone. I turned. Josh was coming in our direction. "I guess he tracked you, too," I mumbled into my drink.

"Yeah, right after I texted him the location."

Josh plopped into the booth next to me and immediately grabbed several fries from his brother's plate. He looked at the burger and frowned. "Rare?"

"Of course," Ethan said.

Josh grumbled his displeasure and looked around for the server. "There's a club down the street, we have to check it out," he told me.

"Our meeting is at noon," Ethan reminded him.

Josh looked at the clock on his phone. "Yeah, fifteen hours from now."

"I don't need you hungover."

He flashed the same miscreant dismissive grin he always did whenever Ethan attempted to control him. Ethan's being the Beta of the strongest pack in the country meant nothing to his younger brother. Josh draped his arm around me. "Can I coax you into a naughty night of fun that is only going to piss off my brother?"

I smiled, but at the situation and not Josh. If nothing else, traveling with the brothers was always a lesson in sibling dynamics and made me appreciate being an only child.

Ignoring the look Ethan gave me, I agreed.

Ethan was a less-than-enthusiastic participant as he followed us to the bar a couple of blocks away down the busy street. For a Wednesday, it was crowded. I immediately knew why Josh had been drawn to this place. Like the club the pack owned and he managed, it was full of the supernatural types. Interspersed between them were the wholly human, drawn to the bar by an enigmatic dynamism that they could never describe. As we made our way through the bar, my gaze wandered and held the attention of the guitarist as the band set up. There was a slight glint in his eyes; he grinned, and I couldn't stop staring. What was he?

When I stopped walking to watch him, Josh whispered, "Mage." His voice had the same derisive lilt it always held when he discussed them. Every so often his elitist views, the result of being a witch, managed to surface. He referred to mages as "diet witches" and said that, like diet soda, it was never as good as the real thing. Mage magic wasn't as strong as a witch's. Their skills were limited to defensive magic. But because of their ability to cast spells, it would be more accurate to describe them as "human plus."

I sensed the were-animals the moment I walked into the room, and the vampires as well, even before seeing the fangs or brushing against their cool skin. Sometimes their dark eyes were the telltale sign, but in the right light, they looked normal, like heavily pigmented brown eyes. You can't tell witches by looking at them, but their magic tingled my skin, a little tickle that let me know they were near. Most were-animals couldn't detect a witch nor sense how powerful they were, but Ethan and I could. I guess it had a lot to do with our mothers being witches. His was a powerful one and it would be odd if he couldn't.

We found a small space at the end of the bar, but Josh was there for only a few minutes before an enthusiastic witch approached him. There wasn't any doubt she was a witch; magic wafted off her in waves, nearly at a level that matched Josh's. She guided him onto the dance floor where he stayed for several songs.

Soon someone had coaxed me onto the dance floor. Bodies moved erratically on it, and we weaved our way through the crowd and found a spot near Josh.

The music played, bodies bumped and gyrated against each other. More than once, I was splashed by someone's drink. And if I had forgotten why I hated clubs, that was a reminder. Josh had made his way back to the bar and scuttled into the corner with people that, to a casual observer, looked like friends he'd known a lifetime and not a couple of random people he'd just met in a club. When I approached, he handed me a shot glass, then tossed the other one in his hand back, wincing slightly before he ordered a couple more for his new friends.

Yeah, you're going to be ready by twelve tomorrow.

There was a level of comfort and sadness about him, and it was then that I realized that Josh didn't interact with other witches often. He wasn't accepted by the ones in the Midwest because of his relationship with the pack, and for many years he had been ostracized. Now he was surrounded by them, there was an instant affinity and connection, and he was enjoying every minute of it.

Ethan hadn't moved from his spot at the end of the bar, nursing the same drink he'd had since we'd walked in. Several women had approached him. I guessed the broody, antisocial type was alluring because nothing about him hinted that he was approachable or wanted a friend. But it didn't stop them from rotating in and out of the seat next to him. Every so often, I looked in his direction and our eyes met, a little clip of amusement, and with a lazy smile he returned his attention back to whatever woman was now in the seat.

Josh had found his way back near my direction and urged me back on the floor. Bodies beat rhythmically around me, and instead of me dancing with Josh it had become a group dance. A crowd of warm bodies moved around me in a hedonistic manner. Bass pounded at the walls, the music blared into the crowd, and more people came on the floor. I usually hated overstimulation—I was sure most were-animals did—but this didn't bother me as I moved around, partnering with anyone I found myself next to. The energy was intoxicating, or maybe it was the shots and cranberry and vodka that I'd had.

When I looked in Ethan's direction, the chair next to him was empty; he lifted his glass and waved me forward to come have a drink with him. I wanted to finish the song, so I let him know it would be a minute by sticking up my finger, but before I could catch his attention again, a curvy blonde had. I didn't have to look at her eyes to know she was a were-animal. More than likely feline, her lithe movements unintentionally sensuous. The appreciative look on Ethan's face gave me the impression she wasn't nearly as ugly as the hideous shirt she wore. It wasn't hideous, not really, but I wanted it to be, and I wasn't sure why. It was a navy sleeveless ruched shirt so low cut that it didn't have any chance of containing her breasts but I doubted that was an issue for her. And her jeans were just as fitting and revealing as her shirt.

It *bothered* me. *She* bothered me, and the way Ethan interacted with her bothered me, and I hated that feeling. Instead of dealing with the peculiar feelings, I turned my back to him and continued to dance until the feeling went away or at least I was too distracted to notice it.

Again the bodies whirled around me, the music pounded, the

energy heightened, it pulsed and pounded as much as the music. Then for a second—it stopped.

We are monsters. I heard the voice against my ear. I felt queasy, like when I traveled with Josh. I stopped in the middle of the floor and grabbed my stomach until the nausea calmed. Everything was back to normal, the music, the bodies moving around and against me, but the energy was off. Not as strong, subdued.

Had the three drinks started messing with me? I shook my head and stopped in the middle of the floor waiting for the voice again.

The "diet-witch" stood on the other side of the room, and when our eyes met, it happened again. *None of us should exist as we do.*

I couldn't pull my gaze from his, wondering if he was the one. But how could a person who wasn't nearly as strong as a witch do that? I dismissed the idea when he started talking to an overenthusiastic fan. Again, the music stopped, and for a blink of a second I wasn't in the club. *Help me stop the monsters.*

It wasn't the diet-witch. The bodies moved, the music played, people drank, and no one had heard the voice or noticed that I had left. For minutes, I stood in the middle of the dance floor, staring through the crowd until I heard someone say, "Whatever she took really messed her up,"

Soon Josh was standing next to me. "Are you okay?" he asked. Seconds later Ethan was next to him, watching me carefully.

I looked around the room at everyone behaving as though nothing had happened. And I couldn't believe not even Ethan had heard it. How could they not hear that? But then I thought maybe I was drunk.

"I think I had too much to drink," I said.

Ethan clasped my hand. "We are going back to the hotel, you can stay, but remember—"

"We have a meeting at twelve," Josh interjected, rolling his eyes. "No, I'm going with you."

His new friends seemed disappointed at the idea that he was leaving. "No, you stay, I'm fine."

Josh's gaze fell on Ethan's hand holding mine and then he frowned. After a few moments, he nodded.

The cool air that hit me once we were out of the club was sobering. Ethan stood in front of me. He cradled my face, staring into my eyes. "You're not drunk."

"No." I liked being close to him, it was comforting.

"Then what happened in there?"

I considered making something up, but decided against it. "I heard voices."

Yep, that was exactly the look I expected to see.

"Voices?"

Then I explained what had happened. I might not have been technically drunk, but saying it out loud made me feel so ridiculous I wanted to claim to be and move on.

"Stay here."

Ethan went back into the club and was gone for nearly ten minutes. "I didn't hear anything or see anything suspicious," he said when he returned. "Josh and I checked out the mage, it couldn't be him. In fact, there isn't anyone in there strong enough to do anything remotely like that." He shrugged. "Maybe there was a witch in there screwing with you."

I wanted it to be something that simple. And if anyone wanted to get rid of the *monsters*, it would be the witches. But I hadn't dealt with the witches on this side of the country. Did they hold the same contempt for were-animals as the witches in the Midwest?

"Maybe the fatigue and the alcohol are getting to me." I really wanted it to be those things instead of someone without a blood connection with the ability to get in my head. When Josh and I had a magical blood connection, we could hear each other's thoughts. The idea that someone could do that to me without me knowing freaked me out.

. . .

Nine blocks later, the city had lost interest for me. Our city was pretty much shutting down around this time and the insistent liveliness of this one was hard to get used to. Ethan's concerned furtive glances just made me wish I were alone.

"How far is the hotel?" I asked.

"About sixteen more blocks."

"Really?"

"Yeah, you walked quite far to find me," he said, smirking, and then he hailed a cab.

"I walked that far to find a steakburger?"

The amused, taunting grin remained.

Ethan lingered at his hotel room door just a little too long, holding it open as I passed his room to go to mine two doors down. I still couldn't believe that he and Josh couldn't stay two nights with each other. He touched my hand and when I turned, he responded with kisses, light and gentle. He pulled away, close enough that his lips wisped lightly against mine as he spoke. "You should stay here tonight."

Lithe fingers ran along my cheek, over the curve of my neck as he waited for an answer that didn't quickly come. A carnal urge made denying him hard, but that goddam logic was a true killjoy. Good sense dictated that a relationship with Ethan wasn't a wise decision. The longer I thought about it, the more I cared less about his history and wanted to give in to a primal lust that balked at logic and common sense. He planted a light kiss on my cheek, and his lips lingered against my ear as he spoke, his breath warm against my skin. "If you have to think this long about it, you should say no." With that, he slipped into his room.

~

The next morning, a variation of the pancake song played in my head. Of course, there wasn't a pancake song; just a constant upbeat chorus of "I want pancakes.". My stomach growled and I couldn't focus on anything else except the carb-loaded breakfast and I was prepared to pay the hotel's exorbitant prices, which somehow made me think that their food had to be laced with gold. I walked into the restaurant and my attention immediately went to Ethan sitting on the other side of the room across from a strawberry blonde. It was the same woman from last night, but with different clothes. Her hair was swept into a messy ponytail on top of her head. I could only see glimpses of her wrinkled button-down. I tried to slip out unnoticed, but his eyes raised to meet mine the moment I saw him.

I backed out of the restaurant in a hurry and walked several blocks until I found a small café hidden off the main street. The moment the server walked up to my table, I placed my order: five buttermilk pancakes, French toast, eggs, and bacon. I ignored the stunned look.

My stomach grumbled to be filled, but all I did was stare at the plate when it was placed in front of me. *Stop it!* I scolded myself for thinking about Ethan and the blonde. When had he called her? Had he even waited until I closed my door before he did? Was she offended that he discarded her for me, only to return to her last night?

The audible growling of my stomach continued and I shoved pancakes into my mouth, ignoring Ethan, who had come into the café and taken a seat in the chair across from me. Head down, I concentrated on my food as though I hadn't encountered anything more interesting in my life.

He wasn't going away.

I reminded myself how ridiculous it was for me to feel this way, but my emotions were pretty fragile and I was jealous.

"What?" I asked, looking up just enough to glance at him before returning my eyes to my food.

He rubbed at his face. It had been a couple of days since he had shaved and it was more evident now. He sat back in the chair.

"Her name is Sara, she lives here—"

"Good. Now you can refer to her by name instead of 'what's her name that I screwed in New York.'"

He sighed. "She is considering moving to Indianapolis to be closer to family and wanted some information about the liaison, but I don't think she really liked my opinion. I only know her by reputation and she seems like a wild card. She will not fare well under his direction." Packs were huge, and Sebastian used liaisons in each large city to help to manage them. Calling them an Alpha was a misnomer, but in a smaller pack, most of them could easily be one. They worked as an extension of Sebastian and an infraction against them was just as serious as one against him.

I attempted to finish my food, shooting furtive glances in his direction as we did what we did best: ignored the obvious and let that elephant roam free in our space.

"Do you think about it?" he asked.

"Huh?"

"Do you think about what Logan told us about spirit shades?"

That is exactly what we were going to do. Ignore the obvious and move on to something else. We were so good at it now, there had to be some type of commendation for our expertise in the game of avoidance.

I nodded. "All the time. Maya could be a Faerie. Wouldn't it make sense? Elves and witches can bring a vampire back from reversion, but to the best of my knowledge, they can't manipulate magic. I am assuming Faeries can." Then I stopped and considered another less than desirable option. "Can demons feed vampires?"

I waited impatiently while he thought about it. Based on what Logan had said about the Faeries, was being a demon any worse?

"Not to my knowledge," Ethan finally said.

"And elves?"

He nodded.

Giving up the pretense of completing the meal, I slid the plate away. "I can read the Clostra. Josh can't nor can you. You are —*were* holding the magic of an elf and can't read it. Josh is a witch and can't read it...." I just couldn't finish. The only thing it left was Faerie.

"So can Senna," he pointed out.

"Yes, but we don't know what she is. We just know that she isn't really related to me. This means she probably isn't a witch."

I had said it aloud, but the concern was there on Ethan's face, a flashing warning that this was just another problem added to the many we already had.

"We'll deal with that later. We need to remove the curse so that you can get the Aufero back."

I couldn't have agreed more, but on the subject of Logan, there was something that bothered me even more. "The Tre'ase that created Maya, I really want to know who it is. After all, my survival is based on his. If he dies, so does Maya and so do I."

"When we get back, we should pay Logan another visit." His voice was rigid and coarse; the idea of going to Logan's was as grating of an idea for him as it was for me.

But I couldn't stop thinking about what he had said about the host and hosted relationship. If Maya was indeed a Faerie, was I strong enough to counter her actions and motives? At what point would my actions be hers and not mine?

Ethan didn't leave immediately. Instead, he remained near my table. "Skylar, don't make things awkward between us. Okay?" His deep-seated gaze held mine, waiting for an answer.

Don't make things awkward? We had slid past *awkward* at record speed and were loitering in an odd spot between *weird* and *complex*. Instead of pointing that out, I simply nodded my head.

Yeah, let's just pretend things between us aren't awkward.

We drove through the heart of Brooklyn and I wished we had time to stop to see some of the historic sites that we passed. Some areas were still fighting off gentrification, with dilapidated buildings with tattered signs advertising long-ago specials. Debris, broken glass, and refuse cluttered the streets. The buildings had character, the dusty homes told a story, and older people sat out on front porches watching children as they played.

Josh kept looking in my direction, his lips lifted into a little smirk. "Go ahead Sky, ask."

"I just don't get it. Fae magic is vastly different from the witches'. How will they be able to help?" Especially since most fae magic was very limited: defensive magic, cognitive manipulations, premonitions, and minor spells. "What are they going to do, will the curse away?" I hoped they could help us, but since our conversation with Logan, I had put the fae, along with mages, in the innocuous file.

"Yes, the majority of fae's magic is limited, but just like we have levels, so do they. There are some that are quite strong, and their minor spells are not very trivial at all."

"But it's not the same. You told me that elven, fae, and witches' magic worked differently, like being on a different frequency. How will a fae be able to remove a curse made by a witch?"

"Just think of it like opening a door. Using a key is ideal, which would be equivalent to a witch removing it, but a sledgehammer or locksmith tools will do the trick. Let's just say that if these fae can help us, it will be like taking a big axe to the door," he said.

I wasn't sure what to expect when meeting the fae, but the bearded man who answered the door definitely wasn't it. The long, full brown beard was a peculiar difference from his bald head. A red long-sleeved shirt peeked out from under his green Kermit the Frog t-shirt. A pair of charcoal, trendy square-rimmed glasses completed his look. He greeted Ethan and Josh with a hug, patting them firmly on their backs. His smile was so broad and welcoming it surprised me, not with Josh, but with Ethan. Most people weren't that ecstatic about meeting him, and definitely not about a second visit.

"Austin, thank you for meeting with us," Ethan said.

"Orchid, they're here," he shouted as he stepped aside to let us in and revealed an eclectic, rustic dust-colored brownstone. The brick was adorned with metal wall art, and the other plain beige walls were spruced with brightly colored abstract paintings. The furniture was a mishmash of eccentric urban chic and Bohemian. I hadn't decided if it was wondrously distinctive to the point I couldn't fully appreciate it, or simply lazy and haphazard decorating.

I still hadn't come to a decision when a woman squealed as she entered the room. She jumped into Ethan's arms and planted a long, lingering kiss on his lips. Austin didn't seem at all upset by the display. And he was just as apathetic when she did the same to Josh. I was the only one startled when she pulled me into her arms, hugged me, and planted a kiss just as enthusiastically on my mouth. When a menthol breeze nicked at my lips, I remembered Winter's warning that a fae could bind you to truth with a kiss. I was sure that Orchid had dealt with Ethan enough to know that he gave the answer you needed, which wasn't always necessarily the truth.

She straightened her dark ivory slouch beanie and brushed away sapphire and black long bangs, the only hair she allowed to peek from under the hat. The dark hair made her deep apricot skin more vibrant. The button-down plaid shirt of interlocking shades of yellows, beiges, browns, and golds blended well with her odd gold eyes that seemed a little too pale. One look at Austin and I realized his glasses were distracting from eyes that were just as pale and golden. Taking both Josh's and Ethan's wrists, she flounced away as she guided them into the house.

"Come in, have a seat."

I couldn't help but watch her the way I did those hyperactive toy dogs at the park. She zipped around the room, straightening pillows, aligning the trinkets on the tables, all the while speaking like a person on an espresso rush. She was going to wear herself out.

We had a seat on the overstuffed sofa while Orchid went to the kitchen. She came back with bottled water, milk, and cookies. The cookies didn't look like anything one should serve to guests. In fact, they looked like something you would discreetly toss in the garbage before pulling out a bag of store-bought ones. They looked dry, with a few morsels of chocolate chips scattered in them. And who puts out only five cookies?

"Have one. That's all you'll need," Austin said as he lifted the plate toward me.

I started to grab one when Ethan clasped my hand and held it. "Thank you for the offer, but unfortunately this trip is strictly business."

Austin nodded politely and placed them on what they were trying to pass off as a coffee table, but was actually a piece of charred wood cut in an odd misshapen clover atop a brass frame. Our "strictly business trip" didn't stop Josh from reaching for a cookie. When Ethan shot him a sharp disapproving look, he simply took a napkin off the coffee table and wrapped three "fun" cookies in it before shoving them into his pocket.

The narrow features of Orchid's face sharpened as her lips pulled into a barely visible line as she scowled. "So, Marcia must really be causing trouble," she said as she plopped into Austin's lap and relaxed back against him. With his neck cradled against her neck, they were a perfect fit. He was as calm as she was hyperactive, or perhaps he had already had a couple of the cookies.

"What isn't she doing?" Josh stated, exasperated, his hands wiping over his face.

She smiled. "Ethan, what brings you to us?"

His face turned an odd shade of red as the corded muscles of his neck pulled taut. "We discussed what I needed on the phone" was all he said, in a strained voice.

She sighed heavily. "Ethan, I am stronger than I was as a teenager; you aren't going to be able to resist it. Just relax and talk to me."

But he didn't. He repeated his statement again.

She rolled her eyes and turned to me. "Skylar, can you tell me what happened?"

Ethan spoke up. "I would prefer to handle everything."

"Of course you would. Ethan, I understand your need for discretion in many things, but I need as much information as possible." Then she grinned. "You are going to hurt yourself trying to deny me my answers. I can't do that to you." She turned to me. "Skylar, please answer my question."

The information dam broke. Everything that had occurred since I acquired the Aufero was revealed to her in annoyingly specific detail. Her eyes widened when I told her about Ethan's grandmother being a dark elf and what had happened to him after she died. She chuckled when I told her I had tried to drown Marcia and that one of the witches smelled like onions, and she listened very carefully as I went over the spell, interjecting occasional questions. And I told her everything I could without a filter. She asked: Did I remember the spell? I wrote down as many of the words as I could remember. Then she inquired about the animal they had used. I went into detail about everything they did, before, during, and afterward, giving her a descriptive reenactment of what had been done. The level of intrigue on her face was surpassed only by that on Ethan's face. Orchid's small smile widened.

For a long time she took in the information, processing it, with both her and Austin's faces void of anything usable. "Will we be the first to try to remove the curse?" Austin asked.

Josh nodded. "The moment I bring up Marcia's name, most witches refuse to be involved. Even those that I know despise her will not do anything to provoke her wrath. And the rest don't like to mess with curses, it is too dangerous."

While Austin and Orchid occasionally asked questions, Josh and Ethan sat in anticipation. I couldn't anticipate anything because I wasn't that confident in the first place. My lack of knowledge regarding fae made me pessimistic.

"We will not be able to remove the curse, but we can weaken it. Josh and Ethan, we will need you for it."

They agreed without hesitation and with blind confidence. "How do you plan to do this and why do you need them?" I asked.

It was bad enough I was cursed. I didn't want to bring them into it. What if things didn't go as expected? I had become a cynic, something I wasn't happy about.

Orchid grinned. "I like you."

I think that people who kiss me on the lips should like me, at least a little, so it was good that she did.

"We will dilute it. I will find which of my animals is your compatible and transfer it through them and then transfer it back. It will need to be done quickly, because I don't want to kill them."

Images of little kittens and puppies dying from being used as compatible animals were persistent thoughts in my mind.

Sensing my concern, she made a melodious, deep sound, holding the note for a long time, progressing to a crescendo of high-pitched sounds. When she stopped, there was a synchronized swooshing sound, and within minutes a group of snakes slithered in our direction, various sizes and colors. They sidled in so close I lost count after twenty-four. They wound across the floor and over the legs of the chair. It was only when they reached Austin and Orchid that they formed a single line splitting off toward them.

I tried to be as calm as Josh and Ethan, who didn't seem to have a problem with a nest of snakes coming toward us. *They're just a group of Winters, nothing to be alarmed about,* I told myself. But I had only seen Winter in animal form a couple of times and she was gross and scaly, just like the ones coming our way. There wasn't any way to sugarcoat it.

Austin and Orchid each held one in their hand, clasping the head and holding eye contact with it for a few seconds before releasing it. The serpents came toward us, some slithering around our legs while the others slipped up them. After several minutes, we each had a snake near us. A black one with odd patterns lay at Ethan's feet. Mine was silver, beige, and rose and so long its body could wrap around my thigh. The snake that picked Josh had coiled around his leg, rubbing its snub head against him. His compatible was more affectionate than ours, which didn't seem to bother him.

When Orchid made a low, deep, throaty sound, the snakes reared back and then struck out, latching on to our legs, drawing blood. A collective gasp filled the room as the snakes sucked blood from us. It was a few seconds before the grip loosened. Ethan was able to pull his off his leg. He held it in a stranglehold.

"Ethan, let go of Franky," Orchid commanded softly. The moment he released it, the snake sidled in next to Ethan while he glared at it. The snake hissed at him several times. It may have been Ethan's magically compatible animal, but it definitely didn't like him.

Is that how it worked? Shouldn't they have said, "Hey, I am going to bring a nest of snakes out, one of them is going to bite the hell out of your leg. Are you cool with that?" You warned people about something like that.

Josh and I waited patiently for our compatible snakes to finish while Orchid snuggled with the others, as though she were playing with little dogs. Their split tongues darted out, planting kisses on her face. Gross.

"Very well, I will need a couple of hours to get the others. I suspect I will only need two more fae," she said.

We received the same farewell, a kiss to remove the spell and an overenthusiastic hug. Orchid was affectionate so it was expected, but I was surprised at how friendly Austin had become. He hugged me after unraveling Tara, my compatible, from around my arm. She had become quite fond of me and had to be torn away.

Three hours later we returned to Austin and Orchid's and were greeted with two other fae. Austin attempted a quick introduction, but the nervous tension was too high and everyone just regarded one another with a casual nod.

Strong but calm magic wafted throughout the room. It was like standing on the beach and feeling the breeze that came off the ocean. It was too soothing, which made me doubt its effectiveness. How could magic like that hold up against Marcia's and the Creed's, which felt like a bristling windstorm.

We surrounded the table that was placed in the middle of the living room, where Orchid had been since we arrived. After several moments, she finally looked up and with a confident smile, she laid out powders, salts, and a large dark stone. She asked us to get closer before she placed the serpents in the middle of the items, and they busied themselves with crawling over and around the stone.

"Are you ready?" she asked us, radiating a level of assurance that chipped at my doubt. She handed us our compatibles and once again their fangs sank into our arms, drawing blood, holding on longer than they had before. The powders were spread around each of them once they were placed back on the table, and another pale stone in front of each snake.

Then things happened quickly. The four fae chanted, then Orchid pierced the skin of each snake, just enough to draw blood, which mixed with the powder that surrounded them. The mixture took form, molding together before it covered the stone, the chanting came faster, and the fae's pale eyes were nearly white. Their magic was no longer a gentle breeze off the ocean, it was a blizzard chilling the room, tugging at our breath. A fiery force of power engulfed the room, expanding and retracting with ferocity.

Thrashing into us with such force it was painful. Josh was the first to collapse to his knees, and I followed. Ethan stood—barely. Orchid slammed to the ground convulsing. The other fae soon dropped to the ground, their bodies writhing uncontrollably for seconds and then—nothing. They all lay on the ground motionless, their pale eyes rolled back, their last breaths taken only moments before, bodies stiff and warm.

Ethan's movement was sluggish as he went closer to the table and smashed everything on it. Josh's lips moved fervently as he performed several reversal spells, but it didn't stop whatever was going on. The fractured pieces of stone glowed on the table. The snakes went wild; their bodies moving in short spastic jolts for several moments before all movement came to a stop. They lay motionless on the table.

We started CPR on the fae, although there was no evidence that they had a chance of being saved. But we couldn't stop rotating between the four of them, compressing their chests, trying to push life back into them as we delivered rescue breaths.

After ten minutes, we stopped and stood in the middle of the room, looking around it at the dead bodies that surrounded us. Bile stuck at the back of my throat. Thick pulses of magic clouded the room and the smell of death was a noxious odor that tainted the air.

Ethan finally said, "Josh, leave the bodies as is, but you will need to remove all evidence that we were here."

Josh didn't move very quickly, still staring at the dead bodies surrounding us, a somber look on his face.

"Josh!" Ethan snapped. "Get it together."

He nodded, withdrawn, and his hands waved over the room. Sparkles of blue illuminated and he looked at each place they were. He whispered a spell with a quick flick of his hands and they disappeared, and our existence and prints vanished from the premises. He did it with such ease, it was apparent he had done it many times before.

CHAPTER 19

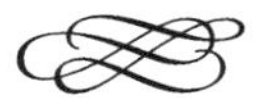

The drive back to the hotel was solemn and silent with poorly concealed grief. Neither Ethan nor Josh would look at me the entire drive. The moment Ethan parked, they both got out as though they were expecting the car to catch on fire. But they weren't running from a pending danger. Or maybe they were—me.

I couldn't stay in my room, and the walk down the busy street was a welcome and needed escape. The smell of wet asphalt from a recent rain shower helped cleanse the memory of fae lifeless bodies. Guilt wrenched at me, and the faster I walked, the more the memory sharpened, a surreal replay in my head. The curse couldn't be broken and anyone that tried would suffer the same fate as the fae. I would die if I came close to the Aufero, a protected object that I was responsible for protecting. When I didn't think about the string of events, things didn't seem like such a mess—but they were a mess.

I focused on the dewy fragrance of rain, ignoring the distraction of perfume and asphalt that also wafted through the air. The clicking of shoes on the busy street was another distraction I welcomed. I passed several restaurants, but nothing interested me. I finally stopped at a pizzeria. I started off watching a man pressing out the dough to make another pizza, but my focus quickly went to the rich, decadent red velvet cake on the counter. It was going to be dinner.

The restaurant was nearly empty. I was about to take a seat near the door when I saw Ethan and Josh sitting in a booth at the far end. I started to turn around and leave. I guess we all had the same idea: solitude. Josh beckoned me over, and the thought of leaving anyway crossed my mind several times.

Josh was stuffing a slice in his mouth as though he expected it to sprout wings and fly away. By the time I was at the table, he had started on another. It was safe to assume that he had buried his sorrow in pot cookies. Ethan hadn't touched the pizza on his plate. Instead, he was sipping on a mug of beer. Each time he swallowed, he grimaced. He'd never struck me as a beer drinker. Scotch was always his drink of choice.

"Have a seat," Josh said, chomping on his third slice as he slid over to make room for me.

Ethan's lips pressed into a tight line and he stared at me in silence. Between devouring the pizza and chugging down his beer, Josh managed to ask me if I had gotten their message. Too busy trying to distract myself, I had forgotten to look at my phone. There were two text messages from him telling me that our flight was at eight the next morning.

Ethan remained quiet the whole time. Occasionally I could feel his eyes on me, deep and penetrating, as he took more drinks from his mug and then finally a few bites of his pizza. He finished up his beer, tossed his napkin on his plate, laid out some money on the table, and slid out of the booth without saying a word.

"Are you going back to the hotel?" Josh asked.

He shrugged. "I just need to get out of here," he admitted as he frowned in my direction as he left.

"You know how he is, don't take it personally," Josh said mildly, but I could tell he was holding back a snarky comment.

How could I not take it personally? Because of me, four fae that had nothing to do with this situation were dead.

We settled into awkward silences that were occasionally broken by clumsy small talk. Eventually Josh put our attempts out of their misery and excused himself to leave. I stayed. The music was nice and I needed the distraction.

When the server returned to the table, I was glad no one I knew was around when I ordered a half of a red velvet cake. I ignored the sympathetic smile that said "Cake will not make it better."

I devoured the dessert and needed to leave before I ordered the other half while I tried to wait out the rain. It had been coming down pretty hard for half an hour, but I was too restless to stay. With my head down, I walked through the streets still busy with people leaving the subway. The rain splashed off the pavement, and my clothes and hair matted to my skin. I could hear the footsteps around me, most of them a steady pattern that remained consistent, but then I heard steps close behind me. The sloshing steps hastened whenever I picked up my pace. Pulling my purse close to me, I balled my hand, ready to strike if necessary. A burst of magic whipped against my back and things happened too quickly for me to react. An arm banded around my waist as he pulled me into him. The crowd disappeared.

Folded onto the ground, I tried to hold on to the food I had just eaten as everything spun around. I grabbed my head, staring down at a pair of battered loafers. Wedged between two buildings in an alleyway, I tried to devise an escape route. Winter always considered hitting a man in his private area beneath her; I didn't hold such beliefs. That was my go-to tactic. Yes, I was skilled enough to protect myself, but why make things harder than they had to be? It was crass and using an unfair advantage, but I wasn't above it. But Samuel stayed too far away for a good kneeing in the groin. When I stood, he handed me my purse. "You are not alone often, are you?"

"Good thing, I can only imagine how many times I would be abducted if I were."

I went into a defensive stance. He held up his hands and stepped back. "I don't plan to harm you," he said. His deep, sand-colored gaze appraised me for a long time.

"Then drop those," I said, jerking my head toward the translucent barriers that blocked me on the left and right.

He nodded once and they fell. The quiet was uncomfortable, and the thick waves of magic that reverberated off him were like I imagined it would feel being near a tornado. It felt like Josh's on overdrive. There is such a thing as too much of a good thing, because it was bringing back the memories of Marcia submerging me in her pool as I fought for air.

"I want the books," he finally said.

"I want to have peppermint bark chocolate available all year round. I guess we can only keep hoping, right?"

He smiled, genuinely. It was odd; I expected him to be a lot more menacing. He kept a fair amount of distance between us, but the smell of tobacco drifted off him.

"What do you know of me?" he asked.

Dammit, I didn't know there was going to be a quiz. But I didn't need to think long; everything came out so quickly it was like I had a dossier on him. "You are strong. Based on how I feel around you, perhaps the strongest witch I've met. Marcia doesn't consider you dangerous enough to kill, because she would have done it when she had the chance. I assume she will want you as an ally, which makes me believe you can be reasoned with and/or bribed."

I waited for him to add something, but he remained silent. The deep inquiring gaze remained on me and the subtle curl of his lips made it hard not to relax. I should have been more afraid. But his mannerisms didn't evoke an instinctive urge to protect myself.

"Go on, please. I am sure there is a great deal more."

I wanted to say that it seemed like Sebastian and Ethan really hated him. But that wasn't really true. They didn't hate him; there was a level of apprehension, and if I didn't know better, I might have called it fear. "The Creed kicked you out, but I don't know why. Those hounds weren't anything you can find at your neighborhood pet store. They look like a product of elven magic, which means someone is afraid of you or you were owed a lot of favors."

"I find working off fear to be counterproductive. People seek to conquer fear. Those who like you deal with you more amicably, show compassion and camaraderie when necessary."

"Unfortunately, you are very powerful. People will fear you because of that."

"True. Is there more?"

"Isn't that enough? On paper you don't seem like a very nice person."

His features were pleasant enough. If I weren't standing with him in a dark alley with strong magic teeming in the air, a constant reminder of how dangerous he could be, I wouldn't have been apprehensive at all. The gentleness of his smile seemed to reflect mildly in his eyes as well.

"On paper you come off worse as well," he said. "You're a Moura Encantada who doesn't have her protective object. A werewolf that has the distinct feel of dark magic on her. I wonder how you've managed that. And Marcia is very vocal about telling people that you came to her home to kill her. Of course, she conveniently leaves out the reason. Should I judge you by what I know of you, or how I feel standing in front of you?"

Well, I liked how I sounded on paper—I came off like a real badass. He stepped closer, and I changed my stance. He didn't seem threatening, but it was never a good idea to underestimate how dangerous a person could be. Was this going to escalate to violence? Clutching my purse closer to me and shifting my weight to my back leg, I was positioned perfectly for a front kick that would send him far enough for me to get away. His movements were lithe, controlled, and it was evident that he could handle himself in a fight if he needed to. His build was sturdy, and although I might have been stronger than he was, he had a magical advantage. As the distance between us closed, I wasn't thinking about a fight. I was considering what it would be like to possess his magic. Each step closer, the desire increased.

I hated that if I had a knife I would have tried to find out. A whip of the blade, an exchange of blood, a quick chant, and I could have it. The thought consumed me and I nearly forgot that he was so close. Would I be able to control it or would magic that strong be too much for me? Would I submit to it before ever gaining true control? What happened in a case like that, rampant magic uncontrolled by its possessor? What type of chaos could it bring? Josh always rationed what he gave, and still at times I found myself in need of his help to control it.

Samuel was oblivious to the nefarious thoughts that plagued my mind because if he weren't, he wouldn't have stood as close. I glanced at the broken glass that glittered against the ground, and thought for a mere second how it could be used like a knife. I tossed the idea aside and focused on him.

"The books that your pack has should not be in their possession," he said.

"Let me take a wild guess: you think you should have them?"

"No, they should be destroyed. Some things are too evil to exist. Those books are such things."

"They can't be destroyed."

"Did Sebastian or Ethan tell you that?"

"No one had to tell me. I saw it with my own eyes. They tried to destroy one of them by burning it. It used magic to save itself from destruction."

He nodded slowly. When he reached, I suspected, to brush the damp hair that kept matting over my eyes, I blocked his hand. "Don't."

"Sorry. I can't see your eyes. I need to see them."

I raked my hands through my hair, pushing it back and away from my face.

"The spells in the books are strong, and yes, I want them, but not for what you think. I want to help."

"Help do what?"

The rain stopped and he seemed pleased. Pulling out a package of cigarettes from his pocket, he lit one and took two long draws before offering me one.

I frowned at it. "No thanks, my lungs and I have a deal. If I don't try to poison them, then they soldier on whenever I decide to go for a jog. We get each other."

He took another long pull, then exhaled slowly before tossing the cigarette to the ground and smashing it with his foot. "There are things in this world that shouldn't exist. Whoever thought it was a good idea to have the books, but never use the spells in them, was a fool."

"So you think it's okay to just do a spell and kill all the were-animals, vampires, elves, and fae?"

"Those aren't the only ones in there. There are spells to release the beast, to make you and your kind whole. The same for the elves, fae, and I do believe witches as well."

"And the vampires, what happens to them?"

"They will return to what they were," he said.

"They were dead. Before they were changed into vampires, they were dead."

He pulled out another cigarette and had it lit before I could make a snide comment about my lungs. "I think that it is a small casualty of the situation."

"Why are you coming to me?"

"You are a Moura Encantada, one of the few people who can read the spells in the book. I've heard there are others, but I think you would be the best for the job."

"In this little dossier that you have created about me, is there something about me being gullible and stupid? Because obviously you seem to think I am. I don't consider myself some type of god and will not behave as one. Who are we to decide that were-animals and vampires shouldn't exist? Or that the fae, elves, and witches should be stripped of their magic?"

Each time he spoke, I expected his voice to be rough and disconcerting, but it retained its mild timbre. "You can't be happy living like this. Pulled into a world where monsters lurk, thrive, and vie for the position of lead monster. It is chaotic and unchecked. Magic and anomalies of nature that can only be managed through drastic means, magic, and even death. Yes, you can try to live a normal life, but once a month you are reminded that you aren't normal. You are one of those monsters, a creature of circumstance. You deserve to be relieved of that burden. They all deserve to be relieved of the burden."

"Says the guy who used magic to abduct me."

"You are right. I include the witches, elves, and fae among the monsters as well, just to a lesser extent," he offered.

I wished I had an impassioned rebuttal, but I didn't. For a fraction of a moment I considered what he had said. Life without the existence of the otherworld didn't seem like a bad thing.

"Even if you can release me from this curse of lycanthropy, I am still a Moura Encantada; I will never have a normal life."

There was an odd delight that pranced over his gaze and lingered for a long time. "Without an otherworld, the objects do not need to be protected, because there is nothing to be destroyed. Humans wouldn't be able to use them, because they only work with magic."

We didn't speak for a while, and the silence didn't seem to bother him. "So you are just an altruistic stranger that wants to save the fae, elves, and were-animals by giving them a normal life."

He took another long draw from the cigarette. "Not at all. I see them as all monsters, creatures that shouldn't exist. They are intrinsically amoral, but only because the things that dwell in them seek a level of satisfaction only gained through power."

I listened to his gentle, compelling words of truth. He wasn't a knight in shining armor, but rather a mercenary with an altruistic agenda. But his logic was flawed. The magic didn't make people monsters or create their desire for power; in the real world they would not behave any differently.

"'Help me get rid of the monsters'—that was you?"

He nodded. "I used a glamour of the image that seemed to have intrigued you the most, then I took you out of the bar, just for a moment."

That is why I had felt so queasy. *Traveling,* magical transportation, was something that only some vampires could do, and higher-level witches. It was often draining on them, which made me wonder how strong Samuel must be to be able to do it three times after performing a glamour.

"What if I decide not to help you?"

He shrugged. "Then you are free to leave. If you like, I can take you to the hotel."

"I want to leave."

He stepped closer, I guess to touch me, so we could travel to the hotel.

"No, I will walk."

He nodded, slowly taking another pull from the cigarette.

I had only taken a few steps when he spoke. "Be careful. My intention is to release the were-animals from their animal half. Marcia's goal is to destroy them. She knows that you are a Moura

Encantada and I am sure she is getting her affairs in order to have you help perform the spell."

"I will not help her, either."

"You will not have to. Although were-animals are immune to our magic and elven magic in animal form, fae still have the ability to compel your mind in any form. I suspect, even as we speak, she is trying to find one that is willing to betray your pack. It is inevitable that you will be the one that will be used; but you can choose in which way. Will you save them from the animals that live within them, or will you be the one responsible for killing your kind? Although I find us all vile creatures, Marcia only considers the were-animals to be. The rest will exist in a world without were-animals. Who will be there to keep the vampires in check?"

My long, thoughtful silence had somehow provided implied agreement between us. He smiled.

"I will not help you," I reiterated.

His face was blank, but his tone remained the same, gentle and entreating. "Will you take my number in case you change your mind?"

I nodded and handed him my phone. He entered his number and gave it back. As I walked away, all the new information didn't comfort me at all; there was just too much and I needed to sort it out. I had made it to the edge of the alleyway when I stopped, feeling his presence still there. "How many protected objects are there?" I asked.

"Five: Gem of Levage, Aufero, Clostra, Fatifer, and Vitae."

Vitae? I had to learn Latin.

"Who oversees the Mouras?" I asked.

"I don't know. I would like to find him as well. He's like a shadow. I thought I found him when I found the Moura for the Gem of Levage. But it was too late when I got there. She was dead and he was gone. You don't have the Aufero, but as I said before …"

He didn't have to finish it. I risked being found and used by one faction or another.

"You thought if you found him you could find the Clostra?"

He nodded. I tried to make my expression blank, but based on Samuel's face, I failed. I wanted to help him. If he was right, then life would get uncomplicated fast.

As a light rain started again, I wanted it to wash away the guilt that wore heavily on me, because half of my walk was me trying to rationalize helping Samuel and betraying the pack. If I brought the idea to Sebastian, would he automatically reject it? They didn't seem to have a problem with this world, in fact, they enjoyed dwelling in the darkest part of it.

If he was right and he could remove the magic, I wouldn't be cursed anymore. Whether or not Maya was a Faerie, elf, or witch would be irrelevant because their magic wouldn't exist. This world would be better; the battle for dominance in the other-world would be a futile endeavor because there wouldn't be any power to be obtained. But there was one thing that dampened my fantasy of a simple life: if the spirit shade could only exist as long as the Tre'ase that created it did, then when the Tre'ase was without magic, could the shade continue to exist? I was alive only because I hosted her. If she ceased to exist, would I as well? Was there a way to work around it?

The Vitae, the elusive fifth object that meant "life," needed further investigation. Life of what? The objects were never simple and usually used for something nefarious, even the Clostra, which in witches' Latin meant *key*. But what did it really unlock? It was books of riddles and inconclusive spells that were so dangerous they had been placed in three different books.

Ethan's eyes shifted from his phone to me the moment I entered the lobby. I ignored him as he followed me to my room, keeping his curious scrutiny on me. My attention stayed on my screen as I scrolled through my e-mail, fully aware that Samuel's number was just a few clicks away.

My wet clothes and hair matted against my skin, so I went to the bathroom to grab a towel and slipped off my shirt. Modesty, much like many of my qualities pre-pack, was fading into nonexistence. When I slid off my shirt, Ethan's glance was one of indifference, as though it was just another naked body. Ethan was the furthest thing from my thoughts. I was preoccupied by the things that Samuel had told me. If he could find a way to allow me to continue to live and remove magic, would I betray the pack and take the books for the chance at a normal life? I wished I were more confident in my assertion that I wouldn't. I wasn't.

"What do you want?" I finally asked.

Ethan moved with such natural predacious grace, I had to learn to control the fight-or-flight reaction his presence sparked in me. When he looked at me, I felt trapped. His sharp gaze tracking my every move, I stopped in the middle of the room. A twinge of curiosity made me wonder if he knew what had happened. He watched me in silence for a long moment.

"Occasionally, I can be a little rude," he said softly. "Today I was. I'm sorry."

Were we using *occasionally* the same way? His eyes narrowed ever so slightly as my conscience began to get the best of me. Ethan just waited in silence for me to confess my sins. I hadn't betrayed them; it was only a conversation. Yet I bore its shame as though I had already given the books to Samuel.

"I went back to the restaurant, but you weren't there. Where were you?" he asked.

My lips rolled slowly over my teeth as I bit back the truth. "I went for a walk."

I wasn't sure why I didn't tell him the truth. Feeling like I was in a state of perpetual limbo between trust and mistrust, I needed to sort things out. There was truth to what Samuel had said, and perhaps there was some in what Sebastian and Ethan had told me as well. But how much of it had been edited for me to see the reality they wanted me to believe? This uncertainty was the result of years of deception.

He focused on me, but I couldn't hold his gaze for very long. Intense and disarming, it left me feeling exposed.

"Did you enjoy your walk?" He inched closer, making slow deliberate steps as he walked in front of me, stopping periodically to assess me.

Now I had his full attention as he waited for an answer.

I swallowed the confession and nodded.

"Thirteen," he whispered.

"What?"

"When you are not giving me the full truth, your respiration drops from fifteen to thirteen times a minute. You blink six times instead of your usual eight times, and your heart rate jumps to between sixty-nine and seventy-seven instead of sixty-four. Shall we try this again? Where were you?"

Most times I remember how sharp my teeth are, but at that moment I didn't. I tasted blood from my lips as I bit into them.

The heavy stare remained on me, entreating an honesty that I just couldn't give. I wasn't ever going to be a good liar. The were-animals considered it a tool in their arsenal of weapons to keep them safe, but I still considered it the behavior of psychopaths. It was not a skill I wanted to work at improving because to me there wasn't anything brag-worthy about it. "Hey guys, I can lie with the best of them." Not who I wanted to be. Detecting lies was a skill I wished I could master. But how useful would it be for me? I would have to be more skillful than the ones that could detect them.

Ethan's hand intertwined with mine; disenchantment and

disappointment washed over his face. "I hate when you lie to me," he said.

"And I celebrate with a dance-off each time you do it to me."

"I don't enjoy keeping things from you. Often it is to protect you when I hold back information from you." His lips pulled into a tight line.

"I don't want to tell you." And that was the truth.

He nodded and let go of my hand. "Our flight is at eleven fifty. I will meet you in the lobby at nine," he said, but his back remained to me as he spoke.

"What is the Vitae?" I asked.

He stopped and took a long, controlled breath and wore the tension harshly on his face as he turned around. He looked instinctual and predacious. It was the look one gave another predator once confronted. The very look that made me remember the many times I had seen him in a fight, the bodies that he walked over when he was done, the fear that people showed at the mention of his name. Sometimes I forgot who I was dealing with, because I had become comfortable with him. Somewhere in the back of my mind, I knew that, despite the odd tension and animosity, Ethan protected me and I was a little happy to have a person like that in my corner. Now he seemed to have turned on me and I wanted him gone.

"What do you know about it?" he asked, closing the distance between us, studying me with a new intensity.

"It's the fifth protected object that you and Sebastian want to pretend doesn't exist."

"Did you discover this on your *walk*?" The strain of his thoughts placed a harsh scowl on his face.

His lips were pulled tight into a frown and I knew I wasn't going to get anything from him. He turned for the door in silence and started to leave.

"I met with Samuel today," I blurted out.

He took several steps back, away from me, as if I had just done the vilest thing and he needed to distance himself from it. "And?"

I shrugged. Now I was just as careful about watching him as he was with me. Although I still couldn't read him as well as he could me, something was off, unbalanced. "We discussed the protective objects. He says that the Clostra is rumored to have spells that will not just kill us, but that can dissolve the symbiotic relationship between us and our animal halves. A spell to remove magic from the world. We wouldn't change anymore. He thinks it can make us all whole, normal. I wouldn't have to worry about protecting the Aufero, because without magic, there wouldn't be a need for it to exist. We would be normal."

His face relaxed into interest. "And you believe him?"

"Yes. He could have been dishonest about a lot of things, but he wasn't. He doesn't think that magic should exist in any form, and I think I agree with him. Think about it. If we can do a spell that rids this world of magic, that makes us all normal, then this ... this world of dominance, curses, bad magic, and manipulation ends. It would just be an ordinary life that I think we all deserve."

Ethan was expressionless, nodding occasionally, and when I finished, he took a moment before he spoke. "Where did you meet him?"

"Well, he kind of grabbed me off the street."

"Did he drop you off at the hotel?"

"No, I walked."

"Do you have a way to contact him?"

I nodded.

"A phone number or an address?"

"A number."

"Is he still here in the city?"

"I don't know."

The more the questioning continued, the more I realized that Ethan wasn't on board; he was gathering intel, and like a fool I was giving it freely. Whatever boundaries that had separated us and slowly dissolved over the years were now erected again, and stronger than ever.

"You should call him. Let him answer whatever questions you have, and when you're done listening to his spiel, you pick whose side you want to be on," he said.

"There isn't a side to choose. I am trying to help. He's not our enemy."

"You don't have to be enemies to be on opposite sides of an issue. He wants to rid the world of were-animals and magic, and the way I see it, that seems to be where you stand, too. I guess I was right about you all along. We shouldn't trust you," he said acerbically.

I sighed into the moment, my frustration getting the better of me. "Now you know how I feel about you and this pack," I snapped back.

"Whether you believe it or not, I have never enjoyed keeping things from you, or from anyone. Often it is necessary."

"I think you and Sebastian go to great lengths to keep this pack safe. You act as gatekeepers of information that I think people should know, and because of that I don't—no, I *can't*—trust you. I get it: I spilled my guts to a fae and gave in to their magic while you held strong. I am weak. Yay for you … you were right. I hope you enjoy whatever prize you win for being correct."

"I don't think you're weak," he said softly, moving closer.

"Whatever you think, it's a hindrance. You think things are easy for me? Three years ago I had a boring life that I kind of enjoyed. Now I am part of a pack I can't fully trust because of all the secrets. I am a Moura Encantada without the object I am supposed to be protecting. I host a spirit shade that I'm afraid may be Faerie, that I may not be able to control. I watched four people die today because of me. You think I am okay with it? Well, I am not. I'm tired, frustrated, and scared."

Ethan hugged me. A gentle caress that enveloped me in warmth. I closed my eyes, but it didn't make things better.

His touch was tender as he stroked my hair, and when he finally spoke, his tone was soft. "The Vitae has nothing to do with you. I swear it does not. The less people know about it, the better. Will you please trust me on this?"

He pulled away, beseeching eyes waiting for an answer. "Please trust me," he said quietly.

Finally, I nodded.

Ethan started toward the door, but barely made it to threshold before he stopped, and remained for a long time. Turning around he came back. Taking my hand, he led me to the bed. "Have a seat," he said.

His fingers ran over his hair several times. This had to involve Josh. His brother had a tell, which was biting at the bed of his fingernails whenever he was nervous. Only one thing ever made Ethan nervous, and it was always centered around his brother and his safety. "Children always bear the sins of their parents," he whispered, sitting next to me. "My mother was very similar to Josh: very powerful and very tenacious, which gained her quite a few enemies and provoked the Creed too many times. She had performed a forbidden spell to help a friend and it was discovered. The punishment was death—but not hers. They wanted her to live with the consequences of her mistake, so she had to choose one of her children."

"Did she perform a *rever tempore*?" I asked.

His brow crinkled with curiosity, but he didn't inquire how I knew. I wouldn't forget the one spell that altered time, the one Josh said was considered the most egregious violation by the Creed and often was punished with death. Of course, Marcia, being the type of person she was, would choose a punishment that would hurt a mother the most—having to offer her child's life as penance.

Ethan stared at his hands, occasionally looking in my direction. I tried not to let the look of horror show, but I wasn't doing a very good job. The only thing I could think about was the brother he must have lost. *Stop dammit,* I scolded myself, but the tears were already forming and I blinked them back.

"She chose Josh."

Josh. Well, the curse didn't work. "Josh?"

"Never underestimate their cruelty when defied. Josh's eighteenth birthday, he was supposed to die."

Josh was a year older than I was; someone had botched that curse by eight years. "But he's still alive."

Ethan nodded. "Yes, but not without great effort on our part. You want to know where the Vitae is? It's on Josh. Well, part of it is on him." Ethan pulled out his wallet and sorted through the multitude of cards and handed me a folded picture of a small, metal, helix-shaped object. "This is it."

Blinking back the confusion, I tried to make sense of the information. How had they used the Vitae to save Josh?

A half-smile came through and he didn't seem to bear the same stress. "There is a quarter-sized mark just above the top of one thigh that he believes is a birthmark. The metal is in the ink."

I stared at the crinkled picture, speechless. I wasn't really speechless; the hundreds of questions running through my head were fighting for their turn to be asked.

"What about the Moura, what became of her?" I was happy that Josh was alive and the curse had been circumvented, but I couldn't forget the dead Moura that I had seen as a result of her losing her protected object. Someone had died so that Josh could live.

"She's fine," he said with confidence. Too much confidence.

"It's Claudia, isn't it?"

He nodded.

"And Josh has no idea?"

He shook his head.

"Why wouldn't you tell him?"

"Do you think that is something he really needs to know?"

"Yes, I would want to know."

"When you found out about the specifics behind your birth, do you remember how you reacted?"

I hadn't taken the news with the level of grace that I had reconstructed in my mind. I went a little berserk, but who wouldn't have? I had found out that I had died at birth and the only thing keeping me alive was a spirt shade that had died years before. You don't take that type of information with a grin and a nod.

"But this is different."

"How? He will have to deal with the fact that, when my mother had to sacrifice a life, she chose me over him," he said. "I don't want him to know that. To live with that."

"She chose you to live because of the age difference. You all were given six extra years to remove the curse."

"I know, and I am sure he would understand, but I can't imagine knowing something like that would not mess with him. I don't see why he needs to know. And you can't tell him." He turned toward me. "Promise me you won't tell him."

I wasn't promising that. There was no way in hell I was promising that. As a person who was on the other side of the secrets, I couldn't do that to someone else. "I can't do that."

Ethan stood, pacing the floor in long sweeping steps, and the tension weighted his movements. "Do you remember how easily we destroyed the Gem of Levage?"

It wasn't that easy. It was a spell that only Josh could perform from a spell book that only the pack had. I ignored the fact that something that powerful was in their possession, opposed to that of the Creed. I nodded.

"The Vitae is the only thing that is keeping Josh alive. That spell book has the ability to contain such objects, a spell that even a mediocre witch can perform. Do you think that is something he needs to know?" he asked.

I held my breath as he watched me, waiting for an answer. "I will not tell him, but you should," I said. Secrets were what my life had become. I was so out of my depth in this world and each day was a constant reminder of it. He knelt in front of me, inches away. His head rested against mine and he kissed me lightly on the cheek.

"Thank you," he said quietly.

CHAPTER 20

I walked up the gravel pathway to Logan's house again, still unable to get the image of the four dead fae out of my head. Desperation made fools out of people, and I was desperate. I needed the curse removed and I needed the Aufero. The rest I would have to figure out later. In the back of my mind, I kept thinking that if he could help me then he could do the same for Josh.

The smell of juniper wisped through the door, much different than the scent of brimstone and lemon that I had always smelled in Gloria's home, the first Tre'ase I had met. Logan opened the door before I could knock, the broad smile welcoming.

"Do come in," he said. He kept looking past me expectantly.

"Ethan's not with me." When he continued to look behind me, I said, "Winter isn't with me, either. "

He said Winter's name softly to himself. "It is quite fitting for her." He said her name again, just as low as before. "You came alone." His brow raised and his voice was light with amusement. "Is there a reason you left them behind?"

What was this, an interview? "I wanted to talk to you alone."

He moved closer, his smirk gilded with deviance. "I'm flattered. How can I help you?"

I looked around the room, trying to figure out how to handle this. Practicing over and over on the drive there didn't help. He didn't follow the script I had in my head. "Can you remove a curse?"

"Done by whom? Witch? Fae? Elf? Or Tre'ase?"

"Witch."

"Of course I can."

He slowly moved around the room, his hands clasped behind his lower back. "Their magic is strong and complicated, but if you've dealt with them as long as I have, you find a workaround to all their little tricks. If I remove this curse for you, then will you accept that you owe me a debt?" His odd lavender eyes bored into me, expanding and relaxing as the art on his arms roiled up them, moving and changing. "Do we have a deal?" he asked, extending his hand to me.

"No."

"No? Did you come here for a visit? Because I am all out of free favors."

"I will not make an open debt with you. Give me specifics. I need to know exactly what you want from me in return."

He assessed me for a long time before he walked into his living room and took a seat. "Come sit with me."

I hesitated. Was he trying to make me comfortable so I'd let my guard down? I followed him, but stood instead of taking a seat in the chair across from him.

"Oh, sit down, you silly woman. I need to explain what I want."

I sat down, keeping a careful eye on him. He was absolutely relaxed, sinking back into the chair.

"I've lived many years and very few people interest me. Those who have, die. I need someone that has a little more longevity and that I am fond of. Chris is a vampire, am I correct?"

"Yes, for about three months now."

He nodded slowly. "Did you know that vampires can be bound to humans?"

"No. Bound in what way?"

"Like the bond between that of a vampire and the one that created them, but it is stronger—much stronger."

"Okay, and?" Since I wasn't considered wholly human, I wasn't sure why he was telling me this.

"Well, a bond between you and Chris can be established."

"I am a were-animal. Some only consider us part human."

He smiled. "Those people are fools and wouldn't believe such things if they had seen your origins. Nevertheless"—he waved away the thought—"as long as you are like this, in human form, it can be done."

"How does Chris being bonded to me benefit you?"

He chewed on his lips for a while, and when he released them, there was blood. His tongue slid over it. His voice lowered to almost a whisper, barely audible even from my location just a few feet from him. "She'll be your servant, and answer to your wishes. The spell that binds you will not allow her to deny anything you request of her." He smiled, leaned forward in his chair, and waited a long time to finish. "You can wish her to me."

I guess he thought enough time had passed that he could slide that little tidbit in unnoticed.

What?

But I hadn't opened my mouth to say it out loud. Was he kidding? "You want me to form a bond—"

"A *servus vinculum*. That is what it is called," he offered in a casual timbre.

"I don't care what it's called. I am not forming a magical bond with someone so I can give them to you as a gift!"

He relaxed back in the chair. "Then the curse, it is something you are okay living with?" he asked coolly.

I should have just left. Stomped away with my self-righteous anger in tow after giving him a piece of my mind—but I didn't. Instead, I said, "She'll never let it happen."

"We will hammer out the specifics later. Do we have a deal?" He smiled, his eyes widening, the marks on his arm scrolling slowly and his lips moving lazily in an invocation.

"No."

Everything stopped: the art halted mid-movement, his eyes shrank to normal, and he bit back his words.

"What will you do with her?" I asked. "Are you going to hurt her?"

"Of course not. She would be my companion and come and go as she pleases, but she would return to me when I wanted her to. Nothing nefarious about that, is there? I will live a long time, inevitably outliving the connections I have. She will be that link, and liaison to the outside, the companionship I long for. Why would I hurt her in any way?"

That didn't seem bad, yet it didn't sound good, either. "Fine, if that's all you are looking for then I can visit you daily," I offered.

His long sweep of disinterest trailed over me as he dismissed the idea. "That is not an offer that interests me. I would agree to your friend—Winter, isn't it? But I don't know of a spell that can bind a were-animal to another. I doubt she will stay as long as I like or visit as much as I desire without some form of incentive. Therefore, I would need someone more acquiescent. Winter doesn't strike me as the type."

"Chris isn't, either. You've met her, right?" I asked, knowing it was ridiculous to be offended by his rejection, but it didn't stop me from feeling that way.

"With the *servus vinculum,* she will be far more cooperative."

I crossed my arms over my chest and started pacing the floor, unable to ignore the satisfied look that remained on his face as I pondered the situation. I couldn't believe that I was considering this. But if the roles were reversed, there wasn't a doubt that Chris would do it to me. "You won't hurt her?"

His lips drew into a tight line. "*Hurt* is a subjective word. One person's pain is another's comfort. She will never be damaged by me under any circumstances" was all that he offered.

And I was desperate enough to cling to that as a promise that he wouldn't hurt her. But I just couldn't commit, although he took my extended consideration as a tacit agreement.

"As long as you are alive, she remains gifted to me. I would then have a vested interest in keeping you alive. I think that is a good thing for you. Am I wrong?"

"But she is immortal, I am not. She will outlive me, too."

"You'll live longer than most. I am confident you will not outlive my interest. Perhaps if you don't, she will not need to be bonded to desire to stay," he said in a wistful tone.

A Tre'ase who benefited from me being alive was a very good thing. But did it trump the very bad thing I needed to do to achieve this?

His deep, assessing gaze settled on me, waiting for an answer I couldn't freely give. Finally, he said, "I will give you time to think about it. But if you decide this is a good deal for you—and I believe you will—take this." He walked over to a cabinet and pulled out a small ring with a sharp prong on it. He pulled out a vial filled with a pink shimmering liquid, whispered a spell, and the liquid sparked into a vibrant blue before he dipped the ring in it. "Wear it on your finger. All you have to do is prick her with it. She'll be disabled for just a couple of hours. You will, too, if you stick yourself. Do be careful. Then bring her here. And I can perform the *servus vinculum*."

He placed it carefully in my hand and I looked at it. In my mind, I tossed it at him and stormed out the door. In reality, I left quietly with the poisonous ring in my open palm, walking away as though it would detonate at the slightest movement.

I drove away from Logan's home, wishing the feeling of indignation would somehow rear its head—but nothing. Instead, I could only think about Chris trying to kidnap me and give me to the vampires to be killed during a ritual. To her, I wasn't a person, I was just a job. I was doing the same thing. This was a job. My job was to keep me alive. Wasn't it poetic justice that I did the same thing to her? It was justified. Right?

I didn't think about Logan's fascination with death or what he wanted to do with her. I put aside his fondness for her. The entire drive to Chris's home, I dredged up memories of her trying to kidnap me two years ago. I needed to remember what she was capable of.

I had a job to do. My job was keeping me alive. And I repeated that over and over until it was a loud, distracting loop in my head.

It continued to play as I walked up to her door and knocked on it. The ring was on my third finger, the only one it would fit on.

She opened the door with a sheer look of annoyance, her tone bitter and uninviting. "Look, Bambi—"

I lunged at her, but she quickly moved. A hip toss forced me to the ground with a thud. I swept her leg and she landed next to me. Chris was faster than I was, faster than Winter. She hovered over me. Two quick right hooks landed squarely on my jaw, and blood spurted in my mouth. I blocked the next blow, and when she tried to hit me from the left I grabbed her wrist. The prong of the ring pierced her skin. Making a futile attempt to release herself, she yanked at my wrist, hammering at the inside of my arm. Her fingers started to rake across my face when she collapsed on top of me.

The drive back to the Tre'ase's home seemed shorter than the original thirty minutes it had taken to get to Chris's. I slung her over my shoulder and slowly went up the gravel path, playing the mantra over and over in my head. Her body, cool against my shoulder, was a constant reminder that she was a vampire who had died during an alliance with us, presumably at the hands of Michaela for whatever reason. My pace slowed the closer I got to the house.

Once I was nearly thirty feet away, Logan opened the door and started toward us. Pleasure drenched his appearance as he moved in a slow, languorous gait, savoring each moment as he approached, making the debauchery of the situation worse. The longing smile found an ugly place between salaciousness and joy. His eyes twinkled, and whether it was intentional or not, his glamour dropped for a few seconds, longer than the time it had with Ethan.

This is a job. My job is to keep me alive. I need to do my job. But the little affirmation wasn't enough. It wasn't my job to do it at the expense of others. Collateral damage was a concept eloquently and flippantly thrown around, one that I had started to think of as an inevitability. But was it? Treating people like pawns was something I just couldn't do.

The reality of the situation felt heavy on me, shocking me back into myself where desperation had somehow allowed me to abandon who I was. I was delivering her to a monster— as a gift. The bile was thick and nauseating as it clogged my throat, making it hard to breathe.

When I slowly backed away, his pace quickened.

I turned and was at a full run back to the car when I heard him growl, "No!"

The pounding of his heavy steps crunched the gravel. Something brushed against my back, hands, claws, making an attempt to grab me. I sprinted. Running as fast as I could toward the restrictive magical barrier that prevented him from leaving the area, I slammed into the car, dropping Chris. As I gathered her in my arms, I forced myself to look at him. His odd lavender eyes glowed with anger as his glamour faltered. Long teeth protruded from his maw. The gruesome elongated snout widened as he snorted. Horns lifted out of his scalp. He inched closer to the barrier and lunged toward it and then crumbled to the ground, howling in pain. Scooting back from it, his body folded into itself. He looked up, and the anger was gone, replaced by sadness and desperation. I mouthed an apology, but I knew it wasn't enough. Cold, narrowed eyes followed me as I placed Chris in the car.

Nearly ten minutes later I was on a side street, next to my car, hunched over everything I had eaten that day and most of the day before. The monster that Logan had shown me was nearly as ugly as the one that he had unleashed inside of me. I slid to the ground and sobbed. I didn't know how long it was before the tears finally stopped and I could move without them forming again.

Lying on the sofa in her home, Chris looked as limp as she had when we had found her lifeless body in the woods several months ago, before she was turned into a vampire, except this time she wasn't brutalized beyond recognition. I couldn't just leave her without making sure she would awaken. She stirred, just for a moment, and then again. She vaulted up with a start, screaming. In one swift move, she pushed the sofa back with her feet, picked up a gun I had not seen, and stood and aimed it at me. Her trembling wouldn't stop and I raised my hand, prepared to duck if the twitching caused her to accidentally fire.

She used her other hand to try to steady the gun and keep it on me. The breathing was habit and it came hard, I was sure as an effort to calm herself. Her gaze darted around the room, looking for others, then refocused on me.

I eased to my feet, keeping my hands up in surrender. "Put the gun away. If you were going to use it, I am confident you would have already," I said.

She blinked several times and looked around the room. It took a moment before she slowly lowered the gun. After extended moments of contemplation, she placed it on the table and returned to her seat on the sofa, across from me. "My head hurts," she said.

"I bumped it pretty hard."

The extended silence continued. "Who was it for?" she finally asked in a low, detached voice.

I shook my head. I had messed up. This never should have happened, and I wasn't going to tell her so she could get revenge when it was entirely my fault.

"I will eventually find out."

"Perhaps, but it will not be because of me." I said, taking a seat. She kept holding her head. It must have really hurt. "I have aspirin in my purse, do you want some?"

"No, I handle pain pretty well."

Why did she think that was a good thing? What had occurred in her life that made her consider the ability to endure a great deal of pain an attribute? I'd always wanted to hate her, and in fact she really deserved it, but I couldn't help but wonder, as I did with Quell, what had happened in her life to make her like this? What horrific things had occurred in the real world that made people seek comfort in the otherworld?

She quickly came to her feet and I jumped to mine, but she went to the kitchen and came back with two glasses and a bottle of vodka. She filled them both up too full and slid one in my direction. She drank hers down, filled it again, and had nearly emptied it by the time I had taken a couple of sips from mine.

"I'm sorry for what happened to you. For what I did and what happened to you to cause you to become a vampire," I said.

"Don't be," she responded in a curt tone. Cool marble eyes scrutinized me for a long moment. "I know this seems like it is going to be one of those 'kumbaya' moments, where we give our apologies, reveal personal things about ourselves, and you start to feel like you really misjudged me. Then we become cordial to each other and maybe eventually friends. And eventually during one of our fun girls' nights out we get nostalgic and reminisce about the horrible shit we did to each other and how we overcame those obstacles to become best gal pals. I can assure you that is not going to happen."

"Your optimism is infectious. I'm absolutely giddy right now." I took a sip from my glass.

She emptied hers and poured another. "I am realistic. You still look pallid and nauseated and I am sure you will be for a while. You'll leave here and unnecessarily castigate yourself for what you did. You'll do that while I will speculate about it: what has you so desperate that you reduced yourself to kidnapping? Who have you left righteously pissed off because you didn't complete your job by bringing me in? And do I want revenge for what you did to me? And now you are going to think about it, too, and be thankful that you have the pack. But I am sure you're not concerned about the revenge thing, because I did something similar to you? Right?"

I considered finishing the glass. I really needed it. This had been one of those nights that I wanted to be too drunk to remember, but instead I placed the half-full glass on the table before I headed for the door. "No. I don't consider it the same thing, because I doubt *you* would have changed your mind. *You* would have completed the job."

"You're right. I wouldn't have changed my mind, because I am good at my job."

"Yeah, probably one of the best. I will never be good at anything like that because I don't want to be what you have become. But looking at your lot in life, how is 'being the best' working out for you?" And with that, I closed the door behind me.

By the time I had made it to the car, she was just a few feet from me. Her jaw worked in an odd manner, chewing on the words that were having trouble coming out, so she simply bit them back.

I waited for her to say something, but instead she stood still, her face absent of anything decipherable. I nearly jerked away when she lightly touched my arm and squeezed it gently. And it stayed there for a long moment. She remained silent. Her mouth moved ever so slightly, but the words were obstructed by her pride.

I smiled. "You're welcome."

"You have a good night, Skylar," she said in a low voice. Then she was back at her door, closing it, but not before looking back at me, her lips barely moving into a smile.

CHAPTER 21

Maybe I was a masochist, because I stared back at Ethan, Josh, and Sebastian expecting more than just the limpid gazes that looked at me as I told them about the situation with Logan and Chris. Stolid expressions, even on Josh, who in the past had proven unskilled at hiding his emotions; somehow he had now perfected it. "Did you make a formal agreement to do this?" Sebastian finally asked.

"No, it was an implied agreement," I said.

"One that you did not fulfill," Ethan added. Always the emphatic narrator.

Their response was just thoughtful silence, no more questions. Ethan and Josh looked at each other a few times. Long, careful glances that just supported my ongoing suspicion that they communicated differently than other people did.

Sebastian shrugged off my confession as nothing more than a simple peccadillo.

I waited for Ethan to respond and add something, but his relaxed casual silence remained. Something roiled in me. "Did you hear what I did?"

"Yes, you went over it in great detail. Do you have more to

add?" Sebastian asked.

I snapped my mouth shut, trying to decide what was more appalling: what I did, or how they were responding to it. I needed someone to be disappointed. To have a chastising spark in their eyes, a diminutive frown. Nothing. Not one of them thought I was better than this. I felt a little shattered, and that fragments of who I was had floated away in the wind. I hated this feeling. Or was it the opposite? Had the trials I faced inured me to this kind of moral trespass? Was I being prepared to survive in a world that would have devoured the old me?

Assessing Sebastian's and Ethan's dismissive looks, I thought perhaps I wasn't the hardened knave that my overactive mind had painted me to be. But I damn sure wasn't who I had been two years before.

They still hadn't responded in the manner I expected. Did they believe it was just another day in Sky's life? I wasn't sure what I wanted. Disappointment? Offense? Indignation? Disgust? Something that ensured that they expected better? But why would I think that they would expect more from me than they did of themselves? The only thing I did was initiate a job that I couldn't complete, and I was no better off having not completed it. They just wanted to make sure there weren't consequences.

Eventually, Sebastian spoke. "Can Samuel be reasoned with?"

I shot Ethan a quick glance. His gaze narrowed with balmy indifference as if I were a fool to think he wouldn't have shared the information I had confessed to him.

"In which way? He doesn't seem like a psychopath, if that is what you are asking. Just an extremist with an agenda. He doesn't think we should exist because we are monsters, and he thinks I am naïve enough to help him and fall for his rhetoric. Besides that . . ." My voice trailed off, because I wanted to say that he wasn't any more dangerous than they were.

"Call him," Sebastian said.

"Now?"

"No, six days from now. Of course now. We need the third book—"

"He's not going to give it to you."

"Then I would like to hear that from him." Sebastian started to slowly walk the large space in his office. "Josh believes that there has to be a spell in the Clostra that can remove all curses."

I should have been ecstatic, but I had the same portentous thoughts that also seemed to occupy Sebastian. The various emotions played on his face, and the most profound was apprehension. If it removed my curse, how many other curses would be removed? Would we remove curses that were necessary in this world, to control dangerous people and things?

"We don't have many choices," Josh admitted, looking just as despondent about the situation.

"I need to talk to him," Sebastian said.

I called him.

"Skylar," answered Samuel's raspy light, optimistic voice over the speaker. It wasn't the voice of a fanatical madman that wanted to divest the people of the otherworld of their magic and power. He could easily sway the right unsuspecting individual to his side.

"No, it's Sebastian."

Palpable silence remained for an extended time before Samuel spoke. "I am not giving you the other book." His tone was like a knife, and before Sebastian could respond, he said, "And it is not for sale, either."

Sebastian's humorless chuckle was a deep rumble that resonated through the room. "I am quite comfortable with you having the third book."

And I was sure he was. Sebastian just needed to know where it was, but he didn't want them ever to be in the same place. As long as the pack had two, then the chances of anyone ever getting all three were slim. "But I need to borrow it."

"Borrow for a borrow," Samuel suggested.

"No. I don't agree with your cause. Frankly, it's a fatuous

agenda. You will waste your life trying to end this world. It will not happen, but if you want to go on with your lost cause, have at it. You will never succeed, because in order for that to happen, you will need the other two, and you get those over my dead body. I have no concerns with that. Stronger and better than you have tried to best me and failed. But let me humor you. This magicless utopia that you dream of doesn't have an iota of a chance of success without allies."

"I have no desire to be allies with beasts that present themselves as human."

"The feeling is mutual; I don't want you as an ally, either. However, I know a lot of really angry witches that have had their magic stripped from them by Marcia using the Aufero. You loan me the book and I can guarantee that their magic will be returned to them." Sebastian paused. "I assure you their allegiance will no longer be to the Creed and Marcia, and they would be willing to align themselves with anyone who is against her. Don't you think?"

Samuel was very careful with his words. "I don't need alliances. I do fine alone."

"Yeah, I saw how fine you did back at your little hideaway. Marcia and the Creed pretty much handed your ass to you and then made you thank them for the pleasure of doing so by forcing you into an agreement that restricts you from ever retaliating. What I saw wasn't 'fine' by a long shot."

Samuel didn't agree immediately. In fact, it took so long for him to respond that Sebastian had to call his name several times.

It was a reluctant agreement, but an agreement nonetheless after several long moments.

CHAPTER 22

Samuel had settled on coming to us, although I suspected it had little to do with our convenience and a lot to do with his curiosity about the pack's home. It wasn't their only one, but it was the compound that most knew about or the one that the pack didn't actively hide. I knew of three others, but not their actual locations, and I had a sneaking suspicion that, like most things that revolved around the pack, the addresses were revealed only on a need-to-know basis.

Samuel assured us he could meet us in a couple of hours, which left us all wondering where he lived. I was curious whether he lived in the Midwest and had followed us to New York, or if the latter was actually his home state. The anticipation of his arrival left everyone ill at ease, claiming most of their patience. I found Ethan in the basement drilling into a heavy bag, his sweaty shirt clinging to his body. Forceful kicks and hard punches nearly separated the bag from its cable. He gave me a brief sweeping look before he returned his aggression to the bag.

"You aren't imagining that bag is me, are you?" I asked.

He held the bag, his forehead pressed against it. "Why would I?" he asked before he returned to pounding into it. The unrestrained energy resonated off him. An overwhelming influx of primal power filled the room. Different than I was used to, but just as strong. "How was she when you left her?" He grabbed the swinging bag after a brutal hit.

I thought about it for a while. "She was Chris."

He turned. "I don't know what that means."

"She's a broken, dysfunctional person. And not in a hyperbolic way, but truly. She wasn't angry—she just wanted to know who the job was for and made a snide comment about me not completing it. Even though my job was to kidnap her."

He chuckled. "That sounds like her."

Clarity shone over their dysfunction and what held their relationship together when by all reason it should have ended. She was the personification of the pack. She was the "good" and the "bad" guy or whatever she needed to be to complete her objective. Lines blurred, ethics skewed, alliances were made with the devil. In the end, even if an egregious act were directed at her, she understood that she was just a consequence of a job. I couldn't admire it, because it was too disturbing. But Ethan did and was unable to hide how he felt.

My mind had wandered to a place that I didn't really like. Was I slipping into that ambiguous place of misplaced integrity that blurred the lines and fractured conscience that failed to appreciate the difference between good and bad?

Ethan, standing just inches from me, snapped me back to the present. Acutely aware of how close he was, I tensed as his gunmetal gaze watched me. He needed to get back to the bag; he had too much pent-up energy that needed to be released. His fingers trailed along my cheek and then over my lips. Then he kissed me—I didn't respond. Instead, my lips stayed rigid, my hands balled at my side. "You said back at the restaurant that we shouldn't let things between us get awkward," I whispered against his lips.

Stepping back, his hands that encircled my waist fell away. "This is awkward?"

His long, lingering gaze trailed up me, his head tilting slightly, and I was fully aware of how attracted I was to him and how horribly wrong it was to be. "You don't think it's awkward," he said.

I shook my head. "No. But I think it is the king of bad ideas."

His lips kinked into a miscreant smile as he gave me another lascivious look that forced the night in my bedroom to the forefront of my thoughts. My id was telling me to shut the hell up, and my body wanted to listen. But common sense was the nagging overlord that wouldn't have any of this foolishness.

"Maybe you're right." He stripped off his shirt and went back to expending his energy on the bag. I turned to leave and he asked, "How many times did you get sick tonight?" while planting a side kick into the bag.

"I didn't," I said, as I kept my back to him.

"Seventy-seven."

I could hear the arrogance and humor in his voice. How did he hold a conversation and count someone's heart rate? That was how he knew when I lied.

"That's a stupid skill to have," I mumbled as I continued up the stairs. I didn't wait around the pack's home until Samuel arrived, but instead decided to go home and wait.

Samuel, Josh, and I were in the pack's library. It wasn't unexpected that Samuel wouldn't leave us with the books, so he and Josh both scribbled on their notepads as I read from all three volumes. It went slowly at first, Samuel unable to resist looking at the books over my shoulder and becoming increasingly irritated when the words quickly disappeared from the pages.

When he wasn't scribbling on his pad, he was studying me

with interest, although he never asked any of the questions that were gilded on his face. The tranquil ocher eyes rooted on me whenever Josh would leave us alone. Which he had done reluctantly several times.

"You are a special oddity. I suspect Sebastian has great plans for you," he said softly.

I never thought I would long for the day when someone would call me *plain, simple, ordinary,* or just *unremarkable.*

"And you suspect that he has some grand plan? Like what, taking over the otherworld in an epic battle?"

"No, I suspect it will be something subtler. He is impressive. I applaud whatever he has done to warrant such naïveté and blind loyalty."

"And I will give the same accolades to those who have twisted your mind and instilled such beliefs in you. You can stop their ability to change into monsters, as you put it, but you will not change their personalities. Those that are savages will remain that way even if they no longer have the ability to change. Every full moon, I change into a wolf. Sometimes I do it just for the hell of it, but that is where that part of me ends. And that is true for many of us."

His smile was genuine, and off-putting. Why did I expect him to go off into a tirade revealing his crazy face? Instead, what echoed back were delicate eyes, void of any insanity, a light unwavering smile that implored for some understanding—and a few times I had to fight not to give it.

"But are you really? You aren't the first were-animal that I've dealt with. You are different, but it will eventually be overshadowed by the horrors of this world. You'll do unthinkable things—for the good of the pack. That is what you all like to use, right? Yes, you will do heinous things for your pack. It will be hard at first, and then it will become easier to do because it is acceptable in this world. And eventually you, too, will be lost to it. As much as you want to believe I am a fanatic with nefarious intent, I am not. I came to you because I see someone different. You aren't like them, although you pretend you are."

The image of Chris's drugged body on the ground prior to me taking her to Logan flashed in my head. But it wasn't for Logan; it was for me and it all had started with the pack, hadn't it?

He had started to get me. For a brief moment I gave myself over to the idea of living in a magic-free world—normal. The books lay in front of me and Samuel sat across the table. My gaze slipped over Josh's notes. So many spells.

As if he had read my mind, Samuel said, "We could leave with them now. I could get us out of here."

I took out my phone and pulled up Google translate. It was slower than working with someone that was versed in Latin, but I had a feeling Samuel was too distracted by his agenda to be of any use. "We need to finish and find the spell we need," I said firmly. He had gotten to me, and for a few moments I had given myself over to the fantastical thoughts of what-if. But the abstract world of what-if just didn't work. I had jumped down the rabbit hole, and there was a lot of crazy stuff down it, but I would adapt and survive. I was determined to do so. How could I make a decision for everyone about whether or not they should be a were-animal or possess magic? What type of world would I create by doing that?

He relaxed into the painful resolve that he had failed to convince me to side with him. Working hard not to look angry at his failure, he took a seat, but the rest of the night I garnered a great deal of his attention.

Nearly three hours later we had gone through one-third of the book, revealing spells stronger and darker than any of us had imagined. When we found the right one, we stopped. Samuel wanted to continue. He looked at the books with longing, an unequivocal lust for the knowledge that the books held. But we reiterated that the spells would be no good to him without the books, and they would never be in the same room again, if any of us had anything to do with it.

His disappointed, shadowed gaze barely left me even as Josh performed the spell. He was furled over the books, speaking the invocation in Latin, as a whirl of jasper, orange, cream, and teal flowed from them. There was a shift in the air, and a dank feeling hovered as the large library became too small to contain its power. The walls shuddered and the bookcases collapsed, sending books all over the room. Sharp whips of magic, so far removed from the natural form that both witches possessed, overwhelmed the space. Samuel gulped for breath that just wouldn't come until he gave in to the indomitable power that would settle for nothing less than submission. Darkness overtook Josh's eyes as he continued with the spell. The ragged sharp breaths stopped as he slumped over the books. After fulfilling their task, the books closed, settling next to each other in a quiescent state.

"How do you feel?" Samuel asked me.

I didn't feel anything. Should I have? I didn't feel any different and I had no idea if it had worked. I guessed we would have to see.

It was déjà vu once again. Ethan and I were entering the little store that was a front for the Creed's sanctuary, but now he was in wolf form, and Josh and Samuel, who refused to be left behind, followed behind us.

Little had changed, except the lock was easier to break with two powerful witches at our side. After a quick invocation, it disappeared. I cautiously walked toward the windowed armoire in the corner. I stopped fifty feet from it, waiting for the sickly feeling that overtook me when the imprecation was invoked. Nothing. I eased closer. Nothing.

It had worked.

I moved with more confidence, pushing aside the thought of

all the other curses that we had abolished. The Aufero glowed, still the odd color that it had turned since we had removed the magic from Ethan. Extra measures had been taken to keep it safe. Now secured with locks, the Aufero pulsated, expanding, working at the locks, yanking them apart. I wasn't a foot away before it shattered the glass and slammed into my chest, hard enough to push out a gasp. Shoving it into a satchel, I headed out the door.

On the other side of the door, we were met with a blistering wind as hard rains pounded us. Thunder crackled and a bolt of lightning drove into Samuel, thrashing him into the wall. The car that we came in was there, but Sebastian was gone. Liam and the army that had accompanied him in Elysian came from the west. Vision blurred by the rain, I could barely make out the mass of people who descended upon us, overtaking the small space behind the store. Ethan lunged into the crowd, knocking down three of them, his fangs tearing into their throats. The others surrounded Liam, protecting him as they retreated.

A wave of Samuel's hand, and most of the cadre was leveled. Another bolt of lightning hit him, and he collapsed to his knees. The odd twins from Elysian held balls of light, prepared to release them, and hail pelted into us like stones. Marcia slinked in between them with the rest of the Creed just steps behind. Josh surrounded us with a protective field, shielding us from the elements as Samuel recovered, coming to his feet. The witches shattered the field. There was a flash of light and Josh was slammed to the ground. Before I could respond, Samuel quickly erected the field again. Samuel and Josh worked to keep it up against five witches.

Sebastian, in wolf form, lunged at the twins, and in a riot of screams and gurgled gasps the elemental attack stopped, but it only cleared the way for Marcia to advance without injury. Carrying the same knife she had had when she encountered Samuel, she approached me. The field shattered again. Samuel waved his hand, but stopped, his face red, spastic quivers overtaking his body forcing him back as he pressed against the wall of the building for support. Marcia smiled, aware that the spell they had performed earlier prevented him from hurting them.

Slipping my hand in my bag, I touched the Aufero. Their lips began moving quickly the moment I erected my protective field. It fell at the hands of five very powerful witches. Wet hair obstructed my vision and I tried to brush it away. Josh whispered an incantation. The knife was no longer in Marcia's grasp but in his as he charged toward her. Her eyes were just as dark as Josh's, and she sent him catapulting into the brick wall with a crash, pinning him against it. They both called forth stronger magic, their pupils black chasms. Marcia clasped hands with the others, and her shrill voice reverberated against the closed-in surroundings. Josh pushed against the force of her magic but remained fixed to the wall. She released one of the hands she held, keeping the other in contact with the Creed. Lifting her finger, she guided the knife that Josh held in his hand toward him. He panted, his hand quivering, trying hard to override her command. The blade dipped into his throat and blood spilled.

He let out a shrieking sound. He didn't even look like himself: his eyes were black, face feral with rage, and the knife flew in her direction, embedding itself into her arm. She dropped to the ground, screaming. The other witches fell, too. Josh pushed them back in a violent wave. Again he slammed them to the ground. I'd never seen him like this. As savage looking as a beast, he approached them quickly, but before he reached them they vanished.

The commotion continued: bodies falling, blood soaking the wet pavement and mixing with the rain. Liam had somehow escaped, but three of his men had fallen victim to Winter's sword and Gavin's claws. Steven and a few others had come in behind them. Steven disappeared, I assumed to track down that one that had attempted to escape.

Bodies surrounded me, some injured, others dead. I looked

around. Josh was okay: he had only superficial wounds along his neck, but he hadn't recovered from the use of strong magic and for the first time I saw a side of him that I would soon like to forget; violent, baleful, and as close to primal as a human could get. Ethan was several feet away, his fur matted with blood and dirt. I quickly moved toward him, but not fast enough. An arm slipped around my waist and the last thing I heard was Gavin calling my name before there was nothing but silence.

I stood in the middle of the empty cornfield, Samuel's arms hooked around me, my back confined against his chest. I dropped to the ground, trying to keep from getting sick.

"I didn't want it to be this way," he said as he went for the satchel with the Aufero.

I jabbed my elbow into his throat, and while he gasped for air, I swiped his leg and he plowed into the ground. With a wave of his hand, I soared through the air, skidding across the grassy plain. His steps were heavy and labored as he approached. I pulled the Aufero into my chest and put up a field. He walked around it with slow, weary steps.

"I thought you were better. I thought you of all people would see the danger of letting this continue," he whispered. "Why can't you see it? Why can't you see that they are monsters and we are the only ones that can save them?"

His bedlam babble continued, but the gentle topaz gaze was a contradiction to his hateful words. "Did you see anything good out there tonight? Who were the good? Who were the bad? Self-interest, darkness, and the pursuit of indomitable control is all that I saw. Monsters. What did you see?" he asked as he circled the field. I knew what he was doing, just as Josh had when we practiced, looking for a weakness in the barrier.

The air was stifling, dark power pulling the oxygen from it in the same manner it had at Ethan's house. I endured it because I didn't know what to expect. Did Samuel think the pack would trade me for the books? Did he want the Aufero for his pseudo-altruistic purposes?

"I saw a fight. Nothing worse than what I see on the news or in a bar. You are trying to save people who don't need to be saved."

He shook his head, his hand pressed on the field. "Sebastian will give me the books for you and the Aufero."

The field trembled and bucked under his touch. As he pressed his hand ever so slightly on it, a spark flicked off it. He whispered a spell, and the field fell. I quickly put it up again. Concentrating, I made it stronger. His words came at a more fervent pace as he called on stronger magic, and his body molded against the protective field.

Then his eyes rolled back. His breaths were ragged and sharp, and I could hear the oxygen being pulled from his lungs, the dragging of his heart as it fought to beat once more, the slow collapse of his body into the field.

"Let go of it," I said.

He ripped himself from it and stepped back so fast he stumbled to the ground. I dropped the protective bubble and started toward him, but he scuttled back.

"Get away from me!"

"I just want to make sure you are okay."

"Get away from me!" Shock and disgust laced his words as he looked at me with the same revulsion and awe he reserved for Sebastian and the others.

When I made another attempt to step closer, he vanished. I considered looking for him. He was too weak to have gotten very far. But there wasn't a purpose. We were done. Perhaps it was better that he considered me one of the monsters, too, that he couldn't convert to "Team Samuel." But I hated that little tug that I felt at lumping myself with the others. But I still didn't know why. Was I really that different?

. . .

I looked around the bleak land, trying to get my bearings. I had no idea where I was. Closing my eyes, I just inhaled the air and stayed quiet for a few minutes trying to figure out which direction to go. Nighttime made it hard to use nature's compass. I lived west of the pack, south of the city, but in the middle of nowhere I had no idea which way to go. I started walking east. When I came to a main road, I stayed closer to the street, hoping to get a glimpse of something familiar. A car crossed over the median, and once it was closer, I recognized Ethan as the driver.

I exhaled a sigh of relief as I got in the car. I couldn't ignore the odd look of intrigue on Ethan's face as he called Sebastian to let him know he had me. We drove a couple of miles in silence when he finally said, "Why did you head east?"

I shrugged. "I don't know."

"That's twice," he said softly.

"What?"

"Samuel was too weak to be able to go any farther than a twenty-mile radius. Sebastian went west, Winter north, Josh south. We knew you would go to a major road."

It was the first time that it really seemed strange. How did I end up at the same restaurants with Ethan? Why did I go east?

I didn't want to think about the oddness between Ethan and me. We had enough to fill a room. "Something is wrong with the Aufero," I said. And I went on to tell him about its behavior since we had pulled the magic from him.

"Are you sure it is the magic pulled from me?"

He didn't have to say it, because it had floated around in my head for some time. Was this the result of Maya? We were convinced that she was a Faerie, one of the original badasses of the otherworld. Was this her becoming more of a force in my life, taking over, and now my actions were no longer my own?

"For now, don't use it until we can figure it out."

"When did Marcia align with Liam?" I asked, ending nearly ten minutes of silence.

He shrugged. "I am trying to figure it out. There's something at hand and I think it is directed toward us." He never looked troubled, but now he did, entrenched in an odd worry. It made me a little afraid. What were Marcia and Liam planning?

But for me, the weight of the world seemed a little lighter. I was no longer cursed, I had the Aufero, we knew where the third Clostra was, and I knew what the fifth object of power was. So many of the veils of secrecy had been lifted. I refused to have it dampen my mood.

Just as I started to get out of the car, Ethan stopped me. In front of my porch, his odd-colored eyes were narrowed to slits and focused intensely on me. A fixed scowl stayed on his face, and, like a statue, Logan stood in front of my house.

Ethan cursed under his breath. The consequences of us removing my curse was glaring at us. How much of the otherworld had we changed?

What had we done?

MESSAGE TO THE READER

~

Thank you for choosing *Midnight Falls* from the many titles available to you. My goal is to create an engaging world, compelling characters, and an interesting experience for you. I hope I've accomplished that. Reviews are very important to authors and help other readers discover our books. Please take a moment to leave a review. I'd love to know your thoughts about the book.

For notifications about new releases, *exclusive* contests and giveaways, and cover reveals, please sign up for my newsletter at www.mckenziehunter.com

www.McKenzieHunter.com
MckenzieHunter@MckenzieHunter.com

Printed by Amazon Italia Logistica S.r.l.
Torrazza Piemonte (TO), Italy